James Becker spent over twenty years in the Royal Navy's Fleet Air Arm and served during the Falklands War. Throughout his career he has been involved in covert operations in many of the world's hotspots; places like Yemen, Northern Ireland and Russia. He is an accomplished combat pistol shot and has an abiding interest in ancient and medieval history. His previous novels, *The First Apostle* and *The Moses Stone*, are also published by Bantam Books. *The First Apostle* was one of the biggest selling eBooks of 2009.

www.rbooks.co.uk

Also by James Becker

THE FIRST APOSTLE
THE MOSES STONE

and published by Bantam Books

THE MESSIAH SECRET

James Becker

BANTAM BOOKS

LONDON • TORONTO • SYDNEY • AUCKLAND • JOHANNESBURG

TRANSWORLD PUBLISHERS
61–63 Uxbridge Road, London W5 5SA
A Random House Group Company
www.rbooks.co.uk

THE MESSIAH SECRET
A BANTAM BOOK: 9780553825046

First publication in Great Britain
Bantam edition published 2010

A CIP catalogue record for this book is available from the British Library.

Addresses for Random House Group Ltd companies outside the UK can be found at: www.randomhouse.co.uk
The Random House Group Ltd Reg. No. 954009

The Random House Group Limited supports The Forest Stewardship Council (FSC), the leading international forest certification organisation. All our titles that are printed on Greenpeace approved FSC certified paper carry the FSC logo. Our paper procurement policy can be found at www.rbooks.co.uk/environment

Typeset in 11/14.5pt Sabon by Falcon Oast Graphic Art Ltd.
Printed in the UK by CPI Cox & Wyman, Reading, RG1 8EX.

2 4 6 8 10 9 7 5 3 1

To Sally, as always, and for everything

Acknowledgements

My thanks go to a very talented duo – Selina Walker and Jessica Broughton – a pair of 'slash-and-burn' editors who together took the bones and flesh of this book and imbued it with real life. And they, of course, are just a part of the experienced, dedicated and gifted team at Transworld who all worked to ensure that the book was as good as we could possibly make it.

And, as always, my thanks to Luigi Bonomi, the best literary agent an author could have, a good friend and real inspiration to me.

Prologue

AD 72 Ldumra

The nine men had made slow progress ever since they'd left the last village and started the final stage of their long climb. Now, the simple stone houses were a distant ghostly monochrome in the grey light of pre-dawn.

There was no road, barely even a track, leading to where they were going, though they knew exactly the route they needed to follow, a route that would take them high into the mountains and finish in a blind-ended valley. Each of them – bar one – also knew that they were making the last journey of their lives. Only one man in the group would ever leave the valley, or would want to. That journey or, to be exact, the reason for that journey, was the culmination of everything they'd worked for throughout their adult lives.

They were well-armed, each man carrying a dagger and a sword, and all but two of them also had a bow and a quiver of arrows over their shoulders. The whole area, and especially Ldumra, was a well-known haunt of bandits and thieves. Their principal prey were the laden caravans travelling along what would later become known as the Silk Road, but they would show no compunction in attacking any group of travellers, especially if they believed those people were carrying valuables. And the nine men were accompanying a treasure that every member of the armed escort was fully prepared to die to protect. Only when they reached their destination would they be able to relax, when the treasure would at last be safe, safe – they hoped – for all eternity.

Two of the men rode slowly at the head of the group, each mounted on a woolly two-humped Bactrian camel, an animal surprisingly well-adapted to the harsh terrain. Following them, two yaks were hitched to a small and sturdy wooden cart, one man sitting on the bench at the front, whip in hand. Two other yaks followed, tied with short ropes to the rear of the cart, then half a dozen donkeys, each bearing a single rider and with heavy packs on their rumps.

In the flat loading area of the cart was a heavy wooden box, perhaps eight feet in length, four feet wide and two feet high. The box was hidden from view, covered in piles of furs and other garments, baskets of food and pitchers of water and wine. The men hoped they looked like a group of simple travellers, transporting nothing of value, and would be of no interest to bandits.

And their appearance was unremarkable. With one

exception, they all looked – and indeed were – indigenous to the area. Their skin was brown and heavily wrinkled from a lifetime's exposure to the sun in the thin air at high altitude, their eyes Mongoloid, their faces broad and flat, their hair black and worn long.

The youngest man was the odd one out, riding one of the donkeys near the centre of the group. Perhaps twenty years old, less than half the age of the youngest of his companions, he had fair skin and almost a ruddy complexion. His eyes were a bright and startling blue and his hair – hidden under his hooded cloak – was reddish-brown. He was known to his companions as 'Sonam', the word translating as 'the fortunate one', though that was not his given name.

The track from the village ran for less than a mile, and then crossed a mountain stream. The small caravan stopped by the bank and the travellers took the opportunity to drink and refill all their water containers. It would be the last stream they would cross before the steepest part of the ascent began and, although the valley was cold, with blankets of snow covering the peaks that surrounded them, an adequate supply of drinking water was essential.

The two men riding the camels remained mounted, alert for any signs of danger lurking behind the hills and within the scrubby vegetation that bordered the tumbling waters, but saw nothing. In a few minutes all the members of the caravan had remounted and resumed their journey, fording the stream and climbing the bank on the opposite side.

The going became rougher the higher they ascended, the track – such as it was – barely wide enough to accommodate the wooden cart, and their progress was reduced to little more than a slow walking pace.

It was mid-morning before they saw the first sign of anyone else on the mountainside. The leading camel walked around a bend in the track, and as the animal stepped forward, a shadowy figure dressed in grey melted back into the rocks fifty yards in front.

Immediately, Je-tsun, the leading rider, reined in his mount and raised his hand to stop the caravan. He glanced behind him, checking that his companions had seen his signal, and at the same time grabbed his bow, drew an arrow from the quiver on his back and notched it, ready to fire.

'What is it?' the man riding the second camel asked, stopping beside him and readying his own bow. His name was Ketu, and their language was a local dialect that would, in time, become known as Old Tibetan.

'A man,' Je-tsun said shortly. 'In the rocks on the left.'

The two men scanned the track that meandered along the side of the mountain in front of them. If the figure was a bandit, he and his fellow thieves hadn't picked a particularly good place for an ambush. The caravan – apart from the cart, obviously, which was unable to leave the track – could move well over to the right, away from the rock-strewn mountainside, which would give the riders space to manoeuvre, and to fire their arrows.

'Not where I'd have chosen to mount an attack,' Ketu muttered.

As if in answer to his remark, a figure wearing a grey cloak appeared some distance away from the track and, behind him, a handful of goats could be seen, moving erratically across the rough and rocky terrain towards a small level area studded with patches of green.

The two men sighed in relief.

'Was that the man you saw?'

Je-tsun nodded. 'I think so. It looks like him, anyway.'

After a few minutes, the caravan resumed its slow but steady progress along the track and the increasingly uneven ground. Fallen rocks and trees frequently blocked their route, and several times three or four of the men had to dismount to drag and lever the obstacles to one side to create sufficient space for the cart to continue on its way.

Just after the sun reached its highest point in the sky, Je-tsun ordered the caravan to stop on a small level plateau that offered good visibility in all directions. They dismounted and clustered around the cart where their supplies were stored. They chewed hunks of heavy unleavened bread and strips of dried meat, washed down with water – they wouldn't touch the wine until they reached their destination.

Less than fifteen minutes later they were on the move again, and about half an hour after that the bandits hit them.

They rounded another bend to see a tree trunk completely blocking the track. In itself, that wasn't a cause for concern – they'd had to shift half a dozen already – but when they reined in their mounts the silence of the mountains was shattered by a sudden shouted command, and then a volley of arrows erupted from the rocks over to their left.

Most of them missed, but two hit Je-tsun squarely in the chest, knocking him backwards in his saddle. He grunted with the double impact, but didn't fall.

Beside him, Ketu swiftly notched an arrow on his own bow and fired at one of the attackers who they could now see clearly. A gang of about a dozen bandits, clothed in grey and brown cloaks, were standing among the rocks to the left of the ambush site, all armed with bows and arrows or throwing spears.

Behind the two men on camels, the rest of the group surged forward, yelling defiance as they dismounted. They used the bodies of their animals for cover, unslung their bows and fired at the bandits. The exception was the blue-eyed younger man, who was quickly dragged behind the yak-drawn cart by one of his companions.

'Sonam, stay down!' the man hissed, seizing his own bow and pulling an arrow out of his quiver.

In seconds, the air filled again with arrows, the missiles clattering against the rocks and thudding into the wooden sides of the cart. The driver jumped off the vehicle and ducked for shelter – he had no bow – while his companions fought for their lives.

Three of the bandits fell screaming, tumbling back into the rocks, their bodies pierced by the well-aimed arrows of the travellers.

The driver of the cart suddenly howled with pain as an arrow slammed into his thigh. He fell backwards, both hands clutching at his injury, and the two other men dragged him behind the cart, desperately seeking shelter from the hail of missiles that still whistled across the mountainside.

One of the donkeys fell, three arrows striking it almost simultaneously and killing it instantly, and Je-tsun's camel roared in pain as a spear grazed its side. Two of the travellers collapsed to the ground, one with an arrow through his neck, the point glistening red in the weak sunlight, the other pierced by two spears.

Then another shout rang out, and for an instant the volley of arrows diminished as the bandits stared at the scene in front of them.

Both of the men mounted on the camels were still in their saddles, but each of them had sprouted a handful of arrows, their points embedded in their chests and stomachs. Yet neither man appeared in any way affected by this – they were still aiming their bows and firing arrows without any obvious discomfort.

The sight was unsurprising to the travellers, but was clearly unnerving the bandits, who obviously believed both men should be dead or at least mortally wounded. The men pointed, shouting at each other in disbelief, then stopped the attack and simply took to their heels, vanishing into the jumble of rocks that covered the slope behind them.

For a few seconds, nobody on the track moved. They just stared at the hillside, making sure that their attackers really had gone, and weren't regrouping to launch another assault.

Behind the cart, Sonam and his companion stood up cautiously and looked round, then turned to give what assistance they could to the injured driver.

Je-tsun issued crisp orders. Two of his men drew their swords and ran across to the side of the track where the attack had been launched, and where a dull moaning sound could be heard, coming from one of the wounded bandits. Moments later, the moaning rose to a scream, then there was the sound of a blow and the noise stopped completely. Seconds afterwards, Je-tsun's men reappeared, one of them cleaning the blade of his weapon.

At the same time, two other men stepped forward to check on their fallen companions, but it was immediately apparent that they were both dead. Swiftly, the bodies were stripped of their weapons and belts, and then they were carried over to the opposite side of the track. There was no time to bury them, but Je-tsun ordered the two corpses to be laid out and covered with rocks, to try to keep away the vultures and other scavengers.

Only then, when he was sure the attack was over, did Je-tsun nudge his camel to make it kneel on the stony track, and dismount. Behind him, Ketu did the same.

'It worked, my friend,' Ketu said, stepping towards the other man with clumsy movements.

'It worked,' Je-tsun agreed, and awkwardly pulled his cloak over his head, the front of it stuck fast to his chest by the handful of arrows. Underneath it, secured by wide leather straps over his shoulders, he wore two thick planks of wood, covering his chest and back, a rudimentary form of body armour.

Je-tsun placed the wood on the ground and plucked out the arrows, one by one, then donned the planks again and replaced his cloak.

He turned to look at the wound his camel had sustained, but it was little more than a graze. The spear had obviously struck the animal a glancing blow that had left a shallow cut on the skin. One donkey was dead, pierced by three arrows, and two others had minor wounds.

Je-tsun walked across to the yak-drawn cart and looked at the three men there, one injured, the other two ministering to him.

Sonam stood up as he approached, and Je-tsun bowed down in front of him. 'You are unhurt, my lord?' he asked, standing erect again.

Sonam nodded. 'Yes, but Akar is bleeding badly from his thigh. The arrow has cut through several blood vessels, I think.'

Je-tsun nodded, clasped the younger man by the shoulders and then bent down to look at the injured man.

Akar looked up as Je-tsun knelt beside him. He was quivering with shock, and blood was pumping out of both sides of his thigh – the arrow had penetrated right through his leg, and was still lodged in the wound.

Je-tsun looked at the pain-racked face of the man he'd known for decades and shook his head. He knew that the injury was life-threatening simply because of the blood loss, but there was more to it than that. The bandits were known to smear the tips of their arrows with poison or excrement and, even if the wound wasn't fatal in itself, there was a good chance that infection would follow in the days to come, killing the victim more slowly but just as surely.

Akar stared at Je-tsun, knowledge of the reality of his situation written on his face. He nodded slowly, lifted his right hand and seized the other man's arm. 'Make it quick, my friend,' he said. Then he leaned back on the rocky ground and closed his eyes.

Je-tsun nodded in his turn, drew a short dagger from the scabbard at his belt and swiftly drove it into Akar's chest, straight through his heart. The man on the ground shuddered once, then lay still, his features growing slack as the pain ebbed away for the last time.

About half an hour later, the small caravan, now three men down, moved off again. For the rest of the journey the remaining men neither saw nor met anyone else, and finally they reached their destination, high up the valley, just after sunset.

Je-tsun ordered torches lit, then sent two of his men inside to check the structure thoroughly, and to ensure that nobody else had taken refuge there, though at that altitude it was unlikely. They emerged a few minutes later, to report that the place was exactly as it had been the previous year, when they'd found it for the first time, and when they'd spent almost six months preparing it, a task that had proved to be physically demanding and had also required considerable ingenuity.

Je-tsun nodded in satisfaction. He ordered the yaks to be unhitched from the cart and had them turned loose, together with the remaining donkeys. They wouldn't need those animals again. But the two camels were tethered securely on a patch of level ground nearby, where scrubby bushes would provide them with something to eat.

The men removed all the furs and other goods from the cart to expose the heavy wooden crate, lifted it between them and carried it into the entrance, where they laid it on the ground. Then they lit more torches to provide enough light to start their work. Baulks of timber had been piled against the opposite wall, and it took over an hour to remove them all, and to reveal the inner chamber.

Before they entered, Je-tsun walked in and inspected it. The small room was almost square, and for obvious reasons devoid of windows or any other openings. At one end was what looked almost like an altar, an oblong shape made from hewn chunks of solid stone, the gaps between them filled with some kind of mortar, and the top covered with half a dozen slabs of stone.

The men picked up the heavy box again, carried it into the chamber and set it down beside the stone structure. Je-tsun issued another order, and his men began removing the slabs, leaning the heavy pieces of stone against the wall. Their actions revealed that the structure was completely empty, just an oblong cavity formed from shaped rocks. When they'd removed the last slab, Je-tsun peered inside, ran the tips of his fingers along the inner surfaces and nodded in satisfaction.

Building this cavity of stone had been one of the tasks he and his men had carried out the previous year, and his only concern had been the possibility of damp inside it, because their treasure was very fragile. But he could detect no signs of moisture on the cold stones that formed the cavity, the structure that would be the last resting place of the wooden box and its precious contents.

Getting the box inside the stone cavity was not going to be easy, just because of its size and weight, but they had foreseen the problem and Je-tsun had come up with a simple and effective solution.

One of his men laid three short lengths of wood in the base of the stone structure, to provide a platform on which the box could rest. Then, together, the six men lifted the box up to waist height, and then lowered it on to the top of the stone structure so that it lay across the opening. They slung heavy ropes underneath it, looped the ropes around their shoulders and, when Je-tsun gave the order, lifted the box again just using the ropes. They shuffled awkwardly around, manoeuvring the wooden box until it lined up exactly with the opening, then lowered it carefully into the structure.

Once it was resting on the floor, they pulled out the ropes from underneath it. Then they carefully replaced each stone slab on the top of the stone structure, sealing the cavity again.

Once he was satisfied that it was properly sealed, Je-tsun took a hammer and chisel and, in the middle of the central slab, carved two symbols that, in the Tibetan dialect, equated to the letters 'YA'. Each of the men touched the carving once, then all but one filed slowly out of the chamber – that man had a single final task to perform. Then they closed the door for the last time.

It was too late to complete their task that night, so they ate some of their provisions and drank a little wine before wrapping themselves in the furs and sleeping as best they could on the cold and rocky floor.

The following morning they rose to finish their work. Concealing the entrance to the inner chamber took a couple of hours, but when they'd finished the result was impressive. Without knowledge of what was hidden there, nobody would have any idea that it even existed.

Je-tsun inspected the result and expressed his satisfaction.

'We have done well,' he told the men who'd followed him on this, their final mission. 'Now it is time.'

The men filed outside and followed Je-tsun up the valley floor to the edge of a cliff, where a deep gully split the rock.

As they approached the edge, the man known as Sonam moved a little to one side, his expression troubled.

'Is this necessary, Je-tsun?' he asked. 'You have all been loyal to me and to our master. Such loyalty should not have to be rewarded in this way.'

The older man shook his head. 'We would not speak out willingly, my lord, but we know not what the future holds, and this is the only way we can be certain the secret will be preserved.'

Sonam shook his head. 'I cannot witness this,' he muttered. 'I will leave you now.'

He stepped forward and clasped Je-tsun around the shoulders, then turned and walked away without a backward glance, down the slope to where the two camels were grazing contentedly.

Behind him, he heard the first cry of pain as Je-tsun began the willing slaughter of his faithful and trusting companions.

England

1

Present day

2 a.m. Total darkness. Oliver Wendell-Carfax was wide awake. An unusual noise had echoed through the house – Carfax Hall was old and creaked at the seams – but for the moment he couldn't identify it. Maybe a window catch had sprung, or perhaps he hadn't closed one of the doors properly and a draught had moved it?

He lay completely still in the ancient four-poster bed he'd slept in since he'd reached adulthood, eyes wide open and staring up at the ceiling – the bed's canopy had vanished long ago.

Then he heard it again. A scraping, rattling sound that he knew instantly wasn't caused by a door or window banging. Somebody was in the house, moving things around, searching for something.

Wendell-Carfax had lived alone all his life. He'd never married and the days when he could afford live-in staff were long gone. He'd had burglars in the place twice before, both times kids from the local village, looking for something they could grab and sell to pay for cigarettes or alcohol or drugs. Each time he'd taken care of the problem himself because he knew if he called the police they'd take at least an hour to get to him, and wouldn't do much when they arrived.

He heaved himself out of the bed, pulled a dressing gown around his thin frame and grabbed his walking stick from the chair beside him. Trying to move as quietly as possible, he made his way along the corridor to the head of the central staircase. There he stopped, staring down towards the ground floor. Somebody had switched on the lights in the grand salon.

Not only did he have burglars, he had cheeky burglars.

Holding the end of his walking stick, so that he could use it as a club if he had to, he crept down the stairs to the hall and walked slowly across to the partially open door of the salon.

He peered through the gap into the room, and almost muttered his displeasure aloud. Somebody – Wendell-Carfax could only see the figure from behind – was sitting in his favourite chair beside the empty fireplace, smoking a cigarette and tapping the ash on to the carpet.

Wendell-Carfax straightened up, changed his grip slightly on his walking stick and opened the door. He raised the stick, fully intending to bring it crashing down on the head of the intruder – and froze. An ugly black automatic pistol was pointing right at him.

'Sit down,' the stranger said, his voice little more than a sibilant whisper. He gestured towards the chair in front of him.

He was stockily built, about forty or fifty years of age, and there was an air of confidence, of menace, about him that was frightening in its intensity. He had tanned skin and black hair, and his eyes were so dark they almost seemed to have no pupils. But it wasn't the man's face that most arrested Wendell-Carfax's attention – it was what he was wearing.

'You're—' he began.

'Be quiet,' the man said softly, but there was no mistaking the power his words conveyed. 'You have something I want and I've come to collect it.'

'What is it?' Wendell-Carfax demanded. 'And who the hell are you?'

The stranger stood up, and stepped across to where Wendell-Carfax was standing.

The old man raised his walking stick threateningly, but the stranger brushed aside his pitiful weapon and with the fluid power and casual malevolence of a striking snake, he smashed the barrel of his pistol into the older man's stomach.

Wendell-Carfax folded at the waist, gasping for breath, as a second blow crashed into the back of his neck.

* * *

Consciousness returned slowly and painfully. His stomach and his neck ached, but the greatest pain Oliver Wendell-Carfax was feeling was in his wrists and arms – an aching, tugging sensation. When he looked up, he saw the reason.

His attacker had dragged him out into the hall, looped a thin rope over the banister rail of the main staircase, tied the end of it around his wrists and then hauled him upright, securing the rope around another banister. He was suspended, his toes barely touching the floor, completely helpless. Already he had lost almost all feeling in his hands. But that wasn't his biggest problem.

In front of him, the stranger sat in one of the chairs he'd obviously brought from the salon. His face was calm and relaxed.

'Who are you?' Wendell-Carfax demanded again, his voice made harsh by pain and fear.

The stranger bent down and picked up a leather whip from the floor. It was a handle with about a dozen thongs attached to it, and at the end of each was the glint of steel. He walked across to the suspended figure, stepped slightly behind him and swung the whip at the old man's back.

The pain was shocking, sudden and overwhelming, a red ribbon of agony that stretched the whole width of Wendell-Carfax's unprotected back. He howled in pain, his body arcing forwards. He felt a sudden dampness as he lost control of his bladder.

The stranger swung the scourge again, sending a second

bolt of pain lancing through the old man's thin frame. Then he walked back, resumed his seat and waited until Wendell-Carfax stopped screaming.

'I'll ask the questions,' the stranger said, his voice still soft and controlled. 'The scourge will encourage you to speak the truth, as it has done through the ages.'

Wendell-Carfax nodded.

'I want the parchment,' the man said. 'You know the one I mean.'

'I don't have it,' Wendell-Carfax gasped.

'Don't play games with me. I know it's here. Somewhere.'

'You don't understand—'

'No, *you* don't,' the man said, raising his voice very slightly. 'I will have that parchment, wherever it is.' He took two swift strides forward and again swung the leather scourge.

Wendell-Carfax shrieked in pain, then sobbed his agony.

The man stepped in front of Wendell-Carfax again. 'I can do this all night. The scourge will cut you to shreds unless you tell me what I want to know. Where's the parchment?'

'I don't have it,' Wendell-Carfax whispered. 'It's gone.'

'What do you mean?'

'It fell to pieces. It was two thousand years old. My father didn't know how to look after it. It discoloured, then it just fell apart years ago. It's gone for ever.'

For the first time the stranger's expressionless face

changed. It was as if a cloud passed across his eyes, to be replaced by a kind of cold fury.

'You stupid, stupid old fool. Didn't you know what you had in your hands?'

Once more he stepped behind Wendell-Carfax and swung the whip, again and again, the old man's thin pyjamas turning deep red as the skin of his back split open.

The assault stopped as suddenly as it had begun, leaving Wendell-Carfax dazed and barely conscious, bleeding from dozens of wounds, his back flaring with the agony of ripped skin and torn flesh. Then Wendell-Carfax felt a new pain as a hand grabbed what little hair remained on his scalp and pulled his head up.

'But you copied it?' the stranger demanded. 'Your father must have made a copy of the parchment?'

'Yes.' Wendell-Carfax's voice was slurred and faint, his eyes virtually closed. 'Yes, he did.'

'Where is it?'

Wendell-Carfax's mouth moved but no sound emerged.

'Where is it? Say that again.' The stranger stepped closer to Wendell-Carfax, turning his head so that his ear was virtually touching the old man's lips.

Wendell-Carfax's eyes flickered open, and in that instant he knew what he should do.

'It's . . .' he began, the words scarcely audible, and the stranger leaned closer still. Then Wendell-Carfax bit down on the stranger's ear with all the strength he could muster.

Blood spurted into his mouth and he felt his teeth meet through the thin flesh.

The stranger howled his own agony. He dropped the leather scourge and jerked away involuntarily and, as the flesh of his ear tore further, the pain reached a new crescendo. He reached up to Wendell-Carfax's face, trying desperately to force the old man's jaws apart, but he couldn't reach, couldn't get a purchase.

But he had to get free.

He swung his fist, hitting Wendell-Carfax in the stomach, but the blow was badly aimed and weak, and had no apparent effect. So he hit him again, and again, until at last he managed to land a solid punch on the old man's solar plexus.

Wendell-Carfax gasped with the pain, and his jaw muscles relaxed, allowing the stranger to escape.

'You bastard,' the stranger snapped. He grabbed the whip and swung it savagely against Wendell-Carfax's body, lashing him mercilessly.

But even as the first blows landed, Wendell-Carfax's face changed. A kind of spasm, a rictus of agony resonated through him, and a sudden gripping, clenching pain exploded in the centre of his chest. And in that instant, at the very last moment of his life, Oliver Wendell-Carfax knew he'd achieved a kind of victory, knew he'd defeated the violent psychopath facing him.

He gasped a breath, grunted once and his head slumped to one side. Finally he hung motionless, his eyes wide open, the grimace on his face slowly softening.

Cursing softly, the stranger stood still, his gaze locked on the body of the elderly man he'd travelled so many thousands of miles to find. Then he shrugged, swung the scourge once more across Wendell-Carfax's chest – a last, pointless act of violence – before folding it up and putting it into his pocket. He needed to refocus.

Three hours later, he gave up his search. Wherever the copy of the parchment had been hidden, he couldn't find it, and now dawn was approaching. He had to get away from the house before anyone – a gardener or a cook – turned up.

His best hope was that the copy of the ancient parchment would never be discovered. If it was, he'd have to recover it at any cost, even if it meant killing those who got in his way.

2

'This really isn't my field, Roger,' Angela Lewis said, irritation showing in her voice.

'You work with ceramics.'

'I'm a *conservator*, not an *assessor*. My job is putting the broken pieces back together again. You need a specialist, somebody who can identify and value the relics – someone like Jane or Catherine.'

Roger Halliwell leaned back in his swivel chair and looked at his subordinate across his cluttered desk.

'I can't spare either of them,' he said simply. 'They're both working on important projects for me here at the museum.' Halliwell lifted his arm in an all-encompassing gesture that appeared to include the entire premises of the British Museum, rather than just his fairly small section of it. His domain encompassed only pottery and ceramics, and he was in nominal charge of a small staff of about a dozen people.

'More important than anything I'm doing, you mean?' Angela snapped.

'You said it, Angela, not me.' Halliwell sat forward and rested his hands on his desk. 'Look, I never intended to ask you to do this. Jane was supposed to be the ceramics expert on this team, but something else came up on Friday afternoon and I've had to re-assign her. Right now, there's nobody else here with enough experience to do the job.'

He smiled at her across the desk. 'I know it's not your specialization, but you certainly know enough about ceramics to identify the pieces that have any real value. All I want you to do is be a part of the team we're sending to the estate and separate the good stuff from the dross. We don't need you to assign accurate values. That can be done later, when whoever ends up in charge of this decides what to do.'

'So you want me to do a sort of ceramics triage?'

'Exactly. It'll take a week of your time, no more. Look at it as a kind of working holiday in the country. And there's something else that might interest you. A story about the house, especially after all that time you spent digging about in Jerusalem and Megiddo.'

'What story?'

'Apparently the deceased owner's father claimed that he knew where a really valuable treasure was hidden. He told anyone who'd listen that it was the most important treasure of all time.'

'Which is what, exactly?'

'I haven't the vaguest idea. Anyway, he spent a long time somewhere out in the Middle East, digging for this hoard in several different places.'

In spite of herself, Angela felt a tingle of interest.

'And did he find it?'

'No, obviously not.' Halliwell leaned forward again. 'But there might be some clues left in the house, clues that you and Chris could follow, I mean – if you're interested.'

Angela sighed. 'Look, Roger, I'm not some adolescent schoolgirl you can send off on a treasure hunt. I'll go to Carfax Hall and look at these ceramics, but that's all I'll do. If you want somebody to waste their time looking for buried treasure, you'd better look elsewhere.' She paused, irritated by Halliwell's look of relief.

'Where will we stay?'

'There's a pub not far from the estate with about eight or nine rooms. We've block-booked half a dozen of them for all of this week, with an option for next week as well, just in case the assessment takes longer than we expect. The museum will pay for your food and accommodation, of course, and even your mileage.'

'I'm not sharing a room with anyone on the team.'

'I wouldn't expect you to. There are only six of you, so you'll have one room each.'

Reluctantly Angela bowed to the inevitable. It was only a week, after all, and maybe the house would be interesting. 'When do I leave?'

Halliwell glanced at the wall clock above the door of his

office. 'The sooner the better. In fact, right now would be a good time.' He passed a sheet of paper across the desk. 'Here's the address of the pub where you're staying, and of the estate itself. I suggest you go to the house first of all to see how the land lies. Richard Mayhew is in overall charge of the team, but you're all working as individuals, of course. And remember, if you do find a treasure map, I want to know about it.'

3

Jesse McLeod almost always arrived at work early, typically at about six in the morning, for two good reasons.

Firstly, it meant he could leave early in the afternoon and head for the beach with his surfboard, as long as the sun was shining. If it wasn't, or if he had a lot to do, he'd climb back on his Harley, track over to his penthouse apartment just south of Carmel, right on the Californian coast, and spend the rest of the day working on one of his computers, using his administrator access to remotely monitor the company's network. Of course, leaving early only worked if nobody had broken anything or otherwise screwed up the system, which didn't happen quite as often these days because they'd ditched Vista, which only occasionally did what it was supposed to do, and reverted to XP, which was clunky but usually reliable. He was still evaluating Windows 7.

The second reason was that arriving at work two hours before anyone else allowed him to run his usual checks on the operating system, application software, back-up devices and the various linked databases – getting on with his basic network housekeeping, in other words – without any of the non-geeks interfering or asking the usual idiot questions.

McLeod had been the network manager, database designer and just about anything else to do with the NotJustGenetics Inc. – colloquially known as 'NoJoGen' – computer system for over ten years, pretty much since the day the company was formed. He'd done well out of it. Not as well as the guy who'd come up with the idea of genetic research and gene manipulation to attempt to cure or at least help combat specific diseases, but well enough. He had a six-figure salary, could dress just about however he liked, and turn up pretty much whenever he wanted, as long as the network and software were stable. And there were other bonuses as well.

McLeod pressed the code to open his office door, dumped his crash helmet on the table in the corner and peeled off his leather jacket. It was already getting hot outside, but he wore the leather for protection in case he crashed the hog, not for warmth. Under it he wore a faded CalTech T-shirt – unlike most people who affected such garments, he had actually been there – and tight-fitting black jeans that emphasized his height and lean build. They were cinched around his waist with a leather belt which was fastened with a solid silver buckle depicting a fist giving the finger. It was, in many ways, an accurate indication of his outlook on life.

Then he switched on his monitor. Like most commercial operations that relied on computers, which meant almost everybody these days, the NoJoGen system ran 24/7. Only the flat-panel monitors were shut down when the offices were closed.

McLeod sat down in his swivel chair, ran his fingers through his untidy mop of dark curly hair, opened up his master diagnostic program and started it running. He'd designed the software suite himself. It was a management program that executed a series of commercial diagnostic routines one after the other and displayed the results at the end, and it usually took no more than about ten minutes to run to completion. That gave him enough time to plug in his coffee machine and load up the first brew of the day – in McLeod's opinion, a supply of decent coffee was almost as important to him as good diagnostic software.

Only when the system analysis results popped up on the screen – all showing green – and his first cup of java was sitting on the desk beside him, did he take a look at the search routines his machine had been running overnight. These weren't normal internet searches. The wide-area search routines McLeod had put in place accessed private databases as well, many of them run by government agencies and commercial organizations, databases whose managers fondly believed were secure against hackers.

But Jesse McLeod wasn't just any old hacker. He'd narrowly avoided a prison term at the age of fifteen when he'd wormed his way past three separate firewalls and numerous intruder detection systems to get inside a network at the Pentagon. He'd gained administrator access there, given himself a username and password, and used that network as a gateway that had allowed him to jump straight into another network based in Pennsylvania Avenue and operated by the White House. The reason he wasn't prosecuted was probably largely due to embarrassment that a kid of his age had managed to outwit the best security consultants and computer experts in the American government and military.

He had been ordered to show these experts exactly how he'd managed to effect his intrusion, however, so that those loopholes could be closed, and he'd also been instructed to test all the Pentagon's and the White House's access points – under close supervision – to see if he could defeat those as well. He had, twice, which had resulted in four civilian administrators and three senior military officers losing their jobs within the next three weeks.

In the ten years since then, the FBI had watched Jesse McLeod very closely, but the threat of prison had frightened him, and after that episode he had become what was known as a 'white hat hacker'. That meant he still trawled the internet, and still probed the sites he found, but if he worked his way into a system he announced the fact to the network administrator and suggested ways of closing the loopholes he'd exploited. He never copied data or did any damage inside the networks he cracked, and a handful of times he'd even been paid 'consultancy fees' by the target companies for his efforts.

At least, that was what the FBI believed. But like a lot of things the FBI believed, they were wrong. Jesse McLeod was constitutionally incapable of obeying the law, and that was one of the reasons why NoJoGen paid him such a large salary. The company needed access to the kind of data that was unavailable in the public domain – a less mealy-mouthed description of this activity would be industrial espionage – and relied on him to hack his way into whatever system held it, and then retrieve it.

But these days he was a lot more careful, and a lot more secretive. He had set up dozens of fake identities in China and Pakistan and the new states that had emerged following the break-up of the Soviet Union, places where he knew that American law enforcement would find it difficult, or even impossible, to track him, and used those as the apparent origin – the technical term was a 'zombie server' – for his probes. He'd even set up an account that purported to be located in North Korea – a country that offered no internet access at all to its population – just to see what the Fibbies would do about it. They hadn't noticed.

And so, every night, while he slept peacefully in his penthouse, the sound of waves breaking on the shore below him, his untraceable electronic proxies trawled the web, probing systems and networks and looking for any references to whatever subjects the founder and majority shareholder of NoJoGen, John Johnson Donovan – known simply as 'JJ' – had asked him to locate.

His proxies never left any evidence of their intrusion, and merely copied whatever data they could find that related to the search string McLeod had loaded into their programs. When they'd completed their mission, each proxy automatically accessed one of several web-based email accounts and pasted the results into email messages. But these messages would never be sent, because all emails leave an electronic trail across the internet. Instead, all the messages were left on the servers as drafts, and McLeod was then able to access each email account, copy the contents of the draft messages and afterwards delete them, which left no trace at all.

The whole process was automated, and McLeod would only get personally involved if the hacking software he'd designed failed to breach the defences of a particular network. Then he'd flex his hacking muscles and spend a pleasant few hours working out how to get inside that system. But normally, he just scanned the results when they were displayed on his monitor, weeded out the obvious rubbish, and sent the rest up to Donovan's workstation on the top floor of the building.

Because it was a Monday and the offices had been closed since Saturday morning, there were dozens of results to analyse. As usual, most of them were of neither interest nor relevance, but when McLeod looked at the nineteenth search result he sat back in his seat and whistled.

'I'll be damned,' he muttered to himself.

He checked the source of the data, but that turned out to be no surprise at all. He'd seen immediately that the information had been posted on the front page of a small local newspaper, and the version his proxy had located had been in the on-line version of the journal, hosted on an entirely unprotected server.

McLeod read the article in its entirety, and one short paragraph caught and then held his attention. He sat in thought for a minute or so, then clicked his mouse button a couple of times to bring up an internet search engine. He entered a simple search term and looked at the results, which gave him the name of the website he was interested in. He opened up one of the hacking programs he'd written himself and started probing the distant server, looking for a way inside. There was something there he definitely needed to get a look at.

In less than fifteen minutes he was looking at a list of police case files, listed by number. Then he changed the parameters and generated an alphabetical list of the names of the claimants or victims. Most of the files were small, the incidents fairly pedestrian – muggings, car thefts, burglaries, and so on. And then he saw something big. There were numerous statements, reports by the attending officers, forensic analyses and the like, and a whole sheaf of crime-scene photographs, all neatly labelled and catalogued.

He flicked through the forensic stuff until he found the one that related to the paragraph in the newspaper story, and made a copy of it on his hard drive. Then he glanced through everything else he'd found, and despatched the original newspaper report up to Donovan's computer with the rest of the stuff. When his boss got in, he guessed he'd get a call.

But he had a completely different recipient in mind for the forensic report he'd copied from the police database.

4

Two hours later, Angela had turned off the M25, where the traffic was actually moving, for a change, and was heading up the A10, the old London Road. Her satnav had protested when she made the turn, but she'd decided to take the scenic route because she had two ulterior motives. First, she wanted to treat herself to lunch in a country pub somewhere, and there were no such facilities on the M11. And, second, she wanted to be able to stop somewhere and ring her ex-husband, Chris Bronson, to explain why she'd be out of town for the rest of the week. She'd called his mobile from her flat in Ealing before she left, but it had gone straight to voicemail. Knowing Chris as well as she did, she knew she'd be able to reach him at lunchtime.

Nearing the village of Wendens Ambo, she spotted an old pub and parked her Mini in one of the few remaining spaces in the front car park.

She ordered a Caesar salad and a bottle of Perrier, and

carried the drink over to a seat right beside a window that overlooked the main road outside. While she waited for her food to be served, she pulled out her mobile. This time, Bronson answered almost immediately.

'Hi, Angela. Where are you?'

'How do you know I'm not in my office, slaving away over a broken pot?' she said, a little annoyed with herself for feeling pleased to hear his voice.

'I'm a detective, remember. Actually, I called your office. So where are you?'

'Suffolk, I think.' She looked up and nodded her thanks as the barman placed an enormous bowl of salad on the table in front of her.

'Suffolk?' Bronson was clearly surprised.

'Yes. I've just stopped for lunch in a pub near a village called Wendens Ambo, and I'm heading for a country house somewhere near Stoke by Clare. Wonderful names, don't you think?'

'A country house party, is it?'

'Sadly not. Actually, I've been sent up here to work. An elderly minor aristocrat named Oliver Wendell-Carfax was murdered in his home near here about two weeks ago—'

'I know about that,' Bronson interrupted, sounding concerned. 'I saw one of the reports. Somebody strung him up from the staircase and then beat him, but the autopsy showed that he actually died of a heart attack. I think the local police have drawn a blank on the case so far – no obvious suspects and no apparent motive, though somebody had searched the house. It's a nasty business. But what's it got to do with you?'

'Well, the museum has now become involved – not because of who Wendell-Carfax was, or how he died, but because of what he did. He was pretty much the last of a long line of avid collectors of antiques and ancient relics. Apparently his country house is full of the things. He was also, according to Roger Halliwell, a typical grumpy old bastard. Over the last ten years or so he managed to alienate just about every member of his family, and almost everybody else who knew him. When he died, the firms of solicitors he'd used opened up his last will and testament and had a bit of a shock.'

'"Firms of solicitors"?' Bronson asked. 'In the plural?'

Angela sighed. 'Yes. Over the last year Wendell-Carfax visited four different solicitors in Suffolk and deposited his last will and testament with each of them.'

'Different wills, I suppose?'

'All completely different, and each cutting out one or more different family members. The trouble was, each time he made a new will, he never bothered telling the new solicitor acting for him about the earlier ones, although he made sure he told the beneficiaries of the new will.'

'But not the people he'd just disinherited?'

'Of course not. That wouldn't have been any fun, would it? So as soon as he was found dead, various family members crawled out of the woodwork, each of them expecting to inherit about two hundred acres of prime Suffolk real estate and a country house stuffed full of antiques.'

'So who is the beneficiary?' Bronson asked, sounding puzzled.

'For the house and land, I've no idea – but in his final will, or at least the last one that's turned up so far, the old man gave everything inside the house – the entire contents, that is – to the British Museum.'

'So you're up there to assess the bequest?'

'Yep.' Angela drove her fork into the salad and took a mouthful. 'The Suffolk Police have finally allowed museum staff to go into the house. Until now, it's been out of bounds as a crime scene.'

'So you'll be away all week, then?' Bronson asked.

'Hopefully no longer than that. Until I get there, I really don't know how much there is to do.' Angela paused and crossed her fingers surreptitiously under the table. She hoped her next question didn't make her sound too desperate. 'We're staying in a local pub, if you fancy popping up one evening?'

5

As befitted the founder and major shareholder of NotJustGenetics Inc., JJ Donovan's office was on the top floor of the building. It occupied most of the top floor, in fact. Two of the walls were almost entirely glass, offering spectacular views of Monterey and the ocean beyond, but these days Donovan rarely bothered looking out in that direction. He'd even had his desk moved closer to one of the inner walls and positioned a couple of couches and several armchairs by the picture windows in its place.

His desk was a wide expanse of bird's-eye maple supported by a stainless-steel frame and legs, his chair a futuristic combination of chrome, steel and leather. Opposite the desk, about half of one wall was entirely given over to video displays. Eight digital plasma screens displayed a selection of domestic and international news feeds. In the centre of the desk, a smaller digital screen displayed exactly the same feeds, but was touch-sensitive, so Donovan could simply press the tip of his finger on any of the video pictures to select the sound for that particular channel.

Also on the desk were three telephones and two computer screens, one displaying the logo and the status of the NoJoGen network, and which showed the progress of any of the development programmes being run by the company's scientists. The other was just a regular PC hitched to a broadband router, which allowed him to surf the web or do anything else he wanted. This machine was an obvious area of vulnerability, so it was separated from the company network, which was shielded behind a physical firewall, and the most powerful software firewall, anti-virus and anti-intrusion programs money could buy. Jesse McLeod had stated that even he couldn't hack his way inside the system and if *he* couldn't do it, he'd added modestly, nobody else could.

The only incongruous note in Donovan's hi-tech office was a large display cabinet positioned beside the door, containing a collection of old books. Really old books. Or, to be absolutely accurate, old copies of really old books. And in a locked safe set into the same wall, a safe that incorporated sophisticated thermostatic controls and devices to regulate the humidity, lay his most prized possession. It was little more than a scrap of papyrus that he'd privately named the Hyrcania Codex, based upon the single name he'd found in the text.

In complete contrast to the work his company did, which was arguably beyond the cutting edge of the science of genetics, Donovan had long had a fascination with ancient manuscripts and codices. As his business had blossomed, he'd had the finance to indulge his passion, and he'd bought relics at auction and from specialist dealers. He'd even learned a little Hebrew and Aramaic along the way, though he usually employed specialists to produce translations of the works he had purchased.

Over two years earlier, a single phrase he'd read in the translation of one part of the Hyrcania Codex had electrified him, and it was this discovery that had driven the non-medical searches that he'd tasked Jesse McLeod with.

That morning, Donovan arrived early at the building and followed his usual routine. He slid his Porsche 911 into his named slot in the underground car park and took the stairs to his office. He never used the lift because he got little enough exercise during the day, and he had never seen the point of sweating away pointlessly on some machine in a gym. Climbing six flights of stairs non-stop every day would, he hoped, give him a short but regular cardio-vascular workout.

Anyone looking at him would probably agree that it was working. Donovan was tall, just over six two, and slim, with thick black hair that he kept trimmed close to his scalp – not a crew cut, but not far off. Dark brown, almost black, eyes and a large straight nose dominated his face, and even when he'd just shaved he still seemed to sport a five o'clock shadow. When he smiled, which he did often, because JJ Donovan was a man with a lot to be happy about, he showed two rows of brilliant white teeth, which he sometimes referred to as his 'forty-grand smile', because this was exactly what they'd cost.

He put his briefcase down on his desk and switched on both of his monitors. On the PC connected to the internet, he pulled up a classical music broadcast and pumped the sound through the desktop's built-in speaker system. Then he flicked the switch that powered up the wall-mounted monitors and watched CNN for a few seconds. Finally, he looked at his network computer and checked the internal message system.

The note from Jesse McLeod was the third one he read. He read the text twice, then reached for the internal telephone.

6

The Mini bounced down the drive, which curved around to the right behind a low hill. As she straightened up the car, Angela could see the hall itself for the first time. She knew from what Roger Halliwell had told her that it dated from the late nineteenth century, a Gothic-revival structure built on the remains of a much older building.

From a distance, the house looked mellow and comfortable in the landscape. Set on a slight rise and overlooking a small ornamental lake, which was a somewhat bilious green in the mid-afternoon sunlight, it featured spires on the corners and a profusion of arched windows, the whole building constructed of what looked like the same type of grey stone as the pillars at the end of the drive.

'Nice,' Angela murmured.

Three cars were parked on the oval gravel area in front of the house, so she assumed the other members of the British Museum team had already arrived. These cars were some distance from the house, which at first puzzled her, but when she pulled up next to one of them and switched off the engine, she saw why.

Along the façade of the property was a temporary fence, just a line of steel posts driven into the gravel surface of the drive and linked by plastic-coated wire, and behind that were several quite substantial lumps of masonry. And when she looked up at the old house itself, she realized that it was in a very poor condition indeed, with large gaps in the stonework where pieces had fallen out over the years. Several of the window panes were broken, and what paint there was had flaked badly.

She left her overnight bag in the boot of the car, but took her laptop case with her, and walked across to the main door of the house which was standing wide open.

She stepped into a large square wood-panelled hall filled with cardboard boxes and tea chests. On one side stood a mounted suit of armour, that to Angela's inexpert eyes looked genuinely medieval, and on the other a life-size wooden carving of an erect bear, one paw raised high, the other held out at about waist height, a wooden plate clutched in its claws, possibly intended to be a receptacle for mail or perhaps keys. Avoiding the bear's glassy eyes, she looked around. At the far end of the hall, beyond the bear and the suit of armour, a massive stone staircase ascended to the first floor of the house. On both sides of the hall were large double doors, open wide.

Choosing the doorway on the right-hand side, Angela

walked straight into an Aladdin's cave of relics. The room ran the entire length of that part of the house and had probably originally been intended as a formal reception room. There were two tall windows at the far end; half a dozen others along the right-hand wall looked out of the front of the building towards the gravelled car park. The long wall opposite them was dominated by a huge fireplace. You could burn an entire tree in it which, Angela reflected, you'd probably need to do in the winter if you wanted to keep the temperature of the room much above freezing. On either side of the fireplace, built-in bookcases extended in both directions, the shelves lined with leather-bound volumes. Just cataloguing those would be at least a week's work for somebody. But it wasn't the elegant proportions of the room or the books or the faded decoration, or even the fireplace, that caught her eye. It was the floor.

Almost the entire surface of the scuffed parquet was covered with boxes and bags and chests, a haphazard collection of containers, interspersed with occasional bronze and marble sculptures and other, unrecognizable, objects covered in white dust sheets or plastic sheeting.

'Good God,' Angela muttered to herself. 'If every room's like this, it'll take months, not weeks, to sort out.'

'Ah, there you are, Angela.' Richard Mayhew's voice boomed out from behind her, stating the obvious. A large – in all respects – and florid-faced man who specialized in objects made from silver and gold, he seemed incapable of ever speaking in anything less than a slightly moderated shout.

'Richard,' she said, shaking his hand. She pointed at the chaotic mass of containers in the room. 'Are all the rooms as full as this?'

Mayhew shook his head. 'No, not at all. This is the biggest room in the house, and it looks as if somebody – presumably the executors – decided to leave the furniture in situ, but bring almost everything else in here and the room on the opposite side of the hall. Personally, I'd have preferred to do it room by room, but there you are. Needs must, and all that.'

He looked round. 'Now, we'll be making a start in here first thing tomorrow morning. The other chaps are checking the rest of the house, making sure that we know what else there is to be assessed. The good news for you is that there's a very large kitchen, and almost all of the china and ceramics we've found so far are already in there. I don't think it'll take you all that long to check them over. In the meantime, let me introduce you to the other chaps and give you the guided tour. It's a fascinating old house with some very interesting features.'

He led the way back into the hall and across to the foot of the staircase.

'What the devil happened here?' Angela asked, stopping short when she saw a missing banister halfway up the staircase.

Mayhew coughed, and turned an alarming shade of

puce. 'That is where the old man . . . er, died,' he said. 'Apparently he was found hanging from that piece of banister. Terrible business.'

Angela noticed a large brown stain on the flagstones near her feet, and looked away. There had obviously been a lot of blood. She decided it was time to change the subject.

'Roger told me about the multiple wills Wendell-Carfax made.'

Mayhew smiled and relaxed a little. 'Mischievous old sod. He was the last of the line, you know. Never married, no children. Just a few cousins who're now all busily fighting each other over their share of the inheritance.'

He led the way up to a wide corridor on the first floor, spacious bedrooms opening up on both sides of it. 'As you've probably guessed, Oliver was a quite a character, probably slightly mad. But his father – his name was Bartholomew Wendell-Carfax – was as nutty as a fruitcake. That's him at the end of the corridor.'

Where the corridor ended was a small sitting area, tall windows offering a view of the parkland outside the house. Between the two windows was a painting, almost life-sized, that showed a middle-aged dark-haired man wearing what looked like a tweed suit. He was seated in a chair and looking slightly away from the painter, towards a roaring wood fire, a coat of arms cut into the wall above the inglenook.

'He doesn't look mad,' Angela said, stopping in front of

the painting and staring up at it. 'In fact, he looks rather attractive, in a sort of avuncular, country-house kind of way. He reminds me of a character you'd find in a P.G. Wodehouse novel.'

'Perhaps,' Mayhew said, 'but he was definitely odd. He had several portraits painted of himself and, even though he was running pretty low on funds, he commissioned four self-portraits from a very minor local artist named Edward Montgomery, and apparently paid quite a lot of money for them.'

'Maybe he didn't know how bad his financial situation was,' Angela said.

'Oh, he knew, all right, but that wasn't what was odd – it was the subjects he chose. According to the guidebook we found in one of the boxes in the salon, two of the pictures were like this one, conventional portraits. But in the other two, Bartholomew was depicted as a young man, in one dressed like a Sioux chief, feathered headdress and all, and in the other like a member of Indian royalty. The artist had to work from photographs Bartholomew supplied of himself when he was about twenty-five. That's what I mean by nutty – what was the point of having a portrait painted showing him when he was young when he was already well over seventy? And why was he wearing such extraordinary outfits?'

'You know, that kind of thing was quite the fashion in the early part of the twentieth century,' Angela said. 'A lot of society figures had their portraits done in exotic outfits.

So where are the paintings now? Somewhere here?'

'The conventional portraits are in the house, but not the other two. Bartholomew managed to sell them soon after they were painted.'

'Well, maybe it was just a money-making exercise after all. So why was he so short on funds?'

Mayhew stepped over beside Angela and they both looked out over the acres of peaceful parkland, so much in contrast, Angela thought, to the chaos of the house.

'According to the guidebook – which is quite a good read, by the way – Bartholomew's parents were very comfortably off. They owned huge tranches of land in East Anglia and had a couple of hundred tenant farmers, plus stock market investments, all that kind of thing. After that, the family fortune shrunk considerably, for all the usual reasons – the First World War and the Depression, plus Bartholomew's Folly. And that's another reason for the damage you saw. There are bits of panelling torn off in various areas of the house, and even a few holes dug through some of the walls.'

Mayhew paused, clearly waiting for Angela to ask the obvious question. She raised her eyebrows, but said nothing. He sighed.

'Anyway, just after the end of the Great War, Bartholomew went off on a Grand Tour of Europe and the Middle East. At the time, that was still a very fashionable way for a wealthy young man to finish off his education, and lucky for us that he did, because a lot of the relics

Oliver has now bequeathed to the museum were bought by Bartholomew on that Grand Tour. I gather he went as far east as Syria, and into what was then Persia, and acted as a bit of a shopaholic everywhere. He must have spent thousands, maybe even tens of thousands, of pounds, and at that time a thousand pounds was serious money.'

'And Bartholomew's Folly?'

'One of the things Bartholomew brought back from his grand shopping tour of Europe was a wooden crate of mixed antiquities from Cairo. Apparently it was a kind of job lot. He only actually wanted a couple of ornamented vases – which we haven't found so far, by the way, so they were probably sold some time later – but ended up having to take the whole crate, at an inflated price, naturally. Anyway, when he got the stuff back here, he opened the crate, took out the vases he wanted and stuck the box with all the rest of the bits in one of the attics.

'A few years later, he dragged it down again and for the first time actually took a good look at what he'd bought. Most of it was rubbish, as he'd expected, but down at the bottom of the crate he found an earthenware jar. Bartholomew believed it was probably first century AD, but the guidebook doesn't say what type of jar it was, or how he came to that conclusion. What attracted his attention wasn't the age of the jar, but the fact that the stopper was pinned and wired through the neck of the vessel and the whole thing sealed with wax.'

Mayhew turned and led the way back down the corridor. Angela followed him, stepping over the occasional missing floorboard.

'So, as you might have guessed, Bartholomew grabbed a screwdriver and attacked the jar. He broke the seal and ripped out the stopper, expecting to find something valuable inside.'

'And did he?'

'According to the guidebook, at first he thought the vase was empty, but then he saw a piece of parchment, or maybe papyrus, inside it – the account I read uses both words to describe it. He broke the jar and got it out, convinced it had to be some kind of priceless ancient text.'

'But presumably it wasn't?'

'No. It was written in a language he didn't recognize – not that that meant much, because the only language Bartholomew spoke or read was English. So he decided to get it translated, but was terrified of anyone else finding out what the text meant, so he copied out each line as best he could, then sent off the individual lines to half a dozen different linguists.'

Angela stopped, interested now in spite of herself. She touched Mayhew on the shoulder to make him turn round. 'Don't keep me in suspense, Richard. What was it – Aramaic? Hebrew? And what did it say?'

Mayhew shook his head. 'The text was an early type of Persian script.'

'Persian? Oh, the Silk Road, I suppose. There was

already a lot of interchange between the Middle East and the other eastern nations by the first century AD. But why was it in a sealed jar?'

'No one knows. As for what it said, when Bartholomew received the various bits of translated text and tried to assemble them into a whole, he discovered that it was part of a much larger text that described a journey in an unnamed part of the world called the "Valley of the Flowers", which was presumably somewhere in Persia or modern-day Iran.'

'Because of the language the writer used?'

'Yes. But what also caught Bartholomew's attention was a phrase. Something the writer referred to as "the treasure of the world".'

'Of course,' Angela said. 'Roger Halliwell told me there was a kind of lost treasure story attached to this family, I presume this is it?'

Mayhew laughed. 'Yes. And because Bartholomew was such a nutter, it was enough to send him off on a whole series of expeditions to the Middle East that—'

'Whereabouts in the Middle East?'

'Iran, obviously, because of the Persian text, but quite possibly Iraq and God knows where else in the region. All his expeditions were completely fruitless, of course. Anyway, that's what became known as "Bartholomew's Folly", because he ran through most of the family's fortune searching for this so-called treasure. When he finally popped his clogs, he left his son with massive debts, and Oliver had to sell off a whole lot of antiques and most of the land he'd inherited just to stave off bankruptcy. The couple of hundred acres around the house is all that's left of the estate now.'

'But how does that relate to the damage here in the house?'

'Bartholomew told his son that he'd fashioned a secure hiding place for the parchment he'd found. According to what Oliver wrote – he supplied the text for the guidebook, of course – his father had promised to tell him where the hiding place was, and also to give him a complete translation of the text, but he never did because he died suddenly of a massive heart attack, here in the house.'

'So I presume Oliver made the holes in the wall and ripped off the panelling?' Angela asked. 'Looking for this piece of parchment or papyrus?'

'Exactly. Oliver spent the last few years trying to discover where his old man had hidden it. And as far as I know, he never did find it.'

By now, they were downstairs again in the hall. Angela looked around her, at the bloodstained flagstones and the missing banister, and shivered. The house felt sad and lonely, there was no doubt about that. But there was something else – an air of lurking evil – that she didn't like at all.

7

'Where did this come from?' JJ Donovan asked, pointing at his system display.

Jesse McLeod barely glanced at the screen. He knew exactly which of the twenty or so search results his boss would be most interested in.

'The on-line version of a local newspaper.'

'Not encrypted or protected, then?'

McLeod shook his head. 'Nah. It's a town news-sheet – you know, births, deaths, marriages, all that sort of stuff, strictly local news. It's entirely open-source and terminally boring if you don't know any of the names, and pretty boring even if you do. The whole thing's a waste of time and in my opinion a total misuse of space on the web.'

He paused for a second or two, then again voiced a suggestion he'd made to Donovan a couple of times before. 'Look, JJ, I know what keywords you gave me, but it was a real broad search and I've still got no idea what you're looking for. If you could tell me why this stuff's so important, I'd be able to get you more targeted results.'

Donovan shook his head. 'Right now, I don't even know if it *is* important. It's just an idea I've got, a possibility of something that could change everything. But I'll tell you this. If I *am* right about what I'm looking for, it could be the single most significant discovery in the history of science. After this, nothing would ever be the same again.'

McLeod was thoughtful as he rode the elevator back down to the computer suite on the first floor. It sounded like Donovan had flipped, and that was a real worry. The company ran so well because Donovan was a genius when it came to genetic manipulation. If he'd lost the plot, it was definitely time to start thinking about finding employment somewhere else. When he got back to his office, he thought, he'd put out a few feelers, just in case.

And he also needed to make a call, because JJ Donovan wasn't the only person he was working for. And his other contact would be a *lot* more interested in the story he had to tell him.

8

It was late afternoon before Mayhew finally led Angela into the kitchen at Carfax Hall. Like the rest of the house, it was constructed and equipped on a grand, albeit late nineteenth-century, scale. A huge oblong solid-wood table sat squarely in the centre of the floor, most of its surface covered with china and ceramics of various types.

A Victorian cooking range, traces of wood or coal ash visible in the fire grate, was built into one wall, and old steel and copper pans and cooking utensils hung from hooks in the walls on either side of it. Incongruously, on the counter-top to the right of the range stood a grubby white microwave oven, and next to that an electric kettle, about half a dozen modern mugs in different colours, a jar of instant coffee, a box of tea bags and an open bag of sugar. Below the counter-top, an ancient fridge emitted a constant clattering and wheezing noise.

Clustered around a cleared area at one end of the table

were the other four members of the assessment team, steaming mugs in front of them. Angela had met them all individually as she and Richard Mayhew had walked around the property, and she knew them all by sight from her work at the British Museum.

Angela and Mayhew made themselves coffee, Mayhew adding milk from a one-litre plastic carton he took from the elderly fridge, then sat down.

'You've inspected this old pile, then, Angela,' said David Hughes, a thin, balding and bespectacled expert on English furniture. 'What do you think?'

Angela shrugged. 'Mainly, I think it's a shame. If Bartholomew had spent less of his time and effort chasing rainbows and collecting antiques that he just locked away, and a bit more money keeping the place properly maintained and repaired, this would still be a great estate. As it is, I guess that as soon as the dust has settled Oliver's heirs will bring in the bulldozers, flatten the house and outbuildings and a modern housing estate will spring up.'

'They might find getting planning permission difficult though,' Mayhew said. 'This is firmly in the green belt, I understand.'

'Seen any decent china yet?' Hughes asked.

Angela shook her head. 'I'll make a start first thing tomorrow morning. Is this everything?' she asked, pointing at the cluttered table.

'That's most of it, yes. There are a few trunks and boxes we've got to check up in the attics, and we've only had a quick look around the cellars, but it doesn't look as if there's anything much down there.'

'Is there anything else you need before you start work, Angela?' Mayhew asked.

'Yes. I might just as well pack the stuff away as soon as I've looked at it, so can somebody find me a couple of crates or boxes, one for the good stuff and the other for the rest? Oh, and tape and bubble-wrap to protect the bits of china?'

'There are about half a dozen tea chests in one of the attics,' Hughes said, 'and we brought a couple of rolls of bubble-wrap with us. I'll bring everything you need in the morning.'

'Right, people,' Richard Mayhew said, glancing at his watch, 'let's call it a day.'

Silence had fallen over Carfax Hall.

About ten minutes after Richard Mayhew turned the key in the lock on the front door, a faint scraping sound became audible in one of the attic rooms, a pile of cardboard boxes was moved slowly to one side and a grubby, sweat-lined face peered out from behind it.

The man listened intently for about thirty seconds, then stepped forward. His casual clothes – jeans and a T-shirt – were covered in dust and cobwebs, and his limbs were cramped from remaining in the same position for the previous three hours, ever since he'd sneaked in through the front door and crept up into the attic to hide.

The man made his way down the main stairs to the ground floor and walked into the huge reception room on one side of the front hall. He strode across to the closest of the tall windows and cautiously looked out, checking that there were no cars left on the gravel parking area.

Then he nodded, pulled a nylon bag out of his pocket and opened it on the floor near the door. He walked over to the closest packing case and started pulling out the contents, his movements urgent, but careful and concentrated. The room was enormous and the number of boxes and packing cases huge.

Within fifteen minutes he'd selected about a dozen high-value silver objects and placed them in his bag. Ten minutes later he climbed out of a ground-floor window at the back of the house, and walked unhurriedly over to the boundary fence on one side of the property, where he'd parked his car earlier that afternoon.

With any luck, he thought, he could probably repeat the operation three or four times that night, and then do the same thing tomorrow. If he picked his prizes carefully, he'd be able to make a tidy sum from their sale. It wouldn't be anything like as much as that devious old bastard Oliver had promised him the last time they'd talked, but it would be a big help to his bank balance.

But the antiques he was stealing were only a part of the story. The big prize, the thing he'd really like to get his hands on, was a few words written on a tattered piece of parchment. He'd never seen it, or even met Bartholomew

– the old man had died several years before he was born – but Oliver had always been going on about it, back in the days when he'd been a welcome guest at Carfax Hall. He knew that Bartholomew had been incredibly secretive about the relic, but it had to be somewhere in the house.

Once he'd stashed his acquisitions in the car, he'd start searching in all the places that Oliver might have missed – and there were plenty of them.

He reached his car, popped open the boot and carefully placed his prizes inside it. He pressed the lid closed carefully, making as little noise as he could, locked it and then headed back towards the old house.

'Up yours, Oliver, you mean old bastard,' he muttered, as he climbed over the boundary fence again. It was a still, clear moonlit night, and the house and its belongings were all his.

9

Jesse McLeod looked across the table at the man sitting opposite him.

Killian had worried him from the moment they first met. It wasn't the man's general appearance he found intimidating, just his eyes – black, dead eyes, seemingly able to pick apart your very soul and lay bare your thoughts. And there was a kind of suppressed energy about him, like a tightly coiled spring, that always seemed about to explode into sudden violence, probably extreme violence.

But McLeod knew he had something Killian wanted, and this gave him a powerful lever to use in his negotiations. He didn't see why Killian would baulk at the fairly modest payment he had in mind. And the consequences of him *not* paying up were real serious. McLeod knew that Killian would realize this.

'I want it now,' Killian growled, referring to the information McLeod had accessed.

'I can give it to you right here, on a memory stick,' McLeod suggested.

'You have it with you? On your laptop?'

McLeod nodded. 'It's right here,' he confirmed, patting the leather bag beside his chair. 'There's just the matter of payment to discuss.'

Killian's face clouded. 'I've been paying you a retainer for two years. Why do you think this information entitles you to more?'

'I think when you see it you'll realize why it's so important.' McLeod was choosing his words with enormous care. 'It's directly related to the previous data I gave you – that stuff about the "treasure of the world" – you remember? That article in the magazine about the old guy in England, and how he thought he'd finally worked out where the treasure had to be hidden?'

Killian stared at McLeod for a few seconds, then nodded for him to continue.

'I found a report in a county newspaper. It seems somebody croaked that old man, whipped him until his heart gave out. That means somebody must have read that article, and maybe they're looking for the same thing as you.'

Killian still said nothing.

'There was one detail in the story that I thought was real interesting, so I did a little more digging. I hacked into the local police database and checked out the forensic reports and a bunch of other stuff. I downloaded it all, and there's a couple of details there I think you need to see.'

'OK,' Killian said slowly. 'Let me have it and then we'll talk figures.'

McLeod nodded and pulled a small laptop computer from his bag. He switched it on, and a few minutes later extracted a slim memory stick from the USB port on the side and put it on the table in front of him.

'That's it?' Killian asked.

'Yep. That's the whole thing. It seems like the old man didn't die too quietly. The forensic examiners found quite a lot of blood in his mouth – blood that wasn't his own, I mean, and traces of flesh. The investigating officers guessed he might have bitten his attacker. They've got samples of that blood and tissue and they're just waiting for the DNA analysis results to come back from their labs, which will give them a DNA profile of the killer.'

He let his gaze rest for a few seconds on the bandage wound around Killian's head, and the heavily padded area over the man's left ear, then switched his attention back to the screen of his laptop.

'You told anyone else about this?' Killian demanded.

McLeod shook his head. 'No, but a guy has to take precautions, if you know what I mean. So there's more than one copy of what you got there – just in case that data gets lost or corrupted, that kind of thing.' He leaned back in his chair, trying to look relaxed and in control. 'So how does fifty grand sound for the data and all the copies?' It was, he thought, a reasonable enough figure.

Killian's smile didn't get anywhere near his eyes. 'Like

about fifty grand too much, McLeod. I've got a much cheaper, and a whole lot more permanent, solution.'

He pulled a small semi-automatic pistol out of his jacket pocket, the weapon made ugly by the bulbous suppressor attached to the end of the barrel.

McLeod's eyes bulged in terror, and he strained backwards in his seat. 'Hey, man, don't do this,' he said, his voice shrill with panic. 'I'll deliver everything to you. You can have it all for free.'

'You should have stuck to computers,' Killian said, his eyes dark, his face expressionless. 'You'd never make a blackmailer in a million years. You're just an amateur, and not even a good one.'

'But the other copies of the data – if I don't make contact, my friends will—'

'I'll risk it, McLeod, and if your friends come knocking I'll kill them too. This isn't about the money. This is about security, about sealing loose ends. I have to make sure you won't talk to anyone else about this.'

'I won't, I promise,' McLeod said, standing up.

'I know you won't.'

The report of the pistol was little more than a cough, but McLeod's body was flung backwards by the impact of the shot. His chair toppled over and he crashed to the floor, limbs splayed, his mouth opening and closing, his eyelids flickering.

Killian stood up and walked around the table to where his victim lay. The shot had taken McLeod almost in the centre of his chest, probably just missing his heart, but it was still a fatal wound.

Taking careful aim, he fired again. The bullet smashed into the left side of McLeod's chest and bored straight through his heart. His body twitched once, then lay still.

Killian slipped the pistol back into his jacket pocket, and almost without thinking he touched his forehead lightly and then his chest three times, making the sign of the cross. He bent down and emptied the dead man's pockets, then he turned away, picking up McLeod's computer bag and the memory stick.

He had a lot to do, and now the clock was ticking.

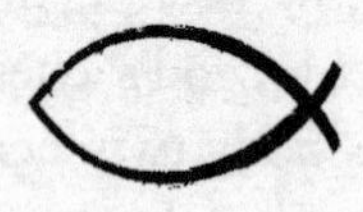

10

'Do you know this man?'

JJ Donovan shivered, and not just from the chill of the mortuary. Lying motionless on the table in front of him was a sheeted figure, only the head and face visible.

'For the record, sir, can you please identify him?'

'His name is . . .' Donovan paused and swallowed. 'His name was Jesse McLeod. He worked for me. At NoJoGen.'

'And that's what, sir? Again for the record.'

'NotJustGenetics Incorporated. It's my company, here in Monterey. Why did you call me? He's not a relative of mine. He just works – worked – for me.'

'A business card bearing your company details was found in his possession. Calling you seemed a good place to start to try to get an ID on him.'

Donovan looked down at the face of the man he'd worked with for more than a decade.

'How did it happen?' he asked the police sergeant. 'Where did you find him?'

'A couple of guys in a patrol car spotted his body on a vacant corner lot in downtown Monterey. It looks as if he was mugged, because his wallet is missing.'

'Did he have a bag with him? A computer bag, I mean?'

The sergeant shook his head. 'No. Apart from a comb and a handkerchief, the only thing we found was the card. No bag, no wallet, no phone, no keys, even.'

'But Jesse lived down near Carmel, and spent most of his spare time on the beach. If he went out in the evening, he normally stayed in Carmel because he didn't much like Monterey. So what was he doing there?' Donovan scratched his head. It was all too much to take in.

'I can't help you there, sir. What we seem to have is a mugging that went wrong, and the only unusual thing about it is the weapon used.' The sergeant pointed down, at the sheeted corpse. 'This body has two small-calibre bullet wounds in the chest. We won't know for sure until the doc does the autopsy, but it looks like he was hit by a couple of point two-fives, maybe even twenty-twos. Most of the bad boys around here use thirty-eights or bigger. A twenty-two isn't your usual mugger's pistol of choice. It's not a serious weapon.'

'Maybe that's all the criminal could find,' Donovan suggested.

'Maybe. Sometimes, a small-calibre gun could mean a professional hit, because with a suppressor fitted the weapon's pretty near silent, but it doesn't look like that was the case here.'

'Why?'

'Because a pro would go for a head shot every time. And this guy was shot in the chest.'

'You said you didn't find any keys on him either,' Donovan said. 'Could you do me a favour and send a car out to Carmel to check his apartment? He had a lot of expensive electronic equipment out there, and some of it belonged to my company. If the mugger took his keys, he might have burgled his home as well.'

'We'll do that today, sir, if you can give us the address. And do you know who his next of kin is?'

'His parents live somewhere in Utah, I think,' Donovan said, writing down the address of McLeod's apartment in Carmel, together with his own mobile number. He passed them to the sergeant. 'I'm going back to the office. Call me if you find anything.'

Donovan climbed back into his Porsche, started the engine – and just sat there, staring through the windscreen at the street ahead of him. So much had happened in such a short space of time. Two weeks earlier, McLeod had come to him with the first, tantalizing snippet of information. He'd found a report in a monthly magazine published in an English county called Suffolk about someone who was trying to raise money to fund an expedition to the Middle East to search for a lost treasure, a relic he'd referred to as the 'treasure of the world'. The old man had been following some clues originally found by his father and, according to the magazine, he finally believed he had worked out where he should start his search.

That single expression – the 'treasure of the world' – had electrified Donovan, because he'd seen it before, in an entirely different context, and he believed he knew exactly what it referred to. That was why he'd turned to Jesse McLeod. If anyone could locate any other references to the man or his quest, he could.

And then there had been the report of the Englishman's brutal death. Now McLeod was also dead; murdered in a way that didn't seem to make sense. McLeod had clearly been murdered: Donovan was certain of that. This was no mugging.

Was there a connection here? That was one other thing that disturbed Donovan: he now knew he wasn't the only person looking for the treasure. Suddenly, what had started out almost as an academic curiosity had turned into a dangerous race. But in spite of McLeod's death, Donovan was determined to find the treasure first, no matter what it took – the potential rewards were simply too great to ignore.

He pulled out in to the busy morning traffic. The search had begun.

11

It was lunchtime by the time Donovan got back to the office and very quiet, which suited him just fine. He'd gone straight to McLeod's workstation, telling his secretary he didn't want to be interrupted, and opened up his computer. Now he leaned back, faintly surprised. He hadn't expected his scan of the hard drive to reveal any useful information at all, but in fact he'd found an entirely unprotected folder named 'Suffolk' in the root directory. Inside it were the statements and forensic reports prepared by the Suffolk Police in their initial investigation into the murder of Oliver Wendell-Carfax, information that McLeod had obviously obtained recently, but which he'd failed to share with Donovan.

He copied the whole lot on to a memory stick, then read the reports on-screen. The old man had obviously died a hard, painful death, and common sense suggested he would have told his killer whatever he needed to know.

His injuries were so severe that he would probably have died from them anyway, even without the heart attack that had actually killed him.

But the blood and tissue found in the corpse's mouth pointed to an alternative scenario. It meant the killer's face must have been right next to the old man's mouth, and that implied that the killer was listening intently to what he said. So maybe Oliver Wendell-Carfax *hadn't* blurted out everything?

Obviously, there was no way of telling now, but that detail from the forensic report at least gave Donovan hope that the other man searching for the relic might not have obtained all the information he sought. The playing field, so to speak, might still be level.

As Donovan shut down the computer, his mobile rang.

'It's Sergeant Hancock at the MPD, Mr Donovan. We sent a team over to Jesse McLeod's apartment and it's been cleaned out, at least as far as electronic devices are concerned. No computers, cameras or even mobile phones. Whoever did it left all the cables in place, but the hardware's gone. You've no idea who the intruder could be, I guess?'

'Absolutely none at all, Sergeant,' Donovan said. But he knew he had to find out – and quickly.

Back in his office, Donovan cleared everything off his desk, then walked across to the wall beside the door where a single piece of modern art hung. He didn't particularly like the picture, but it was exactly the right size to conceal the safe that was set into the concrete wall directly behind it.

He pressed the bottom left corner of the picture to release the spring-loaded magnetic catch and then swung the frame back on a piano hinge to reveal the wall safe and control panel behind it. With the ease that comes from familiarity, he entered a six-digit code on the control panel keypad that unlocked the thermostatic controls and gradually adjusted the internal environment of the safe to allow the air inside it to reach room temperature and humidity, and permit the door to be opened. It would take a little over three minutes, but he never minded the wait.

As soon as the light on the control panel changed from red to green, he inserted a slim steel key in the adjacent lock, turned it twice, and swung open the door. Inside lay a zipped plastic bag containing a piece of papyrus with ragged, frayed and uneven edges, and a single sheet of paper. He picked up both and carried them over to his desk.

Pulling on a disposable mask and a pair of thin cotton gloves, he unzipped the plastic bag and carefully, almost reverently, he slid the parchment out and placed it gently on the bag. For some moments he just stared down at it. He couldn't read the closely written Aramaic script in its entirety, though he knew enough of the language to translate the odd word, but a complete translation – in fact, three complete translations prepared by three different but very experienced ancient-language specialists – was typed on the sheet of paper in front of him.

Those translations had sparked his all-consuming passion and ongoing search for any other clues that might tell him where he should be searching for the relic he believed still had to exist. They were all subtly dissimilar, because each translator had interpreted the Aramaic script in a slightly different way, but there was no mistaking their meaning. The dozen or so Aramaic words in front of him, written in faded black ink, referred to the greatest lost treasure of all time, an object that even now quite literally had the power to change the world.

Just under an hour later, Donovan checked the contents of his leather carry-on bag for the second time, then pulled the zip closed. His didn't need to undo his suitcase – he kept two of them permanently packed with everything he'd need for a two-week stay, one for cold countries, and the other for the tropics. This time his destination was London, Heathrow, so choosing the correct case for the trip hadn't been difficult.

He also had a carry-on bag that contained a small Dell notebook computer, one partition on the hard drive hidden, encrypted and password protected. In that partition were the reports McLeod had copied from the Suffolk Police files, as well as telephone numbers and contact details he'd pulled off his own computer, plus an automatic destruct routine that would repeatedly over-write the contents with random characters if an incorrect password was entered three times. The bag also held a couple of external hard drives and memory sticks, and a selection of chips of various sorts, some of them of an unusual specification. Donovan wasn't a computer expert, but before he'd started NoJoGen he'd worked for a specialist Los Angeles electronics company, which had contributed to the breadth of his technical knowledge.

He paused for a moment, unzipped his carry-on and slid a compact umbrella inside, just in case.

Donovan glanced round his spacious penthouse apartment once again, nodded to himself and then headed for the door. He set the alarm, double-locked the door and took his personal elevator down the ten flights to street level. He walked out of the main door of the building as the cab he'd booked drew to a halt by the kerb.

It was, he hoped, a good omen.

12

By 10 a.m. that morning, Angela was in the kitchen at Carfax Hall, her laptop open and running. The cataloguing software program would, she hoped, allow her to identify most of the ceramics in the house, or at least assign them an approximate date and country of origin. Valuations would take longer, and she really wasn't equipped to do them. The other obvious problem, she thought, as she looked at the china piled at the other end of the table, was that the period she knew most about was the first century AD. Most of the stuff in front of her dated from about two millennia later than that. She sighed. She'd just have to do her best.

By the time she finished her coffee, she'd already taken a preliminary look at the china, ceramic and earthenware utensils, and had picked out half a dozen nice pieces of early English slipware and put them to one side.

Then she settled down into her tried and tested routine.

She created a free-form database on her laptop, named it 'Carfax Hall Ceramics', and labelled the fields from top to bottom. She started with the current date, then moved down to the probable date of the piece of china; the manufacturer, if known; a description of it; a note of any defects she could see and finally a rough estimate of its value.

She also created a second, much simpler, database for those pieces of china – and there were a lot of them – which weren't likely to be of any interest to the museum, and which would probably end up in a local auction house. She'd already decided to look at the less valuable pieces first, to get them out of the way and clear space on the table as quickly as possible.

She photographed each piece from different angles with her digital camera before enveloping it in bubble-wrap and storing it in one of the wooden tea chests from the attics. It was soon apparent that almost everything on the table was going to end up in the 'auction' tea chest, because most of the china in front of her was worth only a few pounds – some even less than that. Periodically, she attached the camera to her laptop and transferred the pictures she'd taken to a new folder on her hard drive.

The other members of the team drifted into the kitchen at intervals to make coffee or tea, or just to chat while they took a break from their own cataloguing activity elsewhere in the old house.

When the team stopped for lunch, Angela had already

half-filled the 'auction' tea chest and in the process had cleared perhaps a quarter of the pieces of china off the table.

'Have you found anything interesting?' David Hughes asked, his spectacles glinting in the sun that shone through the large kitchen window.

Angela shook her head. 'Not really. There's some English slipware and a few bits of early Wedgwood, but nothing that you couldn't pick up in almost any halfway decent antique shop. It doesn't look to me as if Oliver or Bartholomew were really into collecting ceramics. What about you?'

'Actually, quite a few nice pieces. There's a good octagonal Regency rosewood centre table, but my most exciting find so far is a really nice Jacobean wainscot chair, in beautiful condition.'

'Are you sure it's not a mid-nineteenth century repro?' Mayhew had just come in, looking more florid than usual. 'They made a lot of them around that period.'

'You just stick to your specialization, Richard,' Hughes replied, looking at him over his glasses in what Angela thought was a teacher-ish sort of way, 'and I'll stick to mine.'

'You're very quiet, Owen,' Mayhew said, turning to a grey-haired man wearing bifocals who was sitting on the opposite side of the long table. 'Anything to report?'

Owen Reynolds, one of the British Museum's arms and militaria experts, leaned forwards. 'I'm not sure. There's not much here that's obviously within my remit, apart from that suit of armour in the hall, so—'

'Is that the real thing?' Mayhew asked.

'Definitely. It's a particularly nice example of *Gotischer Plattenpanzer*, Gothic plate armour, dating from the fifteenth century. I'll need to research it, but I think it might be Maximilian, which is really exciting. And I've found a couple of 1796-pattern heavy cavalry swords, one an Austrian *pallasch* and the other a British version. But apart from those, I haven't found very much, so I've been checking the contents of the boxes in the salon or whatever that big room is called.'

Mayhew looked at him expectantly. 'And?' he asked.

Reynolds looked round the room. 'Well, I'm not *absolutely* sure, but I think somebody's been searching through them. Not one of us, I mean. In several of the chests the contents have been unwrapped and, as far as I can recall, everything in them was properly wrapped when we first inspected the boxes.'

There was a brief silence.

'A burglar, you mean?' Mayhew asked.

Reynolds spread his hands. 'The problem is that we don't know what there was in the boxes to start with. I mean, we don't have a full inventory of their contents, do we? That's what we're here for.'

'Do you think somebody has been pilfering?'

Reynolds shook his head. 'I don't know. There are a lot of valuable pieces on display in this house – silverware, that kind of thing – that any burglar would immediately realize were worth a lot of money, and I think one or two of those might be missing as well. But because there is no inventory I can't be sure.'

Angela stood up. 'Look, if Owen *is* right, and somebody has been here, the first thing we need to find out is how this burglar – or whatever he is – is getting inside. God,' she lowered her voice, 'you don't suppose he's in the house *now*, do you?'

Richard Mayhew shook his head. 'No. But we have been leaving the front door open while we've been in here, so I suppose it is just possible somebody could have snuck in. We'd better keep it locked from now on.'

Angela nodded decisively. 'I also want a complete sweep of the entire house, right now, just in case there is anyone lurking in the cellar or attic or somewhere.' She was aware of how fast her heart was beating and took some deep breaths. She had narrowly escaped death the last time she'd been away and didn't want to take any chances here.

'OK, OK,' Mayhew agreed, with a heavy sigh. 'As soon as we've finished lunch we'll search the place from top to bottom. Will that do?'

Ninety minutes later, hot and dusty from poking around at the top and bottom of the old house and everywhere in between, the team re-assembled somewhat grumpily in the kitchen. They'd found absolutely nothing to suggest that anybody else had been in the house recently, apart from an unfastened ground-floor window at the back of the house, which they'd now closed and locked, and which Angela had then jammed with a screw to ensure it couldn't be opened from the outside.

'Happy now?' Richard Mayhew snapped.

Angela sighed. She still felt very uneasy. 'I'd rather be back in London, thank you. But at least now I'm sure that there *isn't* someone watching us.'

'OK, now that we've *finally* got that cleared up, let's get some useful work done, shall we?' Mayhew hurried out of the kitchen.

Angela picked up another piece of china from the table to assess and catalogue. She had just opened up her laptop when she heard a startled gasp from David Hughes.

'What is it?' She spun round to look behind her.

'I thought I saw something outside, some movement.'

He strode across the kitchen to the window and stared through the somewhat grubby panes of glass at the unkempt grassland outside.

Angela put down the china plate she'd been examining and stood up, joining him at the window moments later. The land in front of them sloped gently downwards, away from the house, dotted with clumps of shrubs and bushes, many of them easily big enough to conceal a person. And there was something else Angela noticed as well.

'You might be right,' she said slowly. 'Every time I've looked out of this window since we got here, I've seen at least two or three rabbits hopping about out there. Right now, I don't see any. Rabbits are extremely nervous animals. Because they've vanished, it could mean there *is* somebody out there.' She shivered slightly. 'God, I'll be pleased when we're finished and back in London. This place gives me the creeps.'

13

Jonathan Carfax stared through a pair of compact binoculars as the last of the cars drove away from the front of Carfax Hall. He knew he was invisible to the museum people, because he was standing in the shelter of a group of trees just outside the boundary of the property, but with a clear view of the house.

Earlier that afternoon, he'd crept closer to the house, approaching it from the rear and making use of the cover provided by various small groups of bushes, but he'd obviously been seen by somebody. As he'd moved towards the building, two faces had appeared at the kitchen window and looked out, but by that time he'd already run down the slope away from the house, and ducked down into a hollow behind a large rhododendron bush, where he'd lain and fumed. Jonathan was one of Oliver's cousins, and like the rest of his family had only recently discovered that he'd been disinherited. Well, he'd told himself, as he became gradually colder and damper, he was going to do something about that.

Fifteen minutes later, he'd finally eased up into a crouch and then sprinted the last few yards to the boundary fence. Then he'd walked through the woods back to his car, and waited for the last of the British Museum people to leave.

Darkness was falling as Carfax walked back towards the house. The cars had left, and no one seemed to be around. A solitary bat swooped through the gloaming. So far, so good, he thought.

Quickly, he made his way to the window he'd left open at the back of the house. He took one more look round and pushed the sash upwards. Or tried to. It took less than a second for Carfax to realize that somebody – obviously one of the team from the British Museum – must have spotted the open catch and locked it.

'Bugger,' he muttered, backing away and retracing his steps. He had come prepared, though. In the boot of his car he'd assembled a selection of tools that he hoped would be enough for him to slip the window catch if he found it locked.

Ten minutes later he was back at the window, a long thin chisel in his hand, which he slid up between the two sections of the sash window. He positioned it against the locked catch and applied sideways pressure. Nothing happened – the catch remained obstinately closed. He tried again, and then again, each time increasing the level of force on the tool, and each time with precisely the same result – the catch didn't move.

Carfax swore again, more loudly this time. He'd chosen that window because, of all those on the ground floor, that one had the loosest catch. Finding a chunk of stone that had fallen from some part of the house he dragged it across to the window and stood up on it. Almost immediately he spotted the screw jammed into the catch, and knew he wouldn't be able to force it from the outside.

Somebody must have guessed he'd been inside the property. He thought he'd covered his tracks, and had only taken a handful of the choicest pieces. Quickly he tried forcing the other windows in the back wall of the house, but he knew that all the other catches were stiff with rust and disuse. Within ten minutes he was certain he was wasting his time – none of the other catches had budged even a millimetre.

Grumbling to himself, Carfax gathered together his tools and equipment. His best option seemed to be a ladder that he could use to reach one of the first-floor windows. Hopefully he'd be able to force one of them. His only other choice was to break a pane of glass and open a window on the ground floor but then the police would get involved and he really didn't want that.

There were a couple of pieces of really good Georgian silver somewhere in the house that he hadn't found yet, and a tray made by Paul Storr that he guessed would have a five-figure price tag, so being able to get inside undetected was vital.

No, he'd just have to come back tomorrow with a ladder. He had a right to Oliver's possessions, and he was going to make damn sure they came to him, not to any museum.

14

'Nice place,' Chris Bronson remarked as Angela parked her Mini outside Carfax Hall the next morning.

Despite being divorced, he and Angela had remained the closest of friends, talking every day on the phone, and had come to trust and rely on each other perhaps even more than some married couples. Bronson was hoping they might get back together as man and wife, but Angela was still cautious about committing to that, the painful recollection of their separation and divorce still fresh in her memory. He was doing all he could to make her change her mind.

He had taken a couple of days' leave and had driven up the previous evening, after Angela had told him about the possible intruder at Carfax Hall. Angela said she'd feel a *lot* happier having him around, and he'd agreed to come immediately. It was, he hoped, a sign that she might be about to put the past behind her.

'I'm afraid the house is virtually falling apart. All those lumps of stone' – she pointed – 'have fallen off the roof and the upper walls. That's why we can't park any closer. The building's losing bricks and masonry like a snake shedding its skin. We reckon it'll be bulldozed inside a year.'

'That's a shame. I suppose it's just deteriorated too much to save.'

'That, plus the fact that the ungrateful relative who's actually inherited the place – he's a second cousin twice removed or something like that, according to Richard Mayhew – has already applied for planning permission to build houses in the parkland.'

The front door was locked, so Angela rang the bell. 'This is just a precaution,' she said, 'until we – or, to be exact, you – tell us we're all imagining things.'

The heavy door swung open and Richard Mayhew peered out at them, looking the image of a museum curator, Bronson thought.

'Oh, it's you, Angela,' he said, testily. 'Hello, Chris. This is completely unnecessary, you know. Angela's reading far too much into things.'

'If you don't mind, Richard, I'll be the judge of that. In my experience, Angela rarely overreacts.'

Mayhew grunted, pulled the door wide open and stepped aside to let them enter the hall.

'Thanks,' Angela said, leading Bronson around the base of the main staircase and down a corridor towards the back of the house. 'Thanks for backing me up like that. Richard's one of those annoying people who always think they're right.'

Bronson smiled at her. 'If you say there's a problem, there's a problem, and I'm here to fix it for you. Or at least I'll try to.'

Angela pushed open the door at the end of the short corridor and stepped through into the kitchen. 'This is where I've been working,' she said, indicating the old table partially covered in assorted china and ceramics.

'You make coffee and tea for the chaps in here, do you?' Bronson asked.

'In their dreams.' Angela put her bag at the end of the table. 'If they want drinks, they make their own. But I am prepared to make you a coffee, if you'd like one.'

Bronson nodded. 'While you're doing that, let me take a quick look at that window.'

Angela plugged in the kettle and pointed towards a door on one side of the kitchen. 'Down there,' she said. 'That corridor runs along the back of the house. The window we found unlocked was at the far end.'

Bronson strode out of the room. He wasn't gone for long. Angela had only just finished making two mugs of coffee when he walked back into the kitchen.

'Did one of you jam the catch with a screw?' he asked.

'Yes. I did. It seemed very loose, so I thought it was a good idea.'

'I've found what look like fresh scratch marks on that

catch. I think they're recent because there are a couple of flakes of paint still attached to one of the scratches. It looks to me like somebody has tried slipping the catch with something like a Slim Jim – you know, a thin length of steel?'

Angela looked alarmed.

'Well, someone's been using something similar to try to get that window open,' Bronson continued. 'He's been sliding a steel tool between the two parts of the sash window and trying to undo the catch. The marks are quite unmistakable. The good news is that the screw you jammed into the mechanism stopped him from doing it. The bad news is that I found similar marks on the catches of all the windows along that corridor, so it was obviously a very determined attempt to break in.'

'Are you sure? I mean, couldn't those marks have been there for some time?'

Bronson picked up his mug of coffee. 'Not really, no. I reckon your intruder tried really hard to open the window with the loose catch, because there are more scratches on that than any of the others. He didn't get anywhere, because you'd jammed it, so he tried all the other windows at the back of the house, then he gave up.'

Angela shivered and rubbed her arms.

'Come and take a look at this,' Bronson said, moving to the kitchen window.

Like all the other ones in the property, it was a two-part sash window, single-glazed with a wooden frame. The only lock was a simple turnbuckle mounted on the top of the lower frame that locked both halves of the window together when it was rotated through ninety degrees.

Bronson pointed at three or four vertical scratches on the side of the catch.

'That's where he tried to slip it,' he said, 'and if you look down here, at the gap between the two panes, there are scratches there as well, where he forced the tool up to the catch.'

'But he didn't get inside the house?'

'It's just possible he did manage to open one of the windows, but if he did he must have secured it from the inside afterwards, and then left by one of the doors. Could he have done that?'

Angela shook her head decisively. 'Not a chance. The rear door is bolted on the inside – in fact, we haven't had it open since we've been here – and the front door's fitted with a deadlock. I think even Richard Mayhew would have been suspicious if he'd found that open.'

'OK,' Bronson said, putting his arm round her shoulders. He could tell she was still nervous. 'So apart from that first day, when it's possible he got in through the unlatched window, or maybe even strolled in through the front door if he had the balls to do that, he can't have got back inside.'

'So what can we do to make sure he doesn't get inside again? Go to the local police?'

Bronson laughed. 'Unless the Suffolk Constabulary is

very different to the one I work for in Kent, it'd be a complete waste of time. They'll have their hands full trying to solve crimes that have already been committed. They certainly won't have time to try to prevent a possible future crime.'

'So what can we do?'

Bronson glanced round the room, then looked at her. His face softened. 'As I see it, you've got three choices. First, do nothing. Keep all the doors and windows properly secured and hope that'll be enough to keep this tea-leaf out. Second, stop what you're doing here and transport the entire contents of the house straight to the British Museum and do your classifying and sorting out there. That's probably the best option.'

Angela shook her head. 'Most of this stuff is of no interest to the museum – we really don't want to clutter the place up with the kind of things you can find in any provincial antique shop. We'll cherry-pick the very best bits and most probably sell the rest through a local auction house. What's the third option?'

Bronson grinned at her. 'It's obvious, really. You employ a night-watchman. Somebody to patrol the house and make sure nobody breaks in.'

Angela stared at him for a few seconds. 'We can't afford to do that – not on our budget. Have you any idea how much it would cost?'

'That depends who you get. Some people are a lot cheaper than others.'

'You've got someone in mind, haven't you?'

Bronson's smile widened. 'Of course I have,' he said. 'Me.'

15

Michael Daniel Killian stared at his reflection in the bathroom mirror and grimaced. The pad over his left ear, which he'd only changed an hour earlier, was showing spots of red again. Carefully, he unwound the bandage from his head, then teased away the cotton pad he'd placed over his injured ear. Some of the fibres had stuck to the open wound, and he gave a grunt of pain as the pad came free and his ear started bleeding again.

He turned his head sideways and looked closely at the wound. The old bastard in England had done a pretty good job. His teeth had been strong and sharp, and his jaw muscles surprisingly powerful. His bite, and Killian's initially futile attempts to escape his grasp, when he'd jerked away, had actually severed the upper part of the ear, and that section of it was now attached only by a narrow band of flesh close to his head.

He'd not tried to get his injury treated in England – the

old man had died in the house, and any doctor he went to would remember such an unusual wound. His image might even have been recorded on the CCTV system of any hospital he visited. So he'd simply covered the injury as best he could.

He'd also been worried about the surveillance cameras he knew were all over British airports, so he'd dumped his Heathrow to LA ticket and instead had taken the Eurostar to France, then hopped a flight from Paris to New York, and then on to LA, in an attempt to muddy the waters. To anyone who asked about his bandaged head – and only two people had during his entire journey – he'd explained he had a bad ear infection, and was returning to the States for treatment.

But Killian hadn't gone to a hospital or doctor in America because he still feared his injury would excite comment and – far worse – be remembered. Instead he'd placed pads around his ear to hold the loose part in position, hoping that it would somehow re-attach itself without the need for stitches. He could now see that this wasn't happening.

For a couple of minutes Killian stared at his ripped ear as small rivulets of blood dripped off the lobe, splashing into the sink. He couldn't go on without doing something about the injury.

Replacing the cotton pad, he roughly retied the bandage around his head, tightly enough to stop any more blood seeping out. Then he walked out of the bathroom and down the hall to the smallest bedroom of his modest and fairly isolated single-storey house, located in the country-side a few miles outside Monterey.

The moment he touched the door handle, a feeling of peace and contentment suffused his body. He opened the door and stepped inside.

At the far end of the room stood a tall cupboard, the doors and sides hidden behind deep purple cloth. Above it, a richly ornamented crucifix gleamed golden in the light from the candles burning on either side of it, the only illumination in the room. Directly in front of the makeshift altar was a single bare wooden pew, wide enough for only two or three people to kneel side by side. Killian had bought the pew from an antique dealer in France, and knew it was over five hundred years old.

He closed the door behind him, crossed himself and bowed his head, then walked forward slowly, reverently, to the wooden pew. He stepped into the centre of it, crossed himself again, then knelt down, clasping his hands together. For some seconds his lips moved in silent prayer, then he looked up at the crucifix.

'Forgive me, Father, for I have sinned,' he began. 'I need Your guidance and Your help and Your strength to complete the sacred task You have set for me.'

Ten minutes later, Killian emerged from his chapel, bowed once towards the altar, then closed the door behind him. Then, removing his black shirt and clerical collar, he assembled the materials he would need for what he now knew he had to do.

In his bathroom, he again stared at his reflection for a few seconds, then plugged the electric soldering iron into the shaver socket and tested the tip with his finger to ensure that it was getting hot. Taking a small piece of cotton cloth, he folded it until it fitted over his entire mouth. He used one hand to hold the cloth there while he wrapped duct tape around his head to hold the material firmly in place, as a simple but efficient gag. Finally, he made sure that the scissors were close to hand.

His preparations complete, Killian unwrapped the bandage around his head and removed the pad from his ear. Once again, blood started to flow from the open wound.

Picking up the scissors, he opened the blades and positioned them over the thin band of tissue that connected the two sections of his ear. As the steel of the scissors touched his flesh, Killian jumped involuntarily, then steadied himself. He took a deep breath through his nose, and squeezed the blades together.

The pain was instant and startling as the twin blades closed together, cutting deep, and despite the gag, he screamed, the sound emerging as a muffled howl. Tears streamed down his face. For several seconds he couldn't even see his image in the mirror, then he blinked furiously and rubbed his eyes.

The loose flap of flesh was still attached, still hanging

from the rest of his ear. He knew he'd have to do it again. He took several deep breaths, then positioned the scissors once more. This time, he closed his eyes before he applied pressure to the handles.

He heard a distinct 'crunch' as the scissors sliced through the remaining flesh, then a faint wet slap as the top of his ear landed in the sink in front of him. He didn't look down as he was trying very hard not to scream again, and his eyes had once more filled with tears. But, he thought, as his vision slowly cleared, at least the worst of it was over. Or perhaps not. He glanced down at the soldering iron, its tip smoking ominously.

His ear was bleeding copiously, the amputation of the remaining flap of tissue having cut through several blood vessels. Killian dabbed at it with a piece of cotton cloth, which was instantly soaked with blood, turning a deep red. His hand trembled slightly as he picked up the soldering iron. As he lifted it past his face he could feel the radiant heat on his cheek. He hesitated for barely a second, then touched the tip of the implement to the top of his ear closest to his head, where the blood flow was most pronounced.

This pain was different, even worse than before, a searing, burning agony that seemed unbearable. The smell of roasting flesh filled the air. Suddenly Killian felt he couldn't breathe. He reached up and tore the rough gag from his mouth, gulped in a lungful of air and screamed. After a few seconds, the pain faded and he felt more in control. He looked in the mirror again. The treatment, such as it was, did seem to be working. The blood flow had clearly diminished, at least around the fresh, straight cut he'd made with the scissors.

Gritting his teeth, Killian lifted the soldering iron again and pressed it once more to the top of his ear. And once more he screamed.

Fifteen agonizing minutes later, he'd managed to stop all the bleeding, though the side of his head felt as if it was on fire. The wound to the top of his ear looked appalling, a rough crust of red and black burnt flesh, where the tip of the soldering iron had done its work. He hoped it would now start to heal.

Gingerly, taking infinite care, he applied a salve to the injury. That cooled the burning sensation, at least a little, but did nothing for the pain. He took a clean cotton pad, rested it gently against his ear and cautiously wrapped a bandage around his head to hold it in place, grimacing as the pressure increased. Finally he swallowed half a dozen painkillers – three times the recommended dose, but he needed something to reduce the agony.

He walked out of the bathroom – he'd clean up the mess in the sink later, when he felt better – and stumbled down the corridor to the lounge, grabbing a bottle of whisky and a glass. He slumped into a recliner near the window, poured a generous two fingers into the glass and downed it in a couple of gulps. The fiery liquid seared his throat as he swallowed it, then settled warmly, comfortingly in his stomach. He eased backwards, turning his head to avoid his torn ear touching the fabric of the chair, and lay there, glad his ordeal was over.

As the painkillers started to kick in, the throbbing ache from the side of his head began to subside. Killian thought back over the events of the last few weeks, wondering if he could have handled things differently. He shook his head, and instantly wished he hadn't as a fresh spike of pain lanced through his head.

It had begun a couple of years earlier, with a visit from a former colleague, Father Mitchell, a deeply troubled man who'd long been aware of Killian's encyclopedic knowledge of Church history, its doctrine and practices, and without doubt this had influenced his decision to break the sacred trust of the confessional.

Killian closed his eyes and replayed the conversation in his mind.

'Do you believe in the sanctity of the confessional?' Mitchell had asked him.

'Of course. Anything learned in the confessional is to be kept between you, your parishioner and God.'

'Do you think there are any circumstances when that trust can be breached? Suppose one of your parishioners confesses to murder? What then?'

'The position of the Church is unequivocal. What's said in the confessional is sacred. You should encourage your parishioner to surrender to the police, of course, and confess to his crime. But you yourself may not breach that trust and approach the authorities.'

Mitchell had nodded, because he had already known the orthodox answers to those questions. He'd paused and Killian had been struck by his haunted, almost terrified look.

'Then *you* must be *my* confessor, Michael. Hear my confession. Right here, right now.' Mitchell leaned across the table and seized his arm with a grip so firm it actually hurt.

'Very well,' Killian had said, reluctantly.

Mitchell had explained that a couple of weeks earlier, a man named JJ Donovan had entered the confessional box at his church in Monterey. He had seemed over-excited, hyped up about something and eager to talk. Donovan had followed his usual routine, confessing a fairly dull litany of what he perceived to be his sins, and Father Mitchell had granted him absolution, just as he'd done on previous occasions. But then, instead of ending the session as usual, he'd asked Donovan directly if there was some other matter troubling him, something that might account for his very different, almost elated, mood.

What Donovan had told him had shocked him into stunned silence; a silence that had lasted so long Donovan had eventually knocked on the pierced wooden divider between the two sections of the confessional and asked if he was still there.

'I told Donovan that what he was planning to do was a

mortal sin, a blasphemy of such appalling magnitude that nobody would ever be able to forgive him. And I absolutely forbade him to even contemplate proceeding with his plans,' Mitchell told Killian. 'What stunned me most was that he apparently thought I'd be pleased with what he was intending.'

'What was it that so shocked you?' Killian asked quietly.

So Mitchell told him, and what he said was so extraordinary that Killian felt the blood drain from his face.

'Dear God in heaven,' he had whispered, and then pulled himself together. 'Tell me everything you know about that man,' he'd said. 'His address, telephone number, whatever you have.'

Mitchell had passed across a sheet of paper.

'God will reward your courage,' Killian had told him. 'Now you must leave everything to me. If Donovan approaches you again, about anything at all, let me know immediately.'

Killian had prayed for guidance that night, and by the following morning the way ahead had been clear. Donovan himself wasn't the problem. Whatever he had found could also be discovered by others, now or sometime in the future, and that could have disastrous consequences. The only way to achieve a lasting solution was to allow Donovan to locate the relic. And then it would have to be utterly destroyed, as would everybody involved in its search.

He would have to break the first commandment; Killian

knew this. But he also knew that he'd have God's forgiveness. Because the reality was that the killing of one or two men – or even the deaths of hundreds or thousands of people – was completely inconsequential, totally insignificant, in comparison with the stakes he was playing for.

16

'I'm not even going to discuss it,' Richard Mayhew snapped. 'It's completely out of the question.'

'Actually, Richard, it's not out of the question at all, and I'm afraid you're not in any position to make an autonomous decision.' Angela's tone was sweetly reasonable, but there was no mistaking her resolve.

'I'm in charge of this group,' Mayhew snapped.

'According to Roger Halliwell, you're only the administrative head. That means you control the budget that buys our food and pays for the accommodation back at the pub. Otherwise, we're here as six individuals from six different departments, with an equal say in what we do. Chris has volunteered to stay here overnight to make sure that whoever's been burgling this house doesn't get back inside again, and I for one think that's a really good idea. I had hoped you'd think it was a good idea as well but, as you don't, maybe we should take a vote on it.'

'What's the harm, Richard?' Owen Reynolds suggested. 'It's not like one of us staying here – Chris is a police officer, well able to take care of himself. He's the ideal man for the job.'

Mayhew glanced around the kitchen, sensing general agreement among the others there. He made one more attempt to get them to change their minds.

'Suppose he gets hurt? What about the insurance implications, all that kind of thing?'

'It's not your property,' Bronson interjected, 'so you have nothing to do with the insurance of the building or its contents. But if it would make you any happier, I'd be pleased to sign a waiver absolving you and the museum from any responsibility for me being here overnight.'

Mayhew recognized defeat when he saw it, and raised his hands in the air. 'Oh, very well, then. Do whatever you like,' he muttered irritably, and stalked out of the room.

Bronson had nothing to do. His stint as an unpaid night-watchman wouldn't start until the evening, when everyone else had left the building, so he made a point of checking every room in the house, noting possible hiding places, points of entry, and so on. He made two complete circuits of the interior of the old house, then did the same outside, before going back to the kitchen, where Angela was still working her way steadily through the collection of china and ceramics.

'Anything interesting?' he asked, flicking the switch on the kettle.

'Not really,' she said. 'You?'

Bronson shook his head. 'Just one very slight oddity,' he said. 'This house has been owned by the same family for a while, hasn't it?'

Angela nodded. 'Since the middle of the nineteenth century, I think. Why?'

'There's a coat of arms above the main door, cut into the stone lintel, and others on the backs of the dining-room chairs, on the wall over the fireplace in the salon, and so on. There's also a coat of arms in the background of each of the two paintings of Bartholomew Wendell-Carfax that are hanging in the first-floor corridor.'

'So?' Angela was busy packing more worthless china into her auction box.

'Well, the crests in the paintings of Bartholomew are slightly different. Both of those have the head of a fox in the top right-hand quadrant of the shield. All the others have the head of a bird – I think it's a hawk – in the same position.'

'Maybe the painter made a mistake,' Angela suggested.

Bronson shook his head. 'Both paintings were obviously done from life. Bartholomew was sitting in a chair in the salon and the artist was painting what he saw. Why would he get three of the four quadrants of the shield right, and then substitute an entirely different image for the fourth?'

Angela stopped packing. 'You're very observant, Chris,' she said, smiling. 'For a man, anyway!'

'I'm a policeman, remember? I'm supposed to notice things. They're called clues.'

'Well, I agree – the paintings *are* a bit odd.' She explained about the two pictures showing Bartholomew as a young man in exotic dress, both of which had been sold shortly after they were completed. 'And then there was the fiasco of his Folly.'

Bronson poured himself a cup of instant coffee and sat down as Angela explained about Bartholomew Wendell-Carfax's obsession with a lost treasure hidden somewhere in the Middle East, and how it had been sparked by the discovery of a piece of parchment he'd found in a sealed earthenware vessel, a parchment that had then vanished.

'Maybe it didn't vanish,' Bronson said. 'Maybe the old man hid it somewhere and Oliver couldn't find it. Suppose Bartholomew had the paintings done as a sort of a last laugh, so Bartholomew could tell Oliver that the clues had been staring him in the face all along.'

'A fox's head instead of a hawk doesn't seem a particularly helpful clue to me,' Angela objected.

'It could be really simple,' Bronson said with a grin. 'There's a fox in the dining room. Stuffed, of course, and in a glass case. Maybe he just hid the parchment inside it.'

Angela put down the plate she'd been wrapping. 'Lead me to it,' she instructed, her brown eyes shining – always a sign, in Bronson's opinion, that she was excited.

The fox was standing on a small mound, glassy eyes staring sightlessly across the dining room towards the tall windows on the opposite side, mouth open to reveal yellowish teeth and a thin pink tongue. It was clearly old and rather mangy, a few patches of fur missing on its sides and tail. It stood on a wooden base, under an oblong glass dome.

'It doesn't look like much,' Angela commented.

'Maybe that was the point. Bartholomew might have thought it was an ideal place to hide something.'

He lifted off the glass dome. 'The stitches don't look as if they've been disturbed since the poor little sod was stuffed.' He turned the fox around. 'And I can't see any slits or cuts anywhere, so I don't think there can be anything hidden inside the body itself.'

He ran his fingers around the base of the object, then stopped abruptly and bent down to look at the back of it.

'This is more likely,' he said. 'I can see a line running along the base, just here, so it looks as if this section might open, and there are some scratches on the wood as well.'

He tugged at the base, but nothing moved. Then he tilted the fox on to its side and looked at the underside. There were half a dozen brass screw-heads showing, presumably to hold the stuffed animal and the other parts of the tableau in place. One of them looked different to the others.

'That could be a locking screw,' Bronson said. He pulled out a folding pocket knife and selected the correct blade. Rotating the odd screw until it dropped out on to the sideboard, he grasped the edge of the base and pulled. One section of it moved slightly. He returned the fox to an upright position and looked at the back, where a section perhaps a foot wide had now slid clear of the rest of the base.

He could hear Angela's indrawn breath of excitement.

The section of wood opened like a drawer and, as Bronson pulled it clear of the base, they both saw what looked like a small leather-bound book lying inside it. He picked it up as soon as he'd fully opened the drawer and passed it to Angela.

'Don't expect too much,' he warned. 'My guess is that Oliver found this some time ago – he was probably the one who tried to open it – so if the parchment was here, he'll have removed it.'

But it wasn't a book. What they'd actually found was a slim and shallow wooden box, covered with leather, that opened like a box-file. The inside was stuffed with loose papers of various sorts and a couple of large photographs, each of them folded twice so they'd fit into the box.

Angela flicked through the contents briskly, then shook her head. 'No lost parchment,' she said sadly. 'That would have been too easy, I suppose. This seems to be a collection of old bills and invoices, and also some of Bartholomew's expedition notes.' She held up several sheets of paper covered in small and neat handwriting. 'I've spotted a couple of references to Egypt already.'

'What about the photographs?'

'Just pictures of the two paintings Bartholomew sold. Interesting, but not helpful.' She shrugged. 'Back to work for me, I'm afraid. But do keep poking around. You never know what you might find.'

It was early afternoon, and Bronson and Angela had just finished their sandwich lunch. There was an extra sandwich in the fridge, and this would be Bronson's lonely dinner after the rest of the team had left him in the house at the end of the day.

'Look what I've found in one of the attics,' Bronson said, walking back into the kitchen carrying a dusty cardboard box. The label says "First C Corinth", with a question mark after it.'

Angela walked across to where Bronson was standing.

'If that label actually relates to the contents of the box, it could be quite interesting,' she said. 'A first-century Corinthian piece would be a lot more exciting than most of the stuff I've seen so far. Let me have a look.' She lifted the newspaper-wrapped object out of the box. The pot was shaped like a tall water jug, and Angela stood it on its base while she cut the string and removed the wrappings.

'Coffee or tea?' Bronson asked, but got no response. When he turned round to look, Angela was staring at a tall, wide-necked, blue-green vessel with a single handle and some kind of animal images inscribed in horizontal bands around it. There was a scatter of paper and bits of string lying on the table nearby.

'If I had champagne here, I'd drink that,' Angela said at last. 'Do you know what this is?'

'I'm just a simple copper, remember? What is it?'

'I think – in fact, I'm almost sure – it's a proto-Corinthian *olpe*.'

'Really? It just looks like a big green jug to me.'

Angela came over and gave him a hug. 'What you've just found is very rare, especially in such excellent condition. I've seen one similar one, but it's in the Louvre in Paris. An *olpe* is a wine vessel. This one's decorated with registers – these horizontal bands – of what I think are lions and bears, and it probably dates from around six hundred and fifty BC.'

'Not first century, then, like it says on the box?'

Angela shook her head decisively. 'Definitely not. It's over half a millennium older than that.'

'So it's valuable, then?'

'Oh, yes. I'm not an appraiser, but this could be almost priceless!'

'So do you want me to bring the others down?'

'Others?' Angela went white. 'There are others?'

Bronson smiled at her. It felt great to be working together again. 'I've no idea. There are a few more cardboard boxes up in the attic. I'll go up and have another look, if you like.'

Bronson returned about fifteen minutes later carrying another dusty box.

'No other jugs, I'm afraid,' he announced, 'but I did find some bits of a broken pot.'

He placed the box on the table, opened it and pulled out a number of shards of reddish pottery which he spread out in front of Angela.

She dragged her attention away from the *olpe* with apparent difficulty and glanced at the fragments.

'Now those probably *are* first century,' she said, 'and most likely Middle Eastern in origin.'

She picked up a couple of the pieces and fitted them together in her hands. They matched exactly.

'It looks like these might all be part of the same vessel,' Bronson suggested.

Angela nodded and picked up a fragment that looked as if it had formed the neck of the broken vessel. In it was a small hole, and in a band around it was a dark brown deposit. Angela picked at this with her thumbnail thoughtfully, then picked up another couple of the broken shards, piecing them together in her hands to reform the neck of the vessel.

She pressed the pieces together firmly. A few slivers were still missing but she'd found enough of the neck of the ancient pottery jar to see that the hole on one side of it was exactly matched by a second hole opposite. That, and the band of darker material, told her all she needed to know.

'There's a hole driven through both sides of the neck where it's narrowest,' she said, 'and this darker material seems to be some kind of sealing putty or resin. According to Richard Mayhew, who seems to have taken quite a keen interest in the Wendell-Carfax history, the vessel

Bartholomew found was secured with a pin driven through the neck, a pin that went right through the wooden stopper, and the outside was then sealed with some sort of putty. And this,' she finished, 'could well be the remains of that first-century pot.' She paused. 'There was nothing else up there, was there?'

'Just the usual sort of rubbish that seems to migrate to any attic. Look, I'll need to stay awake tonight, so I should get my head down this afternoon. The first bedroom on the left at the top of the stairs still has a bed and mattress in it. Can you come up and wake me about half an hour before you all leave?'

Angela looked troubled. Although she'd eagerly embraced the idea of Bronson staying at the property overnight when he'd first suggested it, now that the evening was approaching she was feeling markedly less certain that it was really such a good idea.

'Are you sure you want to do this, Chris? I mean, suppose there are half a dozen intruders, all armed?'

'Then I'll lock myself in the loo and dial triple nine on my mobile,' Bronson said. 'But most burglars operate alone, and they almost never carry weapons, because the penalties for being caught with a knife or a gun are so severe.' He put his hands on Angela's shoulders and kissed the tip of her nose. 'If I think I'm in danger, I promise I'll put on that suit of armour that's standing in the hall.'

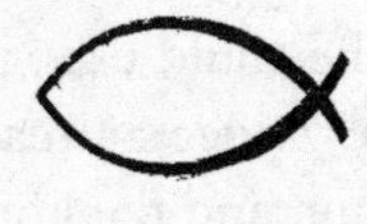

17

6 p.m. Angela and her museum colleagues had left, and Carfax Hall was completely silent.

Chris Bronson walked through to the kitchen and clicked the switch on the electric kettle. Coffee, he knew, would help him keep alert. He'd have no trouble staying awake until well after midnight – he'd always been a late bird – but staving off boredom and sleep in the early hours of the morning would be more difficult.

He'd establish a routine, and prepare the house for his coming vigil. At night, sound travels further and more clearly than during the day because of the absence of other noises to interfere, so there were things he needed to do. The first was to go round the entire house and open every door to allow him to enter any room as silently as possible – a creaking hinge would be an obvious giveaway.

He started on the ground floor, checking that both the front and back doors of the house were securely locked.

Then he walked through each room in turn and opened all the internal doors wide. Some he had to prop open because they were fitted with self-closing hinges, but there were plenty of boxes he could use.

He walked up the wide staircase and repeated the process on the first floor, and then on the attic floor above that. Back on the ground floor, he checked that the cellar doors were also open. There were two doors, one leading to a wine cellar that appeared to have been emptied of its contents, and the other to a general-purpose cellar full of various sorts of household junk, and which also housed a large and clearly elderly central-heating boiler.

Finally, because he hadn't got a torch, he switched on the hall, staircase and main upper corridor lights so he'd be able to move around without walking into doors or tripping over things. Those lights would be enough to let him see where he was going, but hopefully wouldn't raise the suspicions of anyone who'd tried to force the rear windows.

That done, he walked back into the kitchen, made a mug of coffee and sat in the armchair in a corner of the room. He'd found a handful of paperback novels in the library, hidden away amongst the collection of weighty and dull-looking leather-bound tomes. He picked a thriller and started to read.

He'd barely got beyond the first page when he felt his mobile start to vibrate in his pocket.

'I'm in my room at the pub,' Angela announced. 'Are you OK?'

'Of course I am. Don't worry about me.'

'I do – that's the trouble,' Angela said with a sigh, and Bronson couldn't help but feel a little bit pleased. 'We agreed you'll call every hour, on the hour. If I've not heard from you by five past each hour, I'll call you. And if I can't get through to you by ten past, I'll be calling the cavalry, so make sure you answer – OK?'

Bronson glanced at his watch. 'Agreed. It's six fifty now, so let's consider the seven o'clock call made. I'll talk to you at eight.'

'Take care, Chris.' There was a brief, rather strained pause, and Angela rang off.

Bronson drained the rest of his coffee and stood up. It was time to check the house. He wandered through all the downstairs rooms, his feet making almost no sound on the mainly stone floors, and looked out of the windows. Then he climbed the stairs and did the same thing on the first floor, looking inside each bedroom and making sure that the various paintings and pieces of furniture were still there. Apart from a few rabbits hopping around in the long grass at the back of the house, the estate seemed to be deserted. Bronson hoped it would stay that way.

His evening soon settled into a routine. At quarter past and quarter to the hour, he walked all the way through the house, checking every room, which took him about ten minutes. And on the hour, he rang Angela's mobile.

At ten he called Angela, made another cup of coffee, drank it, and then began his usual patrol. He saw nothing until he looked out of one of the windows in the bedroom at the end of the house, a window that offered a good view of the woodland that ran alongside the estate's fence.

Then, in the soft darkness that surrounded the house, a sudden movement caught his eye.

Jonathan Carfax stopped just inside the tree-line at the edge of the wood, panting slightly from his exertions. He'd had to bring a long ladder – it needed to be able to reach the first floor of the house – and it was a lot heavier than he'd expected. In fact, he would have to make two journeys – once he'd carried the ladder to the house he would have to go back for his bag of tools and a couple of other bags to hold his booty.

He rested the ladder against a tree, well out of sight of the house, then moved forward a few feet. There were no cars parked in front of the property, which presumably meant that the British Museum people had all gone for the day. Then he looked more closely at the house itself, and spotted a dim glow in both the upstairs and downstairs windows. Somebody had obviously left a light – maybe two or three lights – switched on.

He wasn't going to go near the house if there was anyone still inside and there was one way he could check this out. He still had the telephone number of Carfax Hall, a hangover from the days when he'd been a welcome guest there, before Oliver had turned against him.

Pulling his mobile from his pocket, he dialled the

number. Faintly, across the intervening distance, he could hear the sound of the house phone ringing. If anyone was in the property, he was sure they'd pick it up.

Watching from the upstairs bedroom window, Bronson jumped slightly as the unexpected sound of a ringing phone echoed from the hall downstairs. The only person likely to phone him was Angela, and she'd call his mobile, not the house phone. Just to check, he pulled out his Nokia and looked at the display. His battery showed a full charge, and the signal strength was near maximum.

It was most likely a wrong number or a cold call, he decided. He'd let it ring. He looked again to the edge of the wood, where he'd seen the movement.

A minute later, the ringing stopped and the house fell silent.

18

Bronson had been standing in the same spot for perhaps ten minutes, and the movement he'd seen hadn't been repeated. He was just beginning to think he'd imagined it, maybe it *had* been an animal – a fox or a deer, perhaps – when he saw it again.

This time there was absolutely no doubt about it. From the undergrowth an object emerged horizontally, about four feet above the ground, and for an instant Bronson couldn't work out what it was. Then he recognized the end of a ladder and smiled to himself.

'Cheeky bastard,' he muttered, easing forward slightly, the better to see the man as he approached the property. He didn't seem to be in any particular hurry, and was walking steadily across the uncut grass towards the back of the house, the ladder slung on his shoulder, looking for all the world like a workman arriving to do a job. Perhaps his lack of haste was a measure of his confidence that the house was empty – or maybe, more prosaically, it was just that the ladder was so heavy that he couldn't run or trot with it. In any case, he seemed to know exactly where he was going, and in a few moments vanished from Bronson's line of sight, moving around to the rear of the property.

Bronson stepped back out of the bedroom, and waited, listening intently for the sound of the top of the ladder being placed against the wall of the house. But he heard nothing, and after a few seconds he walked back to the bedroom at the end of the corridor and peered out of the window.

Then he saw the man again: he was running back towards the tree-line and then vanished among the trees. Less than half a minute later he popped back in to view with a bulky bag clutched in his left hand, and jogged over to the house.

A few minutes later, Bronson clearly heard a metallic scraping sound from the bedroom to his left, and crossed to the doorway. He looked inside the room, checking the window, but the burglar was not yet visible. Bronson slid into the room, walked swiftly across to the rear wall and flattened himself against it, where he knew he'd be invisible to anyone looking in through the window.

He felt in his jacket pocket, checking that the handcuffs he'd collected from the Canterbury station were still there. When Angela had told him what she thought had happened at Carfax Hall, he'd decided that having a pair of cuffs in his pocket made sense. And it looked as if he'd been right.

Using his ears rather than his eyes to measure the burglar's progress, Bronson could hear the man climb up the ladder, a muffled thumping sound as he put his feet on the rungs. Then there were a few brief moments of silence, followed by a faint rubbing sound which Bronson guessed was the insertion of the screwdriver or chisel or whatever turned out to be his tool of choice for forcing the catch.

He heard an irritated muttering from outside and suppressed a grin. Even the first-floor window catches weren't *that* loose. Then a louder noise, a click, as the catch finally gave way, and moments later the unmistakable sound of a sash window sliding upwards.

Bronson kept behind the substantial curtain that framed the window, as the man climbed into the bedroom, an empty nylon bag clutched in his hand, then crept slowly across the bedroom towards the door. Bronson waited until he was about halfway there, then crossed the room in half a dozen swift strides.

As he approached, the man half-turned towards him, a look of sheer panic on his face.

Bronson grabbed his right arm, forcing his hand behind his back and up towards his shoulder.

'I know it's a cliché,' Bronson said, 'but you're nicked, my son. I'm a police officer and I'm arresting you on suspicion of breaking and entering and burglary.'

Grasping the struggling man by the shoulder Bronson held him firmly, he snapped the handcuff on to his right wrist, then grabbed his left arm and repeated the process, securing his hands behind his back.

'We're going to go downstairs,' he said, 'and I'll explain what's going to happen.'

Once downstairs, Bronson pushed his captive into one of the kitchen chairs. 'Now, I'm required to caution you, so please listen carefully. You do not have to say anything, but it may harm your defence if you do not mention when questioned something that you later rely on in court. Anything you do say may be given in evidence. Do you understand the words of the caution?'

'Just let me go, you bastard.'

'I'll take that as a "yes", shall I?'

'I'm not saying another word. I want my solicitor, and I want him now.'

'Fine,' Bronson said. 'That's entirely within your rights. I'm not going to question you – that will be done under caution at the police station – but I am going to search you to see if you're carrying any offensive weapons. Are you carrying anything that might injure me?'

'Go to hell!'

Bronson jerked the man to his feet and checked his pockets, pulling out a small wallet and placing it on the kitchen table.

Then he pushed the man back into the chair, sat down opposite him, and opened the wallet he'd found. Almost the first thing he pulled out was a driver's licence. Bronson looked at the name on it and smiled.

'Well, Jonathan,' he said, 'Carfax is a name I certainly recognize, so I assume this burglary is more personal than professional. I presume the old man cut you out of his will, so you're bypassing the legal process and taking what you believe you're owed.'

His captive didn't respond.

'But it doesn't actually matter why you did it – it's still burglary,' Bronson said. Then he shrugged, reached into his pocket and pulled out his mobile phone. He glanced at his watch. It was almost eleven o'clock, so he thought he'd tell Angela that his mission had succeeded, then he'd call the local police.

'Hi, it's me,' he said, when Angela answered her phone. 'Just thought you'd like to know I'm sitting in the kitchen looking at your burglar.'

'Really? Is he – I mean, was there any trouble? Do you want me to call the police?' Angela asked.

'No, thanks. I know the form. I'll have to go to the local police station with him to make a statement and stuff, so I won't get to the pub for quite a while, but I'll call you once I'm at the cop shop to let you know how long I'll be.'

'OK.' There was a pause. When she spoke again, Angela sounded uncharacteristically nervous. 'Will you come up to my room when you get here? I want you to tell me everything that's happened.'

Bronson smiled. 'It's a deal. I'll see you later.'

But Jonathan Carfax was not looking nearly so happy. 'This is entrapment. I don't believe you're a policeman at all. You're just some bloody thug the museum staff have employed.'

Bronson pulled out his warrant card and showed it to him. 'I'm Detective Sergeant Christopher Bronson,' he said, 'and I promise you that I'm a real police officer. My ex-wife works for the British Museum and asked me to give her a hand here.' He reached across the table and pulled the local telephone directory towards him. As he did so, he looked at his prisoner. 'Just sit quietly and we'll get this sorted out. Are the cuffs too tight?'

The man shook his head. 'No,' he said grudgingly. Then his eyes widened and he looked behind Bronson. 'Look out!' he shouted. 'Behind you!'

Bronson half-turned and, as he did so, saw a sudden flash of grey and then something slammed – hard – into the side of his head.

He saw stars for the briefest of instants, and then nothing at all.

19

'Chris! Chris! Wake up, damn you.'

Bronson's head felt as if it was bursting. There was a massive throbbing ache above his right ear, and all he wanted was for the pain to go away, for the pulsing agony to stop.

The voice was familiar to him, but for several seconds he couldn't seem to place it. Or remember where he was. And then, with a rush, it all came back to him. Carfax Hall. The burglar, and then the kitchen. But he couldn't remember what had happened next, or why he seemed to be lying on the floor with a splitting headache.

He forced his eyes open. Angela was bending over him, some kind of a pad in her hand that she was pressing against the right side of his head. That hurt, and he raised a hand to stop her.

'Oh, thank God,' she whispered. 'No, don't touch it. You've got a nasty gash on the side of your head. There's an ambulance on its way.'

Bronson groaned and eased up into a sitting position. 'I don't need an ambulance,' he muttered.

'Actually, you probably don't,' Angela said, 'but I really called one for him.' She gestured behind her.

Slumped in a kitchen chair, his arms still obviously secured behind his back, and his face battered and bleeding, was the man he'd caught climbing in through the bedroom window.

'What the hell's happened?' Bronson said. 'I never touched him. Is he OK?'

'He's been badly beaten up, but he's alive.'

Bronson took the pad from Angela, pressed it gingerly to the wound then struggled to his feet, the pounding in his skull getting worse as he stood up. Swaying slightly, he gripped the back of a chair with his other hand.

'Just take it slowly,' Angela said.

Bronson stepped across to the man on the other side of the table. His face was puffy and cut from repeated blows, his eyes closed.

Bronson leaned over him. 'Can you hear me?'

The man stirred, looked up at him and nodded.

'Bend forward,' Bronson ordered. He took out the handcuff key, released the restraints and put them in his pocket.

The man leaned back gratefully, rubbing his wrists. 'Am I still under arrest?'

As he spoke, Bronson could see that he'd lost a couple of teeth in the attack. Bronson shook his head, then wished he hadn't as another stab of pain shot through his skull. 'No, as far as I'm concerned, we were here in the house together this evening and somebody attacked us.'

'Are you sure, Chris?' Angela asked.

'Yes. Burglary's a minor offence compared to what's just happened. And you won't be trying it again, will you, Jonathan?'

'Jonathan?' Angela's face registered her surprise. 'Do you know him?'

'He was careless enough to bring his wallet and driving-licence with him tonight. This is Jonathan Carfax, and I presume he's one of Oliver's numerous disinherited relatives. In other words, he's an amateur, not a professional burglar.'

At that moment, they heard an engine outside and the noise of tyres on the gravel drive. A few seconds later the main doorbell rang.

'That'll be the ambulance,' Angela said, getting up.

'OK, Jonathan,' Bronson said. 'Let's get you checked over in the local casualty department. If anyone asks, we were here in the house together, locking up after the British Museum team, when a man burst in and attacked us both. You've no idea who he was or what he wanted. He beat us up and then ran away. Just stick to that – nothing more and nothing less, OK?'

Jonathan Carfax, his face largely obscured behind bandages, pads and sticking-plaster, folded his frame into the rear seat of Angela's Mini. Bronson got into the front passenger seat and strapped in as Angela started the engine.

'Where to?' she asked, starting the engine.

'The nearest pub,' Carfax insisted, his words slightly slurred. 'I need a drink.'

'The doctors said no alcohol for you two,' Angela pointed out.

'All the pubs will be closed by now, but a drink's a bloody good idea,' Bronson agreed. 'We can go to the hotel and get something there.'

'Right,' Bronson said a few minutes later, cradling a brandy schooner. 'The last thing I remember about this evening was looking at your driving-licence in the kitchen at Carfax Hall, Jonathan. What the hell happened next?'

Carfax took a sip of brandy, and closed his eyes. 'You were just about to call the police,' he said, his voice slightly distorted due to his missing teeth and probably compounded by the effect of the painkillers he'd been given. 'The door behind you opened – the kitchen door, I mean – and a man walked in, carrying a cosh or club of some sort. I tried to warn you, but you turned very slowly. And then he hit you on the side of the head, and you just dropped flat on the floor. I really thought you were dead.'

'And then?' Bronson prompted.

'And then he started on me. He checked to make sure I couldn't defend myself – thanks to the handcuffs you'd snapped on me, I was completely helpless – and then he started asking me questions that I couldn't answer.' Carfax's voice quivered slightly.

'Can you describe this man?' Bronson asked.

'I doubt if I'll ever forget him. He was slim, over six feet tall, maybe six three. Black hair, cut very short, almost a crew cut, dark brown eyes and quite a big, straight nose. A good-looking man, really. From his accent, he's American or Canadian, probably American as he had far too many teeth, and they were very white.'

'What did he ask you about?'

'Like you, he looked at my driving-licence, so he found out my name. He assumed I would know all about my family, but I really don't. I'm only a cousin of old Oliver, and I didn't know his father.'

'You mean Bartholomew?' Angela interjected.

'Yes. All this man seemed to be interested in was Bartholomew's Folly – you know, the way the old man squandered the family's money on his treasure hunts.'

'And what did you tell him?' Bronson prompted.

'Everything I know,' Carfax said simply, 'but that's not a lot more than was printed in the local parish magazine when Oliver died, and this guy seemed to know all about that. When I didn't tell him what he wanted to know, he started hitting me, hard. And every time I told him I didn't know something, he hit me again.'

'But why would a few unsuccessful treasure hunts that took place well over half a century ago be of the slightest interest to anyone now?' Bronson asked, almost to himself. The whole thing made no sense at all.

'I asked him that,' Carfax said, 'and he yelled at me that just because Bartholomew didn't find the treasure, it didn't mean it wasn't there.'

'Right,' Bronson said. 'I'd like you to tell us everything you know about Bartholomew's Folly, from the beginning. That's everything you told that American thug, and anything else you can think of that you forgot to tell him.'

By the time they walked out of the hotel and climbed back into Angela's Mini, Bronson thought he knew as much as anyone else about Bartholomew's Folly, and exactly what had happened in the kitchen at Carfax Hall, and he did, in fact, know almost everything.

But there was one thing that Jonathan Carfax hadn't told him about the American and what he'd done after Bronson had been knocked unconscious. He hadn't withheld the information, or not deliberately, anyway. What he'd seen was apparently so innocuous that he'd genuinely forgotten that it ever happened, and it never occurred to Bronson to ask the specific question that would have unlocked Carfax's tongue.

20

'So what now?' Bronson asked.

It was 9 a.m., and he and Angela were drinking coffee in the breakfast room of The Old English Gentleman. Angela had told Richard Mayhew that there had been a fight in Carfax Hall, that Bronson was fine, but that the burglar had been permanently frightened off, which was actually remarkably close to the truth, albeit shaded somewhat.

She'd also told Bronson how she'd grown increasingly concerned about leaving him on his own at the house, especially when he'd failed to call her from the police station as he'd promised, and failed to answer his mobile. Filled with a growing sense of unease that she couldn't quite explain, she'd driven her Mini – in her words 'like a maniac' – back down the country roads, and had arrived at Carfax Hall to find Bronson out cold on the floor and Jonathan Carfax tied up and very much the worse for wear.

Carfax had explained that when their attacker had heard the sound of wheels on the gravel, he had run off. Bronson now realised that Angela had possibly saved both their lives. He leaned forward and put his hand on hers, thinking – not for the first time – how fortunate he was.

Angela looked at him appraisingly. They'd spent the night together in her room, because – she told him later – she felt sorry for him – and thought he needed mothering. It hadn't quite turned out that way, and Bronson had proved that although his head might have been hurting, the rest of his body was in perfect working order. He sat back, stretching his legs in front of him. If getting himself knocked out was all that was needed to get him and Angela back together again – well, he'd have done it long ago.

'What do you mean?' Angela asked now. 'Exactly?'

'I'm not talking about us,' Bronson said. 'I know you too well, Angela. What happened last night caught both of us by surprise—'

'It certainly surprised me. The first time, anyway.'

Bronson grinned at her. 'Yeah. Anyway, I know you're still not sure about allowing me back in your life, and I'm prepared to work at showing you that you can trust me. What I meant, though, was this Bartholomew's Folly thing. I saw the expression on your face when Jonathan was talking about it. Despite the dangers, you want to do some digging, don't you?'

'Yes, I suppose I do, if for no other reason than to find

out why some thug would travel over here from the States – I'm assuming he doesn't live here – to try to beat information out of Jonathan Carfax.'

'So here we go again,' Bronson murmured. 'Another Lewis–Bronson treasure hunt gets under way. Is that what you mean?'

'Maybe.' Angela smiled at him. 'You've got to admit, it *is* an intriguing story.'

'OK. I know what Jonathan told us about the old man's treasure hunt, so if you're serious about this, I'm guessing you've got something else, some other piece of information, that relates to it.'

Angela shook her head. 'Actually, I don't really *know* very much more than you, apart from two things. First, those notes and stuff you found in the base of that hideous stuffed fox are quite interesting, though I'll need to have a proper look at them over the next day or two. The other thing is the translation of the piece of parchment that Bartholomew Wendell-Carfax found in that earthenware pot apparently mentioned "the treasure of the world", which is a fairly unusual expression.'

'You're assuming that the translation from the Persian original was correct, of course. I thought you said there was some doubt about that.'

'There are doubts, yes, and without the original text there's no way of checking it out, so all we can do is assume that the translators Oliver employed managed to get it right. But the thing is that I've read about this before, and the source I'm referring to was nothing at all to do with Bartholomew's Folly. I remember seeing it on a fragment of text written in a different language, from another country and possibly dating from a different century.'

Bronson knew by the look of Angela's dark brown eyes that she was determined to follow this one through. 'Go on.'

'It all goes back to a man named Hillel. He was an important first-century Jewish religious leader, a man involved in the development of both the Mishnah and the Talmud, and he later became the spiritual head of the Jewish people. He was known to be the author of various religious treatises, and his writings aren't all that rare. Bits and pieces turn up fairly regularly, even today.'

'So?'

'So I was doing research at the museum a few months ago and I came across a fragment that had been attributed to Hillel, and which included that same expression – "the treasure of the world". It stuck in my mind because I'd never heard it before. The problem was, though, it was only a fragment of text, just a few disconnected phrases. This was one of them, and it's the only one that I can remember. I'll need to go back to London, to the museum, and check it out.'

'Haven't you got to finish up here first? The cataloguing, I mean?'

Angela nodded. 'Yes, but there's not that much more to do, unless any more bits of china turn up. Basically, the proto-Corinthian *olpe* you found plus a few bits of decent English slipware are the only pieces of any value. I can have it all finished today, I should think.'

'So you can be back at the museum tomorrow morning. And what then?'

'Well, research, obviously. I'll need to take another look at the Hillel fragment and translate the other words on it, just to see if any of that helps.'

'But what sort of thing are you looking for?'

'Difficult to say, but it has to be something quite significant. If you look at other ancient references to hidden treasure, the writings usually describe it quite specifically – the "treasure of the temple" or the "gold of Carthage", that kind of thing. The "treasure of the world" strikes me as rather odd, because it manages to be both vague and specific at the same time. The expression suggests a vast, or at least a very valuable, hoard, but the name gives no clue at all about its origin, where the treasure came from or what it consists of – and that's unusual.'

'What worries me is that if Jonathan Carfax was right,' Bronson said, frowning, 'the fragment of text that Bartholomew found was about two thousand years old, which raises at least one obvious question.'

Angela nodded. 'I know. Surely somebody would have found what it refers to some time during the last two millennia.'

'Exactly. Well, wouldn't they?'

'It's not that simple. History is littered with tales of lost or hidden riches. There are hundreds, maybe thousands, of lost relics that were known to exist because of contemporary accounts, but which then simply vanished.'

Bronson looked thoughtful. 'OK, but even if half of them had been dug up since, that still leaves a lot of buried treasure waiting to be found. And Bartholomew's document was written in Persian, wasn't it? I reckon getting permission to tramp round Iran carrying a metal detector and a few shovels might prove a lot more difficult than actually finding the treasure itself.'

Angela sighed. 'You're missing the point. Just because that fragment was written in an early Persian script doesn't mean that the treasure is now, or ever was, in Persia. In the first century AD, there wasn't a lot of written material available, and texts were routinely copied, and also translated from one language into another. It's quite possible that the fragment of Persian and the Hebrew reference I saw that was attributed to Hillel were both copies of the same text, either one translated from the other, or that they were both translated from an earlier source document written in a third language.'

'So what you mean is that there might be another reference out there somewhere, a reference that will narrow down the search, or at least tell you what it is you're looking for?'

'Exactly.'

'You're determined to follow this trail, aren't you?' Bronson said, smiling. 'When I first arrived here, you seemed pretty nervous. But now I can see that familiar glint in your eyes.'

Angela leaned forward and took his hand. 'You're right. There's something about Carfax Hall that I really don't like, and I'll be pleased to leave it. But a hunt for a treasure that's been lost for two millennia – that's quite different.' She looked into his eyes. 'Will you help me?'

21

The following morning found Angela at her desk in the British Museum. She hadn't expected her search would be easy, or yield any useful results quickly.

Using her desktop computer to access the museum's internal database, she input the name 'Hillel' and scanned the results displayed on her screen. The description showed both the Anglicized name 'Hillel' as well as הלל, the Hebrew equivalent.

There were about twenty references listed, but she quickly found the one she was looking for. The entry read: 'Hillel (attrib) – fragment. Uncatalogued. Possibly part of unknown interpretative text.'

Most of Hillel's known works contained interpretations of various religious matters or analyses of Jewish law, so the listing made sense and, from what Angela remembered, it was such a small fragment of text that the description was as likely an explanation as any other.

Anyway, she'd take another look at it herself, and just see if any of it matched the piece of Persian script that had sent Bartholomew Wendell-Carfax out to the Middle East in his fruitless search for the lost treasure.

Ten minutes later, she had the Hillel fragment in her hands. Or, to be exact, she had the small sealed glass-topped box that contained the Hillel fragment sitting on her desk. Like most ancient pieces of papyrus or parchment, the normal procedure was to handle it as little as possible, and only ever while wearing cotton gloves, because of the damage that the moisture present on a person's bare hands could do to ancient relics over time.

But Angela didn't need to touch it, only to read the translation of the Hebrew text, which didn't take long, because the fragment was so small. Roughly triangular in shape, it contained only four partial lines on one side of the papyrus and a mere three words, two of them incomplete, on separate lines on the reverse. She looked at the translation of those words first.

(Ju?)dea
(Hi?)llel
temple

When she looked at the translation again, it was immediately clear that its authorship was uncertain, that the incomplete second word had simply been assumed to be a part of the proper name Hillel, and that name had then been used to identify the fragment. None of that mattered, of course – it was the writing on the other side of the papyrus that she was interested in.

It had been common practice to write on both sides of papyrus and parchment, so there was no reason to suppose that those three words had anything to do with the text on the reverse. Then she read the translation of that text, the longer piece of Hebrew on the other side of the fragment, which included the phrase that had stuck in her mind:

from whence
followers into the valley of flowers
(hid?)den the treasure of the world for

Angela nodded in satisfaction. She *had* remembered that phrase correctly. She opened her handbag, pulled out the thirty-year-old guidebook she'd taken from Carfax Hall and flicked through its yellowed pages until she found the one she was looking for, the section of the text that described 'Bartholomew's Folly' in tones that still reeked of bitterness at the old man's apparent foolishness. She skimmed through the closely typed paragraphs until she found the translation of the Persian text:

with his trusted followers into the
valley of flowers and there fashioned
with their own hands a place of stone

where they together concealed and made
hidden the treasure of the world for all

Angela smiled again. She'd been right. There were enough points of comparison to show that the Bartholomew's Folly text, as she'd mentally labelled it, had been derived from the same source as the Hillel fragment. It was just possible that one had been copied from the other, but it was much more likely that both were versions of an earlier and separate source document.

It also meant that the British Museum's description of the Hillel fragment was inaccurate, though that wasn't any concern of hers. That particular piece of text – at least the last two lines of it and most probably the whole thing – wasn't interpretative, but was simply a copy of a part of a separate document. It was plausible that Hillel – if he really had been the author – might have then gone on to comment on some aspect of the text, but they'd never know that unless another part of the fragment turned up.

It was a start, of sorts. Angela thought for a few moments, looking at the Bartholomew's Folly text. She could only hazard a guess at the two sections of missing text. Before the expression 'with his trusted followers' there was probably a phrase something like 'journeyed in company' or 'travelled along'. After the end of the text, following the phrase 'world for all', about all she could suggest was either 'time' or perhaps 'eternity'. And if that deduction was correct, then it might mean that the hiding place of the 'treasure of the world' was somewhere fairly secure. The fact that it was buried in 'a place of stone' and that the burial was intended to last 'for all time' suggested both a permanent and a properly concealed hiding place.

And that could mean the treasure, whatever it was, was still buried out there somewhere, waiting to be discovered.

22

Angela had decided to start her search by researching references to 'the Valley of the Flowers,' but this had soon proved frustrating – there seemed to be flower-filled valleys almost everywhere, in virtually every country. But finding places that were known by that name in the first century AD had proved to be considerably more difficult.

She sighed and stretched her back to ease the tension she was feeling. She had found three locations in ancient Persia that more or less fitted the bill. None of them, as far as she could tell, had actually been called the 'Valley of the Flowers', but all three had names that included the word 'flowers' or a synonym. The best match was a place called the 'gorge of blossoms', if her translation of the old Persian name was correct, and she guessed that it was one of the locations Bartholomew Wendell-Carfax had investigated because she'd found two references in the museum records to surveys being carried out there in the first half of the twentieth century by teams from Britain.

There were no indications of the identity of the sponsors of those teams, or the names of any of those involved, and of course the word 'survey' could cover almost any type of investigation, but Angela reckoned it was a fair bet that old Bartholomew had been there. However, it also meant he hadn't found what he was looking for.

What she didn't know was how thorough he'd been. Had he and his men just ambled up and down the gorge looking for the 'place of stone', or had they done a proper, in-depth survey, checking for hidden caves and underground chambers?

The Persian text stated that the people who'd buried the treasure had fashioned the hiding place with their own hands. Angela didn't have a date when this was done, but the age of the Hillel fragment meant it had to have been no later than the first century AD, and that in turn meant the hiding place was probably a fairly simple structure. Unless the 'trusted followers' included a large slave-labour force, skilled masons and a lot of equipment, the 'place of stone' had to be reasonably basic, and would probably have made use of some natural feature – a cave or something like that. And as it *was* a place of concealment, a location where the treasure *was* intended to remain securely hidden for all eternity, if her guess at one of the missing words was correct, it would by definition not be easy to detect. So just how thorough had Bartholomew been?

There was, of course, a more important question: had

he been looking in the right valley? Or even in the right country? She looked again at the search results for the whole of the Middle East. Altogether, she'd identified almost fifty locations spanning countries from Turkey to India. Any one of them could be the place she was looking for, which meant she had no real idea where to start. If this was going to work, she'd have to find some way of narrowing the search parameters.

It was time she tried to track down the other reference – to the 'treasure of the world'.

23

Richard Mayhew was actually quite glad that Angela Lewis and her irritating ex-husband had left the team. She had a way of getting his back up, of usurping his authority, and she was one of those people who always thought they were right. What made it particularly galling for Mayhew – who shared this trait with her – was that she usually *was* right.

She'd correctly guessed that there had been a burglar at Carfax Hall, and had then managed to persuade her ex-husband to frighten him off. Mayhew wasn't entirely sure how he'd done that, although there was an air of menace about Chris Bronson that Mayhew found disturbing. He guessed he was a good police officer, because he could be very intimidating. Mayhew, a man of delicate sensibilities, thought that Bronson was a brute.

Anyway, they'd both gone, which suited him fine. And their work at the Hall was now complete. The individual specialists had prepared their inventories, listing all the items they'd assessed, their historical importance, and where possible their likely commercial value. All he had to do now was collate their data, write a covering letter with his overall assessment of the collections and present the final report to his superior at the British Museum. Then he could get back to his regular work.

But, he reflected, as he stepped outside the Hall for the last time on that Friday evening and looked up at the crumbling masonry of the old building, it hadn't been an entirely unpleasant interlude. A week in the country, all expenses paid, engaged on what amounted to an academic treasure hunt – there were definitely much worse ways to spend one's time.

These pleasant thoughts were interrupted by a brisk tap on his shoulder. Mayhew jumped – the rest of the team had left about a quarter of an hour earlier, and he knew he was alone at the building.

He spun round, and came face to face with one of his personal nightmares.

The man standing in front of him was shorter than Mayhew, perhaps five feet six, and stocky, with the solid bulk that comes from hard physical exercise. A bandage covered his left ear and that side of his face, and his dark unblinking eyes seemed to sear into Mayhew's soul.

The man's physical appearance was disturbing enough, but what Mayhew found alarmingly difficult to reconcile was the clerical collar the stranger wore at the neck of his black shirt, and the pistol in his right hand, a pistol that was aimed directly at him.

Mayhew caught his breath. 'Who are you? What do you want?'

'One question at a time, fat boy,' the man said, his voice quiet and measured, his accent American and the words simple but delivered with such menace that Mayhew felt his bowels loosening.

'I've got no money,' he stammered.

'I don't want your money. I just want you. Open the door you've just locked and get back inside the building.'

Mayhew looked around him frantically. He needed help.

The stranger chuckled softly. 'There's nobody here but us. Just get that through your thick skull. I could kill you right here, right now, and nobody would even hear the shot. So move before I do just that.'

Mayhew's hands were trembling so much that it took him three tries before he got the key into the lock.

'Get a move on,' the man snapped, poking his gun into Mayhew's back.

Finally the door swung open. Mayhew staggered as a powerful hand shoved him forwards, almost fell, then regained his footing as the door slammed behind him. Turning back he saw the American gangster – despite the clerical collar, what else could the man be? – putting the key into his pocket.

'Go into the kitchen,' the man said, pointing towards the back of the house.

Mayhew nodded dumbly and led the way. It never occurred to him to wonder how the man could possibly know where the kitchen was located.

'What do you want from me?' Mayhew asked again, once he was in the kitchen.

The man ignored his question, gesturing with his pistol to a wooden armchair standing in one corner of the room. 'Take off your jacket, then go and sit down.'

Mayhew placed his jacket on the table, then walked across to the chair.

The man followed him, pulled a handful of plastic cable ties from his pocket and tossed one to Mayhew. 'Put that around your right wrist and pull it tight,' he ordered, and watched closely as Mayhew obeyed him. 'That's good,' he said, stepping closer and securing Mayhew's left wrist to the other arm of the chair. Then he drew a small pair of pliers from his pocket and pulled both cable ties tight.

Mayhew grimaced as the thin plastic cut into the flesh of his wrists.

The man pulled another chair across and sat down opposite him, laying the pistol on the kitchen table. From one of the inside pockets of his jacket he drew a leather whip with multiple steel-tipped thongs and placed it beside the automatic.

Gulping for air, Mayhew watched his actions with increasing trepidation.

'This is a scourge,' the man said conversationally, looking down at the whip. 'It's one of the oldest implements of chastisement, used for both punishment and persuasion, and even for self-flagellation. The name is derived from the Latin *excoriare*, meaning "to flay" and *corium*, "skin", and it was used by the Romans to punish offenders. It's been used through the ages in monastic orders around the world, and I'll introduce you to it in a moment. Then I'm going to ask you some questions. I suggest you answer them as quickly, fully and accurately as you can.'

The man removed his jacket, picked up the scourge and stepped towards the wooden armchair.

'No, wait,' Mayhew shouted desperately. 'I'll tell you anything I can.'

'I know you will. There's not the slightest doubt about that.'

'No. Please – please wait—'

'Be silent. Remember that our Lord Jesus Christ endured a scourging during His Passion, before He was made to carry His cross to Calvary. This holy instrument will simply encourage your cooperation and ensure your recollections are accurate.'

The man turned so that he was facing his captive, then swung the scourge against Mayhew's chest, the steel-tipped ends of the thongs ripping apart the thin cotton of his shirt and carving furrows across his torso.

Mayhew howled in pain and leaned back as far as he could in the chair. His fists clenched and more blood appeared around the cable ties as the thin plastic cut deep into his wrists.

The man moved around to the other side of the chair, changed his grip on the scourge and swung it again. Then he moved back to his own chair and sat down.

After a couple of minutes, Mayhew's howls of pain had subsided to low moans of agony.

'Now,' the man said, 'we'll start at the beginning – tell me everything you know about Bartholomew's Folly.'

Whatever Mayhew had been expecting, this wasn't it.

'But it's just a story, a story about a stupid man who lost a fortune searching for something that wasn't there.'

'Then it won't be a problem for you to tell me all about it, will it?'

Mayhew shook his head. 'No, but I mean . . .' His voice trailed away into silence.

The man picked up his scourge, as Mayhew gathered his thoughts, and quickly explained everything he knew or had read about Bartholomew Wendell-Carfax's abortive expeditions to Persia.

'I've read all that in one of the guidebooks,' the man snapped. 'I need more information. Why do you think he was just wasting his time?'

'What?'

'Five minutes ago you told me Bartholomew Wendell-Carfax was just – and I quote – "a stupid man who lost a fortune searching for something that wasn't there."

Unquote. That's what you said. So how do you know it wasn't there?'

'Well, I don't *know* that, of course,' Mayhew wailed. 'What I said was an educated guess.'

'So educate me. Give me your reasons.'

Mayhew paused, trying desperately to think clearly amid the waves of panic and fear that were threatening to overwhelm him.

'There are two reasons,' he said finally. 'First, the fragment of Persian text probably dated from the first century AD, and it's likely that in the next two thousand years somebody would have stumbled across this so-called treasure – if it ever existed – and recovered it.'

'And the second reason?'

'From everything I've read, Bartholomew Wendell-Carfax had no real idea of where to look. He might not even have been searching in the right country. The only clue to the location was the "valley of the flowers", and I suspect that that would have been a fairly common-place name in many cultures around that time. Unless, of course, the remainder of the fragment Bartholomew found contained some other information that we don't have.'

'You mean what's printed in that guidebook isn't the whole translation?'

'No.' Mayhew struggled briefly against his restraints. It was no good – he was held fast. 'If you read the section, you can see that what's contained is only the part of the text that Bartholomew showed to Oliver. He must have kept the rest of it hidden somewhere. Oliver spent quite a lot of his time in later life looking for the original, and that's the reason for all the damaged walls in the house. He was certain there was a hidden passage or panel somewhere that held the Persian parchment.'

'What do you think?'

'I've no idea. It's well established that Bartholomew did find a piece of parchment, and that it subsequently vanished. But whether it's hidden somewhere here in the house or locked away in a bank safety deposit box we know nothing about, or even got destroyed in the last eighty-odd years, is another matter entirely.'

The man tightened the grip on the scourge. 'Give me your best guess.'

'I think it's probably hidden here somewhere. Bartholomew was planning another expedition when he died, apparently, and he would have wanted the entire text available to him. He might have thought that there were still clues hidden in it, and he would probably have studied the text regularly.'

'If it was parchment, handling it all the time wouldn't have been such a sharp idea, though, would it?'

Mayhew took a breath that sounded – even to him – like a sob. 'But if he sealed the parchment in a plastic bag or mounted it between a couple of sheets of glass, and kept it away from moisture and sunlight, it would have lasted quite well. And he would also have made a copy of the text and kept that to hand. And I still think he would have kept it here, somewhere. It wouldn't have been convenient to keep it in a bank, and it was a very precious and important relic for Bartholomew.' Mayhew sighed. 'But I've no idea where you'd start looking.'

'That's not bad,' the man said, looking at Mayhew keenly. 'Oliver told me the parchment did fall apart, several years ago. He also told me his father made a copy of the text before that happened.'

'Oliver Wendell-Carfax told *you*?' Mayhew whispered, an appalling realization suddenly crowding into his brain.

The man nodded, a slight smile playing over his lips. Then he picked up the whip and walked across to the chair Mayhew was sitting in. This time he stepped behind the chair. The wooden back was tall and reached almost up to Mayhew's neck.

'Bend forward,' he ordered, 'or I'll whip you twice.'

Mayhew muttered something inaudible, then bent forward, his whole body trembling in anticipation of the agony to come.

Instantly, the man swung the scourge down, opening up a line of new wounds on his prisoner's back.

Mayhew screamed again, as the man lashed his back a second time.

'You said you'd only hit me once,' Mayhew protested, between sobs of pain.

'I make the rules,' the man said simply, sitting down again, his voice still calm and controlled. 'Now I need to know what else you found here. You've had all week to explore this place. What did you discover?'

Mayhew shook his head, the pain of the lashes across his chest and back still clouding his mind. 'We didn't—' he began, but the stranger again picked up the whip.

'Wait, wait,' Mayhew stammered desperately. 'We did find something. It wasn't much, but—'

'I'll be the judge of its value. Just tell me what it was.'

'The vessel. The first-century pottery jar that the parchment had been sealed inside. We found that – at least we think we did – up in the attic. It was in pieces. Bartholomew broke it when he tried to remove the parchment.'

'Who found it? And where is it now?'

'One of our ceramic specialists – Angela Lewis – took it away with her.'

'Tell me about her.'

Sobbing, Mayhew described Angela and told the man where she lived and worked, and then fell silent. He'd apologise to her when he next saw her, he told himself. For now it was a matter of survival.

'Did you find anything else?'

Mayhew nodded miserably. 'Chris Bronson – Angela's former husband – found a small leather box full of papers, mainly notes Bartholomew had written. Angela said they were expedition records, that kind of thing, and a few bills and receipts.'

'And she took them away with her?'

'Yes.'

There was silence as the man stared at Mayhew. 'Anything else?' he asked at last.

'No, nothing to do with Bartholomew's treasure hunt.'

The man nodded and picked up the scourge again.

'No more, please,' Mayhew begged him. 'No more. I can't take it.'

The man walked over to the kitchen sink, ran the cold tap and washed away the sticky drying blood from the leather thongs. He dried the scourge carefully on a tea towel and tucked it away in his jacket pocket, then shrugged the garment on to his shoulders.

'Thank you,' Mayhew croaked.

The man turned back and looked down at him. 'You have done your best to help me, I think, and so I shall be merciful.'

He pulled a small bottle from another pocket of his jacket and unscrewed the stopper.

'What's that?' Mayhew asked, his voice trembling with fear.

'It's holy water, nothing more.'

The man dabbed a little of the water on to the tip of his right forefinger and traced the sign of a cross on Mayhew's forehead. Then he replaced the bottle in his pocket and strode back to the table.

He turned to face Mayhew, crossed himself and softly intoned '*In nomine padre, filii et spiritu sancti.*' Then he picked up the pistol and aimed it at Mayhew's chest.

'No, no! Wait! Please wait! I'll do anything. Don't kill me. Please.'

The man shook his head. 'Begging is undignified, and, in any case, I have no option. You've seen my face.'

'No! I'll do whatever you want me to do. Please! I'll never tell anyone anything about you. And why didn't you wear a mask?'

The man shook his head again. 'I would never hide my face. I believe God's work should always be done openly.'

'God's work?' Mayhew whispered incredulously, as the man took careful aim and squeezed the trigger.

Mayhew's body shook with the impact of the bullet. He remained upright for a couple of seconds, then slumped forwards lifelessly.

The man walked over, felt for a pulse but found nothing. Then he turned and looked out of the window. His next step was clear. He'd go to London and find the woman who was also hunting for the treasure. His treasure.

24

For a few seconds, Angela stared at the page of text displayed on the computer screen in front of her, then glanced down at the copious notes she'd made on her laptop. She stood up, stretched her arms above her head and rotated her shoulder joints, trying to work the kinks out of her muscles.

She realized she'd been working on the computer for almost four hours without a break – once she got her teeth into any project, she tended to become remarkably single-minded about it. She needed to take a short walk, let her eyes relax for a few minutes and maybe grab a cup of coffee.

Twenty minutes later she sat back at her desk, put down her mug and took another bite of the salad sandwich she'd bought at a delicatessen a few dozen yards down Great Russell Street, across the road from the museum.

She still wasn't entirely certain, but the references she'd

uncovered were beginning to make sense, and a tantalizing hypothesis was starting to take shape. The 'treasure of the world' seemed to be almost a code phrase that had echoed through the last two millennia, and appeared to refer to something quite specific. Exactly what was meant by the expression, Angela still didn't know, but there were one or two hints, and it did seem to be an ancient relic of considerable importance.

She also started to search backwards. Instead of looking for further first-century references to the 'treasure of the world', she'd started at the other end of time, trying to find much more recent documents that contained the expression. Her rationale was that if she found a reference to that expression in a later book or manuscript, there might well be a note about where the author of the work had found the phrase, and that would enable her to establish a trail back through the historical record, to back-track the references to the relic. Hopefully, each mention of the expression would amplify her knowledge and narrow down the search area – always assuming there was still something left to search for.

She'd consulted a wide range of late-medieval books without finding any reference to the phrase, and almost as an after-thought she'd decided to check the contents of a number of grimoires – a grimoire was essentially a textbook of magic. She wondered if that might be worth doing simply because, although such books mainly contained nonsensical spells, curses and incantations, they also often drew on a wide range of earlier sources.

The third grimoire she looked at was the *Liber Juratus*, also known as *The Sworne Booke of Honorius*, the *Liber Sacer* and the *Liber Sacratus*, a medieval grimoire written in Latin that dated from the thirteenth century. The original text had vanished long, long ago, but two fourteenth-century copies had survived, and the vast British Museum database had a scanned copy of the Latin text, as well as a copy of the only known English translation of the work.

Angela's Latin was reasonable, so she'd carried out a full scan of the Latin text using the search string *thesaurus mundi*, which she thought was close enough to the expression 'the treasure of the world'. That produced no results, so she altered the search term to *arcarum mundi*, and that generated two hits, not as part of any spell, but just in a passage that described a number of hidden relics. The author of the grimoire imbued one of these lost objects with the most extraordinary abilities, claiming that it could confer incredible power on its owner. From what Angela had found out so far, she had assumed that the hidden treasure was simply gold or silver or some other object of high intrinsic value, but the passage definitely suggested that whatever it was had magical properties.

The book also hinted that although the object's hiding place was still unknown, it was most likely somewhere in the Middle East. According to Angela's quick translation, it was described as 'hidden most cunningly in the gorge of the blooms', a location that sounded close enough to the 'valley of flowers'. Unfortunately, the grimoire gave no indication of the country in which the 'gorge of the blooms' might be found and, as far as she could tell, the writer was apparently copying the information from an earlier, but unnamed, source.

Although *thesaurus* translated as 'treasure' or 'hoard', and could also refer to a place where valuables were stored, like a 'treasury', the Latin word *arcarum* had a much wider and more general meaning. Depending on the context – which in Latin meant analysing the declension of the other nouns and the tenses of the verbs clustered at the end of the sentence – it could mean a box, a chest, a strong-box, a coffer, wealth, money, a coffin or a bier, or even a cell or cage. And there was one other possible meaning of the word that came as a complete surprise, and opened up both a whole new field of thought and a tantalizing possibility.

Excited now, Angela started checking texts that dated from the fifth to the tenth centuries AD, finding sufficient references to convince her she was on the right track.

She glanced at her watch: it was already after five in the afternoon. She copied all the documents and references she'd looked at on to a memory stick, copied them on to her laptop, which she shut down, then switched off the screen of her desktop PC – most of the museum's computer systems ran all the time – and locked her office.

Chris was coming to her apartment that evening and they were going out for a meal together. She wanted to make sure she looked her best.

25

'OK,' Chris Bronson said, leaning back in his chair. They were sitting over an after-dinner pot of coffee in a small Italian restaurant a few streets away from Angela's apartment in Ealing. 'Let's look at it like a police investigation. What's your evidence?'

Angela leaned towards him, her brown eyes shining in the candlelight. 'We know about Bartholomew's Folly – at least, we know what's printed in the Carfax Hall guidebook and what Jonathan Carfax told us. I also told you I recognized the reference to the "treasure of the world" on the parchment that old Bartholomew found, and I was right – the same expression was used on the Hillel fragment. In fact, both appeared to be copies of the same source document. The only difference was that the parchment Bartholomew found is written in Persian, and the Hillel piece is in Hebrew, but the text is virtually identical on both.'

Bronson nodded, happy to see Angela so excited. 'What else did you find?'

'I looked at a thirteenth-century grimoire – that's a kind of ancient magician's sourcebook of spells and incantations – and I found the same expression there. It even suggested the treasure was hidden in the "gorge of the blooms", which is close enough to the "valley of the flowers" to suggest it's referring to the same treasure, hidden in the same place.'

'But you still don't know which country?'

Angela put her hand on his. 'No. That's the downside. But I plugged away, going back through all the ancient texts I could find, because I thought there might be some really old source document that other authors had copied from over the centuries, and if I could find that, I hoped it might tell us where we should start looking.' She paused, and Chris raised his eyebrows, so she continued.

'I started with *De Administrando Imperio*. That's a really long letter written in Greek by the tenth-century Byzantine Emperor Constantine VII to his son, the future Emperor Romanus II, telling him how to run an empire. As far as we know, it was never intended to be published – it was just a private letter. I found a single reference in that text to an important treasure that was supposed to be "hidden in the valley", which I agree isn't an exact correlation with the other references. I also checked the translation of a tenth-century geography book written in Persian and called *Hudūd al-Ālam*, which translates as

"The Limits of The World".' She looked at Bronson. 'Following me so far?'

'Sort of,' he said. 'Just don't question me too closely afterwards. And I hope you aren't expecting me to remember any of this,' he muttered.

Angela laughed. 'Point taken. The *Hudūd al-Ālam* described what was then known about the entire world, and its author divided the world into three areas – Asia, Europe and Libya, by which he almost certainly meant the whole of Africa – and described the geography, the people, the languages, the food, and so on. In the section dealing with Asia, I found a phrase very similar to those I'd looked at before. One section referred to "the treasure of the world" and described it as being hidden in a place of stone located in a high valley.'

'But still no mention of where the hell the place is?' Bronson said, sounding frustrated.

'No, and that's probably because the author didn't know either. It's generally accepted that he was just regurgitating chunks of information he'd gleaned from earlier works. And I found similar references in other books that dated from the tenth century. I then went back about half a millennium to the sixth century and a man named Procopius of Caesarea. He left a manuscript known as the *Anecdota*, which means "unpublished things" and which is today normally referred to as the "Secret History", and there's a mention in that of a treasure hidden in the valley of the flowers. But, just like the other writers, he doesn't give any helpful details, like in which country the valley's located.'

'So that's it, then, is it?'

Angela smiled enigmatically and took another sip of coffee. 'Not quite,' she said, 'because two interesting things have emerged. I told you about the grimoire, the *Liber Juratus*. There's a theory that it was written by a small group of magicians and alchemists who had decided to incorporate their entire body of learning into a single volume. It's a big book – ninety-three chapters in all – covering a huge range of topics. But one section is devoted to the finding of treasure, and whoever wrote that bit insisted that this particular treasure had some kind of magical powers.'

'But he was writing a book about magic, so you'd expect him to say something like that, wouldn't you?' Bronson objected.

'Well, the text of the grimoire was written in Latin, so when I did a search I had to use a Latin term, obviously. I tried *thesaurus mundi* first.'

'A thesaurus? I thought that meant a word list.'

'That's what it means today, yes, just a list of synonyms and antonyms, but back then it meant a treasure or possibly a treasury. Anyway, that didn't produce any results, so I tried a different Latin noun – *arcarum* – and that did find a reference.'

Bronson looked interested. 'Go on.'

'The word *arcarum* is more of a catch-all term than

thesaurus, and to find out what the word means you have to analyse the context, which involves studying the sentence in which it occurs. One of the meanings was "money" and another one was "strong-box", but there was a third meaning that hadn't even occurred to me until then.'

'Which was?'

'"Ark",' Angela replied simply.

For a second or two Bronson just looked at her. '"Ark" as in Noah's Ark, or "Ark" as in "Ark of the Covenant"?' he asked.

Angela raised her hand. '*Arcarum* could mean "Noah's Ark", I grant you. But I don't think we're looking for the remains of a wooden boat on top of a mountain somewhere, Chris, do you?'

Chris leaned back in his chair and whistled. 'Are you sitting here in this small Italian restaurant trying to tell me you might be looking for the Ark of the Covenant?'

'And there's something else. The authors of grimoires and other "magick" texts were very fond of using analogies to obscure the meaning of certain passages. It was a kind of rudimentary code – you needed to be educated in the craft to some extent before you could understand what they were talking about. For example, a very simple code would be for the writing to include something like "a box without hinges, lock or lid, yet golden treasure inside is hid".'

Angela looked at him expectantly, but Bronson just shook his head. 'No idea,' he said.

'It's an egg, you idiot. What else could it be?' Angela shook her head. 'Anyway, somebody a lot brighter than you would look at the rhyme and correctly identify the object as an egg, so that when the author of the work later referred to an egg, because of the words used in that rhyme they'd realize he was talking about a treasure chest. The egg would be the analogy for the treasure chest.'

'I follow that,' Bronson said, 'stupid policeman though I undoubtedly am. But what's that got to do with the Ark of the Covenant?'

Angela sighed. 'My point is that there were two references in the grimoire that used almost the same words. But in the second one there was a misspelling – the author had substituted the letter "n" for the second "r" of *arcarum*.'

'So instead of *arcarum mundi* it read *arcanum mundi*,' Bronson said. 'Gutenberg didn't invent the printing press until the fifteenth century, if I remember my history correctly. So, if you're right about the date of the grimoire, the first version must have been handwritten. Those two letters are very similar. Are you sure he didn't just write the "r" with a slightly elongated down-stroke?'

'I don't think so. The two phrases were so similar that I'm certain it was done deliberately. And you haven't asked the obvious question.'

'I know,' Bronson replied. 'What does *arcanum* mean?'

'I'd have thought you'd have guessed it, because it's so similar to a modern English word. *Arcanum* means a sacred secret, a secret known only to a very few people, or a secret of nature, the kind of thing the alchemists spent their time searching for. It's usually found in the plural form – *arcana* – and it's the origin of the word "arcane".'

'So let me get this straight. In the grimoire you found, this hidden treasure is called both the *arcarum mundi* – meaning the "treasure of the world" – and the *arcanum mundi* – the "sacred secret of the world".'

'Precisely. There can't be that many relics that could be considered to be both a treasure and a sacred secret, but without any doubt the Ark of the Covenant has to be one of them.' Angela took his hand again. 'Shall we continue this conversation at my flat?'

26

The night was warm and the streets still relatively busy as Bronson and Angela walked up Ealing Broadway.

'You said there were two things you'd found. Obviously one was the grimoire, so what was the other?' Bronson asked.

'The other was the box of papers we found under that revolting stuffed fox. I've gone through them all now. In the main, they comprise notes of Bartholomew's abortive expeditions, but they also contain his thoughts and conclusions. On his very last expedition to Egypt he writes that he is now certain that he is on the trail of the *sakina*, and that someone he refers to as "Sq" took it to Sinat.'

'And that means exactly what?' Bronson asked.

'Well, he obviously didn't want to write down his thoughts in plain language,' Angela said. 'Maybe he was worried about somebody reading them and stealing a march on him. The "Sq" is almost certainly his own pet abbreviation for Shishaq – he's the only pharaoh I can think of whose name begins and ends with those letters.'

'What about "Sinat"?'

'Look,' Angela said, taking his hand, 'I think Bartholomew used a very simple code here. The word "Sinat" is "Tanis" spelt backwards, and that was where the Pharaoh Shishaq had his capital city, so if he did seize any prize or treasure, that would obviously be where he'd take it.'

'And the "sakina"?'

'It's an Arabic word that derives from *sakoon*, meaning "peace" or "tranquillity". But it has a more obscure secondary meaning as "the Chest in which the tranquillity of the Lord resides". In other words, that sentence says that Shishaq seized the Ark of the Covenant and took it with him to his capital at Tanis.'

'And we both know, from the time we spent together in Israel, that both the Ark of the Covenant and the tablets of stone it protected, actually existed,' Bronson said slowly.

'Absolutely,' Angela agreed. 'Anyway, according to one story in the Bible, Shishaq seized the Ark in about nine hundred and twenty BC. In another account, the Ark was looted from the First Temple, also known as Solomon's Temple, in Jerusalem in five hundred and eighty-six BC, by King Nebuchadnezzar and his army. But nobody actually knows, and there's nothing in the historical record to support or deny either suggestion.' She paused. 'However, I have got a theory of my own.'

They turned the corner towards the Common and Angela's apartment block came into view.

'I think we need to find out what the original Persian text said before we go any further,' Bronson said. 'And unless you've found it in that box from Carfax Hall, I've no idea where we'd start looking for it.'

'It wasn't there, Chris. If it had been, I'd already have told you. But there was something that suggested where we should start looking for it.'

Angela stopped suddenly, looking startled.

'What is it?' Bronson said, his hand on her shoulder.

'I think there's someone in my flat,' she said.

27

Bronson stopped short and stared at the apartment block, seeing immediately what she meant. The lights in her lounge windows were blazing away, and he knew she always switched everything off whenever she left home.

'OK.' Bronson passed her the leather-bound box he'd been carrying, fished in his pocket and pulled out his car keys. 'My car's parked in the next street,' he said. 'Get in it, lock the doors and drive back here. Pick a spot where you've got a good view of the building and keep watch. And keep your mobile on and close to hand.'

'What are you going to do?'

'I'm going inside, of course, and find out what's happening.'

'Shouldn't we call the police?'

'My dear Angela, I *am* the police. If I call the local bobbies, they'll send a squad car along, blues and twos switched on, and whoever's up there will leg it long before the car gets anywhere near the building.'

Reluctantly, Angela passed Bronson her keys. 'Just be careful in there,' she said, shivering a little as she remembered what had happened in Carfax Hall.

Bronson leaned across and kissed her. 'I don't intend to get hit on the head again,' he said. 'So stop worrying, and get the car.'

'Looking both ways, Bronson strode briskly across the road. On the opposite side he stopped and looked back, making sure that Angela had gone, then walked towards her front door. He looked closely at the lock. Even a casual glance was enough to show him that it had been forced.

Angela paused briefly at the street corner and looked back towards her apartment building. Bronson had just vanished inside the front lobby. She muttered a silent prayer for him and walked on.

As she did so, a shadow detached itself from a doorway on the opposite side of the street and moved after her.

Bronson pushed open the lobby door and the automatic hall lights flared into life. He had a choice of the lift or the stairs. Using the stairs would have been the quieter option, but Bronson knew he'd be out of breath by the time he reached Angela's floor, and that wouldn't be a good thing if he was going to have to get physical with a couple of tea-leaves in her flat. So he pressed the button for the lift instead.

When the doors opened, he stepped inside the lift and pressed the button for two floors above Angela's apartment – that way, if somebody was burgling her flat, they'd hear the lift carry on past that floor, and wouldn't expect him to then come creeping down the staircase. Or that's what he hoped, anyway. Then he took out his mobile and pressed triple nine, but not the button to dial the number. If there was an intruder, he'd only have one button to press, and he could do that with the phone in his pocket. The mobile cell triangulation system would pinpoint his position even if he couldn't speak, and he knew that would probably be a faster way of summoning help than talking to the operator, especially if the background noise on the call was the sound of fighting.

The lift shuddered to a stop and he made his way slowly and silently down the two flights of stairs to the correct floor.

Angela's apartment door was ajar. Bronson could see a thin sliver of light between the door and the jamb. It looked as if whoever was inside the flat had switched on most of the lights. It also meant that there could be several intruders, confident they could handle anyone who tried to interfere with them.

If so, it wasn't good news.

* * *

Angela walked swiftly down the street, looking for Bronson's BMW. She spotted it about a hundred yards ahead, and felt in her coat pocket for the keys.

But as she approached the car, a figure dressed in black stepped out on to the pavement from between two parked vehicles a few yards in front of her, and stood there, motionless by the kerb, looking towards her.

Angela's stride faltered. There was something about him, some hint of menace or implied threat, that her heightened awareness picked up. She stepped off the pavement, deciding to cross to the other side of the road in order to avoid him.

She glanced both ways but there was no traffic coming from either direction. When she got about halfway across the road she looked back, and her heart pounded in her chest. The man had also stepped off the pavement, and was angling towards her.

'Oh, God,' she whispered, remembering all too clearly what had happened to Bronson and Jonathan Carfax.

Desperately searching for help, she looked in both directions but the street appeared to be deserted. No pedestrians, no traffic.

For the briefest of instants she considered her options. Then she turned and started to run.

Bronson fingered the mobile in his pocket, wondering if he should make the call to the emergency services before he even stepped inside.

Then he shook his head and crossed to the door. Just like the outside door of the building, the lock had obviously been jemmied. He pressed his ear to the opening, but the only noise he could hear was the regular ticking of Angela's old long-case clock that he knew stood in the hallway.

He took a deep breath, pushed the door open very slightly, just wide enough for him to see through the gap, and looked inside.

Immediately Angela started to run she heard pounding footsteps behind her. She risked a quick glance back, which confirmed what she already knew – her pursuer was much quicker than she was, and was gaining on her with every step. He'd be on her in a matter of seconds.

She'd never reach the main road, she knew. She took a deep breath and screamed; a loud, panicky yell that echoed off the walls of the buildings. But as the sound died away, the only noise she could hear was the thudding of the man's feet behind her. He was getting closer with every second.

To her right was an apartment block, the lighted entrance lobby offering a safe haven. *If* the door was open, and *if* she could reach it before the man caught her.

She changed direction abruptly, cutting across the road towards the lobby, but she was still twenty yards short when a hand seized her shoulder.

Angela screamed again and jinked to her right, shaking

off the man's hand and trying to dodge away from him. But almost immediately he grabbed her again. She spun round, reached for his face and scratched her nails down his cheek, digging as deep as she could.

Then she ran again.

The hall of Angela's flat was empty, and it looked as if nothing had been disturbed. Bronson swung the door wider and slipped into the flat. On one side was the kitchen, the light switched on but the small room clearly empty. To his right, the open door led into the lounge, and it was obvious even from where Bronson stood that the room had been comprehensively searched. Every drawer on the sideboard had been pulled open, the contents scattered all over the floor. But, again, the room looked empty and there was no noise from anywhere in the apartment.

Making as little sound as he could, Bronson stepped over to the lounge door and glanced inside the room. Nobody was there. Moving more confidently now, he strode further down the hall, checking each room. But within a couple of minutes he'd confirmed his initial suspicions – the burglars had already left.

Angela felt a blow to her side that slammed her hard to the right. The next instant, she was gasping for breath, pinned by the man's left hand against the rough brick wall of a building. She stared in terrified silence at her attacker.

He was short and stocky, with a bandage covering one

side of his head. The clerical collar didn't fool her for an instant. Perverts, she assumed, would adopt whatever guise they thought would put their victims off-guard, and most people deferred to priests, even if they never went to church.

But what happened next utterly amazed her.

'You've got something I want, Angela,' the man said calmly, his voice measured and level. Blood trickled steadily down his neck from the ragged scratches on his cheek. 'Give me that case.'

'How do you know my name?' she stammered.

'Just give me that,' he snapped, grabbing for the leather-bound box of papers Angela had removed from Carfax Hall.

But Angela didn't let go. Instead, she pulled back, trying to wrench the box from his hand, and herself out of the man's grasp.

The man reached into his pocket and pulled out a switchblade knife and pressed the button. The 'snick' of the five-inch blade snapping open was ominously loud in the quiet street. He drew back his arm and then swung the knife forward in a vicious under-arm blow aimed directly at Angela's stomach.

Bronson pulled out his mobile phone, cancelled the triple nine that was displayed on the screen and dialled Angela's phone. There was no answer.

In that instant he guessed that something was wrong.

Stuffing the mobile in his pocket, he ran out of the flat, ignoring the lift and pounding down the stairs towards the ground floor.

The moment she saw the knife swinging towards her, Angela reacted instinctively. Grasping the leather-bound box with both hands, she slammed it downwards to meet the blade.

She felt a sudden blow as the switchblade slammed into the wood and staggered with the force of the impact. She looked down. The blade had penetrated both sides, and a couple of inches of it were sticking out.

The man tugged on the knife, trying to pull it free, but the blade was stuck fast.

Angela wrestled the box from side to side, but couldn't loosen the man's grip on it. So she did the next best thing. She kicked upwards, as hard and as accurately as she could, and felt her foot connect firmly with her attacker's groin.

He grunted in shock and his eyes clouded with pain, and for a moment it seemed as if he might let go of the knife. But then he tightened his grip on the weapon and pulled back his left arm to punch Angela in the face.

She did the only thing she could. The instant he released his grip on her shoulder, she let go of the leather-bound box and dodged away from him, ducking under his outstretched arm. And then she ran away – ran for her life – up the street towards safety.

* * *

Running as fast as he could, Bronson reached the corner of the street where he had parked his car and turned into it. She *had* to be down there somewhere.

He'd barely made ten yards down the street when he saw her, dishevelled, panting and running hard in the opposite direction.

'Angela!' he yelled, and ran across to her.

She slumped to a stop and collapsed into his arms, gasping for air and trembling with exertion.

'What happened?' Bronson demanded. As he held her, he scanned the street behind her. It was deserted.

For several seconds Angela couldn't speak. Finally, she gasped out a single sentence.

'He knew my name, Chris.' She flung out an arm and pointed down the street behind her. 'The priest,' she said, 'down there.'

But apart from a couple of girls who'd just appeared from a side street about a hundred yards away, there was nobody in sight.

'Thank God for that,' she whispered.

'What happened?' Bronson asked again, holding Angela hard against his chest.

In short, breathless sentences, Angela explained what had happened to her since they'd separated outside her apartment building.

'And you thought he was a priest?' Bronson asked.

Angela shook her head. 'I meant he looked like one.

He was wearing a black suit and a clerical collar.'

'Would you recognize him if you saw him again?'

Angela nodded decisively. 'Absolutely. I'll never forget those cold, dead eyes. And I left him a souvenir.' She held up her hand and Bronson saw the blood under her fingernails.

'Good for you,' he said, hugging her.

She pushed herself back, her hands on Bronson's shoulders. 'He called me "Angela", but I've never seen him before in my life. He wanted the box of papers and I'm afraid he got it. But it saved my life. If I hadn't jammed it down when he swung the knife at me, I'd be dead by now.' She turned and looked towards the end of the street.

'What happened to the flat?'

'You've been burgled,' Bronson stated flatly. 'You'd better check and see what's been taken.'

'Oh, shit,' Angela said, her old spirit returning. 'Why the hell is it always my place that gets robbed?'

As Angela looked around her flat, Bronson found a couple of long screws in the small toolbox she kept under the sink and replaced the lock assembly on the main door of the apartment.

'You'll need to get that door fixed properly,' he warned her, 'but that should hold it for a day or two. And there is *some* good news.'

'Like what?'

'Whoever did this was a professional, not some

hyped-up junkie looking for something to sell so he could buy his next fix.'

'How can you tell?'

'Those drawers over there.' Bronson pointed at the side-board. 'Amateurs usually start searching in the top drawer, but that means they have to close it afterwards so they can look in the one below it. Professional searchers – or professional thieves – always start with the bottom drawer and work their way up. That way they can leave each drawer open when they've finished.'

Angela straightened up, and put her hands on her hips. 'That makes me feel a lot better.'

'Actually, it should. The other trick amateur burglars are fond of pulling is to take a dump on the floor, preferably in the middle of the carpet, before they leave the place. They seem to think it leaves all the bad luck in the property, and means they won't get caught.'

'Are you serious?'

'Absolutely. So what's been taken?'

'Just my laptop and the broken pottery vessel from Carfax Hall. The laptop wasn't an expensive model, and those broken pottery shards are worthless from a commercial point of view.'

'So whoever took them was clearly looking for those and nothing else.'

Angela nodded. 'Odd, isn't it? Especially as there are lots more valuable things around.'

'It's pretty clear what happened,' Bronson said. 'The

man who attacked you broke in here first and took those bits. Then he waited for you down on the street. And that begs another question.'

Angela nodded grimly. 'Yes. Somebody must have told him what I look like.'

'We've been here before, Angela,' Bronson said slowly. 'Somebody else is obviously searching for this "treasure of the world", and we've no idea who it is, or why they're looking for it.'

'If I'm right and it *is* the Ark of the Covenant, the "why" is a very easy question to answer: the value of that relic is incalculable. I mean, you'd certainly be talking tens of millions of pounds, maybe even hundreds of millions.'

'High stakes, and that means high risk. And now you've lost all your research notes and the box of papers, I suppose we're pretty poorly placed to keep searching?'

Angela shook her head firmly. 'Of course not. What was on the laptop is duplicated on my desktop computer at the museum, and I've got a full back-up of the data on a memory stick in my handbag. I duplicate *everything*. And even losing the papers isn't important, because I scanned everything as soon as I got to the museum this morning.' She stopped and smiled for the first time since she'd escaped from the man on the street. 'That bastard might think he's one step ahead of us, but he's not. However, he now has exactly the same information, and he'll probably eventually make the same connection, so we have to get there first.'

'Get where?' Bronson looked confused.

'Egypt, to see a man named Hassan al-Sahid, and also to visit el-Hiba and the temple of Amun-Great-of-Roarings. Let me just grab my overnight bag. We leave in five minutes.'

Egypt

28

'Bartholomew and Oliver were devious old sods,' Angela said, as they sat in the departure lounge at Heathrow, waiting for their flight to be called. 'We know this because of the way Bartholomew hid his papers and Oliver made all his different wills. So it seems to me that Bartholomew would have planted a trail of clues in Carfax Hall for his son to follow. The trouble is that I don't think Oliver was very good at that kind of thing. He only said a month or so ago that he was planning an expedition to follow in his father's footsteps in the Middle East, so I doubt if he found that hidden drawer under the stuffed fox until quite recently, and he may never have made the connection. He could just have been intending to retrace the route his father took on one of his expeditions, based on Bartholomew's notes.'

'So what *is* the connection you've made?' Bronson asked.

'I found a bill of sale from Bartholomew Wendell-Carfax to a man named Hassan al-Sahid, and a sentence scrawled at the bottom of one of his pages of expedition notes. That read, "The Montgomerys hold the key." Put those two things together, and what do you get?'

'A headache?' Bronson suggested, smiling at her.

Angela sighed. 'The bill of sale is for two oil on canvas portraits, but the terms are a bit unusual, because the purchaser – al-Sahid – agreed to hold the pictures in safe keeping in his family for fifty years or until Bartholomew or his son requested their return, when the purchase price would be refunded, plus accrued interest. So it was really more like an extended loan. The two photographs we found in the box of papers were of the paintings, and I've got scanned copies of those as well. That's the first thing.

'The second point is that the name of the artist was Edward Montgomery. I think the reason Bartholomew had those two portraits painted was so he could conceal the text of the ancient Persian script within them. That's what he meant by "the Montgomerys hold the key". I think he leased them to al-Sahid as a kind of insurance policy, so that there'd always be another copy of the parchment text in existence, just in case Bartholomew lost his version.'

'Or in case something else happened to him,' Bronson said thoughtfully.

'Yes, and Hassan al-Sahid had special significance. His home was in Cairo, and he was Bartholomew's gang master on all his explorations in Egypt, and probably the one man Bartholomew trusted implicitly – his best friend, in fact. His expedition notes make that very clear. The text of that piece of Persian script has to be hidden in one of those two paintings, and that's what we're going to Cairo to track down.'

'What about that roaring-Amun stuff?'

'Amun-Great-of-Roarings,' Angela said patiently. 'Everything I've discovered up to now suggests that the "treasure of the world" is actually the Ark of the Covenant, and one of the likeliest contenders for seizing the relic is the Pharaoh Shishaq.'

'OK,' Bronson said, determined to be practical. He also knew that these discussions were what made them such a good partnership. 'Let's accept that the relic that's referred to in the grimoire and the other places really *is* the Ark of the Covenant. What do we know about it? What does the Ark look like, for instance? And what's supposed to have happened to it?'

'According to the Bible, it was a wooden box made of acacia wood. The acacia was known to the Israelites as the shittah-tree, and it was an important botanical with several uses in traditional medicine. The Ark was built in accordance with the so-called golden ratio – that's the relationship between the dimensions of an object – and it was two and a half cubits long and one and a half cubits high and wide. If we assume they were using the Egyptian royal cubit, that would make it about four feet long and two feet six inches wide and high.

'The box was then covered with pure gold, and the lid, which was known as the *kaporet* in Hebrew, was possibly solid gold, or at least it had a gold rim. The lid was decorated with two sculpted cherubim, facing each other with their wings spread out over the top of the Ark. On each of the long sides of the box were two gold rings, so that gold-covered poles could be inserted to lift the object, because it wasn't ever supposed to touch the ground.'

Bronson smiled to himself: Angela was getting into her stride.

'We touched on this before, when we were in Israel. According to the Bible, the Pharaoh Shishaq sacked Jerusalem in about nine hundred and twenty BC and took away the treasures of the Temple, which might have included the Ark. According to legend, he hid the Ark in Tanis, his capital city, which is about fifteen miles from Cairo.

'Where the Ark is now is unknown, obviously. Perhaps the most widely accepted possible location is the Church of Our Lady Mary of Zion in Axum in Ethiopia. But there's the problem of proof – nobody's allowed inside the building to see or photograph the object, and it's never taken out, so they might just as well claim to have aliens and spaceships and Elvis in there as well.' Angela frowned, obviously frustrated.

'So what do you think happened to it?'

'Well, the Ark was almost certainly in the Second Temple in Jerusalem in nine hundred and twenty BC, and it seems to me that there are only two possible things that could then have happened to it. Either it was taken to a place of safe keeping before Shishaq and his army arrived or it was captured by the Pharaoh. And I'm starting to think that Bartholomew was right – maybe it was seized by Shishaq.

'The problem with the idea of the Ark being spirited away from Jerusalem is where it would have gone. It was the most sacred object held in the temple, and the priests certainly wouldn't have handed it to just anyone. It would have had to have been held by people they trusted implicitly, and that would have meant another group of Jews. And there's a very good reason why they wouldn't have given it to the only other Jewish community that was anywhere near Jerusalem.'

Angela sat forward, a faraway look in her brown eyes. 'Solomon's son was named Rehoboam, and when he ascended the throne he decided to tax the people even more heavily than Solomon had done. This was round about nine hundred and thirty BC – the dates of Rehoboam's reign are disputed – and not too surprisingly there was a revolt. Ten of the northern tribes, under the leadership of a man named Jeroboam, broke away and formed a separate kingdom that became known as Israel, or the Northern Kingdom, or, rather later, as Samaria. Rehoboam's kingdom was called Judah, or sometimes the Southern Kingdom, and it occupied the area to the west and south of the Dead Sea, broadly speaking the area that's now Israel.

'Rehoboam wanted to go to war against Israel, but was advised against it, because he would have been fighting his own countrymen, but the two Jewish nations were in a state of low-level conflict for his entire seventeen-year reign. So absolutely the last people Rehoboam would have trusted with the Ark were Jeroboam's Northern Kingdom tribes, and as far as I know there were no other groups anywhere near Jerusalem that he would have been likely to trust enough to give it to.

'And then, in about nine hundred and twenty BC, the Egyptian pharaoh, Shishaq, invaded Judah and laid siege to Jerusalem. That was bad enough for Rehoboam, but what made it worse was that Shishaq had provided refuge to Jeroboam – Rehoboam's bitter enemy – so his invasion was in support of his ally. And it's known that to buy off Shishaq and the Egyptians, Rehoboam gave them all the treasures of the Temple.'

'And that would presumably have included the Ark?'

'Unless Rehoboam's priests had managed to hide it somewhere else, yes. And if they'd managed to hide the Ark, why didn't they also hide the other Temple treasures, which were known to have been seized by Shishaq?'

'I see what you mean.'

Angela nodded. 'The counter-argument, if you like, is that the Second Book of Chronicles states that the Ark was present in the Temple of Jerusalem in the reign of Josiah, between about six hundred and forty BC and six hundred and nine BC.'

'So if you follow this line of reasoning, the story in the Bible about the Ark being seized and hidden in Tanis by Shishaq must be wrong?'

'Not necessarily. The Bible is inaccurate about almost everything, but especially dates and anything that resembles an historical fact.'

'So how do you know that the stuff about Shishaq is accurate?'

Angela smiled and sat back. 'Simple. It's not just in the Bible. The Egyptians were compulsive record-keepers, and Shishaq's conquest of Judah is recorded there as well. What we have to do as a first step is to go and check on the only relevant primary sources that I know of. Untranslated primary sources, I mean.'

Their flight was being called, and Bronson stood up. 'And where are these untranslated primary sources?'

'The place I mentioned back in my flat: the bas-relief carvings in a small temple dedicated to Amun-Great-of-Roarings at el-Hiba. If I don't find anything definite there, we may also have to trek a long way south to look at the Shishaq Relief on the Bubastis Portal. That's outside the Temple of Amun at Karnak. But first, we must track down the man who has the paintings – Hassan al-Sahid.'

As Bronson and Angela vanished from sight, a tall dark-haired man stood up from his seat on the opposite side of the departure lounge. He strode across to the ground stewardess at the barrier and joined the end of the queue.

When his turn came, he showed her his passport and handed over his boarding card. She tore off one section, handed the remainder back to him, and wished him a pleasant flight.

The man nodded and smiled at her, then followed the last of the passengers down the ramp and on to the aircraft.

29

Cairo airport had been a surprise. Bronson had been expecting a dusty, crowded and inefficient place, probably fairly ramshackle, but actually it was gleaming and ultra-modern, a high-tech steel and glass cathedral dedicated to the needs of the international traveller.

Like all non-Egyptian nationals, they'd needed entry visas but had obviously not had enough time to obtain these before they left the UK. Fortunately, after a few minutes spent queuing at a booth in the terminal building, they were each sold a couple of stamps – entry and exit – that were then applied to a page in their passports. Then they queued again, at a different booth, to get the 'entry' visa stamped. That entitled them to fourteen days' residence in Egypt.

After a short taxi ride they'd checked in to their hotel in the Heliopolis district on the north-eastern side of the city, not too far from the airport, grabbed a late snack at a local restaurant that was still serving food and then fallen into bed.

First thing the following morning Bronson borrowed a copy of the Cairo telephone directory from the reception desk and started looking for Hassan al-Sahid, only to find that al-Sahid was a fairly common name in the area, with about forty or fifty entries in the directory listings.

'We need to narrow this down a bit,' he observed. 'Was there any indication in the stuff you got from Carfax Hall where al-Sahid might live?'

'Hang on a second.' Angela put her laptop – she'd bought a new machine at Heathrow and had transferred all her stored files and programs on to it while they'd waited for their flight to depart – on the table and switched it on. Then she flicked through the scanned images until she found the bill of sale for the paintings and magnified the appropriate section of it.

'Here we are. It's hand-written, so the address isn't that clear, but I think it says he lives in Al-Gabal el-Ahmar, which I presume is a Cairo district or suburb.'

Angela spelt out the name and Bronson ran his finger down the appropriate page in the telephone directory.

'Nothing,' he said, 'no listings at all. Oh, just a second. Could it be spelt Al-*Gebel a*l-Ahmar, not Al-*Gabal el*-Ahmar?'

Angela looked carefully at the image on her laptop. 'It's a bit blurred, but I suppose it could be.'

'Right. If it is, then there are three al-Sahids there, one actually called Hassan, the second just with the initial "M" and the third named Suleiman.' Bronson copied down their numbers and addresses, then closed the directory. 'What we don't know, of course, is whether Hassan al-Sahid is even alive after all this time, or whether he still lives in the same house. Do you want to telephone, or just turn up at the door?'

'We'll go there, I think. There can't be that many Egyptians who would have spent most of their working lives escorting English archaeologists around sites in the country. Don't forget Al-Sahid didn't just work for Bartholomew – he was a professional gang master.' She got up and turned off her laptop. 'At the very least we might find someone who remembers him.'

Ten minutes later, they stepped out on to the street. The heat was brutal – Bronson guessed it was probably already in the high twenties – and the traffic driving past the hotel was heavy, horns sounding a discordant melody, dust and smoke billowing everywhere.

The receptionist had told him where the nearest car hire agency was located, and it was only a fairly short walk from the hotel. The only feature the hire car absolutely had to have, as far as Bronson was concerned, was air conditioning, but in fact every vehicle available was equipped either with that or with climate control, so eventually he settled on a white – all the cars at the agency were white – Peugeot 309.

There was a map of Alexandria and Cairo in the glove box, and another route-planning map that covered the whole of Egypt. While he sat in the driver's seat, both doors wide open, waiting for the air con to haul the internal temperature down to a bearable level, Bronson looked at the latter. Compared to most whole-country charts, it was an unusual map, because almost all the roads, towns and cities were clustered in a fairly narrow T-shape, the top of which ran along the Mediterranean coast from the Libyan border east to Alexandria and then across to the border with Israel. The 'leg' of the T then followed the mighty Nile River all the way down to Sudan. To the west of the Nile there was just a vast empty expanse of desert, studded with the occasional settlement, and even the odd airfield. To the east of the Nile, between the river and the Red Sea, lay a ribbon of roads and settlements, but most of the built-up areas were in the north, where the Nile met the Mediterranean, in a rough 'V' that encompassed Alexandria, Port Said and Cairo itself.

He switched his attention to the Cairo map and fairly quickly found Al-Gebel al-Ahmar. 'It's here,' he said, pointing to an area on the east side of the city, just east of the Northern Cemetery. 'Not too far away. Can you navigate?'

'Of course,' Angela said briskly.

Bronson closed his door, buckled his seat belt, pulled out of the car hire agency parking lot and tried to turn into the street.

'Tried' was the operative word. The traffic was chaotic. Cars, coaches and vans were everywhere, their drivers grimly determined never to give way, never to allow a fellow driver the chance to get in front of them or pass. Bronson looked at the stream of vehicles for a couple of minutes, then decided the only way to beat them was to join them.

'Just hold on,' he muttered, as he waited for the smallest of gaps in the line of vehicles passing down the street. Then he pulled out, accelerating hard. Behind him he heard a sudden squealing of brakes and the inevitable bellows from a selection of car and van horns.

'Jesus, Chris, was that necessary? Couldn't you have waited?' Angela looked pale.

'If I'd waited,' Bronson said, with a grin, 'we'd still be sitting there at the side of the road, and would be for some time. I was just being pragmatic.'

'Which means what, exactly, in this context?' Angela asked. 'Oh, shit,' she muttered, closing her eyes as a coach shot out of a side road directly in front of them, forcing Bronson – and about a dozen other drivers – to hit the brakes hard.

'It means that we're in Egypt,' Bronson said, 'so I think the best option is to drive like an Egyptian. And that means all the normal rules about giving way and leaving a safe distance behind the car in front – all the stuff I was taught as a police driver, in fact – go right out of the window. Over here, if you leave a gap of more than about three feet in front of you, a driver will absolutely force his way into it.'

'Aren't there any rules here?'

Bronson nodded. 'I checked,' he said. 'Basically, there's just one – the car in front has right of way. So if the guy next to us gets his bumper one inch ahead of mine, and then swings across in front of me, he's in the right. That's why they never give way, and never leave a gap.'

Angela dragged her unwilling gaze from the melee in front of them and glanced across at her ex-husband as he changed lanes, braked hard, accelerated and changed lanes again before pulling the car to a halt behind a line of unmoving vehicles which were somewhat surprisingly waiting at a red light. Traffic lights only appeared in Egypt in about 1980, and most of the locals still tended to ignore them.

'You're enjoying this, aren't you?' Angela said accusingly.

Bronson took his eyes off the road for an instant and grinned at her. 'Absolutely. It's like dodgems, but with full-sized vehicles; great fun. Now, stop complaining about my driving and tell me where you want me to go.'

About a hundred yards behind them, a Mercedes with tinted windows was following. In the driver's seat, JJ

Donovan flipped open a pack of Marlboros and extracted one, then pressed the dashboard lighter. Once he'd lit the cigarette, he cracked the window slightly to let the smoke escape, and concentrated on the traffic in front of him.

He'd watched Bronson and Angela Lewis step out of their hotel that morning, followed them to the car hire agency and then sat waiting in his own vehicle until they drove out. Then it had been a simple case of keeping tabs on them as they headed towards the centre of Cairo.

In fact, 'simple' wasn't quite the right word. Donovan was used to driving in the States, but even fighting his way through the Los Angeles traffic a couple of times every day hadn't prepared him for the reality of the morning rush hour in downtown Cairo. The two good things were that the Merc had an automatic box, so all he had to do was steer the big car, and he was used to driving on the right-hand side of the road, though Egyptian drivers seemed to drive more or less wherever and however they wanted.

Donovan knew Bronson was driving, and it looked as if he was pretty competent. A couple of times the smaller Peugeot had nipped through gaps that the Mercedes wouldn't have fitted in, and were barely large enough for the French car, but there was so much traffic that losing sight of his quarry had never really been likely.

And, even if he did lose contact with Bronson's car, it wasn't going to be that much of a problem. Donovan just loved technology. After he'd questioned Jonathan Carfax in the kitchen of the old house in Suffolk, he'd walked out of the room, taking Bronson's mobile with him. Out in the hall, he'd quickly opened the phone and installed a sophisticated GPS tracking chip, then gone back into the kitchen and replaced the Nokia on the table. He didn't think Carfax even noticed what he'd done.

Powered by the phone's own battery, and virtually undetectable unless the user knew exactly what his mobile's circuit board should look like, the chip computed its position from signals received from the GPS satellites, and radiated that position to the GSM cellphone network. Donovan could then monitor the chip's signal from his laptop using a combined tracking and mapping program. The chip was one of the latest generation, and allowed him to pinpoint the position of the phone – and by implication its owner – to within about thirty feet anywhere on the surface of the earth.

The chip had allowed him to follow them to Heathrow, and because neither Bronson nor Angela Lewis had even seen his face, he'd been able to get close enough to hear what they were saying to each other. He had actually flown out to Cairo with them on the same plane.

He settled down to follow Bronson's Peugeot. He had a full tank of fuel, his laptop was sitting in its case on the seat beside him, and built into the computer was a WWAN adapter – a wireless wide area network card – that meant he could access the mobile phone network to surf the internet. So wherever Bronson went, he would be able to follow, as long as he was within range of a cell.

Donovan leaned back in his seat, picked up a bottle of water from the cup-holder in the centre console and took a swallow. He was deliberately trying to avoid drinking too much, because he didn't want to have to stop until Bronson and Angela Lewis also pulled up. He needed to find out as soon as possible where they were going and what it was they were looking for.

Angela studied the map of Cairo, then looked out of the window. 'Where are we now?' she asked.

Bronson glanced away from the road for the split second it took to register a direction sign.

'That sign said we're just about to reach Abbassiyya,' he said. 'If I were you I'd forget about road names and numbers and just work out the districts we need to drive through.'

'Good thinking,' Angela said, and looked again at the open map. 'If you're right and we are in Abbassiyya, it means we must have been heading south-west, more or less. When you can, take any street on the left, because we have to cross the main road, the Salah Salem. Failing that, just follow the signs to Al-Gebel al-Ahmar, obviously, or the Northern Cemetery, Manshiyet Nasr or even Muqattam City. Any of those will get us into the right general area.'

A few seconds later, a slight gap opened up in the traffic on their left and Bronson slid his car expertly into the space. He was rewarded with a cacophony of blasting horns. Then he swung down a fairly narrow street, dodging parked cars, dogs and children, and at the end turned right. Here the road was wider, better surfaced and properly marked, and almost entirely full of virtually stationary traffic.

'Bugger,' Bronson muttered. He was completely surrounded.

'It doesn't matter. Once we get off the main road, I'm sure there'll be a lot less traffic.'

'Well, there could hardly be *more* traffic, could there? This is supposed to be a three-lane road but I can see four lanes of traffic heading in each direction.'

Just then it all started moving again – slowly, but it was moving – and Bronson eased the car forward, keeping it no more than eighteen inches behind the battered rear bumper of the vehicle in front. They came to a stop again, then began inching forwards once more.

'It's more modern here than I anticipated,' Bronson said, after a few moments, looking at the slightly grubby skyscrapers that lined both sides of the road.

'In the centre and in Cairo proper, I guess that's true, but I imagine that if you went out of the city you'd see houses that have hardly changed for half a millennium.'

About a quarter of an hour later, Angela spotted a sign for Al-Gebel al-Ahmar, and Bronson hacked his way through the traffic to make the turn. Angela had been right – once they cleared the main road and started heading south, the traffic was much lighter.

They crossed a railway line and kept moving, Angela checking the street signs as they passed.

'That's the first address,' she said, pointing to the left as Bronson drove past the end of a minor road. 'That's where Hassan al-Sahid – or at least *a* Hassan al-Sahid – lives.'

'Right,' Bronson said, swinging the car round in a U-turn to retrace their steps. 'Let's find out.'

30

'Your name is Suleiman al-Sahid?'

The young man standing in the doorway of the large whitewashed house on the eastern side of the Al-Gebel al-Ahmar district looked puzzled. He hadn't been expecting any visitors, and certainly not a black-suited American priest carrying a large and apparently heavy suitcase, with a thick plaster covering most of his left ear.

'It is,' he replied in heavily accented English, 'but I—'

'You don't know me,' the priest interrupted, 'but I know your father, Hassan. How is his health these days?'

Suleiman shook his head. 'He died a few years ago,' he replied. 'But I—'

'I'm sorry to hear that. I also know the Wendell-Carfax family, from England. Now, I have an important message for you from them, so may I come inside?'

Suleiman nodded, and stepped to one side. The priest

picked up the suitcase and followed Suleiman into the house.

'You have a message for me, you said? And what is your name?'

'Daniels. Father Michael Daniels.' The priest extended his hand. 'You have a lovely home here,' he added, glancing around the spacious hallway.

'Thank you.'

'Now, Bartholomew Wendell-Carfax entrusted your father with two large oil paintings. Were you aware of that?'

Suleiman nodded. 'Yes. My father left very specific instructions about them. They're hanging in this room.'

He turned and led the way into a room just off the hall, dominated by a large dining table surrounded by eight chairs.

'My father bought this dining set in England,' Suleiman said. 'It's not to my taste, but he loved the British way of life. And those are the paintings.' He pointed at the wall opposite the doorway, where two oils were hanging.

The priest smiled. 'I've been asked to collect these two paintings ready for Oliver Wendell-Carfax when he arrives here in Cairo to start his expedition. Did he advise you that I was coming?'

A shadow of doubt crept suddenly across Suleiman's face, and he shook his head. 'No. In fact, in his last message to me he specifically told me he would be arriving here in person to inspect the paintings. He also said that under no circumstances was I to release them to any third party.'

The priest looked puzzled. 'How strange. I have a letter here' – he reached into his pocket and pulled out a creased and folded sheet of paper – 'in which he has authorized me to take possession of them.'

He passed the paper to Suleiman. But as Suleiman reached out to take it, the priest moved with fluid, well-practised ease, seizing Suleiman's right wrist and dragging him towards him, pulling him off-balance. Then he swung his right fist, hard, into Suleiman's stomach.

The unexpectedness of the attack caught Suleiman by surprise, but he was a young and strong man and the blow rocked, rather than incapacitated, him. He straightened up and danced backwards, moving away from his attacker, and brought up his fists to ward off any further blows.

But the priest still had the advantage of surprise, and he, too, was very strong, and a trained fighter. He powered forwards, knocking Suleiman's arms aside, and landing two more hard punches on his stomach.

Suleiman swung wildly, one fist catching his attacker on the left side of his head.

The priest howled in pain as the blow slammed into his ruined ear, reopening the wound and sending a throb of agony searing right across his skull. For an instant his vision clouded and he lifted his left arm high to prevent Suleiman following up with another punch.

Suleiman realized instantly his best chance of defeating the priest was to target his head again – the man's reaction to his lucky blow had been extreme. He swung his right fist once more, aiming for the now bloodstained plaster on the left side of the priest's head.

If the punch had landed, that might have been enough, but the priest saw it coming. He expertly blocked the blow with his left hand and swung his right straight into Suleiman's jaw.

Suleiman's head snapped up and he stumbled back, crashing into one of the chairs that lined the dining table. He shook his head, trying to clear the fog that had descended over his vision. But the priest didn't give him the chance. He stepped forwards and slammed two more blows into his face, opening deep cuts on his lips and breaking blood vessels in his nose.

Suleiman lifted his arms weakly to try to ward off the attack, but the priest finished it with two more hard punches to his face. Then he grabbed Suleiman's shirt, hauled him upright, spun his limp body round and slammed his forehead into the edge of the dining table. The Egyptian crashed to the floor, unconscious.

Killian stood looking down at the man for a couple of seconds, then raised his left hand and carefully felt his injured ear. The plaster seemed to be intact, but blood was flowing from the open wound at the top of the ear, and he knew he'd have to change the dressing. But that could wait. He had more important things to do. He kicked Suleiman hard in the ribs, then turned away.

He walked across to the wall where the paintings were hanging and swiftly lifted them both off their hooks. He didn't know where the parchment had been concealed in them, but he guessed it was probably hidden in a secret compartment in the frame. He would need time to inspect them thoroughly.

Killian carried both paintings out into the hall. He opened the front door of the house, checked in both directions, saw nobody, then walked across the kerb to his hire car, opened the boot and slid them inside.

He looked back at the house, wondering if he should just drive away. Then he shrugged and retraced his steps. Better to finish the job properly.

'I have never heard of anybody called Wendell-Carfax,' the elderly Egyptian man said, his tone polite but with an underlying edge to it.

Bronson and Angela were standing outside a small white house on a side street at the northern edge of Al-Gebel al-Ahmar. They'd received no reply at the first property they'd tried, the one listed as the residence of Hassan al-Sahid in the phone directory, so they'd moved on to the second address, the home of one 'M. al-Sahid'. The man's first name had turned out to be Mahmoud, and he obviously wasn't pleased at the interruption to his day.

'I am sorry we have disturbed you,' Bronson said,

speaking slowly and clearly. Mahmoud al-Sahid's English was far from fluent, his accent thick and heavy. 'Obviously you are not the person we are looking for. Our apologies. You do not, I suppose, know where Hassan al-Sahid lives?'

'Hassan al-Sahid is dead, as I told the other man. But his son – his name is Suleiman – still lives in his father's house.'

'What other man?' Bronson asked, alarm bells suddenly ringing.

'The priest,' the elderly man said. 'The priest was also looking for Hassan al-Sahid.'

Angela clutched Bronson's arm. 'A priest?' she echoed.

'Where does Suleiman al-Sahid live?' Bronson demanded.

Back inside the house, Killian opened the large suitcase he'd brought with him. Inside were three two-gallon cans of petrol, all full of fuel. He picked up the first one, twisted off the cap and tossed it away.

He looked round, choosing where to spread the accelerant. There was a lot of wood in the house, so he guessed it probably wouldn't matter too much where he put it – the place would burn anyway. He walked across to where Suleiman al-Sahid still lay unconscious, looked down at the man and crossed himself. Then he splashed petrol over his shirt and trousers, spread it out all around him and poured out still more in a trail that led to the door of the room. He continued laying a river of fuel out into the hall, then closed and locked the dining-room door from the outside.

Killian hoped Suleiman would come round before the flames reached him, and he spent a few moments imagining the look of terror on the man's face as the trail of fire swept under the door and headed straight for him across the floor. Killian knew it would be a painful and protracted, but ultimately cleansing, death. The Church had always believed that fire cleansed even the most unrepentant sinner or heretic, and had used the flames of sacred fires to save the souls of thousands from eternal damnation during the various Inquisitions across Europe.

He splashed the contents of the other two cans liberally around the ground floor of the house, finishing just inside the front door. Then he took a small plastic bag from his pocket, and extracted a stubby candle through which he'd bored a hole from one side to the other about an eighth of an inch below the wick. Then he took a short length of twine which he'd soaked in paraffin and fed that through the hole. He positioned one end of the twine in a pool of petrol and placed the candle a few inches away. He'd experimented with different types of candles and knew that the wick would burn down to the twine in about five minutes, which would give him ample time to get clear of the area before the accelerant blew.

Killian lit the candle, made sure it was burning properly, then strode across to the front door and left the house.

* * *

'Where the hell is it?' Bronson demanded, looking frantically for a street sign – any street sign – that would tell them where they were in the maze of roads that made up Al-Gebel al-Ahmar.

'Stop,' Angela yelled, pointing. 'There's a sign.'

Bronson braked hard, slewing the car sideways, then reversed back up about twenty feet so Angela could see the sign clearly.

She read the letters, checked the map and then pointed ahead. 'Keep going down this road,' she instructed, 'and take the second turning on the left.'

In the hall of Suleiman al-Sahid's house the candle flame burnt steadily, the flame flickering slightly in the erratic air currents that worked their way under the front door. Four minutes after Killian had applied his lighter to the candle wick, the flame reached the length of twine. There was a sharp fizzing from the twine as it ignited, and then the flame started burning its way down it towards the petrol.

Killian had chosen paraffin for his fuse because it would burn more slowly. Even so, the flame reached the pool of petrol in less than thirty seconds. The moment it did so, there was the sound of a dull 'whump', and in an instant the hall was ablaze, the tendrils of burning petrol spreading out in all directions.

* * *

'Are you sure this is the right address?' Bronson asked. 'It all looks really peaceful here at the moment.' He switched off the car engine and opened the door. For a moment he just looked at the whitewashed property in front of them. Then he sniffed.

'Do you smell burning?' he asked.

Before Angela could reply, there was a thump from inside the house, and the first tongues of flame licked under the front door, bubbling the paint as the old wood caught fire.

'Oh, shit,' Bronson muttered, then started to run towards the house. 'Call the fire brigade,' he shouted.

Behind him, Angela yelled out in alarm. 'Chris, don't. Come back.'

Bronson knew something about fires and the way they spread. If he opened the front door, he would probably be immediately engulfed in flames. But there had to be a back door, some other way in to the house. He wasn't bothered about the paintings – they would either survive the blaze or not – but he was worried about anyone inside the property. He didn't know if Suleiman al-Sahid or his family were in there, but he was going to do his best to check out the house before the fire took hold everywhere.

Bronson ran around the side of the house, stopping at every window and peering inside. But he saw nothing until he looked in through the glass panel of a wooden door at the rear of the property and caught sight of the body of a man lying motionless on the floor.

He wrenched on the handle, but the door was locked.

There's a technique to kicking down a door. Charging at it almost never works, despite the way TV detectives always seem to do it. Instead, the energy has to be concentrated, focused, as near to the lock – the weakest part of any door – as possible.

Bronson took a step back and kicked out, the sole of his foot connecting with the door right beside the lock. It didn't budge, and felt as if it never would. The door was absolutely solid.

He looked around desperately, searching for anything he could use to break it down. On one side of the garden were some lumps of masonry, perhaps left over from some repair work. He ran over, grabbed the biggest lump of stone he thought he could handle, then crossed back to the locked door. Gripping the stone firmly in both hands, he swung it as hard as he could, smashing it straight into the door next to the lock.

The wood splintered and cracked, but the door still held. He glanced back into the room. As he did so, he noticed the man on the floor move slightly, little more than a twitch of his leg, but it proved that he was still alive. Bronson redoubled his efforts, swinging the stone as hard as he could.

On the third impact, the door finally gave, crashing back on its hinges, and Bronson immediately smelt the petrol. The sudden rush of air into the room seemed to act like the bellows in a furnace, fuelling the fire. A tongue of flame crawled up the inside surface of the interior door opposite, followed almost immediately by a river of fire that snaked across the room, arrow-straight towards the inert figure.

Bronson dropped the stone and raced inside, getting to the unconscious man a bare second before the burning petrol reached him. He grabbed him by the arm and dragged him bodily away from the flames, heading towards the door to the garden.

But even as he hauled him across the floor, the end of the man's trousers brushed against one of the flaming pools of petrol, and instantly caught fire.

Bronson heard a sudden gasp of pain from the man he was trying to rescue, and looked down. Dropping his arm, he wrenched off his jacket and flung it on to the man's lower legs, pressing it down hard to smother the flames. Then he grabbed his shoulders and dragged him as quickly as he could to the door and out of the blazing room, the flames licking behind them all the way.

Outside, Bronson paused for breath, then bent down and lifted the man to his feet, draping his arm over his shoulder to support him.

'Do you speak English?' he asked, as he half-dragged, half-carried, the man out to the road.

'Yes,' he gasped. 'My legs—'

'You were burnt,' Bronson said flatly, 'and your clothes are soaked with petrol. Somebody tried to kill you, and they very nearly succeeded. Is there anyone else in the house?'

'No. Nobody.'

'Chris!' Angela cried, running over to him. 'Oh, thank God you're alive!' The smell of petrol was strong. 'Are you OK?'

'I think so,' he said, leaning the man against the side of the car. 'Did you call the fire people?'

Angela nodded, and pointed across the road, where an Egyptian couple stood outside the house watching the fire. 'I got them to call,' she said.

Bronson turned back to the man. 'Can you talk?' he asked.

Suleiman nodded, shakily. 'Yes. Thank you,' he said. 'I owe you my life.'

'I take it you *are* Suleiman al-Sahid?' Angela said. 'You look terrible. Why don't you sit down here on the kerb, so we can take a look at your leg.'

Al-Sahid obediently sat down, and Bronson rolled up his trouser leg, the material badly singed. The burn ran most of the way up his shin, but Bronson had obviously killed the flames before there was any serious tissue damage.

'That's not too bad,' Bronson said, and turned his attention to Al-Sahid's head injuries. 'You've got a split lip and you took a punch on the nose, by the looks of it, and that's a nasty bump on your forehead, but I don't think there's any lasting damage. Head and face injuries always bleed a lot and look worse than they really are.'

A sudden roar from the house caught their attention.

The roof had just caved in and, even if the fire brigade appeared immediately, it looked to Bronson as if the house was going to be a total loss.

Al-Sahid stared at the doomed building.

'I grew up there,' he said, a catch in his voice, 'and it was my father's house before me. He and my mother died in there.'

'And today you nearly joined them,' Bronson said softly. 'What happened?'

'Was the fire anything to do with a priest?' Angela asked.

Suleiman's head snapped round. 'How did you know that?' he demanded.

'I know about the priest,' Angela said simply, 'because he tried to kill me as well, back in Britain.'

Suleiman shivered. 'He looked like a priest, and he was smiling and friendly until he got inside the house. But his eyes – I'll never forget his black eyes. But who are you?'

'Chris here is a British police officer, and I'm a kind of archaeologist. We got involved with the Wendell-Carfax family by accident, and we're trying to follow the clues Bartholomew left. You knew about his expeditions out here, I suppose?'

Suleiman nodded. 'My father was Bartholomew's gang master.' He gave a short laugh. 'You probably won't thank me for saying this, but you're almost certainly wasting your time. My father tried to persuade Bartholomew to give up his expeditions, to stop wasting his money, but he wouldn't hear of it. He remained convinced that the treasure was almost within his grasp, and that he'd find it on the very next expedition, or on the one after that.'

They all turned as two fire engines announced their noisy presence and headed straight towards them. A crowd was starting to gather, people staring at the burning building.

'The paintings?' Bronson asked.

Suleiman nodded. 'My father agreed to store them here for Bartholomew. He told my father that the clues to the location of the treasure were hidden in the paintings. I actually looked for hidden compartments, where he might have tucked away a copy of that old parchment, but I never found anything, so I've always wondered if they were just another one of Bartholomew's eccentricities. But they were all that priest was interested in.'

'Did he take them?'

'I've no idea. We were in the dining room when he attacked me. I tried fighting back, but it was no use. Finally, he slammed my head into the side of the table and I blacked out. I assume he did take them.'

'If he didn't,' Bronson said, looking at the house, 'they're totally destroyed now.'

'What treasure did Bartholomew think he was looking for?' Angela asked.

Suleiman shrugged. 'Only the biggest and most famous of them all. He was convinced he was on the trail of the Jews' Ark, the Ark of the Covenant.'

Angela glanced at Bronson. 'And where was he searching?'

'Various places, because he kept on interpreting the clues slightly differently, which led him to different locations each time. My father never knew what those clues were because Bartholomew always kept that information to himself, but he did at least know the starting point of each search Bartholomew conducted, because it was always the same – Moalla.'

Suleiman smiled slightly at Bronson's puzzled expression. 'He was convinced that the Pharaoh Shishaq had seized the Ark when he invaded Judea, and had brought it back to Egypt as one of the spoils of war. He believed that later in his reign Shishaq ordered the treasure to be hidden a long way up the Nile, in a secret valley, where it would remain for all time. According to Bartholomew, the clues he'd found stated that the treasure convoy had started its journey from Moalla, so that's where he always based his searches.'

Angela's face suddenly lightened. 'He must mean el-Moalla,' she said.

'Which is where?' Bronson asked.

'On the east bank of the Nile, about twenty miles south of Luxor. It's a very ancient cemetery,' Suleiman said. He glanced across the road to where the firemen were tackling the blaze. 'Look,' he said, 'I need to go and talk to the fire chief. Is there anything else you need from me?'

'Not for the moment,' Bronson said, pulling a card out

of his pocket. 'This has got my mobile number on it. If you think of anything else, please call me.'

'I will,' Suleiman said, shaking Bronson's hand. 'And thank you again for giving me back the rest of my life.'

31

Killian drove about five miles away from Al-Gebel al-Ahmar, heading east, away from Cairo and the suburbs of the city, until he found a deserted stretch of road. He hadn't wanted to take the paintings to his hotel room because some of the staff would remember him arriving with such unusual items, and he didn't want to be disturbed while he was examining the pictures. He also needed privacy to replace the dressing on his wounded ear.

A narrow, rough and unmade track snaked away to one side of the road, meandering around a series of low dunes that would provide him with the privacy he wanted. He drove down the track until he was about a hundred yards from the road, then pulled the car to a stop.

Getting out of the vehicle, he looked about him. The air was still and silent. Grunting in satisfaction, he took a blanket from the boot of the car and spread it on the ground. Then he placed both paintings face-down on it, ready to examine them. But as he did so, a stabbing pain shot through his skull and a couple of drops of blood splashed on to the dusty ground at his feet. Killian grimaced, then took a medical kit from the car, opened it and sat awkwardly in the passenger seat to change the dressing. With only his reflection in the interior mirror to guide him it wasn't easy, but eventually he finished and stood up, a fresh dressing and plaster covering his injured ear. Suleiman's blow had knocked the scab off the top of the wound and he knew that would delay the healing process still further.

At least the wound was still clean and showing no sign of infection – perhaps surprising in view of the way he had sustained the injury. In his mind's eye he could still see Oliver Wendell-Carfax's yellowish teeth, stained with blood and shreds of flesh, when he'd finally managed to get free of his grasp. God knows what bacteria or worse had been in his mouth. As well as cleaning the wound twice a day, Killian had also been sprinkling it with holy water and that, he thought, perhaps even more than his rudimentary medical care, might be the reason it was still clean. It was yet one more manifestation of the power of God and of the sure and certain way that He protected His servant on Earth.

Killian gave a grim smile. Both Oliver Wendell-Carfax and Suleiman had more than paid for their temerity in resisting God's will. And Wendell-Carfax and the fat man from the museum had felt the teeth of the scourge, the oldest and most sacred instrument of holy chastisement, before they died. If he'd had a little more time, Killian would have taught Suleiman a proper and complete lesson using the instrument as well. But his first priority had been to get the paintings out of the building.

At least that phase of the search was now over. He had the last clues he needed to recover the treasure, and even if anyone was still looking, his actions had ensured that they would get no further than Egypt. All he had to do now was find the hiding place Bartholomew had used to secrete the copy of the parchment.

Killian looked down at the two pictures. Then he crossed himself and for a few minutes knelt in prayer before the small silver crucifix he took from his pocket. It was his constant companion, guide and comfort in times of stress and trouble.

Then he began an exhaustive examination of the frames of the two paintings. Wherever Bartholomew had hidden the text, Killian was absolutely certain he would be able to find it. Once he had, he could destroy both paintings and start the final phase of his search. He licked his lips. The treasure was practically in sight.

32

Bronson and Angela were in their car, outside the still smouldering house.

'So what now?' Bronson asked, starting the engine to get the air conditioning running. 'We came here to find the paintings, and we failed. So now we've got no way of continuing our search.'

'You're right,' Angela said, her tone resigned. 'Even the reference to el-Moalla – which we didn't know about before – isn't much of a help to us because we don't know what directions were specified in the parchment.'

She paused for a moment, considering, then brightened slightly. 'There is one thing we might as well do while we're here. According to Suleiman, Bartholomew believed Shishaq seized the Ark of the Covenant and then later in his reign ordered it to be concealed somewhere up the Nile in a secret valley. I still think he's a good candidate for grabbing the Ark, but there are a couple of things wrong with the idea of him later hiding it way upstream near Luxor.

'First, Shishaq's capital was based at Tanis, quite close to Cairo, so why would he have hidden the Ark so far away from the area under his control? And, second, the Egyptians were compulsive record-keepers, and I would have expected there to be some documentary evidence to support this theory. If there is, I've never seen it, but I'm beginning to wonder if Bartholomew *did* find a reference somewhere, and that's why he was so sure about it.'

She sat forward, enjoying the blast of cold air on her face. 'I think we should do what we planned to do when we came out here. We should drive out to el-Hiba and possibly fly down to Karnak, depending on what we find at el-Hiba.'

'And you are sure we have to go to these places in person?' Bronson asked. 'You can't just look at pictures of the inscriptions on the internet or study translations of them in a book?'

'The images I found on the web aren't clear enough to decipher properly, and I don't actually think anyone's done a complete translation of the hieroglyphs at either site – I certainly haven't been able to find one anywhere.'

'Can you read hieroglyphs?' Bronson asked doubtfully.

'I can read them well enough to check something like this, I think, and I know a little bit about hieratic and demotic too.'

'Which are?'

'They're technically not hieroglyphic scripts: they're more like a kind of shorthand, and were always written from right to left. The problem with hieroglyphics is that each character is quite detailed – a bird, a leaf, a snake, that kind of thing – and takes a long time to draw correctly. Hieratic and demotic scripts developed so that scribes could produce texts fairly quickly on papyrus, and much more easily than using hieroglyphics. What we'll find will be hieroglyphics – they were used for monumental inscriptions all the way through the Pharaonic period. But I've got a computer program that should help – it analyses and translates hieroglyphic characters.'

Bronson looked at his watch. 'You want to go there now?'

'Yes, we might as well,' Angela said, fastening her seat belt. 'We should be able to get there and back today.'

They headed north and picked up the Salah Salem road that ran south-west towards central Cairo. The traffic was flowing much more freely, and they were able to make good progress.

'Where are the pyramids?' Bronson asked, as they approached the centre of the city. 'I'd like to see them while we're here, and I thought they were quite close to Cairo.'

'They are, but they're over on the west bank of the Nile, probably about five or six miles in front of us. You might get the odd glimpse of them through the buildings when we start heading south. Right,' she said, checking the map again, 'stay on the east bank of the river, and keep going.'

'Understood. Which side of the Nile do we need to be on eventually?'

'I don't think it matters. According to this map there are two main roads that follow the Nile south, one running along each bank, and there are several bridges where we can cross to the other side if we have to.'

The traffic was still congested, but most of the vehicles were heading towards the centre of Cairo, so Bronson was driving against the flow and, as soon as they reached the district of Tura, where the road turned due south, he was able to speed up a little as the traffic thinned out. The tall apartment buildings and office blocks were gradually replaced by lower, older and much more decrepit structures, and a couple of times they did catch just the briefest sight of the very tops of the pyramids in the distance, over to the west. On their right-hand side the Nile flowed steadily northwards, a wide, grey-brown mass of moving water, peopled with a variety of boats, including a couple of big Nile cruisers, scores of motorboats and dozens of lateen-rigged feluccas, the iconic sailing boats of old Egypt.

On the west side of the Nile, the built-up area seemed to have petered out, just a few isolated dwellings, but the road Bronson was following, which was right beside the bank of the river, had extensive urban developments extending to the east. He pointed out this oddity to Angela.

'There's a good reason for that,' Angela said. 'Over to our left there's a large urbanization, but the land on the west side of the river has a lot of ancient sites. We're just about level with a place called the Amba Armiyas Monastery, and just below that is Saqqara.'

'That name rings a bell.'

'As it should. It's a huge ancient burial ground – I think it's about five miles long by one mile wide – and it's where you'll find the oldest hewn-stone building complex ever discovered. That's Djoser's step pyramid, which dates from about two thousand six hundred BC, well over four thousand five hundred years old. Egyptologists believe that was the first stone pyramid of all time. They think it was built by erecting a large *mastaba*, a kind of flat-roofed rectangular tomb, on the bedrock, then building a slightly smaller one on top of it, and then another smaller one, and so on.'

'It sounds like that would account for the steps,' Bronson said.

'True. But in fact stepped pyramids are found in several different parts of the world, where *mastabas* are completely unknown, so it could also have been a design that the ancient peoples liked the look of. The best known are the ziggurats of ancient Mesopotamia – that's modern-day Iraq – and the pre-Columbian civilizations of South America.'

'The Incas and the Aztecs?'

'Yes, and the Maya and the Toltecs as well. They all had

a go at building them. Anyway, as well as Djoser's step pyramid, there are pyramids belonging to about fifteen or sixteen other Egyptian kings at Saqqara, in various states of disrepair. And, because the high officials of the court liked to be buried as close to their king as possible, there are shaft tombs and *mastabas* all over the place. And there's also a thing called the *Serapeum* there. That was the burial site for mummified Apis bulls.'

'The Egyptians mummified bulls?' Bronson asked, surprised. 'I thought it was only cats.'

Angela nodded. 'They mummified a lot of animals, actually. Bulls and cows were the biggest, cats were probably the most popular, and they also mummified birds, especially hawks and ibis.'

The road they were on was called the Kornaish El Nile, which they guessed meant 'Corniche of the Nile', and as they passed the built-up area on their left, the road moved slightly away from the bank of the river before swinging back towards it. As they cleared the urbanization, they passed a bridge over the Nile.

'That's the first crossing point of the river we've seen since we left Cairo itself,' Bronson said.

'Yes. According to this map, that's the El Marazeek Bridge,' Angela replied. 'But there are plenty of other bridges further south. Just keep going on this road.'

Within a couple of miles, the river had swung away from them, over to the west, and the road was taking them slightly to the east, so they lost sight of the Nile altogether.

The traffic had thinned considerably, though there were still about a dozen cars in sight in front of them, and at least that number behind, and a fairly steady stream of vehicles heading towards them. The open road and less frantic driving conditions meant Bronson could relax a little. He glanced over at Angela, who appeared lost in thought; he guessed she was thinking about their search and the dangers surrounding them. He knew he'd have to be extra vigilant if they were going to stay safe.

On the right-hand side of the road he saw a sign displaying the universally recognized symbol of a wasp-waisted bottle and a word beside it in Arabic script, which he guessed meant 'Coke'.

'I could do with a drink after all we've been through this morning,' he said, 'and it looks like there's a café or a bar somewhere ahead. Shall we stop?'

About half a mile further on Bronson pulled up outside a bar that was little more than an old and dusty shack. But they heard the sound of a generator running somewhere behind the structure, so at least the drinks should be cool. This, he thought, was a priority. If he was going to spend the day being a chauffer and bodyguard, he was going to make sure he wasn't thirsty.

33

The sun was high in the sky by the time Killian had taken both paintings out of their frames and then systematically reduced the frames to matchwood. The obvious place to hide a small piece of paper or parchment was within a secret compartment somewhere in the heavily gilded wood that surrounded and supported each picture, he reasoned, so he'd started by examining the frames themselves, looking for any writing or marks on the wood itself that might be relevant. But both the fronts and the backs of the two frames were virtually unmarked. Killian had checked every crack and line he could see, searching for the compartment he was certain was hidden there, but no panels or drawers sprang open under his probing.

Then he'd broken the first frame, pulling apart the joints and separating the four component parts. He'd examined each of them individually, breaking the lengths of wood apart until he was surrounded by splinters and chunks of wood, and flakes of gilt paint covered the blanket like golden confetti. But still he found nothing.

He repeated the process with the second frame, with precisely the same result. There was nothing hidden inside the frame of either picture. Only then did he turn his attention to the paintings themselves.

The reverse sides of the two oil paintings appeared normal in every way. The canvases were mounted on oblong wooden stretchers, the fabric pulled taut and secured in place using short tacks. As far as Killian could see, there were no marks on the wood itself, and nothing on the rear of the canvas. The only other place Bartholomew could possibly have concealed the text of the parchment was on the face of the wooden stretcher, the part that lay hidden underneath the canvas of the painting itself.

Killian took a broad-bladed screwdriver from the small toolkit he always carried, then stopped and shook his head. There were dozens of tacks – maybe fifty or sixty in all – studding the rear of the stretcher, and to shift them using the screwdriver would take ages. The painting itself was of no interest to him, so he could remove it much faster using a knife.

Selecting a utility knife, he slid out the blade and, with one swift movement, cut down the entire length of one side of the stretcher. Then he turned the painting and repeated the operation on the other three sides. The canvas fell away and Killian eagerly studied the clean wood his action had revealed.

Again, he could see no marks of any sort. He picked up his screwdriver again and worked the end of the blade under the strip of canvas that was still attached to the stretcher. He levered up the fabric until he could grip it firmly, then ripped the canvas away from the stretcher and tossed it aside. There was nothing on the wood; no marks of any sort.

Killian stood looking down at the stretcher, turning the wooden oblong over in his hands. He knew he must have missed something. The statement by Bartholomew could only be interpreted in one way. The translation of the lost parchment *had* to be hidden somewhere in the paintings, in the 'Montgomerys'. Nothing else made sense.

Groaning with frustration, he tossed the stretcher aside and picked up the painting he'd cut out of it. He examined the back of the canvas but could see no marks of any sort. Only then did he turn the fabric round and look at the painting itself.

Ten minutes later he screwed the canvas into a ball. There was nothing, no clue at all, anywhere on the painting. There was only one possible conclusion he could draw, and he belatedly realized there was one vital question he hadn't asked Suleiman al-Sahid.

He'd badly underestimated Bronson and Lewis. They'd obviously studied the contents of the leather-bound box before he'd snatched it off them, and made the same connections he had. Then they'd flown out to Egypt, visited al-Sahid and removed the clues Bartholomew had hidden in the paintings years earlier. His own exhaustive and destructive search of the pictures, he now realized, had been a complete waste of effort, and more importantly of time. Most likely, Bartholomew had written down the full translation of the Persian text on a couple of bits of paper, sealed the pages in envelopes and tucked them away at the backs of the paintings.

And then Bronson had come along, spun Suleiman some line, and helped himself to what they'd all been looking for.

Killian cursed long and fluently, then gave the wooden debris a vicious kick that scattered pieces of the frames in all directions. The clues simply weren't there.

He bent down and rummaged through the bits and pieces one more time, then reached into his pocket and pulled out a cigarette lighter and touched the flame to the edge of the canvas. In the extreme midday heat, the old and dry fabric caught almost immediately. Killian waited a few moments, making sure that the fire was well established, piled the remains of the picture frames and stretchers on top of the flames, then walked back to his car.

At least he now knew exactly what he must do. Bronson and Lewis obviously had the information he needed and they had to be somewhere in Cairo. He simply had to find them and recover the clues. And then he'd kill them. He smiled, the pain from his ear receding a little. The deaths he was planning would be long and lingering.

34

JJ Donovan had watched the excitement of the house fire – an event which made no sense to him – and the arrival of the fire engines, and then started his car and eased out after Bronson as they drove away from the scene.

Now he watched with irritation as Bronson pulled off the road. He daren't stop there as well, because it was too small a place, and Bronson was a police officer, which meant he'd been trained in observation skills. Donovan knew that if he stopped at the bar Bronson would notice and remember him, and he definitely didn't want that to happen.

So he carried on another quarter of a mile or so and then eased his car off the road and on to the verge. He stopped the engine and waited for a few seconds, watching the scene in his rear-view mirror carefully. When it was obvious that Bronson and his companion were going to have a drink at the roadside café, he realized that he would have to wait, too. And the obvious way to do that was to stage a breakdown.

Donovan dropped all the windows on the Mercedes – it was going to get very hot inside the car without the engine and the climate control running – but the heavily tinted glass was a possible identification feature. With the windows lowered, it was just another light-coloured mid-sized Mercedes saloon, one of thousands on the roads around Cairo.

Then he stepped out of the car and lifted the bonnet. There was very little to see inside the engine compartment, apart from a massive sculpted aluminium plate that covered the top of the motor, but that didn't matter. With the bonnet lifted, any passing driver would simply assume the car had stopped because of some fault – mechanical or electrical.

Then he got back inside the car and sat down, all his attention focused on the café-bar about five hundred yards behind him. The other thing he needed to do was make sure Bronson didn't get a look at the car's number plates as he drove past, and that meant lifting the boot lid. But he couldn't do that until the Peugeot started moving, because his best view of the café was using the interior mirror and, when he lifted the boot, that view would vanish.

So all he could do was wait. Wait and watch.

Bronson switched off the engine and he and Angela got

out of the car, the heat hitting them like the blast from a furnace. About half a dozen men, all wearing either traditional Arab dress or white shirts and trousers, were already sitting at the tables, drinks in front of them. They eyed the two Westerners with a mixture of curiosity and suspicion as Bronson steered Angela through them towards a couple of vacant seats at a table close to the side of the bar, where the noise from the generator was loudest.

'What would you like to drink?' he shouted.

'What I'd really like is a long, cold gin and tonic with bags of ice, but I guess that's not an option here,' she said. 'Get me anything non-alcoholic, a Coke, Fanta, something like that. No glass and no ice, obviously.'

'Right,' Bronson said. A couple of minutes later he returned to the table with two cans of Coke, moisture beading the outside of the metal. He sat down beside her and they both drank thirstily. 'So this el-Hiba place,' Bronson said. 'Why don't you tell me what you know about it?'

'It used to be called Tayu-djayet, which simply meant "their walls", because of the massive stone walls out there. Hang on a second . . .' She rummaged in her bag, brought out a notebook and flicked through the pages that were covered in her neat and precise script until she found what she was looking for. She took a pencil and a blank sheet of paper, and drew a series of shapes on it.

'Time for your first lesson in hieroglyphics,' she said, turning the paper round so Bronson could see it.

She'd sketched a half-moon shape, a vulture, two leaves, what looked like a young chicken, an obelisk, two more leaves and a half-moon surmounting a cross in a circle.

'And this is what?' Bronson asked.

Angela smiled at him. 'That's the hieroglyphic equivalent of Tayu-djayet. The first symbol, this half-moon,' she said, indicating the shape with the end of her pencil, 'is a "T", the vulture is "A" or "AH", one leaf is "I", but two together like that mean "Y".'

'Hang on, let me work this out,' Bronson said. 'That makes "TAY". What about this chicken here?'

'That is *not* a chicken. It's a quail chick, and it stands for "W". All those symbols are consonants, part of the Egyptian alphabet, which is almost all consonants, but the next one is a fire stick or drill, and that's a determinative. Because the hieroglyphic language is pictorial, there can be two or more different meanings of a series of symbols.'

'Like a rebus, you mean?'

Angela blinked. 'I'm impressed,' she said. 'Though I have to confess that I don't know exactly what a "rebus" is – apart from being the name of Ian Rankin's detective, of course.'

'It's a modern type of pictorial statement,' Bronson said. 'Kids' stuff really. Like a drawing of an eye, followed by a heart, followed by the letter "U". That means "I love you",' he said, firmly holding Angela's gaze as he said the words.

She blushed, and looked away. 'OK – back to the hieroglyphics. The determinatives simply eliminated any confusion over the way the other letters – the consonants – were to be sounded and what they meant.' She gestured towards the paper again. 'Next is another two leaves – a "Y" – and finally a "T" with another determinative – the cross in the circle, which means a city.'

'You said you read hieratic and demotic script from right to left, but hieroglyphics are from left to right, just like English?' Bronson asked.

'Not necessarily. In fact, they were usually written from right to left, but they could also be read from left to right, or downwards.'

'Wonderful. So how did anyone know where to start?'

'That was really easy,' Angela said, and pointed at the drawing she'd done. 'See the vulture and the quail chick?' Bronson nodded. 'There were a lot of animal symbols used in hieroglyphics – birds and snakes, and so on – and they were always drawn in profile. The two birds in this hieroglyphic word are facing to the left, so that's the end you start reading from. If they'd been facing to the right, you'd have to read the word from right to left.' She drained the last of her Coke and stood up. 'Come on,' she said. 'I'll tell you as we drive. We've still got a long way to go.'

Donovan had got steadily hotter and more irritated as the minutes passed, but kept his eyes fixed on his rear-view mirrors. Two figures were now moving slowly across the café's dusty parking lot towards their car.

He pressed the button to open the boot, checked the mirror to ensure that it had lifted – that would make the number plate on the boot lid itself effectively unreadable – and walked around to the front of his Mercedes. He stood right beside the front number plate to shield that as well. As Bronson's car accelerated past him, heading south, he lifted his arm to the front of the bonnet to make sure his face was invisible to the occupants of the passing car. In his white shirt and light-coloured trousers he would, he hoped, look like just any other motorist with a broken-down vehicle, wondering what the hell to do next.

When they were safely past him, he closed the bonnet and boot of his car and walked back to the driver's side door, sitting down gratefully in the seat and switching on the engine, relishing the blast of ice-cold air that almost immediately poured out of the dashboard vents.

He waited until three other cars had passed him, then pulled back out on to the road. Bronson's Peugeot was now at least five hundred yards in front of him, but still clearly visible.

All he had to do now was to find out where they were going.

35

The road stretched long and straight ahead of them, shimmering in the noon-day heat.

Angela adjusted one of the dashboard vents to direct cold air straight at her face. 'El-Hiba is one of those places that not many people have heard of, under any of its names. As well as Tayu-djayet and el-Hiba, in Coptic it was called Teudjo and much later, in the Graeco–Roman Period it was called Ankyronpolis.'

Bronson settled back in his driving seat. 'I can see that the Coptic and Egyptian words are pretty similar, but how did they come up with Ankyronpolis?'

'It was a Greek name. Alexander the Great conquered Egypt in three hundred and thirty-two BC, and founded the city of Alexandria. When he died, his generals divided up his vast empire and one of them – a man named Ptolemy I Soter – eventually seized power in Egypt and created a dynasty that would rule the country for almost three hundred years. It was called the Ptolemaic Period – a mind-numbingly obvious name to choose because every king or pharaoh took the name Ptolemy, one after the other. The only breaks were the handful of women who ruled for short periods. They usually adopted the name Arsinoe, Berenice or Cleopatra. The last one was Cleopatra VII – the lover of Antony. When she died in thirty BC, that ended the Ptolemaic Dynasty.

'Anyway, el-Hiba didn't rank with places like Thebes or Luxor or Giza, but from about twelve hundred BC to around seven hundred BC – that was the period spanning the Twentieth to the Twenty-Second Dynasties – it was an important frontier town. It marked the division of Egypt between the High Priests of Amun, who were based upriver at Thebes, modern Luxor, and the kings of Egypt who ruled from Tanis.

'As a frontier town, el-Hiba was vulnerable to attack, and so a massive wall was built there, encircling the settlement, which of course gave the place its Egyptian name. Now, our interest in the town is because the first of the Twenty-Second Dynasty kings, Shoshenq I, built a temple to Amun there.'

'I thought you said the pharaoh's name was Shishaq?'

Angela sighed. 'Actually, there never was a pharaoh called Shishaq, as he's named in the Bible, which is one of the problems, but most experts now agree that the best fit for Shishaq is probably Shoshenq I, and one reason for that, apart from the similarity in their names, is what

Shoshenq did at el-Hiba. Towards the end of his reign, probably about nine hundred and thirty to nine hundred and twenty BC, he had the temple walls decorated with a list of the cities that his forces captured during his campaign in Palestine. And that accords quite well with the biblical account of the invasion of Judea by the pharaoh who was called Shishaq in the Bible.'

'Yes, that makes sense,' Bronson agreed.

The road was following the east bank of the Nile upstream, heading south-west. There were occasional roads heading off to the east, presumably leading to nearby settlements, and they had driven through some small villages that lay on the main road as well. The road was still reasonably quiet, but there were several cars and a few vans and trucks heading in each direction, with the heaviest volume of traffic going north, towards Cairo.

'Where are we now?' Angela asked.

The road ahead swung slightly to the left, and as Bronson steered the car around the bend he spotted a sign on the right hand side of the road. 'Kuddaya,' he said.

'Got it.' Angela looked down at the map, tracing their route with her finger. 'Believe it or not, it looks as if there's a fairly sharp bend coming up in about ten miles. That'll wake you up.'

Bronson laughed. 'And when we get there, you want to look at the hieroglyphic inscriptions?'

'Exactly,' Angela said. 'I already know that the inscriptions include a list of the towns that Shoshenq captured in Judea – that's been well established – but what I haven't been able to find out is if there's a list of the spoils of war there as well.'

'Did they usually show that kind of thing?' Bronson asked.

'Normally, yes, because that would show the pharaoh as a supremely powerful and all-conquering leader of his people, a living god, in fact. Quite often the temple inscriptions would show him in a war chariot, personally leading a charge against his enemies, or executing captives with a sword or mace after a battle, that kind of thing. If the Egyptian forces managed to capture a treasure as important as the Ark of the Covenant, the pharaoh would want that fact to be recorded in stone as well.'

Bronson sighed and stretched his shoulders. 'Bring it on,' he said.

36

'We're here,' Angela said, folding up the map and putting it back in the glovebox. 'That's el-Hiba up there on the hill.'

In front of them, a vast area of ruined mud-brick walls and other structures extended from the River Nile on their right all the way up the hillside, the bright afternoon sunlight turning it golden. The road climbed steadily up to the village, and had clearly been driven straight through one section of the ruined buildings.

'It doesn't look like much,' Bronson said, disappointed.

'It isn't much, now,' Angela replied, 'but in its heyday it was a busy, populous place. Several thousand people lived here, but now it's probably only a handful. Let's find somewhere to park the car, and then we'll have a look round.'

The village wasn't quite as deserted as it appeared. There were a few locals wandering about, their white clothes grubby from the dust that swirled everywhere each time a vehicle passed through the settlement. Some were sitting beside the road outside a small café, smoking hookah pipes or drinking thick black coffee from tiny glasses. Finding somewhere to park their car wasn't difficult. Bronson pulled over on some waste ground.

'I expected it to be a lot bigger, and a whole lot busier, than this,' he muttered, as he locked the car.

'It's not on the most popular tourist itineraries,' Angela said. 'In fact, I don't think it's on *any* tourist itineraries, so apart from the locals the only people likely to be here are wandering archaeologists, and I don't even see any of them. I read somewhere that an American team came over here five or six years ago to excavate this site, but I've heard nothing about it since. This is one of the few major – by that I mean historically important – places in Egypt that *hasn't* already been picked clean by the archaeologists.'

'They were excavating Shoshenq's temple, I suppose?'

'Probably not just the temple. This place was a fortress, and also a necropolis. There are thousands of tombs here somewhere that date back almost four millennia. I assume the team would have looked at the whole site, rather than just a bit of it.'

'So nobody's ever really studied the place before them?' Bronson asked.

'Not really, though there have been one or two spectacular finds reported here. The earliest known example of demotic script was found here, on a piece of papyrus. That dates from about six hundred and sixty BC. But because el-Hiba is so old, and has had so many influences – Egyptian, Greek, Roman, and so on – any dig here would have to be a long and wide-ranging excavation.'

They walked on, heading for an open area at the very top of the settlement that they guessed would give them a decent view of the whole site.

'Spectacular,' Bronson said, as they stopped and looked around.

Below them, the ruins of the reddish-brown mud-brick walls descended in tumbled waves and terraces towards the surrounding plain and the eastern bank of the slowly flowing River Nile.

'Quite a place,' Angela agreed. 'The high ground would have given the defenders a significant advantage in any conflict, and being so close to the river meant that they were protected from attack on that side. Right, now let's find the temple.'

At the far end of el-Hiba, JJ Donovan stood beside a part of the old city walls and watched his targets through a small pair of binoculars.

About a hundred yards away, Bronson and Angela had their backs to him and appeared to be looking at something. Then they suddenly turned directly towards him, and for a brief, unsettling instant, it seemed to him as if they were staring right at him, their magnified faces clearly visible through the lenses of the binoculars.

Then he saw Angela gesture, and they turned back and started walking slowly down the hill away from him.

The walls were massive. Not just feet thick, but yards thick, the old mud-bricks still largely intact. 'These must be the old city defences,' Angela said. 'They're not in a bad state of repair, bearing in mind how old they are. They date from the Twenty-First Dynasty – that's about one thousand BC – so they've been standing here for three millennia.'

Bronson glanced around. The village nestled in palm trees – this close to the Nile, the soil was obviously reasonably fertile – and more palms studded the settlement itself. But the main road was busy, cars and trucks roaring past them at regular intervals, and they had to be careful to keep well clear of the road itself.

'We've no guidebook or anything,' Angela said, 'so we'll just have to walk around until we find what's left of the Temple that Shoshenq built. All I know is that it's somewhere inside the old walls, which is why I thought we'd start looking from here.'

Slowly they started to retrace their steps, looking closely at all the structures as they passed them. A couple of times Angela thought she'd spotted it, but each time she was mistaken. Then she looked ahead and muttered something under her breath.

'I don't believe it.'

'What?' Bronson looked where she was pointing.

'I think these Egyptian idiots have driven the bloody road straight through the temple. Look, you can see the same kind of stone walls on both sides of it over there.'

It wasn't anything like as clear as that to Bronson. 'You might be right,' he said, 'but perhaps the engineers had no option. There might have been nowhere else here they could have built the road.'

'So they demolished half of an irreplaceable temple just to lay down a strip of tarmac? There's always an alternative in this kind of situation, Chris. This is just archaeological vandalism, caused by nothing more than sheer laziness. They could have routed the road around the hill, down in the valley. It would only have added a few tens of yards to the length, and it might even have been easier to do.'

'Yes, but when this road was built the government may not have realized this *was* an important site. I thought that most of the excavations over here had been undertaken by foreign archaeologists anyway. Essentially, Egypt's been dug up by the British and the French and the Americans, not by the Egyptians themselves. They probably just saw a bunch of old stones and thought they'd do nicely as a hardcore base for the road. I don't suppose it's the first time something like that has happened.'

Angela nodded slowly. 'That's a remarkably accurate assessment, actually, and you're quite right – it's been very common. A lot of people don't know that when St Peter's Basilica was being built in Rome, many of the stones they used for it were taken from the Coliseum, which is one reason why it's in the state it is now. It was only a lot later that the Italians seemed to realize that the Coliseum was an internationally important archaeological site – at least as important as St Peter's, maybe even more important – and started taking steps to give it the protection it deserved.'

Bronson put a comforting hand on her shoulder. 'Let's take a look at what's left of the temple.'

They walked up the slope towards the structure that remained standing beside the road. The walls were very low and the majority were little more than tumbled piles of masonry. Angela crouched down beside one of them and pointed at the carving of a foot and lower leg. The rest of the carving had vanished when the wall fell to pieces – or perhaps was demolished – but there were just a few hieroglyphic characters visible over to one side.

'Anything useful here?' Bronson asked, bending down beside her.

'Not a lot. The carving could have been of Shoshenq, or even of the god Amun, but of course there's no way of telling now.' She bent lower and looked more closely at the hieroglyphic characters, where a curved incision was visible at the edge of a vertical line of characters. 'That looks like the upper edge of a cartouche, so this inscription probably relates to a pharaoh.'

'A cartouche – that's the kind of border they drew around an important name, yes?'

'Yes. The names of pharaohs were always enclosed within a cartouche. In fact, these three symbols above it confirm that the inscription *is* talking about a pharaoh.'

Bronson looked at the characters she was pointing at. He could see what looked like a walking stick symbol with two curved lines sprouting from either side of its bottom end, a half-moon shape and a wavy line.

'That's a word, is it?' he asked. 'What does the walking stick thing mean?'

Angela nodded. 'It's actually a sedge plant, and it's used as a determinative. The letters spell "n", "s" and "w", and that means "nesu", or "king". About the only word which could follow that would be the name of the pharaoh himself and, as this temple was built by Shoshenq in honour of the god Amun, the cartouche almost certainly contained his name.'

Bronson looked beyond the ruined wall at the space beyond it, studded with stones, mud-bricks and bits of masonry. 'It looks as if this was quite a big building,' he said.

Angela pulled out a small notebook and flicked rapidly through the pages. 'Yes, it was. According to the few records that exist, this originally consisted of a brick enclosure and inside that was a temple house nearly twenty yards wide and thirty yards long. Don't forget, Amun was a really important creator god, who was believed to live inside everything. He could appear as a goose or a ram with curved horns – which showed he had a function as a fertility god – or more commonly as a ram-headed man and sometimes as a man with two tall plumes on his head. Later on he merged with the cult of Re or Ra to form Amun-Re, the sun-god. He was *really* important to the ancient Egyptians.'

Bronson looked back at the ruined wall. 'Is there anything here that tells us if Shishaq or Shoshenq did actually seize the Ark of the Covenant?'

'I can't be sure. I'll photograph what there is and translate it later.'

There were a number of surviving pieces of inscription on various bits of wall and even on a few of the fallen stones, and Angela took pictures of every one she could find, checking each image on the screen of her camera to make sure it was clear and legible before moving on to the next.

Finally, she slipped the digital camera back into her handbag and took a last look around the site.

'Is that it?' Bronson asked.

'Yes. It's a real shame. I was hoping there'd be a few complete walls with intact inscriptions still standing. I certainly didn't expect the temple to be in as bad a condition as it is.'

'Did you see anything helpful?'

'Not really,' Angela replied. 'I've spotted a couple of cartouches, both with Shoshenq's name in them, and a few mentions of Amun, but not much else. But obviously I've still got to check the pictures I've taken.'

'Amun's name consists of those three symbols – the feather or leaf or whatever it is and the other two drawings?'

'That's the leaf of a reed plant, a draughts-board and a ripple of water, yes.' Angela sighed, and Chris could see that she was tired. 'I'll take a look at the pictures on our way back to Heliopolis, but I'm not hopeful I'll find anything useful. I had planned to do the work out here, but there's so little material on the site that I don't see any point in trying to do that now. And at least our room is air conditioned.'

Bronson nodded and turned away from the ruins of the temple towards the road. As he did so, he caught a fleeting glimpse of a figure wearing a white shirt and light-coloured trousers ducking swiftly out of sight behind a wall on the opposite side of the road.

He felt a warning stab of surprise. Unlike the citizens of Cairo, the residents of el-Hiba clearly didn't see that many foreign tourists, and he and Angela had been objects of interest ever since they'd arrived there. But most of the people they'd seen had simply stared at them with frank and not unfriendly curiosity. Maybe that man – and Bronson was reasonably certain the figure had been male – was just shy. The only odd thing was that it looked as if he'd been holding a pair of binoculars or perhaps a camera in his hand. Certainly he'd been clutching a small black object. And his Western-style dress was unusual in a place where most people seemed to be wearing the more traditional Egyptian *dishdasha* or *jellabah*.

'What is it?' Angela asked.

'I think there's a man over there watching us.'

'I don't see anything.'

'I know what I saw. You stay here. I'll go and check.'

But Angela grabbed his arm with both hands to stop him. 'No, Chris. Let's just get away from here, right now. It might be that priest again.'

Bronson nodded reluctantly, and looked back up the road to where the car was parked. 'You start running,' he said. 'I'll be right behind you.'

Angela took to her heels, heading back the way they'd come.

Bronson stared across the road for a few seconds more, then followed her.

Two minutes later, Bronson spun the steering wheel of the hire car and powered down the street and away from el-Hiba, the car trailing a cloud of dust as he headed for the open road and Cairo.

37

While Bronson drove, Angela sat in the passenger seat of the Peugeot, transferred the memory card from her camera to the slot on the laptop and copied all the photographs she'd taken of the hieroglyphics on to the computer's hard disk. The LCD screen on her camera offered reasonably good quality, but she needed the better resolution of the laptop screen to be sure of what she was seeing.

And what she was looking at wasn't what she'd hoped for. There was nothing in any of the surviving sections of the inscriptions in the temple that suggested Shoshenq had seized the Ark of the Covenant. In fact, quite the contrary.

'Oh, damn,' she muttered, as she looked at one particular image.

'What is it?'

'On this picture there's a readable section of hieroglyphics, just a few words that probably came from the middle and end of a sentence – the rest of the inscription's long gone. If I'm interpreting it correctly, the top line says something like "the gold from the temple". That sounds to me like part of a description of Shoshenq's foray into Judea or Judah. We know he was paid off by Rehoboam, who gave the Egyptians the treasures of the Temple.

'But the second line finishes with "sacred box" – that's as close a translation as I can get – "which remained". As far as we know, the Ark of the Covenant was in the Temple of Jerusalem when Shoshenq's forces entered Judea, and "sacred box" would be a reasonable description of it. This would mean that the Egyptians may not have seized the Ark. They allowed the priests to keep it in the Temple: the "sacred box which remained". And so—'

'We've been looking in the wrong place,' Bronson said, finishing it off for her. 'Shoshenq didn't seize it, so he can't have taken it to Tanis or anywhere else. Is there anything else there?' Bronson asked, glancing sideways at the laptop screen. 'Hang on – I'm getting distracted by all the pictures. I think I'd better stop for a few minutes.'

He pulled the car to a rapid stop just off the road. The driver of a heavily laden lorry which had been following far too close behind gave an angry blast on his horn, but Bronson ignored him and turned towards Angela.

'There's nothing else in these hieroglyphics that even mention the Ark,' she said. 'These inscriptions, for example, seem to be part of fairly standard texts honouring Amun, and there are a couple that I think are praising

Shoshenq's courage and leadership. Again, pretty much what you'd expect to find in a temple erected by the reigning pharaoh to one of the most important Egyptian gods.'

She pressed the cursor control key and started flicking back through the other pictures on the computer's hard drive. One of the images showed a dark-haired man standing beside a chair.

'Who's that?' Bronson asked, as he glanced down at the picture.

Angela had already moved on to a different image, but then scrolled back and looked at the screen. Then she laughed.

'That's the man who started this hare running. That's one of the paintings of Bartholomew Wendell-Carfax as a young man, one of the two we were looking for. I told you there were decent-quality photographs of the paintings in Bartholomew's box of goodies. They were almost A3 size and folded, in fact, and I scanned them both in my office at the museum.'

Bronson glanced down at the screen of the laptop Angela was holding, and a sudden thought struck him.

'We never really worked out why he had those pictures painted, did we?' Bronson asked. 'I mean, we guessed from that remark about "the Montgomerys" that Bartholomew had hidden the text of the parchment in them somewhere, in a cavity in the frame or something, but why did he choose those subjects? Himself as a young man wearing – what – a Red Indian outfit in one and dressed like an Indian prince in the other.'

'Nobody seems to have any idea. Maybe it was just an old man's vanity, wanting to see an image of how he would have looked in his late twenties.'

'Maybe. Or maybe it was something else. Let me take a look at that.'

Angela looked at him in surprise, but obediently handed over the laptop.

Bronson stared at the screen for a few seconds. 'Where's the other one?' he asked. 'The one in which he's dressed like a Red Indian?'

Angela leaned across and flicked through the pictures until she found the correct one. 'There,' she said.

Bronson studied the photograph, then nodded in satisfaction and passed the computer back to Angela. He checked his mirrors and pulled the car on to the road, accelerating to match speed with the traffic approaching them from behind.

'Well?' she demanded.

'I think I know where Bartholomew hid the text of the parchment he found,' he said, looking very pleased with himself.

'But we know that: in those paintings. The paintings that we haven't the slightest chance of finding.'

'No. I mean, I know *exactly* where Bartholomew hid the text.'

38

Killian had got lucky. He'd gone back to his hotel, grabbed a copy of the local phone directory from the reception desk downstairs, and taken it, along with a street map of eastern Cairo, up to his room. Then he'd started from the airport and worked his way outwards, calling each of the major hotels he had located, asking to be connected to Mr Bronson's room. It wasn't the commonest name in the world, and the receptionist at the fifteenth hotel he rang told him that the guest he was looking for had been out of his room all day.

It was as easy as that.

Killian packed his bags and paid his bill, then set off towards the hotel where he now knew Bronson and Angela were staying. He drove past the building, then pulled in to the side of the road a hundred yards or so beyond it and looked back.

The hotel was situated on a reasonably straight section

that offered good visibility both ways, and Bronson, of course, could approach it from either direction. But the main road ran along one end of the street and that, logically, would be where Bronson would be most likely to appear, so that was where Killian decided to wait. It was essential he spotted his quarry before they arrived at the hotel – once they got inside the building they'd be out of his reach.

Killian pulled out into the traffic and picked a vacant lot close to the main road where he would see any cars turning into the road. He locked the car, walked down the street to a small store where he bought bottled water and several sealed packets of biscuits and cakes, then returned to his vehicle. He opened all the car's windows, and placed his food and drink on the passenger seat beside him. He opened the bonnet and skilfully disabled the Renault's air bag safety system. Then he took a pair of binoculars from his pocket and placed them on the dashboard, where he could reach them easily. Finally, he fastened his seat belt and left the key in the ignition, so that he could start the car and drive away at a moment's notice.

Then he settled down to wait.

39

Bronson paused and glanced at Angela, who was giving him her full attention, and then some.

'Go on, then,' Angela said, obviously irritated. 'Don't keep me in suspense. Where is it?'

At that moment her mobile rang, and she rummaged in her handbag to retrieve it. Before she answered the call, she looked at the screen.

'Damn,' she muttered, 'it's Roger Halliwell, probably ringing to find out where I am.'

'I thought you'd left him a message at the museum, saying you were taking a few days' leave?'

'I did. Maybe that's the problem. Strictly speaking, I should have got his approval first.'

'That *is* the usual routine,' Bronson said mildly.

'Anyway,' Angela said, 'he can wait. I'm up to date with everything, and I've never known anything to happen in the museum that could possibly qualify as urgent. I'll call him tomorrow.'

But as she replaced the mobile in her handbag, they heard the familiar beep indicating that a text message had been received.

Angela again looked at the screen. 'It's from Roger,' she said, 'and he sounds really pissed: "Call me now, vital." Maybe I'd better give him a bell. Can you pull over somewhere – it's not that good a signal.'

As Bronson eased the Peugeot off the road again, Angela selected Halliwell's number from her contacts list.

'Roger, it's Angela. I got your—' She broke off and listened intently for a few seconds.

'What? Good God. Is that a joke? Because if—'

Bronson tried to make sense of the half of the conversation he was hearing, then gave up.

'No, Roger. I wasn't even there on the last day. I was at the museum, remember? You saw me at least twice.' Another pause. 'No. I'm in Egypt. Just a short holiday. I'll let you know when I'm back.'

She listened again for a few seconds, then ended the call.

'What is it?' Bronson asked.

Angela stared at her phone for a moment, then turned troubled eyes towards him. 'It's poor Richard Mayhew,' she said. 'He's dead. Somebody told the local coppers that a car had been left parked at Carfax Hall when we had all left, and they went out there to investigate. They found him in the kitchen.'

'Christ,' Bronson said. 'Did he have a heart attack?'

Angela shook her head. 'No. He'd been tied to that big old chair in the kitchen and whipped with something like a cat-o'-nine-tails, and then shot. It happened on Friday afternoon, according to the police. They want a statement from me when we get back.'

Bronson was shocked. For perhaps half a minute he just sat there, making connections and exploring the ramifications of what Angela had told him.

'I think that explains how that bogus priest was able to call you by name,' he said at last, 'and how he knew about the things you'd taken from Carfax Hall. He tortured Richard Mayhew and forced him to reveal your name and address, and killed him when he'd got what he wanted. Then he burgled your flat and attacked you in the street outside. And he must have killed Oliver as well, or at least whipped him until the old man's heart gave out. He's been one step behind us all the way.'

Angela shook her head. 'I think he's one step ahead of us now, because after the attack on Suleiman al-Sahid in Cairo, he's got the paintings and we haven't.'

Bronson turned to her. 'This worries me. This guy is clearly utterly ruthless. He's killed two people that we know about, and it would have been four if you hadn't got away from him in London and if we hadn't pulled Suleiman out of his house. We need to decide if this search is worth the risk.'

'But we're not taking part in any search at the moment,' Angela said. 'Face facts, Chris – he's got the paintings and we haven't, and without them, we might as well pack up and go home right now.'

But Bronson shook his head. 'Here's the question. If I could produce the entire text of the parchment for you, would you still want to carry on? Knowing that the priest is still at large, and that we would have to face him again some time?'

'I wouldn't *want* to meet him again,' Angela said, 'but it would be different if you were with me. But it's academic, isn't it? We don't have the paintings, so we can't find the text of the parchment.'

'So you'd carry on with the search?'

'Definitely; the prize is too big to ignore.'

Bronson smiled. 'I knew you'd say that,' he said. 'I've got another question for you. What does Persian script look like? I mean, is it a plain and simple font – or something more elaborate?'

'It's quite elaborate. You could call it flowery, I suppose. It's got lots of curves and twists. Why?'

'That's what I hoped you'd say,' Bronson replied. 'If I'm right, Oliver Wendell-Carfax was wasting his time tearing panels off the walls looking for the hiding place where Bartholomew had hidden the papyrus text. I think the papyrus itself probably fell to pieces quite soon after he pulled it out of the sealed pottery vessel – it *is* quite fragile, isn't it?'

'If it's not stored under the right conditions, yes. And Bartholomew wouldn't have had the knowledge or the experience to know that. Or the equipment, obviously. If he didn't keep it in a sealed envelope, and especially if he handled it a lot, it wouldn't last very long.'

'Right. So my guess is that he carefully copied out the Persian inscription as soon as he saw that the papyrus was starting to deteriorate. Then, later on in his life, he decided to create a more permanent record, and that was why he had the two pictures painted.'

'We know that. Presumably there's a secret compartment in the frame of one or other of them. Bartholomew seemed to like things like that, if that drawer under the stuffed fox is anything to go by.'

Bronson shook his head. 'I don't think he did anything so complicated. I think he decided to hide it in plain sight. Look at the picture. You'll see a young man wearing a highly embroidered Indian-style tunic. But look closely at the collar and the lapels. It might look like a random pattern, but I don't think it is, because it's not symmetrical. I think that's a form of writing, a form that most people simply wouldn't recognize as being writing.'

For a few moments, Angela stared at the image displayed on the screen of her computer.

'My God, Chris, I think you might be right,' she said slowly. 'Now that I know what I'm looking for, it doesn't seem to be a random pattern. In fact, I think I can make out several individual letters here.' She looked across at her ex-husband. 'You are brilliant – do you know that?'

Bronson smiled. It had been an educated guess, but a good one.

'And the painting of Bartholomew wearing a Red Indian outfit,' she said, finding the appropriate picture. 'I suppose it's in the band of this headdress that goes around his forehead?'

Bronson looked at the screen and nodded. 'And perhaps running down the front of the tunic as well. Can you read the script?'

'I hope so. The photographs Bartholomew had taken were done professionally, as far as I can see, and my guess is that he would have insisted that the lettering be readable on them. Otherwise, what would be the point in having the pictures taken at all? Then he sent the paintings to Cairo for safe keeping. If you're right, and I think you are, these two photographs would have been his personal record of the Persian text, there for all to see, but only if you knew exactly what you were looking for.'

'What about your scans? Did you lose any of the details of the photographs when you did them?'

'Maybe a tiny bit, but nothing significant. These scans are probably just as good as having the original photographs, and we also have an advantage – using the computer, I can enlarge the areas we're interested in and keep them displayed on the screen, which is a lot easier than trying do the same thing with a magnifying glass standing in front of a canvas hanging on a wall.'

Angela leaned over and gave Bronson a kiss.

'Let's get back to the hotel as quickly as possible. I'll have to transcribe the letters and then find an on-line Persian translation program to sort out what the text says. With any luck, I might be able to do all that today.'

She looked at Bronson, her eyes shining with excitement.

'We're getting closer, Chris. I can feel it. By this evening, we might have a very good idea where the Ark of the Covenant is buried.'

40

Nearing the centre of Cairo, Bronson indicated left and pulled the hire car over towards the middle of the road, looking for a gap in the oncoming traffic. Nobody seemed particularly inclined to give way, so he eased over further, forcing his way into the traffic stream until a couple of vehicles finally and reluctantly slowed enough to let him swing across in front of them.

'I'll never get used to the way they drive over here,' Angela muttered as Bronson straightened up and headed down the street towards their hotel.

Fifty yards ahead of Bronson's car, Killian tossed the binoculars aside, reached down and twisted the key in the ignition. The engine sprang to life immediately. As the Peugeot approached him, Killian engaged first gear and accelerated hard, powering it out of the vacant lot and aiming for the side of Bronson's vehicle.

* * *

'Look out!' Angela yelled, as she saw another car lurch into motion just beside them, the driver apparently not having seen them.

Bronson registered the other car at the same instant and reacted the way he'd been trained, turning the wheel away from the impending collision and accelerating hard to get clear of the path of the other vehicle.

Angela looked more closely at the driver and registered the bandaged ear, pale skin and dark, almost black, eyes of the man behind the wheel.

'It's that priest!' she shouted. 'He's trying to kill us.'

Bronson glanced to his right, but his concentration was on the traffic, not on the driver of the other vehicle.

His options were limited. There was a line of vehicles – cars and light vans – heading towards them, but only a couple of cars in their lane ahead of them. No side streets, or not for about a hundred yards, and all the side turnings Bronson could see were dead ends. The last thing he wanted to do was get trapped somewhere that the priest could attack them. He didn't know if the priest was armed, and had no desire to find out.

But a car is a weapon. A ton or so of metal able to travel at high speed, and in skilled hands – perhaps even more so in *unskilled* hands – can be lethal. He had to keep moving, keep them ahead of the other car.

He accelerated hard down the road. The single ace he

held was that his car had already been in motion, and this gave him a tiny speed advantage.

He checked the mirror on the passenger side. The priest's car was now perhaps ten feet behind him, and dropping back slightly. Fifty yards ahead was a lumbering grey van, the rear doors wedged open to reveal a motley collection of carpets and other unidentifiable materials inside it. To the left, an almost unbroken stream of cars was heading towards them.

Angela looked behind them, then tensed, pushing back in her seat, her arms pressing against the dashboard, as Bronson changed up and mashed the accelerator pedal again.

The priest was still close behind, maybe fifteen feet back, clearly visible in Bronson's mirror and now matching speed with him.

Ahead, the back of the van loomed ever closer. At the last second, Bronson swung the wheel to the left, heading straight towards the oncoming traffic, gambling that the drivers on the other side of the road would give way.

But they showed no signs of moving over, and at the last second before a collision was inevitable, he slammed on the brakes and swung back on to the right-hand side of the road.

There was a bang and a scream of tortured metal as the front of the priest's car crashed into the boot of his. The priest had braked as well, but too late.

'There goes my no-claims bonus,' Bronson muttered.

Angela spun round to look behind them.

'He's still coming after us,' she said, her voice choked with fear.

Bronson had been hoping that the air bags in the priest's car might have deployed as a result of the collision, but there was no sign of that having happened. Behind the wheel he could see the man's black eyes staring right at him as he wrestled with the steering wheel.

Bronson swung his car to the right, back on to the correct side of the road, then moved even further over. He took a quick glance down the right-hand side of the slow-moving van, trying to see what was in front of it, then hit the accelerator again.

'Hang on,' he muttered, as the right-hand wheels of his car mounted the pavement. He sounded a long blast on the horn. With the left wheels of the car on the road and the right ones bouncing over the uneven paving slabs, Bronson powered past the van, scattering pedestrians, chickens and dogs as he did so.

Just as he reached the front of the van, a pile of boxes stacked four high on the pavement loomed in front of the car.

'Brace yourself,' he said, and hit them squarely, his eyes closing at the moment of impact. Cardboard and debris flew in every direction but, as he drove over their remains, he could see that the boxes had contained nothing more solid than a few dozen packets of crisps.

Bronson steered his car back on to the road. It bounced

hard as it left the pavement, the suspension banging in protest. Behind them rose a clamour of angry shouts as crowds of people surged on to the streets. The van driver gave a long blast on his horn and gesticulated angrily. But Bronson had got past him, and that was all that mattered.

Then, as he straightened up, he saw the Renault drive around the outside of the grey van behind them – the priest had found a way through the opposite-direction traffic.

Angela saw the vehicle at the same moment and shouted a warning.

'I know,' Bronson said, desperately looking for a way out.

He slammed on the brakes and slewed his car over to the right-hand side of the road, on to a small open area. Behind him, the driver of the grey van also braked, but Bronson was gambling that he'd take longer to stop.

He swung the wheel hard round, spinning the car until it faced back the way it had come, then accelerated across to the other side of the road behind the grey van. The priest's car was now the wrong side of the van, and Bronson hoped it would take him at least a minute or two to get back in pursuit.

The traffic was still heavy, but he forced his way into the line of vehicles, keeping on the outside and overtaking every time a gap appeared.

'Where is he?' Angela demanded, turning in her seat to stare back down the road. Her face was white, her eyes panicked.

'Hopefully he's still trying to turn round,' Bronson said.

He checked his mirrors again, but there was still no sign of the other car. The traffic started slowing for some unseen obstacle ahead, and Bronson began to relax. Now his car was just another in a line of white cars, effectively invisible.

And then, just seconds later, the priest reappeared from a side street over to their right, and forced his way back into the traffic stream perhaps half a dozen vehicles behind them.

'Shit,' Bronson said. He dropped down a gear and accelerated past a couple of cars.

'How on earth—'

'He must have used a parallel street,' Bronson snapped. 'Either he knows the area well or he just got lucky. We've got to lose him.'

He pulled out, tyres screaming, and dived in front of a Mercedes saloon and down a street to the right, praying that it wasn't a dead end.

It wasn't, and it took several seconds before the other car appeared behind them. But Bronson knew he couldn't keep running. Somehow he had to finish the chase and stop the priest. And he had the glimmerings of an idea.

Ninety yards back, Killian smiled grimly. Bronson's car was in front of him, and despite the earlier impact, his own was apparently undamaged. And on these quieter streets, he should easily be able to finish the job.

He accelerated, starting to close the gap, and looked well ahead, searching for a spot where he could drive Bronson off the road. Once he'd forced his car to stop, he could kill Bronson – the switchblade was still in his pocket – and then Angela would be easy meat. It was just a shame he wouldn't be able to take his time over the killings, and make them truly appreciate the exquisite beauty of the divine agony he could offer them before death ended their rapture.

Bronson saw the priest getting closer and accelerated to maintain the distance between them. He needed to make a couple of rapid turns, but not so quickly that the priest would lose sight of him.

He picked a wide street on the left and turned down it, his car's tyres howling in protest. Fifty yards further on, he swung right, just as the other car appeared around the previous corner. There were narrow streets on both sides of them. It would have to do.

Bronson slammed on the brakes, pulled the gear lever into reverse and backed his car down one of the streets on the right, stopping just a few yards from the junction.

'Get down,' he snapped, grabbing Angela by the shoulder. They ducked down below the level of the windscreen and just waited, listening for the sound of the engine of the pursuing car.

The priest raced past. Bronson immediately slipped the gear lever into first and drove out of the side street.

'Thank God. Let's get out of here,' Angela breathed, then stared at Bronson as he turned right to follow the priest, not left, as she'd expected. 'What are you doing?' she demanded.

'Ending this,' Bronson said simply.

Killian stared down the street in front of him and lifted his foot from the accelerator pedal. For the moment, he'd lost sight of Bronson, though he knew he had to be somewhere nearby.

He slowed still further, checking every opening on both sides of the street, his head snapping from side to side as he searched for his prey.

'Can't we just get back to the hotel?' Angela pleaded.

'He must have found out where we were staying,' Bronson pointed out. 'That was why he was waiting on the street nearby. It's the one place we can't go back to.'

'But if we just drive to the airport?'

'That's where we're going, eventually. But first I'm going to make sure that priest is stuck here in Cairo long enough to let us get out of Egypt without seeing him again.'

Bronson turned the next corner and saw, just as he'd expected, the priest driving fairly slowly down the street in front of them.

'Get down,' Bronson said. 'He'll be checking his mirrors, looking for two people in a white Peugeot.'

Angela ducked down as low as she could.

Bronson looked ahead, weighing up the situation. He was closing up on the priest quickly, and knew it was only a matter of time before he realized who was behind him.

He'd closed to about ten yards when the priest suddenly accelerated hard. He knew he'd been recognized.

Bronson floored the accelerator pedal to increase speed, then eased out until the front wing of his car was level with the rear wing of the other. Then he swung the steering wheel hard over to the right, still keeping the speed up. In America, it's known as the 'PIT manoeuvre'. Bronson had no idea what it was called in Egypt, but it worked just the same.

As he kept up the pressure on the steering wheel, the rear wheels of the priest's car suddenly lost adhesion and it started to spin anti-clockwise. Bronson quickly turned the wheel left again, so that the front of his car hit the rear of the other, finishing the manoeuvre.

The priest's car spun sideways across the road, tyres howling as shreds of rubber were torn away from the tread, and slammed hard into the jagged edge of the pavement on the left-hand side of the road. As the car hit, Bronson distinctly heard the bang as at least one of the tyres blew. He smiled in satisfaction.

'Now you can sit up again,' he said to Angela. 'He won't be bothering us any more.'

In the rear-view mirror he saw a figure climb out of the wrecked Renault. Then he swept round a corner and out of sight.

'Now where do we go?' Angela asked.

Bronson shook his head. 'We'll drive to the airport and climb on to the first flight out of this country, ideally one heading back to Britain.'

To his surprise, Angela shook her head. 'I haven't finished with this yet,' she said firmly. 'Going to the airport's a good idea – there'll be armed guards and police there, because of the terrorist situation. As soon as we arrive I'm going to start translating that text. Then we'll decide where we go next, but I can pretty much guarantee it won't be Britain.'

Half a mile away, Killian picked up his bags and walked away from his crashed car, ignoring the shouts and protestations from the crowds of people who'd gathered at the scene.

Though he realized a British police officer would be a competent driver, Bronson's move had taken him completely by surprise. His car was undriveable – not only had one of the tyres blown, but the sideways impact with the kerb had snapped one of the front suspension components, and that wheel leaned drunkenly to one side as well.

He'd have to find a taxi and get away from the area as quickly as he could, before a car-load of cops turned up and started asking awkward questions. Then he'd have to decide what to do next. He tried to put himself in Bronson's place. He guessed that Bronson and Angela would either return to their hotel or, perhaps more likely, head straight for the airport to follow whatever clues they'd found in the Montgomery paintings. And if they were following the clues, he would be able to follow them.

A taxi squealed to a halt in response to his raised arm.

'The airport,' he snapped. 'And make it quick.'

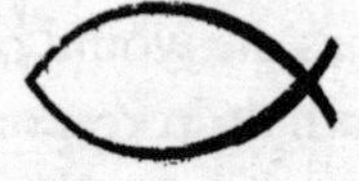

41

'I'll be as fast as I can with this,' Angela said, sitting down at a table in one of the cafés and switching on her laptop.

Bronson bought some food and drinks at the counter, then sat beside Angela as she downloaded a Persian–English dictionary from the web and fed the letters and words she could see in the photographs into it, jotting down the results on a piece of paper.

But it wasn't a quick job. They sat in the café for well over an hour before she finally leaned back in her seat.

'I think that's it,' she said.

'Right,' Bronson said eagerly. 'What's it say?'

But Angela seemed strangely reluctant to read out the text. 'Look, there are a couple of words in it that could have alternative meanings, and a few that aren't in the dictionary at all, so maybe they're proper names. I've transcribed them exactly as they're written. Here. See what you think.'

She turned the sheet of paper round so that Bronson could see what she'd written on it, and slid it across the table.

He scanned the lines Angela had written down. 'I recognize some of it from what you told me before, the bit you found in the guidebook, I mean. But there's no mention of Judea or a temple, which were the other two words you found on the Hillel fragment, if I remember rightly. So what do you think all this means?'

'That's the problem. I'm reasonably certain this is the whole thing, but it's still not clear to me where – or even what – it refers to. It looks as if the first verse is a statement of intent, if you like. Then the second appears to be a general description of what the people involved did, and the third section looks as if it provides some details about the location they picked.'

Bronson looked down again at the text, and then read it aloud, his voice low-pitched and almost reverent as he spoke Angela's translation of the two-millennia-old verses.

And then the son of Yus of the purified,
instructed that the light which had become
the treasure was to be taken from Mohalla
and returned from whence it came.

And Isaac journeyed long and far
with his trusted followers into the
valley of flowers and there fashioned

with their own hands a place of stone
where they together concealed and made
hidden the treasure of the world for all
eternity until the heavens shall be rent asunder
and all shall tremble in the face of judgement.

With their shadows ever before them
from the rising to the setting
beyond the meeting point where waters tumble
towards the mighty river that flows never.
Then turned to face the glory
between the pillars and beyond their shadows
into the silence and the darkness formed of man
to rest forever.

'More information, but a whole bunch of new questions,' Bronson muttered. 'Why couldn't it be easy for once?'

'If it was easy, it wouldn't be fun,' Angela said, 'though I wouldn't mind trying "easy" just once in a while.'

'Which are the two words that have multiple meanings?' Bronson asked.

'In the first line, "purified" seems to be the best meaning of the word, but it also has something to do with lepers, and I can't quite pin that down. Then in the fourth line, "it" can also be translated as "he" or "she", but in that context the word has to mean "it".

'What about the last two lines of the second paragraph – they're a bit apocalyptic, aren't they?'

Angela nodded. 'Yes, but you quite often find that kind of thing in ancient writings. If the author of the text wanted to emphasize that he was talking about a really long time, he might well include some kind of reference to a day of judgement. Don't forget, this idea of the world ending and the souls of all the living and dead being judged by some kind of god is very common in most civilizations. In the Bible it's the Book of Revelations and in Islam—'

'Yes, I remember,' Bronson interrupted. 'All the dead are supposed to assemble in the Well of Souls on the Temple Mount to await judgement.'

'Exactly. I think almost every civilization believes the world will end, one way or another, but most seem to think it'll be with a bang, and with some sort of a creator god involved who'll weed out the good from the bad. I'm not sure that passage is significant – it looks to me like it's just a bit of poetic licence on the part of the author.'

Bronson looked again at the piece of text. 'Well, it seems to me that there are at least three new clues worth following up,' he said. 'The three proper names – Yus, Isaac and Mohalla. And you've spelt "Mohalla" wrong. That should be "Moalla" or "el-Moalla", shouldn't it?'

'That's how it's spelt in the Persian,' she said, 'with the "h".' She shook her head. 'Maybe the original author of the text spelt the name wrongly, though I would have expected the "el" prefix to be included.'

'Or perhaps he really didn't mean "el-Moalla", but somewhere completely different?'

'That's possible, I suppose.'

Bronson looked back at the translation. 'Two of them are the names of people, obviously.'

'And they're the key to this whole mystery. Isaac is still used today, of course, and it was a fairly common name in biblical times, so it's probably not even worth looking at that. There'll be hundreds or maybe thousands of references. But I'm not familiar with the name "Yus", so I'm hoping that's sufficiently unusual to give us some kind of a lead.'

'And do you still think this piece of text is referring to the Ark of the Covenant?' Bronson asked.

'Yes. In the early biblical accounts, the Israelites believed that the Ark was a lethal weapon as well as a treasure. They claimed it was so dangerous that simply touching it could kill you, and that the Ark emitted a powerful light that destroyed their enemies. That seems to me to be a reasonably good match for the early part of this text, where it says "the light which had become the treasure".'

'Yet it sounds as if it had changed somehow,' Bronson suggested. 'Could the Ark's powers – always assuming it had any, of course – have waned? Could the dangerous weapon have become just a richly decorated box? Or do you think there's another meaning?'

'Well, there is one theory that suggests the Ark might have contained some unknown highly radioactive source, something so powerful that touching it could literally kill you – not within seconds or minutes, obviously, but within a few days.'

Bronson grinned at her. 'I think that's getting a bit too wacky for me, Angela, not to mention the questions it raises. Like where the source came from, how the Israelites managed to handle it, and what it was. The most dangerous radioactive elements are things like plutonium, and you can't just find lumps of the stuff lying around. It has to be manufactured in a reactor. Take my word for it – there are no unknown radioactive elements out there that could exist in a stable form on Earth.'

'OK,' Angela said, sighing. 'Scratch that idea. But maybe what the author of that text meant was that the Ark itself hadn't changed, but what they were doing with it had. Suppose they no longer needed to use the Ark as a weapon. That would fit very well with that phrase "the light which had become the treasure". They weren't fighting wars any more, so they no longer needed the destructive power of the Ark – the "light" – but, of course, they would still recognize the value of the relic, so they would treasure it.'

'But what about Mohalla?'

'I think what's important is that the relic – the treasure – was taken *from* Mohalla and "returned from whence it came". So it's not Mohalla we have to find, it's wherever the Ark was taken after it left. And that phrase suggests it was transported back to wherever it was created.'

'So where did it come from originally?'

'According to the Bible, it was made by Moses following the orders of God, to act as a repository for the original Ten Commandments, so I suppose you could say that the place "from whence it came" was most likely Mount Sinai. That was where Moses was meant to have received the Covenant.'

'And Mount Sinai is where, exactly?'

'Somewhere in the Middle East, but there are several different suggestions as to exactly where.'

'So if the Ark *was* taken and hidden somewhere on a mountain in the Middle East, where the hell would you start looking for it? I'm assuming you didn't find anywhere conveniently named the Valley of the Flowers when you were doing your research?'

'Actually, I found quite a lot of them,' Angela replied, 'but none of them were located at any site that could conceivably have been mistaken for Mount Sinai.'

Bronson nodded. 'And with all the activity in the Middle East – by archaeologists as well as by invading armies – it would have to be a really well-hidden "place of stone" that could have escaped detection over the last two millennia. And if anyone *had* found the Ark, I presume we'd know about it by now.'

'Almost certainly.'

'OK,' Bronson said, 'here's a thought. I know you said that finding out where Mohalla was didn't really matter, but actually I think it might be worth doing. We're talking two thousand years ago, when the fastest way to move something like the Ark would be in a horse-drawn cart that might cover twenty or thirty miles a day. I know the piece of text says that Isaac and his mates "journeyed long and far", but that would be "long and far" in the context of that time. If they travelled for a solid week and managed thirty miles a day, which would be pretty good going, they'd still only have covered about two hundred miles. I think if we can find out where Mohalla is, we'll have a much better idea about where to start looking for the "place of stone".'

Angela was silent for a few moments, then she looked across at him, a slight smile on her face. 'Actually, Chris,' she said, 'that's a pretty good thought. These days we're so used to the concept of high-speed travel – five hundred miles a day in a fast car, ten times that distance in an aircraft – that you have to take a couple of steps back to really appreciate the difficulties involved in covering any distance at all that long ago. Right, we'll have to find Mohalla.'

Bronson sat back and stretched his legs. It had been a long hard day, and he knew there was some way yet to go. 'I've just had another thought,' he said, 'and I'll make you a prediction.'

'What?'

'You told me that Bartholomew Wendell-Carfax died suddenly?'

'Yes. He had a heart attack at home, when he was in the

middle of preparing for yet another expedition to search for the treasure.'

'And he'd had those two pictures painted a short time before?'

Angela nodded.

'Maybe the biggest clue of all has been staring us in the face all along. Why do you think Bartholomew chose those two subjects for the portraits?'

'Because he needed to be able to hide the Persian text in the paintings, and those two costumes were ideal for that purpose.'

'Well, I think Bartholomew had a sense of humour. I think he was looking forward to pointing out the Persian writing in the paintings to his son, and I also think he'd finally found out exactly where Mohalla is or was, and the paintings tell us that as well.'

'How?' Angela asked.

'It's right in front of you. Just look at the pictures again.'

Angela flicked back through the images stored on her laptop, found the ones that showed the two paintings and stared at them, one after the other.

'It might be obvious to you, Chris, but it certainly isn't to me.'

'Think it through. Bartholomew could have chosen any number of subjects that would have allowed him to hide the Persian text, so why did he choose these two?'

'I've no idea, and if you don't tell me this instant, I'm going to— '

'India,' Bronson said simply. 'In one picture he looks like an Indian maharaja, and in the other like an Indian chief. The paintings are linked, obviously, because each one has about half of the Persian text on it, but apart from that the only common feature is the subject material. And that's two things – both the paintings show Bartholomew and both of them link him with India.'

Angela shook her head. 'I'm sorry, Chris, but that's just too obvious.'

Bronson grinned. 'I disagree,' he said. 'And I'll make you a bet that when you do dig up some reference to Mohalla, you'll find that it's somewhere in India.'

Sitting in a plastic chair on the opposite side of the airport lounge, completely hidden behind a copy of the *Wall Street Journal* that he'd purchased from the airport shop, JJ Donovan slightly adjusted the position of the shotgun mike resting on his lap as the sound in his earphones – they looked like the type you use with an iPod – faded slightly.

The equipment he was using was state-of-the-art. The shotgun microphone was tiny, but sufficiently powerful to allow him to listen to and record a conversation taking place as much as fifty yards away. Bronson and Lewis were a lot closer to him than that, but the airport was far from an ideal location for detailed surveillance. The problem was people: the passengers arriving and departing, who walked across the open space between Donovan's seat and the café table where his targets were sitting. Sometimes people even stopped in his line of sight to hold a conversation, and there was very little Donovan could do about that. The location wasn't perfect, but his equipment had proved good enough to capture about three-quarters of the conversation Bronson and Lewis had just had, a conversation that Donovan now had stored on a solid-state digital audio recorder.

Once he'd been certain Bronson and Lewis were heading back to their hotel in Cairo from el-Hiba, he'd quickly caught up with the Peugeot in his hired Mercedes and then overtaken it. Then he'd tracked them around the streets of Cairo and followed them out to the airport.

He still didn't know the full story, but he had managed to record the translation of most of the Persian text as Bronson read it out, and now he probably had enough information to work out exactly where he should be looking next.

42

Angela and Bronson watched the computer screen as the first page of search results appeared on it.

'It doesn't look like it's an actual place,' Angela said. 'Or at least there's nowhere named Mohalla in any of the gazetteers. If there was, I'd have expected Wikipedia or one of the other encyclopaedia sites to have popped up with its location.'

'The first result is from Wikipedia,' Bronson pointed out.

'I know, but it's not a location. It's a description of some kind.' She clicked on the result.

'You see? It gives the name Mohalla, or Mahalla as an alternative spelling, but the word means a neighbourhood or a district in some of the villages and towns in Central and South Asia. And that second sentence makes no sense in the context we're investigating.'

'What does it say?'

'That Mohalla often describes a Muslim area, and can

also be a derogatory term. Well, one thing that we can be absolutely certain about is that the Ark of the Covenant pre-dates Islam by millennia; and this Persian text we've been working with is at least half a millennium older than the Muslim religion.'

'And what about that last bit?' Bronson couldn't see the screen as clearly as Angela could.

'It says the word could be a reference to Shahi Mohalla, and that's somewhere in Lahore in Pakistan.' Angela glanced at Bronson. 'OK,' she said, 'I know what you're going to say. India and Pakistan are neighbours, so maybe you're right. But I'm still not convinced.'

'Let's just treat it as a working hypothesis,' Bronson suggested. 'What you've found already suggests that Mohalla could be an Indian place-name. We just don't yet know where it is – or rather where it was. So why don't we assume that Mohalla *is* in India until we've managed to prove that it isn't?'

'OK,' Angela agreed cautiously. 'I'll just take a quick look at the rest of the search results to see if there's anything else there.'

She scanned down the page of results generated by the Google search engine, clicking on anything that looked interesting, then moved on to the second page, but found nothing there.

'I'm going to alter the parameters slightly,' she said, adding a couple of words to 'Mohalla' in the box and checking the results of the new search.

About halfway down the page one result looked interesting. Angela clicked it, they both read it, then Angela sat back, turning the laptop slightly to face Bronson.

'Could that be it?' She looked at Bronson, frowning slightly.

Bronson shook his head. 'I don't believe it.'

'If it is correct, it does explain exactly who "Yus of the purified" was, and where Mohalla was located.'

'Yes, but after all this time – I mean, there'd be nothing left now, surely?'

'We don't know that. It all depends on what they did, how they did it, and where they ended up.'

'So all this time we've been looking for the wrong relic?' Bronson asked.

'We've been looking for the wrong treasure, from the wrong time period, and in the wrong country.' Angela rubbed her eyes. 'How the hell could I have got everything so badly wrong?'

'We were just following the clues,' Bronson said softly, taking her hand. 'We made deductions based on the best evidence we could find. The problem was that once we thought we knew what we were looking for, it was easy enough to make each new piece of evidence fit our preconceptions. It happens all the time in police work.'

'But to be *so* wrong—'

'At least now we know what the Wendell-Carfaxes were looking for. But is it worth following up, after all this time? Wouldn't we be better just packing up and going home?'

Angela looked shocked. 'But we're only just getting started.' She pointed at the screen of her laptop. 'If this information checks out, this would be the single biggest find in the history of the world – bigger than Tutankhamun, bigger than anything else. If there's even a one in a million chance of finding this treasure, it's definitely worth trying.'

For the next few minutes Angela scoured the internet, copying the information she found on some websites, discarding others. Finally she found one that held her attention for several minutes.

'You ever heard of somebody called Holger Kersten?' she asked.

Bronson shook his head.

'Or Nicolai Notovitch?'

'No. He sounds Russian.'

'He is Russian. And how about Hemis Gompa?'

'Never heard of him, either.'

Angela sighed. 'It's a place, not a person.'

'Can you stop the twenty questions routine and tell me what you've found?'

So she did.

Ten minutes later, Bronson sat back in his seat, his face a mask of disbelief. 'You're serious about this, aren't you?'

Angela leaned towards him and took both his hands.

'Damn right I am. Most of this information's been out there in the public domain for years, but without the translation of the Wendell-Carfax Persian text, it's just been a story, and a tall story at that. But when you add the Persian text into the equation, absolutely everything changes. We simply have to check this out.'

'What about the "valley of flowers"?'

'If Mohalla is where I think it is, I've got a good idea where the valley is, too,' she said. 'The difficulty is going to be getting there. It's not what you might call a particularly hospitable part of the world.'

Bronson nodded slowly, recognizing the determination in her eyes. 'OK,' he said. 'Let's do it.'

India

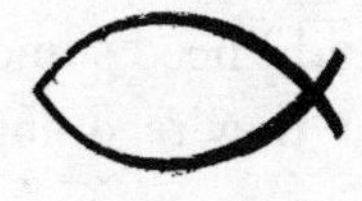

43

In his apartment in New York City, a man called Nick Masters sat upright and looked at the illuminated display of his bedside alarm clock: 3.17. He'd been in bed for less than two hours. 'Have you any idea what time it is?' he said.

'How long have we known each other?' JJ Donovan asked.

'What? You call me up in the middle of the night to ask me that?'

'This is important. How long?'

'Ten years, maybe twelve, I guess. Why?'

'And do you trust me?'

'As much as I trust anyone else in this goddamn country, yes.'

'And I trust you, Nick, which is why I'm calling. We go back a long way. We know each other, and we've worked together before. I need some help. I need somebody who can handle whatever's about to kick off out here.'

'Where are you?' Masters asked.

'India. I need you and I need some of your men as well. Men who know what they're doing. Guys with combat experience.'

'All my people know what they're doing. That's why I recruit them. So what do you want from me?'

In his small hotel room in Mumbai, Donovan looked at the list he'd prepared, wondering if there was another way to achieve his aims. Then he shrugged. He had to prepare for all eventualities, and that meant assuming they might have to fight when they got to the search area. He figured that the more firepower his team could muster, the better.

'I need at least half a dozen men on the ground, plus personal weapons and two or three four-by-four jeeps or trucks.'

Masters was scribbling notes as he listened.

'What's the target?'

'I'll get to that in a moment. I'm following two people, and they're getting real close to something that I've been looking for.'

Donovan quickly explained about Bronson and Angela Lewis, and the trail he'd been following.

'Whereabouts in India are they heading?'

'They'll have to fly to either Mumbai or Delhi, but they'll be making for Kashmir, right up in the north, heading for a place called "the valley of flowers". What I don't know is exactly where in that valley we should be looking. That's why you have to locate them as soon as possible. I'll send you an email with all the data I've got. There's even a photograph of Bronson. Check your inbox in five minutes.'

'OK,' Masters said, thinking fast. 'The quickest way to get to Kashmir is to fly to Islamabad or Lahore, and then cross the border. I've got a couple of friends in the Pakistan military machine, which should solve the problem of getting weapons and vehicles into India. I'll borrow everything I need from them, and then find a nice quiet place to slip over the border. And I'll try to get a couple of my guys to Mumbai or Delhi right now, see if they can pick up Bronson's trail. Whatever happens, I'll have some of my people out there within twenty-four hours.'

'Good. And just tread softly, will you? That part of India's a sensitive area – I don't want any official entanglements.'

'I always tread softly,' Masters replied. 'Like the saying goes, I walk softly and carry a big stick – except that these days that normally means an assault rifle or a Browning fifty cal.'

He looked over the notes he'd scribbled down on the pad beside his bed. 'You still haven't told me what the target is,' he pointed out.

Even over the satellite telephone link, there was no mistaking the suppressed excitement in Donovan's voice.

'You remember that tiny piece of papyrus I bought at

auction ages ago? The one I named the Hyrcania Codex?'

'Yeah,' Masters replied, smothering a yawn. 'You thought it might be a clue to ...' His voice died away as he recalled what Donovan had told him a couple of years earlier. For a few moments he sat there in silence. Suddenly he knew exactly what his old friend was talking about and, despite himself, he felt a sudden chill as he realized the implications.

'You mean you've found something that might lead you to it?'

'That's exactly what I mean,' Donovan said. 'You know that I've been looking for it ever since I read the translation of the papyrus text, how I've had my people scouring the web, checking museum databases, doing everything I could to track it down. Now I'm real close to finding it – or rather Bronson and Lewis are, because they've got more information than I have. And when they do find it, I'm going to take it from them.'

'But surely it would have turned to dust after all this time?'

'For a while, I thought so too. But now I reckon that it could still be viable, just because of where it's hidden. If I'm right, this would be the greatest archaeological discovery in the history of the world, more important than anything that's ever been found before. And the implications for science are just mind-blowing.'

'You're serious about this, JJ, aren't you?' Masters said slowly.

'You're damn right I'm serious. To recover this object, I'll risk everything. It's been a long search but now – right now – the end-game has just begun.'

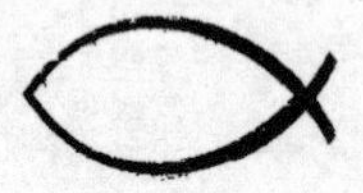

44

In his hotel in downtown Mumbai, Bronson had just woken up. After he'd had a shower and a shave, he announced that he felt a bit better but Angela didn't think there was much visible improvement, and told him so.

'You still look like a jet-lagged zombie,' she said, putting her arms round him. 'Just a clean-shaven zombie, which is only marginally better. Come on. Let's go and find the business centre.'

Downstairs, the receptionist directed them to a small room off to one side of the lobby. Inside were two desktop computers, a fax machine and a laser printer. Angela sat down in front of one of the desktop machines, and plugged a memory stick into one of the USB ports. A few moments later, the printer hummed and began feeding pages into the output tray.

Angela and Bronson knew they had to act as tourists and join the increasing numbers of Westerners drawn to the Leh region of India by its stark and untamed beauty. But they realized that two Westerners wandering about unescorted in some parts of that area, which had a massive military presence because of the sensitivity of the nearby borders with China and Pakistan, might well attract attention – official and otherwise. They also knew they would have to leave the tourist routes to find what they were looking for, so Angela had come up with a cover story that might help.

She had already prepared a mission statement on her laptop, basing it on one of several previous documents she had stored on her back-up disk.

The printer fell silent. Angela retrieved her memory stick, clipped the printed sheets together and tucked them in her handbag. The finished document ran to about a dozen pages and, together with her British Museum identification, it would, she hoped, be enough to satisfy any official who stopped them. According to the statement, the purpose of their journey was to carry out a preliminary survey of the evidence for pre-Indus Valley civilizations in the Jammu and Kashmir regions of India, and to determine whether a full-scale investigation in the area would be justified. The Indus Valley itself ran just to the south of Leh, so it was a plausible explanation.

Such initial explorations occurred on a regular basis all over the world and that would hopefully be enough to keep them out of trouble. Of course, one telephone call back to the British Museum would immediately destroy their cover story, because nobody there had the slightest idea about where Angela was or what she was doing. Neither was there any official approval for any museum investigation in Kashmir, or anywhere else in northern India, for that matter.

The hotel restaurant was closed, so they stepped outside. Bronson was surprised to discover that it was late evening – his biological clock was telling him something completely different. The evening air was pleasantly cool, and they found a decent-looking restaurant that was still serving dinner without having to walk very far.

'The first thing we have to do is get ourselves up to Leh,' Angela said, unfolding a map of the Indian sub-continent on the restaurant table between them and pointing at a spot right up in the Jammu and Kashmir territory, at the very northern tip of India. This area was bordered by China to the east and by Pakistan to the north and west. 'We'll have to use Leh – or somewhere very near it – as our base, I think.'

Bronson studied the map, measuring distances by eye and using the scale that ran across the bottom of the sheet. 'How do we do that? Fly up to Delhi and then take a train?' he asked.

'No – we can fly straight there. Leh's been open to visitors – by which I mean tourists – since the seventies, and it's actually a fairly big town. The whole area has become really popular with what you might call "adventure tourists" – the kind of people who don't expect hot water or comfortable beds at the places they stay. There's an airport, for domestic flights only, a few miles south of the town.'

'Let's see if we can take a direct flight tomorrow morning. Once we're in Leh, we'll have to hire a four-wheel-drive jeep because I think we'll find there are very few roads or even tracks once you start climbing.

'Now,' Bronson continued, 'you spent ages on the internet but you still haven't told me what you've found out.' He looked at her meaningfully.

Angela sighed. 'I now know who "Yus of the purified" was, and how he acquired that name. In fact, he was called Yus Asaph, or sometimes Yuz Asaf. Yus or Yuz simply meant "leader", so his name translated as "the leader of the healed" or "leader of the purified" – and that specifically meant lepers who'd been healed.'

'I didn't know you could cure leprosy.'

'I'm just telling you what I found out, or at least what the records told me.'

'And what about Mohalla? Did you find out where it was?'

'Yes, and you won your bet. The only "Mohalla" that makes sense in this context is Mohalla Anzimarah, which was located in an area called Khanyar or Khanjar, which is near Srinigar, in Kashmir.' She pointed at the map. 'It's some distance from Leh, maybe a couple of hundred miles, so that ties in quite well with your estimate of how far a small band of travellers could cover in about a week.'

'And the man they called Yus Asaph was definitely there?' Bronson asked.

'According to two completely different sources – and one of them is pretty unimpeachable – yes, he was. And there's a slightly spooky element I read about which might be related. According to another source, round about the time that the treasure was hidden away a story started to circulate about the so-called "Ghosts of the Silk Road". That name was tagged on to the story a lot later, of course, because it wasn't actually called the Silk Road until the nineteenth century. But this source claimed that a small caravan was attacked by a gang of bandits as it made its way up a valley. The leaders of the caravan were hit several times by arrows, but the missiles had no effect on them, and the bandits ran away in terror.'

'I guess it could be a legend that was embellished over the years,' Bronson suggested. 'Maybe they only suffered flesh wounds, or were wearing some kind of armour. Or possibly it never happened at all?'

Angela frowned. 'But for the story to have survived this long, there had to be a grain of truth in it. What I found interesting wasn't actually the story about the leaders being bullet-proof, but the fact that the caravan was heading up into the hills well to the north-east of what later became known as Leh, because that area wasn't part of the normal trade route. I think it's possible that the story might even have been an eye-witness sighting of the caravan hauling the treasure itself.'

'And you're still convinced it's worth following this up?'

'Absolutely. If there's even the slightest chance of finding it, we simply have to take it.'

45

The next morning Bronson and Angela stepped out of their hotel to look for a cab to take them to the airport.

Their senses were assaulted in every possible manner and from every possible direction. Above them, the sun blazed down, baking the still air to the point that it almost hurt to breathe. Dust clouds surrounded them, kicked up by the feet of what looked like hundreds of people milling around and the tyres of the dozens of vehicles – everything from trucks and buses down to cars and motorcycles – and literally hundreds of bicycles. And above all was the cacophony of yells and shouts from beggars, hawkers, taxi drivers and numerous other professions, interspersed with the roaring and grumbling of car and truck and bus engines, which virtually deafened them.

'Dear God,' Bronson muttered, pulling their two suitcases to one side of the uneven pavement. He stood there for a few moments with Angela, just looking at the scene in front of them.

'It all looks like total chaos to me,' Angela agreed.

'Well, the sooner we're in a taxi the better,' Bronson said, 'so keep your eyes open.'

He made sure Angela was clutching her handbag and laptop bag, then grabbed the handles on their two suitcases and stepped closer to the edge of the pavement, scanning the road in both directions. Pedestrians thronged the pavements and the edge of the road itself, many of them flapping handkerchiefs ineffectually in front of their faces or fanning themselves with their hats. Some even sported umbrellas against the sunlight.

'It's not just us,' Angela murmured. 'Even the locals are feeling the heat.'

'We mustn't get in any cab unless it's air conditioned,' Bronson instructed. 'I'm not sweltering in a tin box in this heat.'

'How will I tell?'

'Simple. If all the windows are closed, it's got air-con. If they're open, it hasn't.'

A couple of minutes later, they saw an elderly Mercedes draw up beside them, all the windows wide open.

'Ignore it,' Bronson said, looking down the street, watching out for another cab.

The next cab also had its windows open, but then he saw a fairly new taxi going the other way, all its windows closed. He whistled and waved, and was rewarded by the brake lights flaring red as the driver hauled the vehicle round in a tight – and probably illegal – U-turn.

'Here's our ride,' Bronson said. He seized the handles of their suitcases and walked forwards as the car drew to a stop. The driver stepped out, opened the boot and helped Bronson lift their suitcases inside. Angela climbed into the back seat and Bronson sat beside the driver, revelling in the blast of cold air coming out of the dashboard vents.

'Where to, sir?' the driver asked, pulling out into the traffic, his English accented but clearly understandable.

'The airport,' Bronson said. 'We need to fly up to Delhi.'

'Very good. Domestic terminal. I very well know which way. You enjoy ride.'

The drive wasn't perhaps the most enjoyable experience of their lives. Rush hour in Mumbai made the chaos of Cairo seem almost tame by comparison. Several times Bronson was absolutely certain a collision was imminent, and he'd close his eyes, only to hear a squeal of brakes and simultaneous bellowing of horns, and realize they'd somehow managed to scrape through without hitting anything. But the air conditioning in the taxi worked well and, despite the terrifying driving all around them, they were both almost sorry when their journey ended and they had to face the heat and humidity once again.

Bronson paid the driver, retrieved their bags from the boot and together they walked into the terminal building in front of them.

The flight to Delhi left on time, which slightly surprised

them both, and they then had a two-hour wait in the domestic terminal in the capital before their onward flight to Leh.

When their flight was finally called, they picked up their bags again and walked towards the departure gate, and the last leg of their journey.

As they stood up, two middle-aged men of European appearance who'd been sitting about twenty feet away stood up as well. One of them looked down again at the picture displayed on the screen of his mobile phone, comparing that tiny image – showing a man lying apparently unconscious on the flag-stoned floor of a room – with the face of the man in front of him. Then he nodded to his companion. The identification was certain.

As Bronson and Angela walked away, the two men followed about fifty feet behind them, joining the back of the queue for the flight out to Leh, a flight for which they'd already bought tickets. As they waited to pass through the departure gate, the man holding the Nokia flipped it open and then made a twenty-second call to a US mobile number.

46

Nick Masters, his eyes red with exhaustion after a series of long-haul flights, took another sip of thick black coffee and stared across the table at the tall, slim man wearing an immaculate light grey suit. Despite his Western-style dress, his companion's brown skin, black hair and dark eyes marked him as a local. In fact, Rodini was a lieutenant-colonel in the Pakistani military.

They were meeting in a small café close to the centre of Islamabad. Masters had explained what assistance he needed, though not why he needed it. And Rodini knew better than to ask for specifics.

'Tell me exactly which part of Kashmir you need to get to,' Rodini asked, sliding cutlery and plates to one side and opening a military map on the table.

'Northern Ladakh,' Masters said, pointing at the area near Pänämik.

Rodini nodded. 'That helps,' he said. 'We still control

Baltistan and the Northern Areas, so getting you and your men as far as Skardu or Hushe – they're just here, in central Baltistan – wouldn't be a problem. Crossing the border into the area controlled by India will be more difficult, of course, because there's a very large military presence along the border – on both sides of it, in fact. We'll have to work out the best method of achieving that, but it will have to be a covert insertion, because all the roads between the Nubra Valley and Baltistan have been closed since nineteen forty-seven.'

Rodini tapped the map with his forefinger for emphasis. 'Insertion is one thing, but extraction could be quite another. Depending on what you're planning on doing in Indian territory, your best route out might be to simply drive down to Leh and buy an airline ticket to Delhi or Mumbai. Otherwise we could try to arrange for a chopper to pick you up, but we'd have to select the location very carefully. How many men in your team?'

'Eight in all,' Masters replied. 'That's seven plus me, but two of them are in Leh already, or at least on their way there, so I guess they can leave the same way they came in. That means the infiltration team will be six men.'

In fact, he had only recruited a six-man team, but Donovan would be flying into Islamabad that morning, and was intending to cross the border into India with them. Masters had also sent two men to Delhi. They had spotted Bronson and Angela at the airport, and had managed to get on the same flight.

'We'll need some ordnance as well,' Masters continued, 'but nothing too heavy. A few nine-millimetre pistols, some Kalashnikovs and if possible a sniper rifle with a suppressor, plus ammunition. Will that be a problem? Can we still just go out and buy them here in Islamabad?'

Rodini made a note on a piece of paper and shook his head. 'The sniper rifle might prove difficult to source because it's somewhat specialized, and if you find one it'll be expensive, but otherwise there's no problem, especially for the Kalashnikovs. You can buy them in one of the markets. I can suggest traders who supply good quality ordnance and are honest – or at least as honest as anyone else involved in that business. Anything else?'

Masters paused for a few seconds, wondering how best to phrase his final request.

'Yes,' he said, and leaned forward. 'We intend to recover an object from that area, and we will need transport to assist us in the retrieval.'

'What kind of an object?'

'That I can't tell you, but I can assure you that it has no military significance or intrinsic value. It's simply a relic that my principal has located, and wishes to take possession of. He collects such things.'

'Does he always need a team of crack mercenaries armed to the teeth to recover objects that he covets?' Rodini asked, a slight smile on his face.

'Not always, no.'

Rodini grunted his disbelief. 'And may I ask whether it belongs to the Indian government?'

Masters shook his head. 'No. It belongs to nobody. It's been lost for millennia.'

'Very well. How big is it, and how heavy?'

'I don't know for certain at the moment, but I estimate a weight of no more than four hundred pounds, and a box that would fit in the back of a jeep or small truck.'

Rodini still looked unconvinced, but Masters decided this was just too bad. The last thing he was going to do was tell him exactly what he was trying to recover – all his credibility would vanish the moment he did so. Even the men he'd recruited had no idea of their actual objective, only that it was a relic that had been lost for a couple of thousand years.

Rodini looked down again at his few notes. 'OK,' he said at last. 'The only major problem is getting you across the border. Give me a call when all your men have arrived.'

47

After the noise and dirt of Mumbai, the relative peace and tranquillity of Leh provided a stark but welcome contrast to Bronson and Angela. The airport was crowded, groups of white-clad Indians bustling around or standing in groups, and there were several clusters of Westerners, mostly wearing utility clothing, heavy walking boots and carrying backpacks. A babel of voices speaking a wide variety of languages and accents greeted them, but it sounded as if English was one of the dominant tongues.

It hadn't the same sense of frantic urgency as Mumbai either, and outside the terminal building the sense of tranquillity deepened. The scenery was spectacular, mountains, hills and valleys extending in all directions. There was what looked like a monastery on the side of one hill that Bronson had actually seen before – it had flashed past the wing of the aircraft, alarmingly close, as the plane had come in to land.

But there was no sign of the town of Leh itself.

'Is this the right place?' Bronson asked, a little breathlessly.

'Yes. The airport's about seven miles south of the town, so we'll have to take a cab there. Now, just a warning. We're up at about eleven and a half thousand feet here, so don't over-exert yourself – it'll take time to acclimatize to that altitude. Within about twenty-four hours we should be feeling fine again.'

'I'm already out of breath,' Bronson said. 'But at least it's nothing like as hot here as it was back in Mumbai.'

'That's the low humidity. The temperature's probably not a lot different; it just feels a lot cooler.'

The cab ride didn't take long, but the road was far from the smoothest surface Bronson had ever driven along. From the research he'd done before they left Cairo, he knew that in the winter much of the area was impassable because of thick snow, and he guessed that the harsh weather conditions contributed to the very broken and potholed road surface.

'It's bigger than I expected,' Bronson said, as the cab – an elderly Mitsubishi four-by-four – drove down Main Bazaar Road, where there seemed to be plenty of shops and restaurants, including a vehicle hire outlet, then turned off into Fort Road and pulled up beside the kerb.

'Hotel, guest house, here,' the driver said, gesticulating in both directions along the street as he lifted their bags out of the boot.

'*Jule*,' Angela said, bowing slightly.

'*Joo-lay?*' Bronson asked, mimicking Angela's pronunciation. 'What does that mean?'

'It's perhaps the single most useful word in the Ladakhi language,' she replied. 'It's a kind of multi-purpose word that can be translated as "hello", "goodbye", "please" or "thank you". What it means really depends on the context and the circumstances.'

As the taxi drove away, they looked up and down the street. There were numerous signs outside the buildings indicating the locations of guest houses, small hotels and various restaurants.

'This is great,' Bronson said. 'My kind of place!'

'Just don't expect too much, Chris. En-suite and five-star these hotels aren't, but all the reports I've read say that they're good and clean, and the owners are usually very welcoming.'

They chose one of the bigger guest houses, and after Angela's prediction about the lack of facilities, they were pleasantly surprised to find that the twin room they chose *had* got an en-suite bathroom, or rather a shower room, with running hot and cold water. They left their bags in their room, then walked back outside. They had several things to do, and not much time to do them in.

'The first thing we must find is a travel agent,' Angela said. 'We've got to get the Inner Line entry permits so we can visit the Nubra Valley.'

There were a number of travel agents in the Main Bazaar Road. They chose one, who promised that their documents would be ready for them if they returned at the end of the afternoon.

They then walked on to the car hire agency Bronson had spotted on the way into Leh. They already knew that the two most common forms of transport hired by tourists in the area were motorcycles – trail-bikes, in fact – and four-by-four jeeps.

Bronson finally settled on a Nissan Patrol with a diesel engine – big, tough and hopefully unbreakable – with extra fuel cans strapped inside the rear compartment, and with two spare wheels and tyres. It looked like the kind of truck that could cross the Sahara Desert without the slightest problem.

He drove it to the closest filling station, topped up the tank and all the extra cans with diesel, checked the tyre pressures and then parked it just down the street while they sorted out the rest of the things they'd need. They walked into a trekking hire shop and rented a tent, two sleeping bags and ground sheets, a portable stove and cooking equipment, because they didn't know where they'd end up each evening, and it was obviously better to be prepared, just in case they did get stuck out in the countryside.

They knew that the overnight temperature could plummet to below zero, even in the summer months, so they bought warm clothing – woollen shirts, anoraks and padded trousers – that they'd certainly need once they left the shelter of the vehicle to begin their search. Finally, they bought a dozen water containers and filled them all to the brim, and then bought sufficient tinned and packet food to last them at least four days.

They still had a little while to wait until their permits would be ready for collection, so they headed towards the old town that lay at the base of Namgyal Hill. It was a labyrinth of narrow alleys and passageways, lined with houses.

Bronson could see piles of wood stacked outside most of the properties, and other heaps of a lumpy brown substance that was more difficult to identify.

'I suppose that's firewood for the winter,' he said, pointing at the stacks of wood, 'but what's that other stuff?'

'Shit,' Angela replied.

Bronson raised his eyebrows.

'No, it really is. It's dried dung, mainly from camels – they use it for fuel in the winter as well.'

'Ah,' Bronson said, looking with renewed interest at the piles of knobbly brown stuff. 'Doesn't it chuck up a bit when they burn it?'

'The guidebook doesn't say, but I guess it's probably best to be upwind of Leh when they light this stuff.'

They walked on, past a couple of small stone structures shaped something like miniature towers or domes.

'Those are *chortens*,' Angela said. 'They contain holy relics of various types. And that's a *mani* wall.'

She pointed at a wall directly in front of them. It was inset with a couple of stone slabs, and each of them was carved with some kind of script.

'That's the sacred invocation *Om mani padme hum*, which translates as "Hail to the Jewel in the Lotus". You're always supposed to walk past *mani* walls clockwise – and do the same with prayer wheels and *chortens*, in fact – which means you keep them on your right. I've no idea why.'

Then, as the sun slipped beneath the top of the hills lying to the west, they returned to the travel agent. Only a few weeks earlier, Bronson had been driving through the English countryside to meet Angela. Now, here he was on the roof of the world looking for a priceless treasure that had been lost for two millennia. He felt a surge of excitement at what lay ahead.

'These your permits,' the agent said with a smile, his English surprisingly good. 'And these photocopies for you.'

He handed over several sheets of paper, and Angela and Bronson looked at them with interest.

'Why so many photocopies?' Bronson asked.

'For checkpoints,' the agent explained. 'Each checkpoint look at original, and take one copy. I give you each ten copies. Should be enough. Later you want more, you come back see me, yes?'

Bronson nodded agreement.

'They're valid for seven days from tomorrow,' Bronson

said as they left the agency. 'Will that be long enough?'

'I bloody well hope so. The valley's pretty big, but I think I know where we should start looking.'

48

'It's all set,' Rodini said when Nick Masters sat down opposite him in another café in a quiet street in the centre of Islamabad – a different café this time, just in case anyone was taking an interest in either of them. Rodini had set up the meet in a five-second call to Masters' mobile phone thirty minutes earlier. 'Have all your men arrived now? And you've sourced the weapons you need?'

'Yes – everyone's here. The assault rifles and pistols weren't a problem, and we even found a sniper rifle. We're ready,' Masters replied.

Rodini nodded. 'Good. Now, as I told you before, we can only take you as far as the territory just north of the Indian border. Obviously we can then suggest places where you can cross, but that whole area is under a heavy Indian military presence because of problems over the border – they're worried about China as well as about us.'

'So what do you suggest?'

'Well, the safest option would have been for you all to have entered India legitimately, though obviously you couldn't have done so carrying weapons.'

'I'd have preferred to do that as well,' Masters said, 'but the timescale didn't allow it.'

Rodini nodded. 'Our only other choice is to get you across the border in one of the less well-patrolled sections. The biggest problem here lies in satisfying the Indian troops you'll meet in the Nubra Valley area. I've done what I can to help with this, and I have got another idea I'm still working on.

'As for transport I've got a pool of vehicles our troops seized while patrolling the border. I've picked out a couple of Indian-registered four-by-fours that you can use. The bonus is that they were both used for smuggling, so the false floors and other hidden compartments will conceal most of the weapons you've bought. I'm having those jeeps delivered to one of our forward bases down to the south-east of Hushe, in eastern Baltistan, which is only about ten miles from the Indian border. I can arrange to fly you and your men over there by helicopter, but before that happens I'll need your passports. If you're going to stand any chance of surviving scrutiny by Indian Army troops, you must have both India visas in your passports and Inner Line permits, which allow you to travel in the Nubra Valley and other areas close to the border.'

'No problem,' Masters said. 'I'll collect them as soon as I get back to the hotel.'

'Then, once you've made it across the border, you can move around without any difficulty, as long as your passes are good enough and the Indian troops don't realize you're carrying weapons. The next problem is communications. I can provide you with a two-way radio, but it probably won't work properly in that terrain because of the mountains, so a satellite phone is the better option. I can let you have two of those. I'll also supply dashboard-mounted GPS units for the jeeps and a few hand-held ones as well.'

'This is beginning to sound expensive,' Masters remarked.

'It will be, my friend, but never fear. I'm sure your boss – whoever he is – can afford it.' A smile spread slowly across Rodini's face.

'Now, the final matter is the recovery operation. I know you won't tell me what the object itself is, or where you're hoping to find it, so I've had to make some assumptions myself. Presumably it's buried in the ground or hidden in a cave?'

Masters nodded.

'And I presume your plan is to recover it and load it into the back of one of your vehicles?'

'If it will fit, yes. Ideally, we'd like to recover it, move it only as far as a safe helo landing site, and then air-lift it back to Islamabad and put it straight on to a transport bird heading for the States. We can organize the last part of the journey easily enough, but can you lay on a big helo – something like a Sikorsky or a CH-53? It'll need to be a troop-carrier, big enough to carry the recovered object inside. I definitely don't want the object swinging around on the end of a winch cable. And the chopper needs to be at Alert Sixty or better. We won't have time to wait around for it.'

Rodini considered the request for a few moments, then nodded. In fact, he'd already earmarked a troop helicopter for the operation. He even knew which pilot he'd instruct to fly the mission, and had made sure he'd be in the chopper himself, once it was en route to the pick-up point.

He wanted to see the relic with his own eyes, because he didn't believe for a second Masters' claim that the object was of no value. No collector, no matter how wealthy, would mount an operation of the sort Masters was running to grab something that was worthless.

'You were right. This is getting more expensive by the minute,' Rodini said.

'Ballpark?' Masters asked.

Rodini checked his notes again, then gave Masters the figure he'd had in mind from the first. 'One hundred thousand American,' he said. 'That includes the vehicles – you can keep them or dump them, as you wish – and the chopper on standby and at Alert Thirty with effect from nine tomorrow morning.'

'That's totally bloody extortionate, and you know it,' Masters snapped. 'I figured fifty grand, tops. It's two jeeps, a couple of flights in a chopper, two sat-phones and a bit of forgery. How the hell did you come up with that figure?'

'You know how. Because I can supply everything that you need and because I won't ask you questions that you don't want to answer. You're very welcome to try to find somebody else if you think that's too expensive. And it's half now, as in right now.'

'Meaning what, precisely?'

'Meaning a transfer to my Swiss bank today, or the price goes up ten thousand. I'll want the second half on completion of the operation.'

Masters knew Rodini had him over a barrel. He didn't know any other high-ranking military officers in that part of Pakistan, and if he tried to use one of his other possible contacts Rodini might well hear about it and block him. And a junior officer couldn't just snap his fingers and a helicopter would appear – yet Rodini could, and frequently did. And, Masters reflected, it wasn't as if it was his money anyway.

'OK, you blood-sucking bastard, it's a deal,' he said. 'I'll tell my principal to wire you the money. I can guarantee the instruction will be given within the hour, but I can't be certain when the funds will arrive in Switzerland. That's completely out of our hands.'

'Your credit's good with me,' Rodini said. 'As soon as the first fifty thousand gets to my account I'll keep my side of the deal. But if it doesn't arrive, you and your men will have a really long wait for the helicopter.'

49

A Dhruv – the utility helicopter built in India by the HAL company – came to a hover and then settled on to a concrete hardstanding at a small Indian Army base just outside Karu, on the east bank of the Indus and about thirty miles south of Leh.

The howl of the jet engines diminished as the pilot closed the throttles and lowered the collective, the parallel steel skids spreading slightly apart as the weight of the aircraft settled on to them. Safely on the ground, the pilot initiated the shut-down procedure, the engine noise dying away even further. The four-bladed main rotor slowed visibly, and eventually came to a stop, the blades dipping and weaving slightly in the wind blowing across the army base. Only then did the doors of the Dhruv open.

Two men emerged, one climbing out with the ease that came from long familiarity with the aircraft, the other man – a shorter and stockier figure in a set of faded green flying overalls – clearly having some difficulty. The pilot walked round the nose of the helicopter to assist him, then both men walked away towards an adjacent single-storey building, the shorter man carrying a bulky leather carry-on bag.

Just under an hour later, Father Michael Killian sat in a hard wooden chair in the briefing room and wondered yet again why the place wasn't air conditioned. It wasn't the clinging, muggy heat that had assaulted him when he'd stepped out of the aircraft at Delhi, but it was still hot enough inside the room to be uncomfortable, even in the relative cool of the early evening.

He had drunk two bottles of ice-cold water and pecked impatiently at a tray of snacks he'd found on the self-service bar on one side of the room while he waited to speak to the officer in charge.

The door finally opened and a smartly dressed Indian Army officer stepped inside. Killian was unfamiliar with American military ranks, and knew virtually nothing about the insignia of foreign armed forces, but simply from the man's bearing it was clear he was a senior officer.

'You're Father Killian?' the man asked, his English fluent.

Killian nodded.

'Colonel Mani Tembla,' the officer said, extending his hand. 'I've been instructed to assist you in any way that I can. But first, I have a few questions, if you don't mind.'

'Actually, I *do* mind, Colonel,' Killian said. 'Time is of

the essence here, and it's essential that we find these two people before they begin their search.'

Tembla looked mildly amused by Killian's tone.

'We already know where they are, and exactly what they're doing,' he said calmly. 'What happened to your ear?' he added.

'I had an accident,' Killian snapped, reaching up to check the dressing on the left side of his head. His fingers strayed across his cheek, feeling the scratches inflicted by Angela Lewis. They, at least, were healing well. 'So where are they?'

'They're in Leh, in a guest house.'

Killian stood up in frustration. 'What?'

'I gave orders earlier today that Bronson and Lewis were to be identified as soon as they arrived in Leh. That wasn't difficult – there aren't that many flights up here, and my men spotted the English couple almost immediately. I'd already advised the local police, and they quickly discovered where they were staying and identified the vehicle they'd hired. All perfectly routine stuff, I can assure you. But it did raise one important question.'

'And what is that?' Killian demanded.

'All in good time. Now sit down. Calm yourself,' Tembla instructed. 'My orders have been both specific and vague, which is somewhat unusual. I'm aware that tracking these two people has a very high priority for somebody in my government – the fact that you, an American citizen, are sitting here in this base is sufficient proof of that – but what nobody has bothered to tell me is why. The wording of the orders I was given suggested that they might be terrorists, and this is a very sensitive area, because of the borders with Pakistan and China.

'But this does not explain why you are tracking them. We are perfectly capable of following and intercepting terrorists without any assistance. If we do work with entities based outside India, it's invariably with the military or intelligence agencies of other countries. You, as I understand it, have no official standing or authority. As far as I can tell, you're just an American priest. So what, exactly, are they doing here?'

Killian looked appraisingly at Tembla. 'Are you a Christian, Colonel?' he asked.

Tembla shook his head. 'I'm a Hindu, like about eighty per cent of the population of this country.'

'But there is a Christian community here in India, isn't there?'

'Yes, of course. Sikhs and Christians form about five per cent of the population, and the Syrian Church here in India is the second oldest Christian Church in the world, after Palestine. One of the earliest of all the saints – St Thomas – is believed to have landed at Kerala, down in the south-western tip of the country in AD fifty-four. So Christianity is a very old religion here, and a very important one, at least for a small part of our population. What's your point?'

'My point is very simple, Colonel. The man who signed

your orders is a major-general, but he's also a Christian. He issued those orders after he received a telephone call from a man sitting in an office in the world's smallest state.'

'You work for the Vatican?' Tembla demanded.

Killian shook his head. 'Who I work for is irrelevant. All you need to know is that a short time ago some information came into my possession that had the potential to cause irreparable damage to the Catholic Church, and I brought it to the attention of a senior Vatican official.'

'What information?'

'I was forbidden to reveal that to anyone.'

Tembla looked at him levelly. 'If you're expecting to use the equipment and personnel of this base, which I command, you're going to have to do a lot better than that. I need to know exactly what you're looking for, so I can commit the appropriate resources to the task.'

'You have your orders, Colonel,' Killian said. He was still standing and was conscious that he had the upper hand. 'Very clear orders, I believe. Why can't you obey them?'

'Without knowing exactly what you're looking for, I'm not prepared to commit any of my troops or equipment,' Tembla said harshly. 'And that's what my report to my superior in Delhi will say when I file it.'

Killian looked at him for a few moments, then shook his head. 'Very well. What I'm about to tell you must not leave this room, Colonel. Do I have your word on that?'

Tembla inclined his head. 'Of course.'

Killian leaned forward and began to speak in a low voice.

Two minutes later, he sat down in his seat and waited for Tembla's response.

Tembla nodded a couple of times as if he couldn't quite take in the implications of what he'd just been told, and sat down heavily. 'I see your problem,' he said at last. 'And I do appreciate the crisis your religion will face if this relic is recovered.' He sighed. 'You've got what you need.'

'Thank you. You said you had another question for me?'

'Yes. I ordered one of my men to conceal a tracker on the jeep Bronson has rented. But when he attempted to position the device, he found that there was already one fitted, lashed securely to one of the chassis members. Somebody else is following this man as well. Do you know who that is?'

Killian nodded. 'A man named Donovan. I know something about him, and he's even more dangerous than Bronson. So what did your man do? Remove the other tracking device?'

Tembla shook his head. 'I told him to leave it in place, to use a hand-held scanner to identify the frequency the device was using. This will allow us to track the vehicle from a helicopter. And I also ordered him to use a tin of red spray paint to mark a small circle on the roof of the jeep. That will make it even easier to follow from the air.'

Tembla got to his feet. 'I'll be told the moment Bronson or Lewis leave the guest house. I have a team of men watching the property. Now I suggest you get some sleep. Tomorrow could be a very long day.'

50

Bronson and Angela woke early the next morning and got on the road that led north-east out of the town, and which started climbing almost immediately.

Behind them a dusty grey Land Rover appeared from a side street, and turned in the same north-easterly direction.

Two men were sitting in the driving compartment of the Land Rover, and the equipment stored in the back of the vehicle almost exactly mirrored what Bronson and Angela had obtained in Leh, except that there was a lot more of it. The rear compartment held four tents, not one, and far more food and water than they'd bought, and also a number of planks of wood and a small carpenter's toolkit.

In front of the passenger on the dashboard was a topographical map of Ladakh, but he hadn't bothered to open it. Instead, all his attention was focused on an electronic device attached to the windscreen with a sucker. It looked something like a satnav unit, and comprised a five-inch screen with controls positioned around its rim. But unlike a normal satnav, as well as the symbol for the vehicle in which the unit was mounted, there was an additional moving dot showing on the electronic map. It was this symbol that was holding the passenger's attention.

Although the road out of Leh towards the north-east was reasonably straight, albeit with a rough and potholed surface, in reality it was little more than a metalled track, defined only by its slightly flatter surface. On both sides, rocks and boulders marked the limits far more starkly and positively than any crash barriers could. The ride in the big Nissan jeep Bronson had rented was jarringly firm, so it wasn't the most comfortable of drives, but Bronson would trade reliability over comfort any day, and especially in the kind of terrain that he knew they'd be encountering later.

'Are you happy about the route?' he asked, after they were well clear of the town itself.

'More or less,' Angela replied. 'We carry on climbing along this road until we cross the top of the Khardüng La pass – which until recently was considered to be the highest pass in the world accessible by road – and then keep going straight to the bottom of the valley. Then we should swing left and follow the river that runs along the valley floor until we get to Thirit. There must be a way we can cross the river there. The trouble is, I have no idea how big the river is and we've no way of knowing until we see it. According to the map it's fed by tributaries from both sides of the valley, so my guess is that it's quite substantial, and driving through it, even in this truck, might not be such a sharp idea.'

'Makes sense to me.'

'Anyway, somehow we'll cross the river at or near Thirit, and then take the northern fork in the road and head up towards Pänämik, which lies near the southern end of the Nubra Valley. The word "Nubra" means "green" in the local dialect, because it's supposed to have the best climate in the whole of Ladakh – its own microclimate, I suppose. And "Ladakh", as a matter of interest, means the "land of the high passes".' She gestured at the hills and valleys visible all around them.

Bronson nodded, concentrating on the road, which had now started to climb quite steeply. 'Now we're on the last lap, can you just explain to me why you're so sure the Nubra Valley is where we should be looking?'

'Because it all fits so well with the Persian text. The first verse specifically refers to Mohalla, and the second states that they buried the treasure in the "valley of flowers".'

'I thought you told me a few minutes ago that "Nubra" meant "green".'

'I did, and it does. But the old name for the Nubra Valley was Ldumra, which means the "valley of flowers". Some people think that "Nubra" means flowers, but it doesn't – that's just a linguistic echo from the old name in the local dialect. And a small caravan would probably be able to reach the Nubra Valley from Mohalla in about ten days, which again matches the Persian text.'

'OK,' Bronson agreed. 'And I assume there's no other location that you've identified in this area which matches the description so well. But I've looked at the map, too, and the Nubra Valley is shaped like a triangle about forty miles long with a base around twenty-five miles wide. That means it covers an area of roughly five hundred square miles, and the northern end of it is in territory that's controlled by Pakistan, not India, which adds a whole new level of complication. So the question I'm asking,' he finished, 'is where do you suggest we start looking?'

'Your calculation is right, and trying to locate a cave in an area that size would be a complete waste of time and effort without some kind of directions. But, it so happens that we do have some directions,' Angela said, smiling across at him. 'Because of the third verse of the Persian script.'

51

Killian woke before dawn and paced his small room as he waited anxiously for some word from Tembla's watchers a few miles up the road in Leh. Finally, when he could take the strain no longer, he walked down to the briefing room he'd been in the previous evening and helped himself to coffee.

Tembla strolled in about thirty minutes later, nodded to Killian and poured himself a mug.

'Well?' Killian asked.

'They're on the road already,' Tembla said.

'What?' Killian jumped to his feet. 'I need to get up there.'

'Patience, Father. We launched a Searcher at dawn. That's a UAV – an unmanned aerial vehicle – and it was programmed to loiter overhead Leh. It picked up Bronson and Lewis as soon as they left the guest house, and it's been following their vehicle ever since. It's tracking them visually using a high-definition camera, and it's receiving the electronic signal from the tracker, so we know exactly where they are. I got the last update just before I came here, and at the moment they're climbing up the road towards the Khardüng La pass.'

Tembla unfolded a map of the area and spread it out on one of the desks.

'We're here,' he said, pointing at the settlement marked 'Karu' on the map. 'Leh is just here, and Khardüng La is almost due north of the town. At the other end of the pass is the River Shyok and the towns of Khalsar and Diskit. This area, the Nubra Valley, was originally called "Ldumra" and that's the best match for the "Valley of Flowers", as you called it. Now I know this valley, and there's nothing much there, just a handful of old buildings at one end of it, so how sure are you that your information is correct?'

'As sure as I can be; and in any case I need to get there as soon as possible. Can you arrange a jeep or something for me?'

Tembla shook his head. 'There's no point in leaving until Bronson and Lewis stop, and they've still got a long way to go before they even reach Khalsar. At best they'll be making perhaps fifty kilometres an hour. When they stop, we'll use helicopters which can reach them in a matter of minutes.'

'What about weapons? Donovan will be following them too, you know, and he will be armed.'

Tembla smiled thinly. 'That won't be a problem. You can fly to the Nubra Valley in the Dhruv, but I have a couple of Hinds as well, and I'll send one of those up with you.'

'Hind?'

'A Russian-built helicopter gunship. It can take on a main battle tank, so no matter how many mercenaries or what type of weapons Donovan might have assembled, I can promise you that he'll be outgunned by the Hind.'

52

'Are you sure you've deciphered the paragraph?' Bronson asked.

The faintest shadow of uncertainty clouded Angela's face, and just as quickly vanished. 'I think so,' she said. 'I tried to analyse what the writer was describing, and then match his description with the geographical features that I know still exist in the Nubra Valley.'

'And it worked?'

'Yes, I think so,' she repeated. 'Let's see if you agree.'

She pulled a sheet of paper out of her bag and unfolded it. 'Right. The first line is, "With their shadows ever before them". Any idea what that might mean?'

Bronson thought for a few moments. 'I suppose it means they were walking north, with the sun behind them, because that would cast their shadows forward, so they would always be visible to them.'

'Very good.' Angela applauded silently. 'That was

exactly what I thought as well. The second line is slightly easier, I think. It reads, "from the rising to the setting".'

'That has to mean the rising and setting of the sun, so what the writer is saying in those two lines is that they walked north for a full day, which means they probably covered about twenty or thirty miles, no more. But to make any sense of that, you obviously need to know the starting point – the place they set out from.'

'And that,' Angela said, 'is given in the third line. It says, "beyond the meeting point where waters tumble". I took that to mean either a crossroads near a waterfall or, probably more likely, a place where two streams or rivers merge to become one. The problem is that the whole of this area, including the Nubra Valley, is punctuated by rivers and streams. That could have meant almost any location around here.'

'And?' Bronson asked.

'I figured that the same thought must have occurred to the author of this text, so I looked at the next line to see what else he told us. This reads, "towards the mighty river that flows never", and that marks the end of the first sentence, so that's the entire description.'

'Maybe he meant a dried-up river?' Bronson suggested. 'Did you check to see if there are any in the area?'

Angela shook her head. 'I thought the same thing as you at first, but then I quickly realized it didn't make sense. If he really was describing a dried-up river, why would he use a word like "mighty" to describe it? Actually there is a huge river near the Nubra Valley that never flows. Or, to be exact, it flows incredibly slowly.'

Bronson took his eyes off the road for a second or two to look where she was pointing on the map. Beside the end of her finger was a small patch of white.

'What is that?' he asked.

'That's the Siachen Glacier up on the Saltoro Ridge. It feeds the River Nubra, and from the dimensions given on the topographical chart, it looks as if it's about a mile wide in some places. I reckon that fits the description quite nicely. It's certainly "mighty", and it flows so slowly it's almost as if it doesn't flow at all.

'If we put that lot together, what we end up with is a description of a group of people walking northwards for between twenty and thirty miles, heading towards a glacier and starting at a point where two streams or rivers join.'

'And you found somewhere that matches that account?'

Angela nodded. 'That's where we're heading right now. I said we'd cross the river at this place called Thirit. Just north of that village, the two rivers that define the Nubra Valley, the Nubra itself and the Shyok' – Angela pronounced it 'Shay-ock' – 'meet. The road that we'll be following runs almost directly north from there, so that fits the description of their shadows being in front of them; and about twenty-five miles north of Thirit is a road that branches off to the east, and I believe that fits the second part of the verse.'

She took another look at the piece of paper in her hand. 'The third verse begins with the line "Then turned to face the glory". I think that has to be another reference to the sun, the rising sun, meaning that when they set off the next day they headed east, into the sunrise, and that also more or less matches the direction that the present road follows. From what I can see on the topographical map, there aren't that many other routes the road could take, so it's a reasonable assumption that the track they followed two thousand-odd years ago runs in pretty much the same direction as the road that's there now.'

Angela paused briefly. Up to that point, she'd been reasonably happy with her interpretation of the meaning of the three verses they'd found. But she was really guessing about the end of the last verse and that, of course, was the most important bit of all.

'Now,' she said, 'the last three lines, which read, "between the pillars and beyond their shadows / into the silence and the darkness formed of man / to rest forever", are, shall we say, a little more open to interpretation.'

'Basically, you don't know what they mean?' Bronson suggested.

'I didn't say that,' Angela objected. 'The last line – "to rest forever" – is simple enough, and that's just a repeat of the last part of the second verse. And I think the second line is most likely a reference to a cave, either a man-made cave or, probably more likely, a man-made structure within a cave. That is what I believe is meant by the phrase "a place of stone" in the second verse. I don't think Isaac and his followers would have had the time or the equipment to excavate a cave. It would have meant weeks or months of hammering away into solid rock. It's far more likely that they found a suitable natural cave and created some kind of a stone chamber inside it. Or maybe even hid the relic at the back of a cave and simply built a rock wall in front to hide it.'

'So where should we be looking, once we've started heading east along that road north of Thirit? What do you think that line means?'

'It's a bit ambiguous. The first part – "between the pillars" – reads as being descriptive and geographical. Somewhere along that road, and presumably over to the north because the river runs along the bottom of the valley, to the south, there must be a couple of stone pillars or a kind of rock formation that looks like a pair of pillars. Maybe some vertical fractures in the rock, something like that. I'm just hoping that when we drive along there we'll recognize whatever feature they saw two millennia ago.'

'And the second half of the line?' Bronson asked.

'That's the tricky bit. The phrase "beyond their shadows" could refer to the pillars, perhaps, if they were free-standing structures. So it might mean that the entrance to the cave is close to the pillars, just beyond the furthest point that the sun casts their shadows. But I suppose it's also possible that "their shadows" refers to

Isaac and his company, in which case it might simply mean that they kept on going north, heading for a point "beyond their shadows". Or it could be a description of something completely different – something that's not so far occurred to me.' Angela sighed in frustration.

'Look, we're at the top,' Bronson said, pointing through the windscreen.

They'd been climbing steadily ever since they'd left Leh, the road steep and rough, but it now looked as if they'd finally reached the crest of the Khardüng La pass. As he spoke, he saw a sign at the side of the road bearing characters he didn't recognize, but underneath were the English words 'Khardüng La' and below that the height – 5,385 metres, or almost exactly 17,500 feet. The word *La* means 'pass'.

'The last time I was as high as this I was in an aircraft,' Bronson said in amazement.

The view was, indeed, spectacular. Uninterrupted vistas opened up in all directions from their vantage point, and Bronson had the feeling of being literally on top of the world, because almost everything they could see around them was actually below them. In that instant he had a sudden insight into the reasons why mountaineers found climbing so exhilarating.

'I guess it's downhill all the way from now on – at least geographically,' Angela said, as Bronson slipped the jeep into second gear for the long descent down the east side of the pass to the river Shyok that ran along the bottom of the valley. If he used the brakes to keep their speed down, they'd be useless – the fluid would boil and the pads burn out – long before they reached the end of the slope.

The road up to Khardüng La had been steep and impressive, but as Bronson looked ahead he realized that the descent was going to be even more spectacular. He could see a virtual knitting-pattern of steep drops, hairpin bends and only slightly wider turns that marked the route down to the point where the rushing Shyok and Nubra rivers met at the bottom of the valley.

They'd covered about another quarter of a mile down the hill before a scruffy grey Land Rover crested the rise behind them and started the same long descent to the river valley below.

53

On the outskirts of Hushe, in Eastern Baltistan, Nick Masters jumped out of the army helicopter and started supervising the unloading of his men and their equipment.

The weapons were wrapped in sacking to avoid them getting damaged while in transit, although damaging a Kalashnikov with anything smaller than a sledgehammer was quite a difficult thing to do, and the ammunition and pistols were packed in green-painted steel boxes. Masters had even found a Barrett sniper rifle.

At one side of the landing area stood two well-used four-by-fours on Indian plates, and beside them, watching their arrival, was Rodini.

'Come to check on your investment?' Masters asked, walking over to him.

'Just making sure everything is correct,' Rodini replied, looking at the men who'd accompanied Masters. 'Let me show you these vehicles.'

He led the way across to the Land Cruisers and swung open the rear door of one of them. The door was heavy, because a spare wheel was bolted to it.

'This is the clever bit,' he said. 'The bumper's been lowered by about three inches, which is hardly noticeable on a vehicle of this size, and a shallow tray's been made to slide into the body of the jeep just above it. This is how you release it.'

He lifted up what looked like a pair of worn bolt-heads at the rear of the loading area, but when he'd extracted them from the floor, Masters could see that there was no thread on them – they were both completely smooth, like simple locking pins, which in fact is what they were.

Then Rodini took out a knife, slid the point into a tiny gap at the very edge of the floor pan and levered. A tray slid an inch or two out from the floor pan, and he reached down and pulled it out fully. It was the width of the rear bumper, and had been made to fit along the normal panel joint lines, so that it was effectively invisible. The tray wasn't big. It was perhaps five or six inches deep and about three feet long, but almost five feet wide.

'Neat,' Masters said. 'You could pack a lot of cocaine inside this.'

Rodini nodded. 'And that's exactly what they did. Unfortunately for the smugglers, they didn't make the right pay-offs to the right people, and that's why you're now the proud owner of these two vehicles. Your weapons and ammunition will easily fit in there.'

'Definitely,' Masters replied, looking behind him where his men had assembled in a loose bunch, weapons and ammunition boxes and other gear scattered around them. 'John,' Masters called. 'Bring a couple of the AKs over here, will you? And some of that sacking.'

A bulky, bear-like man, most of his face hidden behind a thick black beard, picked up two of the Kalashnikovs and ambled over to the back of the Land Cruiser.

Masters nodded his thanks to Rodini, spread the sacking on the bottom of the tray and laid the two Kalashnikovs on it. Even a casual glance showed that there was room for at least half a dozen of the weapons in the tray, as long as their magazines were detached.

'That's good,' he said. Then, raising his voice slightly, 'OK, you guys. Take the mags off the AKs and put them in these two trays. The Barrett, too. Pack the ammo around them.'

'What about the shorts?' the heavy-set man asked. 'You want them in there as well?'

Masters shook his head. 'No – we'll keep the pistols on us, just in case we need some additional persuasion at some checkpoint.'

Rodini shook his head. 'I would strongly suggest that you don't get into a fire-fight with the Indian Army patrols across the border. I can almost guarantee that you'll lose.'

'Noted,' Masters said. 'But I don't want all our weapons locked away and inaccessible, just in case we do run into any trouble.' He watched as his men stowed away the weapons and ammunition, and closed the two secret trays in the backs of the Land Cruisers.

'Now,' Rodini said, 'crossing the border. You all have your passports and Inner Line permits?'

Masters nodded. He'd personally checked the documents when Rodini had handed them back after the forgers had done their work, and he also had a set ready for JJ Donovan when he finally arrived.

'We're here.' Rodini opened up a map, spread it out on the bonnet of the Land Cruiser, and pointed at a spot about ten or twelve miles from the border between Pakistani and Indian territory. 'On the tracks that pass for roads in this area, the border's about a half-hour drive down to the south-east. What I propose to do is quite simple. I intend to escort all of you down there under guard and then hand you over to the Indian troops.'

54

'We're still pretty high, aren't we?' Bronson asked.

They'd descended all the way to the bottom of the Khardüng La pass, and crossed the bridge over the Shyok, the river that ran along the bottom of the valley. At the T-junction on the other side of the fast-flowing waters, they turned left and again began descending, but this time more gently.

'Yes,' Angela replied. 'This whole area's at an elevation of about ten thousand feet.' She glanced at her map. 'Pretty soon we'll come to another junction, and one fork of the road will go south, back across to the other side of the Shyok. We need to stay on this side, the east side, of the river, and we'll keep on heading more or less north-west until we reach the town of Pänämik.'

In a few minutes they reached the junction.

'Just pull over for a second, could you?' Angela asked.

'What is it? Something wrong?'

'No, nothing,' Angela said. 'Just hop out and follow me.'

She climbed down from the passenger seat of the Nissan and waited in front of the vehicle as two other four-by-fours – a Land Rover and a Toyota – drove past them heading north-west, trailing clouds of dust behind them. She crossed to the other side of the road, Bronson following, and pointed over to the south-west, towards the river.

'Over there,' she said, indicating a wide stretch of the river, 'is where the river Nubra – which is also known as the Siachen, the same name as the glacier that feeds it – and the river Shyok meet.'

Bronson looked across the rocky ground towards the bottom of the valley. Even from the distance he was looking, he could see the tumbling and disturbed water where the two rivers converged.

'And you think that's "the meeting point where waters tumble"?'

Angela nodded.

'Amazing, isn't it?' Bronson said. 'You know, I don't suppose the landscape here looks a hell of a lot different now to how it did two thousand years ago.'

They got back into the jeep. 'If we're right, the road we're following now would have been roughly the same route Isaac and his companions walked,' Angela said, also struck by the enormity of it all. 'It would have taken them at least a whole day to reach the major fork in the road, but we should be there in about an hour. And then we start looking.'

As Bronson drove on, he passed several four-by-four vehicles parked on the rough ground that bordered the road. Most of them were surrounded by tourists dressed in warm clothing – Puffa jackets, parkas and brightly coloured anoraks were much in evidence – looking at maps or taking pictures of the scenery.

But one, a dusty grey Land Rover, stood out slightly, simply because there were only two people in it – both men – and because they were still inside it, sitting with the engine running, parked a few yards off the metalled road. Bronson knew he'd never seen either man before, but he took a mental note of the registration number as he drove the Nissan past the vehicle – just in case.

'If that isn't a bad joke,' Masters said, 'you'd better explain exactly what you mean.'

Rodini smiled at him. 'Think it through. You're driving Indian-registered four-by-fours. You all have India visas in your passports – forged India visas, I know, but they're pretty good quality – and you're carrying Inner Line permits plus about a dozen photocopies each. The simplest way to get you into India is to claim that you were already in it, but somehow you got lost and crossed into Pakistani territory.

'When we get to the border I'll berate the Indians for allowing a bunch of Americans to cross into Pakistan so easily. I will also tell them that we've interrogated you, so if one or two of you can rough each other up a bit –

fake some bruises and maybe a cut or two – that would add realism. My guess is that they'll be so embarrassed that they'll just check your papers, shout at you, and then let you go. And if they decide not to, for some reason, then I can claim that I've just received instructions to re-arrest you all for further questioning.'

Masters nodded slowly. There was a kind of simple genius about Rodini's suggestion that he had to applaud. He'd known all along that trying to sneak across the border was going to be difficult and dangerous, but simply driving to a checkpoint and claiming to have crossed into Pakistan in error eliminated that problem. And Rodini was quite correct – they had all the papers and documentation they needed to be in the Nubra Valley area so, as long as Rodini's forgers had done their work, the Indians should have no reason to detain them.

'You have good relations with the Indian troops?' he asked.

'Good enough,' Rodini replied. 'There are occasional skirmishes, but most of the time nothing happens in the border area, so we do talk to each other, that kind of thing. Before we actually attempt to cross the border I'll call one of the senior Indian Army officers and explain that we've arrested a group of trespassers, just to gauge his reaction.'

'Won't he want to report it, tell his superiors what's going on?'

'I doubt it. If he admits that two jeep-loads of American

tourists managed to sneak across the border in his sector, and on his watch, only to be captured and returned by Pakistani troops, it's going to look as if he and his men have been negligent. The last thing he'll want to do is tell anyone about it.'

Rodini smiled at Masters. 'Time to get going,' he said. 'Next stop, the Indian border.'

55

'You know, I can see why people come here,' Bronson said, gazing through the windscreen at the expanse of the Nubra Valley. 'At this altitude, in this kind of terrain, you just don't expect to see anything like this.'

The broad floodplain stretched out in front of them, flat and comparatively level, but despite the altitude – the valley was about 10,000 feet above sea level – much of it was a carpet of vegetation, vivid green patches that contrasted sharply with the grey-brown of the mountain slopes that bordered it on both sides. Pinpricks of colour, yellows and pinks and reds, marked the positions of wild roses, and darker grey-green patches delineated clumps of lavender, waiting for the heat of August to come before they started to flower.

And it wasn't just the different colours. There was a huge contrast between the plain itself and the mountains, which seemed to rise almost vertically from the edge of the level ground. No foothills, no gentle slopes rising up to meet the mountains. In some ways it reminded Bronson of the Norwegian fjords, where the steep sides of the peaks plunge straight down into the icy waters.

'This valley has the best climate in the whole of Ladakh,' Angela said, 'and, as you can see, it's well cultivated and very fertile. As I told you before, in the ancient language of this area, it was known as Ldumra, meaning the "Valley of Flowers". There's even a theory that this area was the source of the story of the original Garden of Eden.'

'Well, you can see why,' Bronson said. 'For somebody flogging their way along the paths that lead here, seeing nothing but rocks and mountains, and then suddenly being confronted by this sight. I mean, why wouldn't they think they'd found a kind of paradise?'

'But actually, this valley has been quite well-travelled over the centuries. It's only in modern times that it's been turned into a kind of dead end because of the disputes between India and Pakistan, and of course with China. We're not that far from the Chinese border right now. But originally, this was a part of the so-called Silk Route or Silk Road, that ran from the capital of the old Chinese Empire – Chang'an, which is now called Xi-an – to several different locations around the Mediterranean, like Alexandria and Istanbul, and elsewhere.'

A large brown animal moved among a clump of bushes off to one side of the road they were following.

'What was that?' Bronson asked, catching just a fleeting glimpse of it before switching his attention back to the road.

'It's a Bactrian Camel. That's the kind with two humps,' Angela replied, swivelling round in her seat to look at it more closely.

'A camel? I wouldn't have thought you'd find camels at this altitude.'

'They're hardy beasts, well equipped to endure harsh conditions – whether it's very hot or very cold. In fact, about the only animals you're likely to find up here are camels and goats.'

On the opposite side of the river, above a reasonably large settlement surrounded by apricot plantations, a strangely modern-looking building was set into the hill-side. It was square and mainly white in colour, but with some parts of it painted red, brown and yellow, and with tall and thin flags fluttering from its roof. It looked almost like a block of flats.

'What's that over there?' Bronson asked.

Angela looked down at her notes and the map. 'The last place we drove through was called Khalsar, but that was just a small hamlet, so that must be Diskit village. It's one of the bigger settlements in this region. It's got a few hotels and guest houses, and even a handful of shops.'

'I meant that building on the side of the hill.' Bronson took one hand off the wheel and pointed to his left.

Angela checked the map again. 'Oh, that's Diskit

Gompa. It's the oldest and biggest monastery in the whole of the Nubra Valley. It's about three hundred and fifty years old.'

'So the word *gompa* means "monastery"?'

'Yes,' Angela said. 'I think most of the villages here have one, though some have fallen out of use as the population's moved around in the area. Many of them seem to have the same kind of construction – the square corners, flat roofs and square or tall thin windows are typical, and they can be quite colourful. And the monks that live in them are pretty colourful as well – they usually wear dark red robes and sometimes golden headdresses.'

'What about the flags?'

'They have prayers written on them. I think the wind whipping past the flags is supposed to send the message in the prayer straight to Buddha.'

They drove through Sumur and carried on, heading north and occasionally catching sight of the river on their left-hand side.

'Right,' Angela said, as they saw a scattering of buildings on either side of the road ahead of them. 'That should be Pänämik up ahead. We need to check out the condition of the road at the north end of the village.'

'What are you looking for?'

'Roadblocks,' Angela said simply. 'Non-locals aren't allowed to go any further north than Pänämik, and the place we need to get to is quite a way beyond it, so we'll have to either try to talk our way through or drive back and then go cross-country to get around the patrols.'

'And if we're stopped out in the bundu?' Bronson asked.

'We're stupid foreigners. We'll say we got lost and didn't realize where we were.'

'OK,' said Bronson, doubtfully. 'As long as they don't shoot us first.'

Pänämik was the same as almost every other village they'd seen since they'd arrived in Ladakh, but perhaps a little bigger than most. Bronson slowed right down as they approached the northern end, and they both looked ahead. They'd almost cleared the settlement before they saw the barrier across the road, and the handful of Indian Army soldiers standing casually beside it, weapons slung over their shoulders.

'Time for Plan B, I suppose,' Bronson said with a sigh. 'I hope you've got a decent map there.' He pulled the four-by-four into the side of the road and switched off the engine. Angela unfolded the map she'd been using and used a pen to point at a spot to the north-east of Leh.

'There's Pänämik,' she said. 'And this is where we need to get to.'

She indicated a right-hand junction in the road perhaps ten or twelve miles beyond the village.

'And from there?' Bronson asked.

'From there we use our eyes and our imagination,' she said, 'because I think that junction is what the author of the text meant when he wrote that line, "Then turned to face the glory." So once we get there, we'll have to start looking for anything that could fit the expression "between the pillars", which may be somewhere to the north of the road.'

'Because of the phrase "beyond their shadows"?' Bronson offered.

'Exactly.'

Bronson studied the map, working out distances and checking the contour lines. If they were going to venture off the road and go cross-country, he needed to be sure their jeep could handle the terrain. If they got stuck, there would be nobody they could call for help, for obvious reasons.

That was one factor. The other was that they couldn't just pick a nice level route and power along it, because the car would throw up a plume of dust that would be visible for miles, and that would be a pretty sure way of attracting the attention of an Indian Army patrol. So they needed to keep it slow, and ideally drive along valleys or gullies – providing they could climb out of them when they had to.

'I think we need to go back down the road and head south,' Bronson said. 'When we leave the road we can't go west, because we'd have to drive through this village called Arann to rejoin the road. So once we get clear of Pänämik, we'll have to swing over to the east and go along the slopes of this mountain here – I think it's called Saser – in the Karakoram Range. Then we can turn north and join the road that runs east out of Arann without having to go into the village itself.'

Angela nodded. 'It's a hell of a long way round,' she said doubtfully, 'but I don't see any other options, unless we just drive up to the roadblock, wave the letter at the soldiers and tell them we're an advance guard from the British Museum. That might work.'

'Yeah,' Bronson said, 'and it might not. I'd rather hang on to the letter and use it if we're stopped by a patrol out in the hills. If the soldiers at the roadblock don't allow us through, we'll have alerted them that we're trying to get further north. They might radio any roving patrols they've got in the area to warn them to look out for this jeep, and that's the last thing we want. The best bet is to just creep along the side of the mountain and hope nobody spots us. If we are stopped, we just plead ignorance, and then show them the letter.'

He glanced at his watch. 'Do you want to start now or find somewhere here to stay for the night?'

'Let's leave now. I'd rather we got clear of Pänämik and at least tried to get into the right area.'

As Bronson started the Nissan, three men walked past the four-by-four and glanced at it incuriously. Two had the typical features that they'd got used to seeing since their arrival in Ladakh, but the third man had a much fairer – almost ruddy – complexion, and auburn hair.

'Is he a tourist, or what?' Bronson muttered to Angela, as the three men walked past the jeep.

'Not the way you mean it,' she replied. He's almost certainly from Baigdandu, a village about forty miles to the west of here. Every now and then a boy or girl is born there with red hair and blue eyes. There's a local legend that centuries ago a tribe of Greeks arrived and then settled there, and it's their genes that cause the aberration.'

'Greeks?' Bronson asked. 'But why—'

'I know,' Angela interrupted. 'The story makes no sense. Even if a bunch of Greeks did turn up here and inter-marry with the locals, that's still not an explanation for that complexion. I mean, how many Greeks have you ever seen who have red hair?'

'But what was a group of Greeks doing here in the first place? We're a hell of a long way from the Mediterranean.'

Angela paused, then rubbed the back of her neck to ease her tension. 'Exactly the same as us, actually.'

Bronson whistled. 'You're kidding.'

'That's what the legend says.'

'But they didn't succeed?'

'We wouldn't be here, Chris, if I thought there was the slightest chance that anyone had beaten us to it.'

Twelve thousand feet above Pänämik, the Israeli-built Searcher II UAV described a lazy circle in the sky, a near-invisible speck, its engine completely inaudible. Then the craft straightened up and started flying towards the south, anchored to the slowly moving Nissan Patrol by the electronic tether of the signal from the tracking device.

56

'So where are we now?' Donovan asked from the back seat of the leading Land Cruiser. He'd flown in from Cairo the previous day, and joined the group at the military airport at Hushe in Eastern Baltistan, just before the vehicles left for the Indian border.

'For Christ's sake,' the man in the front passenger seat muttered under his breath, then glanced behind him. 'We're about here, between Lhäyul and Gömpa.' He pointed towards the map in his lap.

'How soon before we reach the road junction?'

Donovan had asked the same question at least four times already. He clearly wasn't enjoying the bucking and lurching ride.

'It's about twenty miles away, so maybe forty minutes on this kind of surface. You still sure that's where these two Brits are going, boss?'

Masters, sitting beside Donovan in the back seat, shook

his head. 'Right now, I'm not sure of anything. But according to the guys who followed them to Pänämik, they're going cross-country and it looks as if they're heading towards the road that runs from Arann out to the east and then goes up and over the Saser Pass. So that's where we're going too.'

The border crossing had been much easier than Masters had expected. Rodini's plan had worked just as they'd expected, and all the Americans had had to endure was a vitriolic tongue-lashing from the senior Indian Army officer there.

Now they just had to locate Bronson and Angela Lewis, after which they should be able to wrap up everything quickly. They'd whistle up Rodini's chopper and get the hell out of India and back into Pakistan, where they wouldn't have to sneak around quite so much. And once they got there, they could finally hand over the relic to Donovan, who could load it into the back of his private jet. And then they would collect the balance of their money.

Masters settled back in his seat. Good organization, that was what it was all about. Attention to detail. If all went according to plan – his plan – he'd be back in New York by the end of the week.

If they'd thought the pot-holed and dusty roads in Ladakh were any kind of a preparation for travelling cross-country, they were wrong. Bronson had tried to pick the smoothest route but, no matter what he did, the jeep lurched and bounced, throwing them from side to side.

'I've had about enough of this,' Bronson muttered, as the front wheels of the jeep left the ground completely and smashed down on to the rutted surface a split-second later, shaking the whole vehicle.

The good news was that they weren't leaving much of a trail of dust, because the ground was rocky. Bronson was reasonably sure their progress would be invisible to anyone watching from Pänämik.

'I'm checking everywhere,' Angela said, 'but there are no signs of any Indian Army patrols anywhere ahead of us. Or behind us, for that matter.'

'I guess they just put up roadblocks and patrol the roads. They probably think nobody would be stupid enough to try to drive cross-country anywhere around here. And they've got a point,' Bronson added, as the Nissan lurched particularly savagely.

They were right – there were no Indian Army troops closer to them than the roadblock they'd already seen on the north-bound road out of Pänämik. But they weren't quite alone on the mountain. Nearly a mile behind them, a dusty grey Land Rover was plodding along steadily, not following exactly the same route as Bronson's jeep because the driver didn't need to. The tracking device, securely clamped to one of the chassis members, ensured that they knew exactly where Bronson was. That had been done the first night in Leh, after Bronson had collected the jeep from the vehicle hire company and parked it outside their lodging.

'How much further?' Bronson asked, the quaver in his voice caused by the car's violent jolting.

'No more than ten miles,' Angela replied, trying to sound upbeat about the remaining distance. 'We've already covered five.'

Nearly an hour later, Angela spotted a faint horizontal line on the side of the mountain right in front of them.

'That's got to be the road we're looking for,' she said, checking her map.

She looked over to the left and pointed. 'I think those must be the outskirts of Arann.'

About ten minutes later, Bronson swung the Nissan on to the road and heaved a sigh of relief.

'I vote we go back from here on the road. I'd rather try to crash through a bloody roadblock than do that again.'

'You might not feel that way when we end up in jail,' Angela said. 'Now we head east, but take it slowly. We're looking for anything that looks like a couple of pillars.'

About half a mile away, the driver of the grey Land Rover pulled the vehicle to a halt behind some rocks that completely hid it from the road ahead. Both men climbed out and stepped forward, pulling compact binoculars from their jacket pockets. In the distance, Bronson's Nissan Patrol was heading slowly eastwards.

'You reckon they've found anything?' the driver asked.

'Don't look like it,' the passenger replied. 'He's going real slow. I'll go get the sat-phone, check in with Masters.'

He dialled a number and held a brief conversation.

'What's he want us to do?'

'We stay here and keep eyes on the jeep. If it turns off the road, we tell Masters, then drive over there, stash the Rover and follow on foot, keepin' out of sight. Masters is going to hole up with the other guys near Arann until he knows where Bronson and the woman are going. He doesn't want them spooked, not when we're this close.'

They watched the jeep continue down the road, moving at little more than a crawl, until it was only a distant speck at the limit of their vision.

'You think we should maybe follow them now?'

'No need. The tracker'll tell us where they are if we have to move. Masters seemed to think that whatever they're lookin' for is most likely somewhere at this end of the valley.'

Both men focused their binoculars on the distant vehicle.

'Looks like they've stopped.'

And moments later they watched as the Nissan four-by-four turned round in the road and began heading back in their direction.

In ten minutes, the jeep had covered most of the distance

back to the point where they'd watched it join the road.

The driver stared through his binoculars, then lowered them to his chest.

'Looks like Masters could have been right, and maybe the end-game is near, because the Nissan's just stopped again.'

Bronson pulled the jeep to a halt beside the road and looked over to his right, in the direction Angela was pointing.

'Could that be it?' she asked, her voice clouded with doubt.

On the north, uphill side of the road a fairly narrow gully opened up, a tumble of rocks partially blocking the entrance to it.

'I don't see anything much there that looks like a pair of pillars.'

'Me neither. OK, just go on a little bit further, and see if there's anything else closer to Arann that looks like a better candidate.' Bronson slipped the jeep into gear and eased it back on to the road. But he'd only covered about ten yards when Angela suddenly grabbed his arm.

'Stop,' she said, pointing again.

Perhaps two hundred yards further up the mountain-side, beyond the entrance to the gully, a vertical crack split the rock in two.

'What?' Bronson said.

'Look – over there. It's the closest thing I've seen so far.'

Angela's voice was high with excitement. 'The ancient languages didn't have the huge vocabularies we've got today. "Pillars" might have been the most accurate word the author could find to describe what he was seeing. Anyway, I think it's worth checking out. Can you get the jeep up there and into that gully?'

Bronson studied the rock-covered ground and nodded. 'Probably,' he said. 'Though I'm not sure how far I'll be able to take it off the road. I guess we'll be walking for the last part, up to that cleft.'

He reversed the jeep about twenty yards then swung it over to the right and inched his way off the rutted surface of the road and into the entrance to the gully, weaving his way between the fallen rocks. Beyond the fairly narrow opening, the rocks opened up slightly, and there were fewer fallen boulders to negotiate. He was able to drive about a hundred yards towards the split in the rock, which was further than he thought they'd be able to manage.

But eventually the ground became too steep and the surface too broken up for him to drive any further. He reversed the jeep into a gap between two large boulders and switched off the engine.

'That should be invisible from the road,' he said. 'Now we walk.'

57

In a level area just off the road about a mile outside Arann, Masters ended the call on his sat-phone and grabbed a topographical map of Kashmir. Spreading it out across the bonnet of the Land Cruiser, he studied it for a few minutes, Donovan right beside him. Then he gestured to the other men, who clustered around him.

'OK,' he began. 'Bronson and Lewis have just stopped their vehicle and pulled off the road right here. According to the surveillance team, the jeep drove up this narrow gully about ten minutes ago and it hasn't reappeared.

'So what we can't do is drive up the gully after them. That would be real stupid. We need to sneak up on them.'

The heavy-set man at the edge of the group shook his head. Right then John Cross's surname fitted his mood pretty much like a glove. 'This makes no sense, Nick. These two Brits don't have anything more than maybe a penknife between them. We've got assault rifles and pistols. I don't see why we don't just drive straight up to them, stick a pistol down the woman's throat and tell the guy we'll pull the trigger unless he tells us what he knows.'

A couple of the other men nodded their agreement.

'Oh, and by the way, Nick, we still have no clue what the hell we are supposed to be looking for in this god-forsaken hole.' Cross added, 'because, so far you've told us diddly-squat.'

Masters nodded. 'I'm still not going to tell you why we're here,' he snapped, 'because that guy over there' – he gestured at Donovan, who had walked a short distance away from the group of merceneries – 'is the man who's paying your wages, and he wants it that way. The reason we're not going to give Angela Lewis a nine-millimetre tonsillectomy is because she's the person most likely to find what we're looking for. If you're not happy with this, unload your weapons, put them back in the truck and start walking.'

He looked round at the men. Not one of them had moved. 'No takers? OK, get ready. We leave in two minutes.'

Bronson shrugged a haversack on to his back. Inside it were bottles of water and half a dozen chocolate bars, plus a couple of sweaters and a handful of tools he'd bought in Leh that he thought might be useful. They left the rest of their survival equipment in the Nissan – if they had to spend the night in the open, they'd have to return to the vehicle.

'Are you ready?' he asked.

'Ready and eager to get going,' Angela said with a smile.

Bronson led the way up a gentle slope, clambering around boulders and over fallen rocks, and paused to help Angela over the last section. As he stretched out his hand to her, he saw her eyes widen as she stared at something behind him, something he obviously hadn't noticed.

Bronson spun round. 'What is it?'

'There,' Angela said, pointing directly behind him. 'Just beyond those rocks. There's a straight line. It looks like the corner of a building – something man-made, at any rate.'

Bronson stared at the feature she'd spotted. The rocks closer to them curved slightly outwards, and so only the very bottom of whatever lay around the corner was visible from where they were standing. But from what he could see, it did look like the base of a vertical stone wall.

'Let's check it out,' he said.

'Just over there,' Masters gestured to an area of ground on the left-hand side of the track they'd followed for perhaps a quarter of a mile from the road.

The driver swung the wheel and braked to a halt.

Masters waved the driver of the second four-by-four to park beside it. His four men piled out and stood waiting for orders.

'OK,' he said. 'Break out the assault rifles. Make sure all your magazines are fully charged right now, but do not – I say again – do not chamber a round in either the AKs or your pistols. We can't afford a negligent discharge now. Leave two of the Kalashnikovs and a couple of pistols, plus ammo, between the jeeps for the recce team to collect.'

'Suppose somebody else comes along here?' Cross asked.

Masters just stared at him. 'Out here?' he snapped. 'Get real. The worst that could happen to the weapons is that a goat could come along and crap on them. And gimme that sat-phone.'

Five minutes later they'd locked their vehicles and were heading towards the gully where Bronson and Angela had parked their vehicle.

On the side of the Saser mountain, the grey Land Rover was again mobile, following the same route Bronson had taken. Their plan was to collect the weapons Masters had left for them, drive past the gully, and stop half a mile or so away. They would then position themselves in the hills to the west, too far away to intervene in what was going to happen in the valley, but they'd make sure nobody could get out in that direction.

Caught between two groups of armed men, Bronson and Angela were walking into a trap.

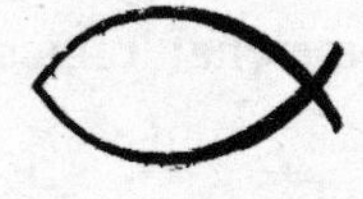

58

'You need to get ready,' Tembla instructed as he walked into the briefing room. He was wearing a set of flying overalls, a survival belt including a holstered pistol around his waist. 'Bronson and Lewis are proceeding on foot up into the valley.'

Killian stepped across to the table and looked down at the map.

'They're here, near these ruins,' Tembla said, 'not far off this road that runs east from Arann. It looks as if they're heading towards the centre of the valley.'

Outside the building, Killian could hear the sound of a jet engine spooling up, and there was a faint whiff of burnt kerosene in the air.

'When do we leave?' he said.

'Not yet. The moment we fly into the valley, everyone will know we are there. Until we're sure they've found something, it's better if we watch what happens through the camera on the Searcher. But I've ordered the helicopters to be manned and their engines started, so we can take off at any moment.'

Killian nodded, somewhat reluctantly. 'Can I see the images?' he asked.

'Of course. Follow me.'

A couple of minutes later, Killian was sitting in an adjacent room staring at a small video screen. On it was an image that moved slightly as the Searcher manoeuvred in the sky, though the area displayed remained reasonably stable.

'This is the jeep,' Tembla said, pointing to an oblong shape in the bottom right of the screen, more or less in the middle of which was a small circle of colour – the mark Tembla's man had painted on the roof of the vehicle. 'Bronson and Lewis are here, standing beside these ruins. But I'm afraid that if they think what they're looking for is inside that building, they're going to be disappointed.'

Bronson stepped around the corner and past the overhanging rock, turned to his right and then stopped.

'What the hell is this place?'

The structure in front of them was very obviously ancient, but at the same time had a strangely modern look, with straight grey-brown stone walls unadorned with decoration. It rose from a level area of ground perhaps fifty yards square, and had two storeys topped by a flat roof, most of which appeared to have fallen down inside the building. All the windows and the two doorways they could see were simply openings in the walls, nothing more. They could see into the building through one of the doorways, where rubble and unidentified rubbish lay scattered across the stone floor.

'I know what it looks like,' Angela said, pulling out her map.

'A deserted monastery?' Bronson suggested. 'A small one?'

'Spot on. Yes, it is – or rather it was – a monastery. In fact, it's even marked on this map.'

She folded the map so that Bronson could see where she was pointing.

'Just there. That symbol and the note right beside it.'

Bronson read the words aloud. 'There's a sort of castle symbol with the words "Namdis Gompa" beside it,' he said. 'I'm a bit surprised it's deserted. You'd have thought some wandering goatherd might have appropriated a place like this for his own use.'

'The locals are very superstitious. This was once a monastery, a holy place, and they'd respect that. They'd never dream of squatting here.'

'Could this be it, do you think?' Bronson said, looking up at the old building. 'The text said something about man-made darkness, which could mean there's a hidden room inside.'

'I wish it was that easy, Chris,' Angela said. 'But we

haven't passed through that cleft in the rock up there, the one the text described as the "pillars".'

'Maybe the writer was referring to the rocks on either side of the gully, down by the road.'

'But the dates don't work. I don't know exactly when this monastery was built, but most of them seem to have been constructed anything from three to five hundred years ago. Even if we're generous with the dating, and assume this was built half a millennium ago, what we're searching for was hidden here fifteen hundred years earlier than that. There's no point in even looking in here.'

'Right,' Bronson said, staring back up the slope, 'onwards and upwards.'

The gully that Bronson and Angela were exploring began as little more than a break in the rock wall. Just to the north of this was an area of sloping ground, at one side of which, and behind a rocky outcropping, the monastery of Namdis Gompa had been built. Beyond that was the cleft in the rocks which Angela had spotted. On the north and north-east side of the valley was a steeper and wider area, dotted with small plateaus where stunted bushes and other scrubby vegetation had gained a precarious foothold.

All this was obvious to Nick Masters as he lay on his belly near the crest of one of the hills that bordered it. He was looking through a pair of binoculars at the scene below him, while about fifty yards back the rest of the men who'd accompanied him sat or lay on the ground, weapons cradled in their hands, bored and waiting for his orders. The exception was Donovan, who was pacing up and down, clearly excited – and irritated.

Masters was careful to keep in the shadow of a rock, because the last thing he wanted was a ray of the afternoon sun to reflect off the glass of his binoculars and alert Bronson to his presence. He kept as low and as motionless as he could, just the way he'd been trained.

He'd already identified the position of their jeep, and now he focused on the two targets themselves. Judging by their gestures, they appeared to be talking about the ruined building in front of them, and for a fleeting moment Masters wondered if this could be the end of the operation, if this old ruin was the resting place of the relic Donovan was so desperate to recover. But then he saw the woman shake her head firmly and point further up the hill. A few moments later they'd both turned and started walking up the slope.

'I didn't expect this,' Bronson muttered as they passed through the cleft in the rocks. In front lay an expanse of rocks and tufty grass. 'It could take us days to search this area properly. Is there any other information that could help narrow down the position?'

Angela shook her head helplessly, then pulled out her notebook and read the lines of the text again. 'It says "between the pillars and beyond their shadows / into the silence and the darkness formed of man". We've passed between the pillars.' She pointed at the jagged-edged gap in the rocks a few yards behind them. 'The next phrase means either that they walked north, so their shadows were in front of them, or maybe that they had to go some distance beyond the shadows cast by the rocks that form those pillars. Either meaning would work, I suppose.'

'Yeah,' Bronson agreed, 'but neither really helps us. It's needle-in-a-haystack time.'

'Don't be so negative, Chris.'

'I'm being realistic.' He waved his arm at the widening valley in front of them. 'This must cover two or three square miles, and over the last two millennia hundreds, maybe thousands, of people must have walked all over it. If there was still anything here to find, surely somebody else would have found it by now?'

Angela nodded. 'But nobody has. When this relic was hidden, the people involved obviously concealed it really well.'

'OK.' Bronson straightened up. 'Let's look at this logically. We're standing on a sloping rocky hillside. The only two possibilities, as far as I can see, are that the treasure is either in some kind of building or hidden inside a cave.' He turned to Angela. 'Let's split up. That way we can cover more ground.'

* * *

Masters watched the two people in the valley below him separate and start to move in different directions. He watched them for a few moments longer, then eased back away from the cliff edge and walked across to where his men were waiting.

'They're moving further up the valley, so you can move parallel to them.' He pointed at an outcropping of rocks about a quarter of a mile north-east of where they were standing. 'Go there, quietly, and make sure you keep out of sight. Keep the sat-phone switched on, but on silent, and wait till I give the word. You stay with me, JJ.'

As his men picked up their weapons and moved off, Masters crawled back to his vantage point and resumed his scrutiny of the valley below.

'Chris!' Angela called out, waving her arm. 'Come here.'

With the constant howling of the wind, Bronson was too far away to hear her distant yell, but he saw her wave and ran across the valley floor towards her.

'Remember the text?' she asked, as he stopped beside her.

'Most of it, yes,' he replied.

'Notice anything?'

Bronson glanced around. 'No.'

'Actually, it's not something I saw – it's something I heard. Listen.'

For a few seconds Bronson listened intently. Then he shook his head.

'Sorry,' he said, 'I can't hear anything.'

'That's what I mean,' Angela said. 'In this area there's no wind noise, and I don't know why. I guess it must be something to do with the shape of the valley.'

Bronson realized she was right. He'd got so used to the constant moaning of the wind that his subconscious mind had tuned it out. But here his brain wasn't having to do any filtering – they were standing there in virtual silence.

'The text says, "between the pillars and beyond their shadows / into the silence." We've come through the pillars and headed north, walking beyond their shadows, and I think we've just stepped "into the silence".'

Bronson stepped towards her and hugged her. 'Did I ever tell you how amazing you are?' he said.

Angela grinned. 'We're not there yet,' she said, pushing him back. 'And this "silent" area is pretty large. It could cover quite a big part of this side of the valley.' She pointed towards the valley wall to the west. 'It's most likely that cliff which diverts the wind. It's probably just blowing right over our heads.'

'But we must be close,' Bronson said. 'Come on – let's keep searching.'

They moved on, further up the valley floor, checking all around them as they went, looking for anything that could possibly match the last half of the penultimate line of the text that had brought them halfway around the world – "the darkness formed of man" – anything, in short, fabricated by human beings rather than a product of nature.

Bronson saw it first. In a small plateau just off to their left he caught a glimpse of a small square structure. He stopped dead.

59

'That can't be it,' Angela said firmly. To their left was a small, cubical building. The stones that made up its structure were the same texture and colour as the surrounding rocks, which was why neither of them had noticed it before. But now they could see it, they also saw the single oblong opening in its front wall – a doorway without a door.

'What?'

'I need to explain something about Lamaist monasteries,' she said, sitting down in front of it. 'Most of them, and certainly all the larger ones, actually consist of two buildings or groups of buildings, in two different places. There's the main structure, like Diskit Gompa that we saw down below, where the two rivers meet, and a second, much smaller building. This is usually quite some distance – maybe three or four miles – from the monastery proper, and usually at a higher altitude. It's like a simple cell, with almost no facilities, and it just provides shelter and a place to sleep.

'Before a monk can become a lama, he is required to spend quite a long period of time in a building like this. He's supposed to meditate in the solitude, completely undisturbed. The monastery provides him with basic food and drink, which is delivered once a day, so that the monk doesn't have to disturb his meditations by preparing meals. It's a bit like the forty days and nights of solitude Christ is supposed to have spent in the desert in Judea after being baptized. And I'm pretty certain that what we're looking at here is the separate house of meditation that belonged to the Namdis Gompa monastery.'

'Oh, shit,' Bronson muttered. 'But it fits the text so well. It's in this weird area of silence, and it's clearly man-made, not to mention dark inside.'

'I agree. It was probably built here precisely because this particular spot is inside this sort of cone of silence, so the constant noise of the wind also wouldn't disturb the meditation of the monks. But you've got exactly the same problem with the dates, Chris – they just don't work. We can take a look inside it, by all means, but it was definitely constructed far too late to be what we're looking for.'

They walked across to the small building and peered into it, but it was empty, just four bare stone walls. There was a tiny cubicle in one corner that had possibly functioned as an earth closet, and a flat stone bench that was presumably intended to be a bed. But apart from that, there was nothing else.

'So what now?' Bronson asked, sitting down beside Angela on the bench.

Angela sighed. 'I still don't think we should be looking for a building, because it just wouldn't be still standing now, not after all this time. I was hoping we'd find a cave, something like that.'

Bronson stiffened. 'I passed one a few minutes ago,' he said.

'Where? Why didn't you tell me?'

'You'd just waved me over,' Bronson said mildly, getting up and pulling her to her feet, 'and I thought you'd found something right here.' He pointed out to the east, back the way he'd come. 'Let's go and see what I found, shall we?'

Two minutes later Bronson led the way in through what actually appeared to be little more than a crack in the rock. But inside, the cave widened out considerably.

'It's a lot bigger than it looks,' Angela said, staring around her in the light from Bronson's torch.

'But no sign of anything that you could interpret as "the darkness formed of man",' Bronson pointed out, shining his torch around the interior of the empty space.

Facing them was a flat rock wall, boulders and lumps of wood resting against it in a tumbled heap. To the right of the rock wall a short tunnel the height of the cave opened up, but terminated in another solid wall of stone after perhaps ten or twelve feet. To the left, there was an even shorter tunnel, just three or four feet deep.

'No,' Angela said sadly. 'To me, this just looks like a cave.'

She turned to leave, but Bronson reached out and grabbed her arm to stop her.

'Doesn't anything strike you as odd about this place?'

Angela shook her head. 'No. It's just a cave, a hole in the rock.'

'But we know that somebody's been in here.'

'How can you tell?'

Bronson pointed at the wall opposite. 'What do you see over there?' he asked.

'Rocks and bits of wood. Why?'

'Exactly. The only way wood can get into a cave is if some person or animal carries it in. Which means that somebody else has been in here too. The question is, when were they here? And what could they have been doing?'

Bronson strode over to the wall and looked down at the debris. 'Some of these look to me like worked timbers,' he said.

He knelt down and started rooting about. Then he picked up a lump of wood, but it crumbled away almost to nothing in his hands.

'These bits of timber must have been in here a long time,' he said slowly, shaking the dust and slivers of wood off his hands. He bent forward and examined the remaining lumps of timber more closely. 'I think this could be a part of a wheel,' he muttered. 'It looks like the rim of a solid wooden wheel. The edge of it is definitely rounded.' He stepped back and looked down again. 'You know, this could possibly be the remains of a cart, something like that.'

'Makes sense,' Angela said dejectedly. 'When the monks from the Namdis Gompa monastery built that house of meditation we've just been in, they'd have had to haul worked stone up here to do it, and they would have needed some sort of cart. When they'd finished it, they probably just stored it here rather than dragging it back down the mountain again.

'They could have worked the stone up here,' Bronson suggested. 'It would have been easier than shaping it down in the valley and then hauling it all the way up here from the monastery.'

'Maybe . . .' Angela said, clearly still unconvinced.

Bronson took another look at the lumps of wood lying on the floor, then turned back towards the entrance. Then he stopped suddenly.

'Just come over here, will you?' he said quietly.

Angela stepped across to where he was standing. 'What is it?' she asked.

Bronson didn't reply, just pointed upwards.

'What?' Angela asked again.

'There, in the roof. See those two parallel lines? There's no way those are natural. Somebody cut those out of the stone with a hammer and chisel.'

On the right-hand side of the rock wall, the cave extended a short distance back into the mountainside, into a short, blind-ended tunnel. What Bronson was pointing at were two straight lines that extended from the side of the vertical rock wall over to their right, a distance of about five or six feet.

'What are they?' Angela asked.

'I know what they look like,' Bronson said, 'though that's almost unbelievable. But there's one way to check.'

'How?'

'Let me show you.'

From his vantage point on the cliffs above, Nick Masters watched the two figures vanish from sight into what he presumed was a cave.

He looked away from his binoculars for a few seconds and stared at his watch. Then he glanced behind him to where Donovan stood, leaning against a boulder, looking uncomfortable.

He slid back from the cliff edge and waved to Donovan to join him. Donovan crouched down and weaved towards him in a clumsy parody of a soldier's advance that would have been funny in any other context. When he got closer, Masters waved him to a stop and knelt beside him.

'Right,' he snapped, his voice low and urgent. 'Keep down, and keep quiet. I know the wind's blowing real hard, but you'd be amazed how far sound can travel at times like this.'

'What's happening?'

Masters explained what he'd seen. 'If they stay in that cave for another ten minutes, I'm giving the go signal.'

Donovan nodded agreement. His instructions to Masters had been very specific – let Bronson and Lewis find the relic, but on no account let them touch it.

'Do you think they've got it?' he asked, his heart pounding with anxiety.

'I don't know,' Masters said. 'But we're sure as hell going to stop them if they have.'

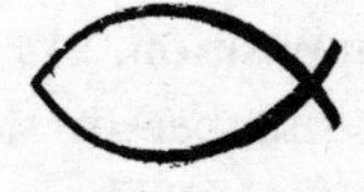

60

Back in Karu, Killian and Tembla stared intently at the video screen. Through the data-link from the Searcher UAV they'd watched two tiny figures look at the ruined monastery building, walk deeper into the valley, and enter another small structure, from which they'd reappeared almost immediately. But now they'd vanished completely.

'They've found a cave,' Killian muttered.

'There are lots of caves in that valley,' Tembla pointed out. 'Let's see if they come out again.'

Five minutes later there was still no sign of the two figures.

'They've found something,' Killian said, standing up. 'We must leave.'

Tembla leaned over to the serviceman who was piloting the UAV and issued a series of orders. Immediately, the image widened as the man switched from the telephoto lens to a wide-angle view that covered the valley walls as well as the floor. Then he began to zoom in on one particular area.

'What are you doing?' Killian asked.

'Checking on the opposition.' As the picture tightened, Tembla pointed at a number of slow-moving dots that were just coming into focus. 'There are the men Donovan recruited. Including Donovan, there are six of them in the valley, the four you can see there and two others who are still watching from the valley wall. There are a couple of others we spotted driving a four-by-four, but they're some distance away, and we don't yet know if they're also a part of the group. And you're right – from the way they move, they are mercenaries. They're also carrying assault rifles, which is good for us.'

'Why?'

'Because it gives us the perfect excuse to eliminate them. You know what we're looking at here, but I'll make sure that all the pictures from the Searcher will just show a group of heavily armed men who've almost certainly entered India illegally. We are entirely within our rights to engage them. Using the Hind might be considered to be overkill, but I'll argue about that later.'

Tembla issued a further instruction and the image changed again, to the view of the rocks where Bronson and Lewis had vanished.

'They're inside the cave,' Tembla said. 'Mark that spot and pass the coordinates to the chopper pilots. Right, Father. It's time we got airborne.'

* * *

Inside the cave Bronson was dragging away the rocks and bits of wood. In a few minutes he'd cleared away most of the debris from a small area, and all that was left underneath it was a thick layer of dust and dirt.

'Look at this,' he said to Angela. He took a knife from his belt – one of the various items of camping equipment he'd bought back in Leh – and pressed the blade into the soil. The tip penetrated no more than a quarter of an inch. Then he moved the blade a few inches away and repeated the operation. This time, the blade slid into the dirt for about six inches. He withdrew the knife blade, moved it even further, and again the tip hit solid rock within less than half an inch.

'You see,' he said. 'There's a groove that runs from the edge of the rock wall across towards the right-hand side of the cave. It's directly below those two lines on the roof.' He paused and looked at Angela. 'In fact, what you're looking at up there isn't a pair of parallel lines at all – it's actually a groove cut into the stone itself, and it's mirrored by an identical groove cut in the floor of the cave.'

'You don't mean . . .' Angela's voice trailed away as she looked from the floor to the roof of the cave, then to the rock wall itself. She stepped forward and carefully felt the stone, running her hand up and down the edge of the wall.

Bronson nodded. 'That isn't a wall of rock. That's a sliding door made of solid stone that somebody went to a lot of trouble to conceal. What we have to do now is find a way to open it.'

Nick Masters checked his watch once more – it was ten minutes and eighteen seconds since Bronson and Lewis had disappeared. He considered his options for a few more seconds then made a decision. Beckoning to Donovan, he moved back from the cliff-edge and made a call on the sat-phone to the small group of mercenaries who were waiting a short distance up the slope.

'The targets have gone into a cave. There's a small stone building on the valley floor – you'll see it when you get down there. The cave entrance is maybe seventy yards east of that. Move forward now, slowly and quietly. Then hold position about thirty yards clear of the cave entrance.'

Next he made a call to the two men who'd been in the Land Rover – and issued orders to them as well.

Finally he checked his Kalashnikov was fully loaded, shouldered the sniper rifle and began a careful descent down into the valley, Donovan following cautiously behind him.

'A stone door, Chris? In your dreams! How would they do it?'

'You're the one who's always banging on about how technologically advanced the ancient races were,' Bronson said, continuing to dig around in the earth with the sheath knife. 'The pyramids have been standing for what – about five thousand years – and you've told me that even today nobody actually knows for sure how the ancient Egyptians managed to build them.'

Angela nodded, almost reluctantly. 'True enough. And some of the passages in them were deliberately blocked by massive stone blocks to foil tomb-robbers, so the technology obviously existed – or at least it did in Egypt. It's just that up here in these mountains, in this country – it's not the kind of thing I expected to find.'

Bronson pointed at the floor, where he'd exposed a long straight-sided groove. 'Once they'd slid the door closed, they jammed rocks under the base of it to stop it moving, filled the channel in the floor with earth and covered it, and the front of the stone door, with rocks and wood. But they couldn't do anything to conceal the channel they'd had to cut in the ceiling.'

He looked up, then back down at the floor. 'They must have used rollers of some kind,' he said, almost talking to himself, 'probably lubricated with animal fat or something like that. I just hope that they used stone instead of wood because of the weight of the door. No, in fact, they *must* have used stone. After two millennia wooden rollers would have simply disintegrated, and the door would have dropped, and maybe even fallen out of the top groove.'

'Can we open it?' Angela asked, her voice trembling with excitement.

'We can have a bloody good try. First, we'll have to shift

all this stuff from in front of it, so there's as little resistance as possible when we try to slide it.'

Together, they cleared all the rocks and bits of timber from the front of the rock wall. Once they'd done so, the edge of the groove the stone door sat in was clearly visible on the ground.

Bronson opened up his haversack and took out a hammer and chisel. Walking to the right-hand end of the stone door, he bent down and started bashing away at the rocks which had been jammed underneath it, and which were acting as wedges to stop the door being opened. In a couple of minutes, he'd chipped them all out and checked under the edge to make sure there was nothing else jamming it in position.

'I can't see anything else locking the door in place,' he said. 'Maybe they relied on those few stone wedges and its sheer weight.'

He stepped closer to the rock, looking for any sign of a hole or another wedge, but found nothing. It appeared that the stone door would slide to the right as long he could find some way of exerting enough leverage to start it moving – though that obviously wasn't going to be easy.

He rummaged in his rucksack and pulled out a crowbar, fully aware that such a puny tool – and even his own strength – might prove inadequate. He looked at the left-hand side of the stone wall, trying to decide where he should try levering it. There were a few gaps that he could see that might be wide enough to let him drive the end of the crowbar into them, but he knew it all depended on how much the stone door weighed and the condition of the rollers that he was sure had to be underneath it, in the groove cut in the stone floor. Then he looked across at Angela, who, like him, was entirely absorbed in the task confronting them.

'Are you ready for this?' he asked.

'She might not be, but I sure as hell am,' JJ Donovan snapped as he walked into the cave, two armed men crowding in behind him.

61

'How long?' Killian demanded. He was strapped into the back seat of the Dhruv and the rubber strap of the throat mike was uncomfortably tight around his neck. His voice vibrated as he spoke, but the other men in the helicopter – the two pilots in the front seats, one of them acting as the navigator, and Tembla sitting beside him – seemed to have no difficulty understanding each other.

'Twelve minutes to the edge of the valley,' the pilot replied. 'And then thirty seconds to the target.'

The Dhruv was flying at about ninety knots – just over a hundred miles an hour – due north and had just reached the Shyok river valley. The pilot altered course very slightly to the west to follow the path of the tumbling river, rugged brown hills and mountains rising well above the helicopter on both sides.

Behind and slightly to the right of the Dhruv was the Hind, a menacing and unfamiliar shape, its stubby wings bristling with ordnance, the light reflecting off the individual windscreens of the tandem cockpits. Tembla had told him that the cockpits and the vital systems on the Hind were armour-plated, and the most that a round from an assault rifle could do was dent it.

Tembla had, of course, been correct. If all the opposition they'd face in the Nubra Valley was half a dozen men armed with Kalashnikovs, using the Hind was overkill. But these were the kind of odds Killian liked. He smiled in satisfaction as he imagined the terror that would follow the totally unexpected appearance of the helicopter gunship.

Tembla tapped the navigator on the shoulder. 'Get me an update,' he instructed.

There was a click as the man went off the intercom to use the radio. A few moments later he had the answer from the UAV operator at the base outside Karu.

'Bronson and Lewis are still inside the cave,' Tembla said. 'And three of the other men we've been watching have just gone in after them.'

Bronson and Angela spun round, shocked by the unexpected sound of the nasal American voice and the sudden appearance of three men, two of them carrying automatic weapons.

'So we meet again,' Donovan said. 'I've been following you ever since that night at the country house in England.'

Bronson looked from one man to the other. The man

doing the talking was unarmed, but obviously the real power lay with him. The figure standing beside him looked like a soldier, tough, composed and sure of himself, the Kalashnikov assault rifle in his hands clearly a familiar tool, another heavy rifle slung over his shoulder.

'You're the guy who hit me,' Bronson said to the American, a statement, not a question.

Donovan nodded.

'But how on earth did you follow us?'

'When I heard you tell Jonathan Carfax that your wife worked at the British Museum, I put a tracking chip in your mobile. I was right behind you all the time you two were wasting your time digging around in Egypt.'

'You were in the cream Mercedes,' Bronson hazarded, 'on the road to el-Hiba?'

'Well spotted. Just satisfy my curiosity – how did you make the connections to find this place?'

Bronson looked at Angela. Since the intruders had appeared, she'd not said a word, but one glance was enough to tell him she was both furious and frightened. Pretty much Rule One in Bronson's book was never irritate a man carrying an assault rifle, and definitely not a man who employed people who carried assault rifles. So before she could say something they might both regret, he intervened.

'We really thought we were looking for the Ark of the Covenant,' he said, placing a restraining hand on Angela's arm. 'At first, all the clues seemed to point to that.'

'So that explains your trip to Egypt,' Donovan said, looking satisfied. 'You thought the Pharaoh Shoshenq might have seized it from the Temple of Jerusalem and taken it to Tanis? But why in hell did you think you were looking for the Ark?'

Whoever the man was, it was immediately clear that he knew what he was talking about.

Angela relaxed very slightly. 'I found a reference in a grimoire,' she said.

'Which one?'

'The *Liber Juratus* or *Liber Sacratus*,' Angela replied. 'It dates from the thirteenth century,' she added.

Donovan nodded. 'Ah,' he said. '*The Sworne Booke of Honorius*, also known as the *Liber Sacer*.'

'So you do know what might be in this cave?' Angela asked.

'Absolutely,' Donovan said, smiling. 'That's why we're here now.'

The armed man at the back of the cave – John Cross – shuffled his feet in irritation. 'Will somebody here just tell me what the hell this is all about?' he muttered.

Angela looked at him, then switched her gaze back to Donovan. 'You haven't told them?' she demanded.

Donovan shook his head. 'What convinced you that you weren't on the trail of the Ark?'

'Two things,' Angela said tightly. 'The first was the expression "the light which had become / the treasure". Making that fit the Ark of the Covenant was a stretch, though we tried. But if the "treasure" becomes the "light", as the Persian text says, then everything changes. The phrase "the treasure of the world" is one thing, but "the light of the world" means something completely different. And then there was a statement about the relic being removed from Mohalla.'

She paused and looked expectantly at Donovan, who just shook his head.

'There's a reference to it in the Quran,' Angela added. 'The full name of the place is Mohalla Anzimarah. Does that help?'

Again Donovan shook his head.

'Anzimarah is in the Kashmir, in the old town district of Srinigar, in the Khanjar quarter. There's a building there called the "Rozabal", an abbreviation of *Rauza Bal*. The word *rauza* means "the tomb of the prophet". Inside the building there are two tombs, and two gravestones. One of them is the grave of the Islamic saint Syed Nasir-ud-Din, who was buried there in the fifth century. The second, larger gravestone is for another man. Right now, Srinigar's effectively in the middle of a war zone, but the Rozabal was investigated by several people a few years back, and details about the building are fairly well established.'

Angela took a breath. Still no one interrupted her. 'Both the gravestones point north-south, in accordance with Muslim custom, but the actual graves are located in a crypt under the floor of the building. In the crypt, the sarcophagus of Syed Nasir-ud-Din also points north-south, as you'd expect, but the other tomb is aligned east-west, which signifies that the occupant was neither an Islamic saint nor a Hindu. Aligning a grave east-west is actually a Jewish custom. In other words, its occupant would have been a follower of Moses.'

She looked at Bronson who nodded for her to continue. 'The name on the second tomb is Yuz Asaf, but he was also known as Yus Asaph, which translates as the "leader of the purified", and that specifically refers to lepers who'd been cured of the disease. The first few lines of the Persian text explained how the son of "Yus of the purified" ordered that the "light which had become the treasure" was to be removed from Mohalla and taken back to the place it had come from. I assumed that meant that the light or the treasure had been located somewhere here, in this valley. The next section of the text described how the treasure was hidden in a "place of stone" in the "valley of flowers". Put all that together and you have a recognizable description of a group of men removing something from Mohalla and hiding it out here.

'There's only one generally accepted meaning for the expression "the light of the world",' Angela stated. Bronson could tell that she had virtually forgotten she was being held at gunpoint, such was the excitement in her face. 'I believe that two millennia ago, the son of Yus Asaph and a band of devoted followers removed one of the bodies from the tomb in Srinigar and transported it here, into this specially prepared cave in the mountains, where they hid it, hoping it would stay hidden for all eternity.'

'But why did they do that?' the man standing beside Donovan asked.

'It may have been instigated by Buddhist monks. Buddhism started around five hundred BC, and by the first century AD travelling monks were visiting India and Tibet. They wouldn't have wanted the location of the tomb to become widely known, for fear that it would become a place of pilgrimage, and they might also have worried that it could dilute the message of their own religion.

'I also think it's possible they spread a story that the man didn't die here, but had returned to his own country and died there years earlier, whereas in fact he lived out his days in Kashmir. And we know he fathered a child here, a man named Isaac, according to the Persian text. In fact, I think that Isaac was either the author of that text or very closely acquainted with the person who wrote it.'

'And there's the Baigdandu anomaly,' Donovan interjected.

'That's a contributing factor, yes,' Angela nodded. 'Whatever the source of the genes that throw up occasional fair-skinned, blue-eyed children in that village, you can be reasonably certain it wasn't some wandering tribe of Greeks. It's far more likely to have been a single source, one very different bloodline that became intermixed with the local genetic make-up.'

'This is making no sense to me,' John Cross interrupted. 'What is this all about?'

Angela smiled at him, half-turned and pointed at the wall behind her. 'On the other side of that stone door,' she continued, 'we'll find a tomb, and in it will be the body of a late-middle-aged or elderly man who in his time acquired a certain reputation, both here and in the country of his birth, which is a long way to the west of here. In India, he was called Yus Asaph or Yuz Asaf, and occasionally Isa-Masih, but you all know him better by another, much more familiar, name.'

She looked around the cave, taking her time. She took a deep breath.

'I believe that in the cavern just behind me is the last resting place of Isa-Masih or Jesus the Messiah – the man better known to you all as Jesus Christ.'

62

'Four minutes,' the pilot murmured.

'OK. Time we sent the Hind in front,' Tembla said, then issued a crisp order.

Almost immediately, the pilot of the Dhruv banked the helicopter to the left, hauling it around in a tight turn.

As the manoeuvre started, Killian glanced to his right and saw the Hind gunship's nose dip slightly as the pilot accelerated ahead of them. Then he concentrated on keeping what little he'd had for breakfast in his stomach as the Dhruv seemed to roll completely on to its side, the 'whup-whup-whup' of the rotor blades clawing at the air rose to a crescendo, the sound exploding through his skull as the chopper seemed to defy both gravity and the laws of physics.

Below the aircraft, the ground spun past at a dizzying speed, a grey-brown featureless blur. Then the pilot righted the helicopter, pulling it straight, the nose dipping as he increased speed.

Killian looked through the windscreen and saw that the Hind was now well ahead of them, maybe half a mile in front.

'Good,' Tembla said. 'We'll let the gunship take out the mercenaries; then we'll go in and see what Bronson and Angela Lewis are up to.'

For a long moment there was absolute silence in the cave, then John Cross muttered, 'Bull*shit*.'

Donovan started a slow, ironic hand-clap. 'Bravo,' he said. 'Impeccable reasoning based upon an imaginative and expert interpretation of the available evidence. It's just a shame you'll never get to find out whether or not you're right.'

Angela looked startled.

'What's behind that wall may be the most important archaeological find ever,' Donovan continued, 'but it means far more to me than that. If the stories in the Bible are true – and I believe that they are – then Jesus had the power to heal the sick and raise the dead. That's why I've been following this trail for so long. Just think what I could do with that kind of power today.'

'But how can the bones of a two-thousand-year-old corpse be . . . ?' Bronson's voice trailed off as he made the connection.

'You're a geneticist,' Angela said flatly, making an

intuitive leap. 'And the whole purpose of all this' – she gestured at the armed men in the cave – 'is so that you can get your hands on the body. Or more accurately get your hands on a sample of tissue from the remains.'

Donovan nodded. 'That's what I've been looking for all along – the DNA of Jesus Christ. Have you the slightest idea what that could be worth today? To medical science? To cutting-edge genetic research? To achieve this, any risk, any price, and any sacrifice is entirely justified. And that's why I'm afraid you're both going to have to die. There can be no witnesses to what happens next.'

'What about the two men with you?' Bronson asked, desperate to keep some sort of dialogue going. 'Have you told them about the sacrifice you'll be expecting them to make?'

Donovan smiled. 'These men are part of my private army. I'd trust them with my life. But I'm afraid you two are surplus to requirements.' He turned to Masters. 'Kill them, will you, Nick, and then we can get started.'

A few yards further up the valley from the cave entrance, one of Masters's men was sitting on a rock, his Kalashnikov resting across his lap, his hand holding the pistol grip. About fifty yards down the slope, another two of the mercenaries were staring down towards the foot of the valley, their AK-47s slung over their shoulders. The three men were covering the two possible approaches to the cave.

They all heard the unmistakable roaring, clattering sound

of a helicopter and for an instant none of them took any notice. They knew they were in a disputed border area, and they had seen and heard several helicopters since they'd crossed into India, so a chopper wasn't exactly a new sight. But then the Hind appeared over the side wall of the valley, nose-down and heading straight towards the cave.

'Take cover!' one of the men yelled, swinging his weapon round to point at the approaching gunship, as his companion opened fire.

The mercenary closest to the cave looked round desperately for somewhere – anywhere – to hide. He knew he'd never make it to the cave entrance, but it was the only possible shelter. He had to try.

His finger slid on to the trigger of his AK-47 and fired a long burst, then turned and started running. But at that very moment the crew of the attack helicopter opened fire. There was a flicker of flame from the nose of the aircraft and a stream of machine-gun bullets ploughed a deep furrow across the rocky ground, ricochets from the impact of the shells and rock splinters flying everywhere.

Half a dozen rounds caught the running man in the chest and almost cut him in two. His momentum carried him forward another couple of steps, but he was dead before he stopped moving.

The Hind's crew switched their aim, and in less than two seconds the other soldiers' weapons fell silent as their bullet-riddled bodies slumped down among the rocks.

* * *

The cave echoed with the sound of automatic weapons' fire. The armed man at the back of the cave reacted immediately, unslinging their weapon and starting to move. Bronson's attention was fixed on Masters.

The former soldier glanced across at him, then at John Cross and what little was visible of the mountain slope outside the cave. Then he reached inside his parka and pulled out a semi-automatic pistol.

For an instant Bronson thought he was going to shoot them both. Instead the soldier turned, and in a single fluid movement reversed the weapon in his hand and tossed the pistol over to Bronson. Then he swung back, snapped off the safety catch of his Kalashnikov and headed for the cave entrance.

Donovan was white with fear and anger. 'What's happening?' he demanded.

'Just get out of sight, JJ, and shut the hell up while I sort this,' Masters snapped. Then he turned away. 'Don't go outside,' he yelled.

But he'd picked his men well – they were all ex-military – and the last thing John Cross was going to do was run out of a dark cave into bright sunlight where enemy troops were probably waiting to cut him down.

Bronson didn't question, didn't hesitate. He caught the weapon in mid-air, grabbed Angela by the hand and pulled her as far away from the entrance as he could.

'What's going on?' she demanded breathlessly, crouching beside him in the darkness at the far end of the short right-hand tunnel of the cave.

Bronson craned his neck as he tried to see outside. 'That sounded to me like two different weapons. One was definitely like a heavy machine-gun, and that could mean—' He broke off as a renewed burst of firing sounded from outside the cave, and then a familiar deep throbbing noise, overlaid by the roar of jet engines.

'That's a chopper.' Bronson pulled back the slide on the pistol to chamber a round and clicked on the safety catch. 'Maybe some Indian Army troops have pitched up.'

He looked around the cave. There was nowhere they could hide. He didn't know how many men the American had at his disposal, although clearly he'd left at least one or two outside the cave, otherwise there would have been no firing. He also had no idea how many troops were in the attacking force, and no clue what the outcome of the fire-fight was likely to be.

But there was one thing he could do that might help their personal odds a little. And he needed to do it straight away.

63

Nick Masters stood in the entrance to the cave. Down the slope he could see the unmoving shape of one of the three men he'd left on sentry duty. Over to his right, in a left-hand turn, the evil light-grey painted shape of the Hind gunship was unmistakable.

'Shit,' he muttered.

'What the hell's that gunship doing out here?' John Cross asked.

As he spoke, the Hind lined up for its next attack, and a short burst from its cannon chewed up the ground immediately in front of the cave entrance. Both men ducked back inside.

Masters tore his glance away from the Hind and looked around the cave. There was no other way out, that was for sure, and nowhere they could hide where the gunship's weapons couldn't find them.

Despite the odds, Masters knew they had to neutralize

the Hind. But how? With three men dead – and a friend whom he now realised was way too greedy and ambitious for his own good – he was fresh out of options.

'Wait here,' Bronson hissed at Angela, and crept forward.

JJ Donovan was cowering behind a pile of rocks, trying to make himself as small as possible. He was staring fixedly at the cave entrance.

Bronson stepped up behind him, smashed the butt of the pistol into the side of his head, then grabbed him by the collar and dragged him to the back of the cave.

'What on earth are you doing, Chris?' Angela snapped, her indignation at Bronson's attack on an unarmed man temporarily overcoming her fear.

'I'm giving us an edge,' Bronson said, resting the barrel of the semi-automatic pistol on Donovan's shoulder so that the end of it rested against the side of his neck. 'As I see it, there are two groups of armed men out there fighting each other. I don't know who this guy is, but if his people come out on top, the fact that he's my hostage might mean we can talk our way out of here.'

'And if the other group wins?'

He sighed. 'Then it won't matter either way.'

When Masters had seen the Barrett on sale in the arms bazaar in Islamabad, he'd immediately decided to buy it. He didn't imagine they'd need to use it, but it was a useful insurance policy. Now he was glad he'd spent the extra money.

The Barrett is arguably the most powerful rifle in the world. In expert hands it is capable of placing a half-inch bullet in a man-size target at a range of well over a mile.

And Masters was an expert. A former SEAL, his particular speciality had been sniping. Thirty seconds after the Hind's heavy machine-gun had annihilated three of his men, he had the weapon loaded and aimed, and was looking through the scope towards his target.

But that, of course, was only half the problem. There was no doubt in Masters' mind that he could hit the Hind. But hitting it wouldn't be enough. The supersonic half-inch bullet would leave a hell of a dent in the chopper's armour plating, but wouldn't penetrate it. There was no point in aiming at the twin cockpits, because they were heavily protected, and the engines, too, would be a difficult target with no guarantee the round would destroy or even damage them.

But there were weaknesses with the Hind, as with all helicopters, and these were what Masters was going to try for. And he would, he figured, have only the one shot. If he missed, and the crew of the gunship spotted he was firing from the cave, they'd torch the area and that would be that.

He had to make the shot count.

He turned to John Cross. 'I need a clear shot at that gunship, and the only way I'm going to get it is if the crew are lookin' somewhere else. Can you exit the cave with your hands up, and then move over to the left?'

Cross looked shocked. 'Sounds like a hell of a bad idea to me.'

'If you can think of something better, just tell me right now.'

Cross stepped forwards and peered cautiously out of the cave entrance. The Hind was quartering the area, the crew apparently looking for anyone else outside the cave.

'OK, Nick,' he said at last. 'This had goddamn better work.'

Lowering his Kalashnikov to the ground he walked slowly to the mouth of the cave.

A sudden noise from his left attracted his attention. Another helicopter, this one a small utility aircraft, was approaching. As he looked, the pilot flared and landed it about a hundred yards away, keeping the rotors turning.

Cross stepped forward and raised both arms above his head in a clear and unequivocal gesture of surrender. He just hoped that the crew of the gunship hadn't been instructed to sanitize the area, and that they would be prepared to take prisoners.

Well, he reflected, as the nose of the Hind swung around towards him, he'd soon find out.

64

The moment the Dhruv touched down, Michael Killian released his seatbelt and fumbled for the door handle.

'Wait,' Tembla instructed. 'We haven't secured the area yet.'

'They've surrendered,' Killian retorted, pointing at the man standing outside the cave entrance. 'It's all over. I need to see what they found.'

He pulled off his throat mike, stepped out of the helicopter and started walking quickly over towards the cave.

'Your orders, sir?' the pilot asked.

'We'll stay here, just in case,' Tembla said. 'We're not carrying weapons, and I'm still not satisfied this situation's under control. There were six men in the area, plus Bronson and Lewis, but all I can see are three bodies and one man who's got his hands in the air. That still leaves four people unaccounted for. Until I know their locations,

I'm not moving. And if the mercenaries are still at large, maybe one of them will do me a favour and shoot that irritating priest.'

As Masters had hoped, when Cross walked out of the cave entrance and over to the left, the Hind moved slightly to follow his path. The pilot brought the gunship to a low hover about fifty feet off the ground and perhaps seventy yards away from the cave. He then selected the public address system and keyed the microphone.

'Step forward five paces, then lie face down,' he ordered.

Cross obeyed, keeping his movements slow and deliberate.

In the cave, Nick Masters took a deep breath, and concentrated on the sight picture. The Hind had swung round slightly clockwise, and he could now see most of the port side of the aircraft.

Helicopters have several weaknesses, but the big three are those parts of the machine that keep it in the air – the main rotor, the tail rotor and the gearboxes that drive them. The gearboxes were probably hidden behind armour plate – Masters didn't know enough about the design of the Hind even to be sure where they were – and because he was looking at the helicopter from the side, the main rotor was almost invisible. So his target of choice – in fact his only target – was the tail rotor.

Slowly, carefully, Masters adjusted his aim, settled down until the sight picture was absolutely clear, then gently squeezed the trigger.

The Barrett kicked into his shoulder – he'd almost forgotten how hard the weapon's recoil was. When he'd recovered, he checked the view through his telescopic sight. There was a neat hole drilled through the rear of the fuselage about six inches forward of the tail rotor disk. Damn, he thought. The chopper had obviously moved very slightly at the moment he'd fired. But the Hind was still in the same position, so he guessed that the bullet had simply passed through a part of the fuselage without armour plating, and the crew had felt nothing and were still unaware what had happened.

Masters settled his breathing – the weapon was semi-automatic and another round was already in the chamber – and again concentrated all his attention on the view through the telescopic sight. Moments later, he squeezed the trigger once more.

Travelling at supersonic speed, the half-inch bullet hit almost the exact centre of the tail rotor disk. The rotors were designed to withstand the impact of rounds from small-arms fire and even bullets from assault rifle, but the Barrett M82 was in a different league.

The bullet tore one blade completely off the hub and splintered and twisted the one next to it. That in itself would probably have been enough to cripple the helicopter, but the round hadn't yet completed its journey.

It ploughed on, smashing through the thin aluminium skin of the fuselage into the tail rotor gearbox. The bullet crumpled and deformed as its kinetic energy was spent, and the effect on the gearbox itself was catastrophic. The casing split, driving fragments of metal between the spinning gears and cogs. In a little under a tenth of a second after the bullet hit, the gearbox seized solid.

As the gunship lurched sideways, Masters saw a portion of one of the tail rotor blades spin away from the fuselage. The nose of the helicopter lifted as the pilot struggled to control an aircraft that suddenly wasn't responding the way it should. He tried to gain height, which was exactly the wrong thing to do, because it made the situation worse. As the nose pitched even higher, the gunship started to spin on its own axis.

And then there was nothing the pilot could do. The moment the tail rotor gearbox seized, he'd lost all directional control. The spin became even more violent and suddenly the Hind was plummeting to the ground, the main rotor blades smashing into rocks, debris flying in all directions as the fuselage impacted. There was a brief moment of silence, and then the fuel in the helicopter's ruptured tanks ignited, turning the wreckage into a massive fireball.

Masters stepped back into the cave feeling drained. It was over. The crew inside the Hind could not have survived the impact – or the fire. There was nothing more for him to do.

* * *

Sitting in the rear seat of the Dhruv, Tembla watched the catastrophe unfold in front of him. He had to get out. The overwhelming tactical superiority afforded him by the presence of the Hind had gone, and he was suddenly uncomfortably aware that he was sitting in a thin-skinned and extremely vulnerable helicopter, and less than a hundred yards away was a group of mercenary soldiers armed with assault rifles.

'Abort! Abort!' he yelled. 'Get us out of here now!'

The pilot reacted immediately, hauling up on the collective and swinging the aircraft in a tight climbing turn away from the cave, accelerating as hard as he could towards the edge of the valley.

Killian was standing open-mouthed, staring at the scene of devastation in front of him. Then he heard an escalating engine note from behind him and glanced back to see the Dhruv taking off.

He watched helplessly as the man who'd walked out of the cave – and then apparently surrendered – stood up and drew a pistol. Holding his weapon ready, he started to work his way across the slope towards him. Killian looked around, but there was nowhere to run, and nowhere to hide, a cliché come hideously to life. He raised his arms and waited.

But even as he watched the armed man approach, he smiled slightly. Whatever happened now, he was content.

If the Lord God had not wanted him to be here, in this place and at this time, he would not be here. God clearly still had a task for him to complete. He closed his eyes. 'Thy will be done, oh Lord,' he prayed.

John Cross strode over to where Killian stood. 'On the ground, face down, arms and legs wide apart,' he ordered.

Killian obeyed, and Cross quickly and expertly searched him.

'Who's this?' Nick Masters asked, walking across to them.

'No idea, but he climbed out of that chopper that buggered off, so he must have something to do with whatever the hell this is all about. Maybe Donovan would like a word with him? Nice shooting, by the way.'

'Thanks,' Masters replied. He reached down, grabbed the recumbent figure by the collar and hauled him unceremoniously to his feet.

'You speak English?' Masters asked, and their captive nodded.

'OK. We're going down to the cave. You try to get away and I'll shoot your legs from under you – you understand that?'

The man nodded again, and the short procession started making its way across the slope towards the dark shadow that delineated the cave entrance.

65

'Masters!' Donovan called out, as the mercenary soldier walked back into the cave. 'Bronson's got a gun. You've got to help me.'

Masters walked over to where Bronson was holding Donovan, the barrel of the semi-automatic pistol pressed into his neck.

'Where did he get the gun?' Donovan demanded.

'I gave it to him,' Masters said simply.

'You did what? Why the hell did you do that?'

'Because I'm a soldier, not a hired killer. That means I don't shoot unarmed people whose only crime seems to be that they're smarter than you are, Donovan.'

There was a commotion as Cross dragged in another man and slammed him against the wall.

'Who are you?' Cross demanded roughly, pushing his gun into the captive's chest.

The man peered around in the gloom, his eyes adjusting slowly to the darkness, but didn't reply.

'Chris, it's the priest,' Angela said, standing up. Her voice carried clearly across the cave. 'He was the one who tried to kill me.'

'Did he now?' Masters murmured. 'Not exactly what I'd expect from a priest.'

'My name is Father Michael Killian, and I am an ordained minister of the Church.' The man's voice was rough and hoarse. 'Whatever I do, I am doing God's work. I know you,' he said, looking at Donovan, who was still being held by Bronson. 'And if it's the last thing I ever do, I'll stop this appalling blasphemy you've been planning. That's what I've been sent here to do.'

'Sent by whom?' Bronson asked.

'By God Himself,' Killian said, pride in his voice. 'I am His messenger, and His agent.'

'Gimme a break,' Masters muttered.

'This isn't blasphemy, you lunatic,' Donovan shouted. 'This could be the greatest single advance in the history of medicine since the invention of anaesthetics or the discovery of antibiotics.'

'And it'll make you a multi-billionaire in the process. But I don't suppose that's influenced your decision in any way,' Killian spat.

Masters looked from one man to the other, almost smiling at the vitriol. 'Well, it doesn't look to me like either of you is in any position to do much, one way or the other.' He paused, then stepped across to the flat wall. 'Let's take a look at what we have here. This *is* the place you wanted to find, JJ?'

Donovan nodded, while Killian struggled furiously against Cross's iron grip. 'This is sacrilege, blasphemy.'

'Can't be both, can it?' Masters remarked, studying the wall carefully. 'Not both at the same time, I mean? And it's interesting that you and your guys were quite happy to follow us here in that goddamned Hind and try to kill us all, but when it comes to opening up a tomb you come over all Old Testament. Sounds to me like you're sending out a mixed message there.'

'Your lives are irrelevant,' Killian shouted. 'What you're trying to do here could damn your immortal soul for all eternity.'

'That's the kind of thing I mean,' Masters said mildly. 'Definitely Old Testament.' He turned to Cross. 'If that idiot says anything else, put a round through his stomach then throw him outside. He's starting to give me a headache.'

'Pleasure,' Cross murmured. He swept Killian's legs from under him and aimed his pistol downwards. 'Just give me a reason,' he said.

'We think it slides,' Angela said. She gave Killian a withering glare, then walked across to stand beside Masters. 'Chris found grooves cut in the floor and ceiling.' She pointed towards the edge of the stone wall.

'Got it,' Masters said. 'So we need to lever on the left-hand side, I guess, to start it moving.'

'There's a crowbar on the floor by the wall,' Bronson said, not loosening his grip on Donovan's collar. 'And if you look in my rucksack, Angela, you'll find a couple of big screwdrivers as well.'

'I like a man who comes prepared,' Masters said, as Angela handed him the bag.

'We were expecting some kind of tomb,' she said, 'not a wall made of solid stone. I don't know if a crowbar's going to be enough to shift that.'

'They must have mounted it on rollers,' Bronson said. 'Nothing else makes sense. Once it's started moving, it should be fairly easy to shift.'

'Yeah, the trick is gonna be gettin' it started.' Masters gestured to Cross. 'Here, John. You're stronger than I am. I'll watch the priest. You wanna try gettin' this sucker open?'

As Cross picked up the crowbar and started tapping the stone wall, working out where to insert the end of the tool, Bronson looked at the expressions on the faces of the people in the cave. Donovan was quivering with what he guessed was a mixture of fury and anticipation, while Killian glowered with impotent anger against the far wall. Between them, Masters and Angela stood together, studying the stone wall with cool appraisal.

'There's a kind of notch just here,' Cross said. 'Reckon I can just about get the end of the wrecking bar into it.'

There was a metallic scraping sound as he rammed the end of the crowbar into the narrow gap he'd found in the rock, then a deep grunt as he heaved on the end of the tool.

'Nothing,' Cross said. 'No movement at all. You sure there's no lock or anything, nothing jamming it?'

'There were some stones wedged under the right-hand side,' Bronson offered, 'but I thought I'd shifted all of them.'

Masters turned to look at Bronson. 'Keep that pistol, but I think you might as well turn Donovan loose. He won't cause you any trouble.'

Bronson released his grip gratefully, flexed his fingers and stood up. He tucked the pistol into the waistband of his trousers, then moved forward to stand beside Angela.

'Just thinking about it from a mechanical point of view,' he said, 'it would make sense if they had done something else to lock the door in place. The last thing they would want would be for an earthquake to shake it open.'

He leaned forward and spent a few minutes running the tips of his fingers over the old stone. On the right-hand side of the door he felt something, and stepped back to see it from a distance.

'Yes, that could be it,' he murmured, pointing at a roughly oval-shaped mark on the stone about six feet off the ground. 'That could be the end of a stone wedge, driven right through the door and then trimmed off flat on this side. It seems to be made of the same stone as the door itself, but the grain, or whatever the correct term is for the marks inside rock, goes the wrong way.'

He picked up the hammer and chisel, strode across to the stone wall, placed the end of the chisel against the oval mark and smashed the hammer on to it. Stone chips flew. He repeated the operation, and again bits of stone broke off and flew all around him. He stopped briefly and peered at the wall.

'I've broken the end off,' he said, 'but now I can see that a hole was cut through the stone and this wedge driven into it.'

Bronson repositioned the chisel in the centre of the mark and hit it again. This time, very few chips of stone flew out, but the whole lump of stone that had been driven into the hole moved slightly inwards.

'That's more like it!' he said triumphantly. He drew back the hammer and hit it again.

The chisel travelled almost all the way through the hole as the stone wedge vanished from sight. There was a hollow thud as it landed on the floor of the cave somewhere on the inside of the stone door.

'Brilliant, Chris,' Angela said, as he stepped back.

'That looks like another one,' Masters said, pointing at a spot about three feet off the ground and directly below the hole where Bronson had shifted the first stone wedge.

'I'll do it,' Cross said, taking the hammer and chisel.

Bronson moved back to where Angela stood watching, when a sudden thought occurred to him.

'Just a moment.' He picked up his rucksack and pulled out a torch then walked across to the hole he'd revealed and shone the light inside the hidden chamber.

'What can you see?' Angela demanded.

'Nothing very much,' Bronson replied, 'except maybe the stone of the wall opposite. But that wasn't what I was looking for.'

'So what were you checking out?' Masters asked.

'The hole itself,' Bronson replied, turning away from the wall. 'It's tapered. It's wider on the inside than the outside of the door.'

'So?' Masters asked.

But Angela had already grasped what he meant. 'So you mean the stone wedges—'

'Exactly,' Bronson said. 'The holes taper from the inside to the outside, so they must have been put in place from within the tomb itself. Unless there's another way out of there, whoever drove those wedges into place is still in there, on the other side of that wall.'

66

'Oh, God,' Angela muttered, and even Masters looked a little pale.

'Yeah, well, he'll just be another stiff, won't he?' Cross muttered, and with a massive single blow of the hammer drove the second wedge completely through the door.

Immediately the whole stone wall shifted very slightly, a movement they heard rather than saw.

'Looks like we could have lift-off,' Cross said. He dropped the hammer and chisel and picked up the crowbar again. He slid one end into the hole he'd found before, and pulled as hard as he could on the other end. This time, the massive stone door moved perhaps half an inch to the right.

Cross changed the position of the crowbar slightly and pulled again. Within fifteen minutes, the three of them – Cross, Masters and Bronson – had moved the door as far as it would go to the right, so that the top edge was resting against another block of stone.

Masters glanced at Bronson and Angela. 'Your privilege, if you want it,' he said. 'You've earned it.'

'What about me?' Donovan called out angrily from behind them.

'You can wait your goddamned turn,' Masters snapped.

'Let me go first,' Bronson said. He picked up his torch and stepped forward. But before he entered, he bent down and looked down at the channel in the stone floor that had been exposed by sliding the door over to one side.

'I was right,' he said. 'They used stone rollers.' Then he straightened up and walked into the inner chamber.

For perhaps two or three minutes the others watched the beam of the torch dancing around the inner chamber, fitfully illuminating the walls and floor and an oblong stone shape. Then Bronson reappeared.

'It's safe,' he said, 'and there's at least one really old corpse in there, though he's just bones and rags. We'll need as much light as possible.'

Masters grabbed a couple of torches and followed Bronson and Angela inside.

All three of them paused just inside the inner chamber and looked around them.

'Did you touch anything?' Angela asked, sending the beam of her torch travelling around the small room.

'Apart from the corpse, nothing at all.'

Directly in front of them was an oblong stone structure,

the top made of large flat stone slabs, the sides from smaller, cubical stones, the whole thing standing about three feet tall, four feet wide and eight feet long, and at first sight apparently devoid of markings or decoration. But Bronson had spotted something.

'There's a mark on the middle slab,' he said.

Angela walked forward to the stone structure, shining a torch directly at the carving. 'It looks to me like an early Tibetan script, and I think the letters are probably Y and A.'

'Yus Asaph,' Bronson murmured.

But it wasn't the marking on the slab that was holding anyone's attention. At the foot of the structure, in what looked like the foetal position, lay the crumbling bones of a skeleton clad in a few wisps of cloth.

'I think,' Bronson said, his voice sounding unnaturally loud in the silent room, 'that he might have died on his knees and then fallen sideways.'

'In prayer, you mean?' Angela asked in a whisper.

'Maybe.'

'You think that's what's left of the guy who sealed the door?' Masters asked.

Bronson nodded. 'The bones are really fragile. I touched one of them and it just crumbled away to nothing.'

'And what we're looking for is in that stone thing at the back? The thing that looks a bit like a big altar?'

'Probably,' Angela said, sounding oddly subdued.

'Right, then,' Masters said briskly. 'You can bet the

Indian Army will be heading this way pretty soon, so we'd best get on with it. I'll get Cross in here, and I suppose Donovan as well. After all, he paid for this little adventure.'

With Cross and Masters doing the shifting, removing the stone slabs from the top of the altar-like structure didn't take long.

When the last one had been lifted off and stacked against the wall, they all stepped forward and peered into the cavity. As well as Bronson and Angela, Masters had allowed both Donovan and Killian to witness what he called 'the unveiling'.

The stone cavity appeared to be just that, three low stone walls abutting the back wall of the inner chamber, and inside it was a large wooden box, much bigger than a conventional coffin.

'Come on, then, get it open,' Donovan demanded, some of his old bravado reasserting itself now he was no longer facing the direct threat of Bronson's pistol.

Killian opened his mouth to say something, but noticed Cross watching him closely, and changed his mind.

'I don't think we should be doing this,' Angela said suddenly.

'Why not?' Bronson asked.

'I don't mean we shouldn't do it at all. It's just that I think this should be done under controlled conditions, in a museum or laboratory somewhere.'

'Not an option,' Donovan snapped. 'We're in the middle of Kashmir. The sort of facilities you're talking about don't exist anywhere within a couple of hundred miles of here, and there might not be any even as close as that.'

'But we don't know what's inside that box—' Angela began.

'I do,' Donovan said. 'A multi-billion-dollar resource for the genetics industry.'

'All you can think about is money, about how you can exploit this situation for your own personal gain,' Killian shouted, unable to keep silent any longer.

Cross waved his pistol again threateningly, and Killian lapsed into silence once more.

Masters looked at the tomb, then nodded, as if he'd just made a decision.

'I'm not coming back here,' he said, 'and nor are my men, so we need to find out what the hell is inside this, and then leave. And, Donovan, if it's what you believe it is, then we'll be taking charge of it until you make the final payment. And the price has just gone up. If this really is a billion-dollar resource, like you just said, then I'm charging you five million for delivery, plus expenses.'

'Agreed,' Donovan muttered. 'Just get on with it, will you?'

'I still think we should wait,' Angela said.

'You're out-voted, I'm afraid,' Masters said. He turned to Cross. 'Get the lid off that wooden box.'

Cross took the crowbar and jammed it into the wooden

crate, where the lid met the side. But as he did so, the two-thousand-year-old wood disintegrated to reveal the dull gleam of metal within. He pulled out the remaining bits of wood and tossed them away.

With the wood removed, a heavy but entirely plain and unmarked metal coffin became visible, resting on the floor of the stone oblong. Cross pulled out a knife and slid the point along its lid.

'I think it's made of lead,' he said, looking at the silvery gleam of the cut surface in the light from his torch.

'That settles it,' Donovan said. 'Even if we wanted to lift it intact and take it somewhere, it's too heavy. We'd never get it out of this room, let alone down to one of the jeeps. We're going to have to open it right here, right now.'

Angela shook her head, and took a half-step backwards. She looked pale and shocked.

Bronson felt a lurch of concern.

'The lid's sealed,' Cross said. 'There are half a dozen separate seals between the lid and the base, and there's a kind of reddish stuff in the joint as well. Looks to me like they did their best to keep the whole thing air-tight.'

'So in that case you might get a decent sample, Donovan,' Masters remarked.

'I should bloody well hope so, after all this,' Donovan said, while in the background Killian snorted his disgust.

Using his knife, Cross sliced through the seals that linked the lid and the base of the coffin, then ran the tip of the blade all the way around the joint, to try to break the seal between the two sections.

'You'll need to give me a hand,' Cross said, motioning to Masters to help him lift the lid. The two men stood side by side as Cross drove the tip of the crowbar into the gap below the coffin lid and levered it upwards. There was a sudden hiss of escaping air as the seal was finally breached. They seized the lid and levered it up and to one side, where it thudded heavily back against the stone wall that surrounded the coffin. Then they both stepped back.

For the first time in two thousand years the contents of the coffin were revealed in the yellow light from a handful of electric torches. For a few seconds nobody spoke.

'So Josephus was right,' Killian muttered.

There was a sudden clang as Angela dropped her torch. She gave a sharp intake of breath that was almost a sob. 'Oh. My. God,' she whispered, and almost fell into Bronson's arms.

67

'It can't be,' Donovan muttered. 'That's wrong. That's so wrong. That can't be Him. That's not Jesus Christ.'

Behind him, Masters crossed himself.

'He wasn't called Jesus Christ,' Killian said, his voice echoing around the tomb. 'Now that we're finally in this sacred place, at the very least you should use His correct name. He was called Yehoshua or Yeshua, and that name in Hebrew means "God is saviour". The appellation "Christ" is just a translation of the Greek *Khristos* or Latin *Christus*, meaning "the anointed one". He was never called that when He was alive.'

Nobody in the cave took the slightest notice of what he was saying. Everyone was looking into the coffin, with varying expressions of disbelief.

'That's not what I expected,' Bronson muttered. 'Not what I expected at all.'

'You're simply showing your ignorance, all of you,'

Killian snapped. 'What *did* you expect? The skeleton of a man six feet tall, maybe still showing the remains of long hair and a beard? The image that almost everyone, Christian and non-Christian alike, has of Jesus Christ? The image that has not the slightest shred of historical evidence to support it? The image that only became accepted as a true representation over eight hundred years after He died? That image?'

Still nobody responded.

What the coffin contained wasn't a skeleton. It was a body. The body of a man which looked so fresh and so vibrant that it was almost possible to believe he was still alive. It was wrapped in a discoloured but probably once-white cloth, the arms lying by its side, bare feet exposed at the end of the coffin.

But the body wasn't six feet in height, nothing like it. Bronson, who was used to estimating heights and distances as part of his job as a police officer, guessed the man had stood little more than five feet tall. He was heavily tanned and almost clean-shaven, just a few wisps of coarse hair dotted on his cheeks and chin. And his patchy fair hair was almost reddish in colour, and parted in the centre.

But it was the face that shocked them the most. Every person standing in that cave – even Bronson, who was a committed atheist – had a mental image of Jesus as a man of noble, even patrician, bearing, but the body in the lead coffin had a face that was almost startlingly unattractive.

It was pinched and narrow, dominated by a long and thin nose under thick eyebrows that almost met in the middle, giving the face a mean and unpleasant, almost equine, appearance. The corpse was about as far removed from the traditional picture of Jesus Christ as could possibly be imagined.

'This must be a mistake,' Donovan muttered, shaking his head.

'If it is, you made it,' Killian retorted. Of all the people in the cave, he was the only one who seemed unaffected by the sight of the corpse. In fact, from the moment the coffin lid had been removed, he'd acted as if the body inside it had been exactly what he'd expected.

'What did you mean when you said "Josephus was right"?' Angela asked him, staring wide-eyed at the corpse. She seemed to have recovered her composure somewhat, and was leaning forward, right over the base of the open coffin.

'There are no extant first-hand contemporary accounts of what Jesus looked like,' Killian said. 'But in a very early Slavonic copy of the *Capture of Jerusalem*, Josephus – you do know who he was, I hope? – describes Jesus as being small in stature with a "long face, long nose and meeting eyebrows". He also said He had dark skin, scanty hair parted in the middle like a Nazarite and with an undeveloped beard. And I think that's a pretty good description of this man, wouldn't you agree?'

There was another long silence. 'Could this really be the

founder of Christianity?' Donovan said at last. 'Just look at him. Short – he's almost a dwarf – and ugly with it.'

'It's not what He looked like that's important,' Killian said, his voice rising in anger. 'It's what He did, what He said and the lessons He gave us. Those are the building blocks, the very foundations, of the greatest religion the world has ever known.'

'Look at the hands,' Donovan said suddenly, and everybody's focus shifted. 'Do you see any nail marks? Stigmata?'

But the corpse's hands and wrists were unmarked.

'That proves nothing,' Killian said. 'Nails were expensive. The Romans often tied their victims to the cross with ropes. It just meant they lasted a bit longer, made them suffer even more.'

'What about the feet?' Bronson asked. He couldn't quite see into the base of the coffin. 'Or did the Romans lash their legs to the cross as well?'

Masters bent down to have a closer look. When he straightened up, his face was pale in the gloom of the cave, and he crossed himself again before he spoke.

'Two old wounds,' he said. 'Looks like something was driven through both heels. He'd have found walking real painful.'

Everyone looked at Killian who nodded. 'Common practice,' he said. 'They usually turned the victim sideways, jammed his feet into a wooden box attached to the cross and drove one nail straight through both ankles.'

His matter-of-fact explanation of the mechanics of perhaps the cruellest method of execution yet devised echoed around the cave.

'Dear God,' Angela whispered.

'But you said they were old wounds,' Bronson said, looking at Masters, and the mercenary nodded. 'So this man must have lived after he was crucified. How?'

'Crucifixion wasn't always terminal,' Killian said. 'There were a few recorded cases of victims being granted a reprieve after they were put on the cross, and being taken down again. Whether they survived depended on how long they'd been hanging there, and the way they had been secured to the cross. If three nails had been used, they'd eventually die from shock and blood loss or infection, but if their arms had been roped to the *patibulum* – that was the cross-piece – then they would have had a chance of living. And this man obviously did.'

'But if this man really was Jesus Christ,' Angela said, 'this proves He didn't die, or rise again – which would cut away the foundations of the entire Christian religion.'

'Exactly,' replied Killian. 'That's why I'm here.'

Silence fell again in the chamber, then they all heard a faint crackling sound, almost like a repeated electric discharge. It appeared directionless, but seemed to emanate from somewhere within the cave.

Masters jumped backwards, away from the lead coffin, his face ashen.

The eyelids of the corpse had flickered open, and the eyes, eyes of a pure and brilliant and unsullied cerulean blue, were staring straight up at the roof of the cave.

68

'You should have waited,' Angela said calmly.

'What?' Donovan asked, still staring at the body.

'You should have waited. You should have opened the coffin in a controlled environment, not way out here. There's no way of stopping this now.'

'Stopping what?'

'You heard that noise, just like the rest of us. And now it's too late. Far too late.'

'Look!' Masters said. 'Look at the body.'

Before their eyes, the corpse had started to change, the flesh shrinking and changing colour, and a sudden odour of decay, sharp and unpleasant, the smell of rotting and long-dead meat, permeated the cave.

'Sealing the coffin would have arrested the decay process,' Angela said, her voice strained. 'That crackling sound was some of the bones starting to crumble, and the eyes snapping open must have been caused by the muscles of the eyelids contracting as they decayed. Now the body's making up for lost time. That's why you should have waited.'

'Nooo!' Donovan howled, the sound loud in the confined space, and he leapt forward.

He plunged his hands into the coffin, grabbing for the corpse itself. Seizing the right hand, he ripped off one of the fingers, holding it up in triumph.

'This is all I'll need!' he shouted. 'This will be enough.'

The others recoiled in horror, but only one of them moved.

'Sacrilege!' Killian screamed, and launched himself across the end of the open stone coffin straight at Donovan.

The two men tumbled to the ground in a tangle of arms and legs, rolling over and over. They crashed into the crumbling skeleton that lay beside the coffin, a cloud of dust erupting from the ancient body as they crushed it against the ground.

Masters took a couple of steps towards them, to try to separate the two battling figures, then stopped, his head cocked on one side.

'You hear that?' he asked.

'What?' Then Bronson heard it too. A dull rumbling that seemed to emanate from the very walls all around them. And one glance told him what was causing it.

'Get out!' he yelled. 'Get out now.'

Bronson grabbed Angela and shoved her towards the entrance to the outer cave. An entrance that was closing fast as the noise grew in intensity, a deafening rumbling that now echoed around the stone chamber.

They were caught in a trap that had been waiting for them for two millennia.

69

Cross darted through the opening, Masters barely a yard behind him. Bronson pushed Angela into the fast-closing gap.

It was now so narrow that she had to turn sideways to slide through. The moment she stepped into the outer cave she reached back for Bronson. But before she could grab his arm, a powerful hand seized her from behind and pulled her away from the entrance.

Masters reached into the gap and jammed the crowbar lengthwise at chest-height between the cave wall and the moving stone door, and the rumbling sound suddenly diminished.

'Now!' he yelled. 'Get out now! This won't hold it for long.'

Bronson didn't hesitate, just ducked down and forced himself head-first into the gap. As he eased his body through, he could feel the stone door vibrating as some ancient unseen mechanism tried to force it closed against the flimsy steel barrier of the crowbar.

'Chris!' Angela was growing frantic in the outer cave.

Bronson thrust his torso through the gap at the base of the stone door, kicking out strongly with his legs to force his body through.

In the cave's inner chamber, Donovan kicked Killian's unconscious body to one side and dived across the stone floor. Somebody was in front of him, trying to wriggle through the remaining gap. Donovan reached out, grabbed the man's leg and pulled as hard as he could.

Bronson felt the tug on his leg and looked back. He could see Donovan right behind him, doing his best to drag him back into the inner chamber, and kicked out. The sole of his foot connected with Donovan's face, and he lurched backwards, blood streaming from his broken nose, his grip on Bronson's leg instantly loosening.

Bronson made a final effort and pulled himself through the gap, rolling across the floor of the cave to clear the opening as quickly as possible.

On the other side of the moving door, Donovan thrust himself forward, diving headlong into the narrow space.

'Nick, help me!' he shouted as he started to force his way through the gap.

Masters stepped forward and reached down to grab Donovan's out-stretched arm.

Then the stone door gave a sudden lurch and Masters looked up. The crowbar was starting to bend under the enormous pressure of the moving slab of stone. He grabbed Donovan's hand and started to pull, but even as he did so he knew it was too late.

Donovan felt an enormous, intolerable pressure on his chest as the stone door started moving again, started closing the gap. He couldn't breathe, couldn't move.

He felt a snap as the first of his ribs broke, then his chest caved in, a sudden excruciating shaft of agony that seared through his very being. And then he felt nothing at all as the crowbar snapped and the stone slab finally slammed into place, the ancient stone rollers crumbling to dust with the impact, jamming the door closed for another eternity.

70

'We're out of here,' Masters said, as they stepped outside the mouth of the cave. 'The Indian Army or Air Force are going to be swarming all over this valley lookin' for whoever blew their shiny Hind gunship out of the sky, so we need to be history before they get here. You gonna be OK?'

'Thanks,' Bronson said, shaking the American's hand. 'Our truck's parked down at the bottom of the valley, but I suppose you knew that already.'

Masters nodded and grinned, then turned, his mind already on his exit strategy as he selected a number on his sat-phone.

In the open space outside the cave, Bronson took Angela in his arms and for a few seconds just held her tight.

'I thought that was it,' Angela murmured, her cheeks

damp from tears of relief. 'I really thought you'd be crushed by that stone door closing. What do you think happened?' She turned back to look through the dark mouth of the cave.

'A clever booby-trap is how I see it,' Bronson said. 'When we pushed the slab all the way over to the right, the top of it was resting against another lump of stone. Somehow that must have tripped a trigger of some kind, because that second slab then started moving down, pushing against the first one. That was the noise we heard – the second slab starting to move.'

Before he'd left the cave he'd looked over the right-hand side of the slab. On the far side of the stone door was another rough-cut lump of stone which had clearly forced the slab closed as it pivoted downwards.

'That's just like some of the pyramids,' Angela said. 'An anti-theft mechanism. Open the first door and something triggers the mechanism. Then gravity does the rest.'

'I wonder why Yus Asaph's followers didn't trigger it themselves, and seal the door using the second slab when they hid the body here?' Bronson asked.

'Maybe it would have made it too obvious that something was hidden in the inner chamber. If you knew that there was a secret room in there, you could hack your way through the stone door.' Angela shuddered against Bronson's body. 'Let's get out of here, Chris. Let's go home.'

Bronson took her hand, and together they started

picking their way over the rutted boulder-strewn surface of the valley down to where they'd left their jeep. Night had fallen, and above them the sky was a black velvet blanket pierced by the light of countless millions of stars. It felt good to be alive.

Several minutes later, Killian recovered consciousness inside the inner chamber. At first, he could see nothing at all, then pulled a small torch from his pocket, switched it on and glanced around him. The others had all gone, which suited him perfectly. Now he had the time to complete the task he'd been set by God himself.

He walked across to the stone structure and ran his hand slowly over the top of the lead coffin and looked down, a contented smile on his face. Inside, the body he believed to have been Jesus the Nazarite had simply ceased to exist, turned to dust by the inexorable process of decay. That was something he'd completely failed to anticipate, but ultimately that was exactly what he'd intended. He had expected to have to destroy the tomb and its contents with explosives, but a force of nature had saved him the job. And it simply didn't matter what Donovan or any of the others said or claimed now – there was not the slightest shred of proof that the coffin had ever contained a human body, far less the body of the Messiah Himself.

Killian's smile deepened. He truly had been blessed. For the first time in two millennia, a small group of people had been granted the most sublime and utterly divine gift possible. For a few moments they had been permitted to stare at the face of the Saviour of mankind, at the man revered by countless millions of worshippers as the Son of God.

He made the sign of the cross and turned away from the coffin, swinging the torch beam in front of him. For the first time he registered the fact that the stone door was closed. Then he saw the spreading pool of blood on the floor of the chamber, and Donovan's body obscenely crushed into the gap.

Killian looked around desperately, seeking another way out, some tunnel or passageway they'd all missed, but in seconds he confirmed that the walls of the chamber were solid.

He ran to the stone door and tore at the edge of it with his fingers, ripping the skin and flesh and tearing off two of his nails. But the stone didn't budge by even a millimetre.

Then he started to scream.

Author's Note

This book is, of course, a novel, but I've tried to base it as far as possible on fact.

The accepted story of the life of Jesus Christ is fraught with inconsistencies, none of which are entirely surprising in view of the passage of time and the perceived need of the Catholic Church, in particular, to produce a seamless and acceptable account of the life of the man who was responsible for founding the Christian religion. Let me list just three of the more common of these misconceptions:

- *Jesus was born on 25 December.* If there really were shepherds tending their flocks in the fields when Jesus was born, as the Gospel of Luke claims, then the month was most likely to have been June. That was the first month of the year when sheep were allowed into the fields to graze on the remains of the wheat harvest. In fact, the date of 25 December was almost certainly chosen by the early Church as the major Christian festival because it was important to subdue all other religions, including paganism, and one of the most important pagan celebrations was the festival of the Unvanquished Sun, held every year on 25 December. It is known that the 'new' festival was established by the fourth century AD, because in AD 334 the 25 December first appeared in a Roman calendar as Christ's date of birth.

- *His name was Jesus Christ.* The name 'Jesus' is actually a British invention. His original Hebrew name was 'Yehoshua', which later became 'Yeshua' or 'Joshua'. The name 'Yehoshua' was translated from the Hebrew into Greek and then into Latin, where it was rendered as 'Iesvs' or 'Iesous', which was then changed to 'Jesus' in English. In those early days, people didn't actually have a second or family name. Instead, Jesus would have been known as 'Yeshua bar Yahosef bar Yaqub', or 'Joshua, son of Joseph, son of Jacob'. He would certainly never have been known as 'Jesus Christ' while He was alive. Jesus was believed by some people to have been the Messiah, which in Hebrew means 'the anointed one'. The oil used for such an anointing is called 'khrisma' in Greek, and so an anointed person is called 'Khristos', which was translated into 'Christus' in Latin and then became 'Christ' in English. And being anointed was not a special privilege reserved for the Messiah – all sorts of people were anointed, including kings, high priests, prophets and even people suffering from some forms of sickness.

- *Jesus lived in Nazareth*. In fact, it's almost certain that Nazareth didn't exist as a settlement when Jesus was alive, and 'Jesus of Nazareth' is actually a mistranslation of an Old Testament passage by whoever wrote the Gospel of Matthew. The name 'Iesous Nazarene' or 'Nazareneus' means that Jesus was a Nazarene, not that he came from a place called Nazareth. If the writer had meant that he *did* come from Nazareth, the correct word would have been either 'Nazarethenos' or 'Nazarethaios'. A 'Nazarene' was an ascetic, a holy person who spent a lot of time praying, and who lived simply with no or few possessions. They were an important sect in northern Palestine, and may also have been known as 'Mandaeans'.

There's also a large gap in the story of the life of Jesus Christ that the Christian Church never mentions. His birth is talked about, then His appearance at the Temple at the age of twelve or thirteen, His ministry and of course His death and apparent Resurrection, but where was Jesus between the ages of about thirteen and thirty?

There's evidence that Christ spent quite a lot of His early life outside Judea, and it appears quite possible that He actually lived in India for at least a part of this time. Such travels were not unknown in the first century AD.

What later became known as the Silk Road or Silk Route was already well established, and there was frequent two-way traffic between the countries around the Mediterranean, especially the eastern Mediterranean, and as far away as China.

In the winter of 1887, a man named Nicolai Notovitch was travelling through India as a correspondent for the Russian journal *Novaya Vremiya*. In November he was in the Kashmir region, near Ladakh, when he fell from his horse and suffered a broken leg. His bearers carried him to the Hemis Gompa monastery for medical treatment. While he was there, Notovitch was told a story that astonished him.

He was slightly puzzled that he'd been given such excellent treatment by the residents of the monastery, and was told by one of the lamas that, as a European, they considered him to essentially share their faith, to almost be a Buddhist. Notovitch objected that he was a Christian, not a Buddhist, but the lama told him that the greatest of all the Buddhist prophets, a man named Issa, was also the founder of the Christian religion. The head lama produced two bound volumes of loose leaves, from which he read the story of Issa to Notovitch, who took notes and recorded as much as he could.

According to these ancient records, Issa was born in Israel, and arrived in India when he was about fourteen years old in company with a group of merchants. For the next fifteen years or so, he travelled throughout the sub-continent, including a six-year stint in Nepal, learning the tenets of Buddhism and acquiring a reputation as a preacher and a prophet. He then returned home to Israel to try to combat the oppression of the Jewish people. These texts, Notovitch was told, were part of a collection of ancient Tibetan writings compiled in Pali, an old Indian language, during the first two centuries AD.

The parallels between the lives of Issa and Jesus were obvious, and on his return to Europe Notovitch attempted to publicize his discovery, but every Church official, including one at the Vatican, warned him in the strongest possible terms not to try to publish anything about this strange story. And the power of the Church at the end of the nineteenth century was sufficient to ensure that when Notovitch did finally manage to publish *La Vie Inconnue de Jésus Christ* in 1895, not only was the work essentially ignored, but Notovitch himself was arrested in St Petersburg and imprisoned in the Peter and Paul Fortress and accused of 'literary activity dangerous to the state and to society'. He was exiled without trial to Siberia, but was allowed to return in 1897. His ultimate fate remains unknown, though he probably lived until about 1916.

Various attempts have been made to debunk Notovitch's claims since then, but without success. An impartial look at the evidence suggests that he really did visit Ladakh and the Hemis Gompa monastery – the basis of at least one of the debunking attempts was that he was simply never there – and other, later, travellers to the area have been told similar stories of books held at Hemis Gompa that contained accounts of the life of Jesus in India.

It's an interesting story, but without sight of the original documents held at the monastery it's unproven. But there is other evidence that suggests Jesus and Issa might have been one and the same person.

First, when Jesus reappears in Judea as an adult, He's clearly already an accomplished prophet, which suggests He had to have learned His trade somewhere.

Second, there are a lot of similarities between what Jesus is supposed to have preached and the Buddhist religion, so if India *is* where He went for His formative years, it's at least possible that when He returned to Judea He was essentially a Buddhist. For example, both religions cite exactly the same story of the poor widow giving two coins – all she has – at a religious gathering, and this tiny gift being fêted by the presiding priest as being more valuable than all the other contributions. As Buddhism was founded about 460 BC, it's almost possible to argue that Christianity is essentially simply a Buddhist sect, the religious message being carried to Judea by Jesus, which then became enshrined in the Christian religion.

The third piece of circumstantial evidence is that when the first Christian missionaries arrived in Ladakh, they discovered that the local people were already very familiar with the story of Jesus/Issa, and they were carrying and using rosaries.

And what happened after Jesus's crucifixion? The accepted story of the death of Jesus is perhaps the most contentious part of His life, because it simply doesn't make sense for a whole list of reasons, far too many to fully discuss here. But one of the most obvious anomalies was that Jesus apparently died within about three or four hours of being crucified, and his body was then taken down from the cross.

The whole point about crucifixion was that it was intended to be a slow, lingering and very public form of execution. That was why the Romans used it – to frighten and intimidate their subject peoples. Victims could survive for as long as four or five *days* on the cross if their legs weren't broken to hasten their deaths. And the bodies of victims were never removed from the cross after death. Again, for the purposes of intimidation, they were left there to rot, and guards were routinely posted at sites of crucifixions to ensure that relatives didn't manage to steal the bodies for secret burial after death.

If the whole episode wasn't purely apocryphal – a cruci*fiction*, in fact – and the execution did take place as described in the Bible, there had to have been collusion between the Roman authorities and the Jewish people, because nothing else makes sense. The strong implication is that Jesus was alive when he was taken down from the cross, and that, of course, provides the easiest and most logical explanation for the Resurrection – there simply wasn't one.

Taking that as a given, it would also be obvious that Jesus couldn't stay in Israel – having a condemned and crucified man walking around would have been unacceptable to the Romans – so He would have had to leave the country. And if He had spent almost half of his life in India, that would have been the obvious place for Him to return to. Which brings us to the 'Rozabal'.

As Angela states in this novel, in Srinigar there's a building known as the 'Rozabal' – it's an abbreviation of *Rauza Bal*, and the word *rauza* means 'the tomb of the prophet' – which contains two tombs. One of them is the grave of the Islamic saint Syed Nasir-ud-Din, and points north-south, in accordance with Muslim custom. The other tomb is aligned east-west, a Jewish custom, and bears the name 'Yuz Asaf'.

This tomb is also unique in that it bears a carving of a pair of footprints – actually a common custom at the graves of saints – but this carving shows what appear to be the marks of crucifixion, a punishment unknown in India, on the feet. Records show that this tomb dates from at least as early as 112 AD.

According to the *Farhang-i-Asafia*, an ancient text that describes the history of Persia, the prophet Jesus – who was then known as 'Hazrat Issa' – healed a group of lepers, who thereafter were referred to as *Asaf*, meaning 'the purified', because they'd been cured of their disease. Jesus or Issa then acquired the additional name 'Yus Asaf', meaning the 'leader of the healed'.

It's reasonably certain that this tomb contains the body of Yus Asaf, a man who was also known as Issa, and also probably known as Jesus, and I based this novel upon that supposition. I should emphasize that there's no evidence the body was removed from this tomb and carried into the high valleys of Ladakh – that is purely a fiction I devised for this book. As far as I know, the body of Yus Asaf – whoever he was – still lies in the grave in Srinigar.

Readers interested in learning more about this aspect of Jesus's life should refer to *Jesus lived in India* by Holger Kersten (Penguin, ISBN 978-0-14-302829-1).

What did Jesus look like? Again as stated in the novel, the current depictions of Him as a tall man of noble bearing with long hair and a beard have no historical basis whatsoever. In the first century AD, the average height of an adult male in Judea was about five feet.

The full description of 'the King of the Jews' from the Slavonic copy of Josephus's *Capture of Jerusalem* states that He was 'a man of simple appearance, mature age, dark skin, small stature, three cubits high, hunchbacked with a long face, long nose, and meeting eyebrows . . . with scanty hair with a parting in the middle of his head, after the manner of the Nazarites, and with an undeveloped beard'. That description is very similar to one found in the *Acts of Paul and Thecla*, which stated he was 'a man small in size, bald-headed . . . with eyebrows meeting, rather hook-nosed'.

And Jesus was, according to several different accounts,

physically quite unattractive. In the *Acts of Peter* a prophet described Jesus as having 'no beauty nor comeliness', and in the *Acts of John* as 'a small man and uncomely'. Celsus described Jesus as 'small and ugly and undistinguished'. Tertullian said that 'he would not have been spat upon by the Roman soldiers if his face had not been so ugly as to inspire spitting'.

The first depictions of Jesus showed Him as a small man, clean shaven and with short hair. In the sixth century, He was first depicted with long hair and a beard, and He'd grown slightly. By about the eighth century, what's now the present picture of Jesus had fully emerged. It's probable that the image on the Turin Shroud, now positively established to be an extremely accomplished medieval forgery, simply served as a reinforcement of the physical appearance of this 'new' Jesus.

Finally, I mentioned the 'Baigdandu anomaly' in the novel. This is real. Every few generations, a child is born in the village of Baigdandu with red hair and blue eyes. A local legend states that centuries ago a tribe of Greeks arrived in the area looking, oddly enough, for the tomb of Jesus Christ, and eventually settled there, and it's their genes that cause this aberration. I'm not a geneticist, but I have met a lot of Greeks and most of them have brown eyes and black or very dark brown hair. The idea that the present anomaly could be caused by this particular intermarriage doesn't seem to me to make sense.

But some of the descriptions of Issa refer to him as

fair-haired with blue eyes, and logic suggests that this is a far more likely explanation of this anomaly. So it's just possible that the bloodline of the man we know as Jesus Christ is still present on Earth after two millennia, and that His genes can still be found among the inhabitants of a tiny mountain village high in one of the remoter parts of the Kashmir.

James Becker
Principality of Andorra, February 2010

THE FIRST APOSTLE

James Becker

An Englishwoman is found dead in a house near Rome, her neck broken.

Her distraught husband enlists the help of his closest friend, policeman Chris Bronson, who discovers an ancient inscription on a slab of stone above their fireplace. It translates as 'Here Lie the Liars'.

But who are the liars? And what is it they are lying about to protect?

Pursued across Europe, Bronson uncovers a trail of clues that leads him back to the shadowy beginnings of Christianity; to a chalice decorated with mysterious symbols; to a secret code hidden with a scroll.

And to a deadly conspiracy which – if revealed – will rock the foundations of our modern world.

Now available in Bantam paperback and as a bestselling ebook

THE MOSES STONE

James Becker

AN ANCIENT CODE
A clay tablet covered in ancient writing is found by an English couple in Morocco. A day later they are dead, killed in a car crash. But where is the relic they died to protect?

A SINISTER SECRET
Determined to uncover a secret that's endured for two millennia, Chris Bronson follows a trail of clues that lead him from the hustle of a Moroccan souk to the deserted caves of Qumran; from the sinister echoes of a water-filled tunnel under the city of Jerusalem to a windswept fortress whose name spells death.

A DEADLY CHASE FOR THE TRUTH...
Threatened on every side by violent extremists, Bronson is plunged into a mystery rooted in biblical times. For the stone he must find is older and far more dangerous than he could ever have imagined ...

Now available in Bantam paperback and as a bestselling ebook